THE SQUARE ROOT OF EVIL

The Peppermint Files

Re`al "Bull" Oney

iUniverse, Inc.
New York Bloomington

This is a work of fiction. All of the characters, names, incidents, organizations, and dialogue in this novel are either the products of the author's imagination or are used fictitiously.

iUniverse books may be ordered through booksellers or by contacting:

iUniverse
1663 Liberty Drive
Bloomington, IN 47403
www.iuniverse.com
1-800-Authors (1-800-288-4677)

This book has been judged five stars reading and edited by:
  Simone Daesch-Jackson
  Literary Manuscript Reviews
  Tuscola, Illinois 61953
  217-433-0131

ISBN: 978-1-4401-2100-5 (sc)
ISBN: 978-1-4401-2101-2 (ebook)

Printed in the United States of America

iUniverse rev. date: 02/02/09

PREFACE

So much for shortcuts, I thought. The steam rose from under the hood of my Jeep and I suspected a rubber radiator hose had ruptured when a big cloud of steam spewed rust-colored antifreeze all over my windshield. The weak antifreeze crystallized, smeared by the wiper blades, then froze to a sickening puke-colored mess immediately, even before the engine sputtered and the dash warning lights flashed once again. I drove off the roadway as best I could with no shoulder left by the snowplow operators.

Pre-warned this morning, just before I turned off the ignition at work, I should have called to have it serviced in town immediately then. This time the warning light waited to flash until I was in the boondoggles, and in only two minutes all hell broke loose under the hood. I reminded myself of Father's words, "Never put off until tomorrow, anything that should be done today." Duh! I was a slow learner, I guess. Now I was in real trouble out here in no-man's land.

My car's battery was quickly going dead, so I turned off the headlights and initiated the emergency flashers. I got out deciding I must leave for help now, for I would certainly freeze to death if I stayed much longer. It started sleeting and the ice pelted me like hail. My cellular read "No signal…unable to send". I was too far into the woods. The smell of the car's antifreeze steaming from under the hood was sickening.

Hesitantly, I started out on foot towards home, flashlight in hand, with my arms jutting straight out from my sides for balance. I tried to overcome my slip-sliding clumsiness, while trudging down that dark, snow-packed, backcountry road. I figured I was still almost fifteen miles out.

One large and very fast moving SUV, possibly a yellow or light green Hummer, threw up mud as it cleaned out the ditch on the opposite side of the narrow road to miss me, for I was in the middle of the road and could not move fast enough to get out of its way. It did not stop, nor after twenty very cold and lonely minutes did another vehicle pass. I just kept putting one foot out in front of the other.

Now I was really freezing. My neck scarf whipped around in the wind gusts, slapping me in the face, completely blinding me sometimes, as I struggled to maintain my upright position. I followed some very deep tire track ruts, obviously left from that speeding SUV vehicle. I still hoped for some emergency assistance, even though I did not expect there were going to be other passersby.

A sub-zero, gusting 30-knot northerly wind blew snowflakes everywhere, continuously mounting up their deep drifts. Their streaking, white, crystalline-like bodies swirled in front of me like little tornados, each one glistening in the dancing beam from my flashlight. The hidden iced-over potholes, crackled loudly under my weight. I suddenly slipped, then stumbled forward headfirst, down upon my hands and knees into a three-foot snow bank. My big flashlight hurled out of my grasp, nevertheless it safely landed unbroken, still focused, and shining ahead of me. As I picked it up, the flashlight's beam crossed over an object only a few feet away. First, it looked like a log to me, but it certainly was not. This particular nighttime log look-a-like was shoeless, and had bare feet sticking out towards me, with painted human toenails.

That scared the holy hell out of me. I struggled to get up, but could not. No longer was I worried about being cold. My adrenaline was peaking and I grew stronger. The frigid air I breathed in stung my lungs as I gasped for more oxygen.

Still hunched over there on my knees and very flustered, I quickly rubbed the blown sleet from my eyelashes with my dampened gloves. I refocused my flashlight upon that prone body, and then shook the lifeless torso by her foot. Her coatless body revealed her all. I ran the beam to her head quickly. In only the light from the flashlight's beam, I could immediately recognize the person's face, even in her condition.

She lay there, disheveled, motionless, so cold looking, and apparently stiff. The flashlight's beam showed her beautiful, brown eyes, dilated in fixation and wide-eyed. They stared aimlessly up toward me, although partially hidden by the fresh Canadian snow. Her once pretty face, now seemingly frozen almost solid white, apparently was wreathing in horror at the time of her demise. Her throat-slit, blood-spattered, half-naked body showed trauma everywhere. Her lips were bloody and very swollen. Those beautifully arching eyebrows shone gashes from the beating she apparently had received, right before she died. Her skirt, pulled above her waist, exposed torn panties and a firm midsection. It all made me queasy. I immediately got up staggering away and sucked air. I tried not to vomit, but failed. I fumbled with my cellular, and managed to dial the 911 number. My distress call found coverage this time and then went out, thank God!

CHAPTER 1

"911, what is your emergency?" a female voice quickly asked.

"I'm broken down on Highway 22, east of Didsbury...I...I... found a girl's dead body, please...send the police, now," I pleaded.

Almost instantaneously, my damn cell phone died out from my letting the battery absorb the coldness that blew in the night air...it was well below freezing. I hoped the message went through all right; hoped is crucial, I thought, or I would be left standing here in the middle of nowhere simply horrified.

Nevertheless, within minutes, a distant yelping of an emergency vehicle's siren broke the dead silence, just as blue lights appeared upon the horizon. I became impatient and began waving my flashlight to hail whoever it was headed my way. As it turned out, it was an ambulance. Apparently, the 911 dispatcher thought she better not rely on my judgment that the girl was dead.

The ambulance skidded to a halt upon my flagging them down. The EMT rolled his driver's side window down and asked me if I had called. However, all I could do was point to her. I was getting dizzy as I used the big vehicle's engine heat and frame to block the cold winds.

After one EMT shined his flashlight in her eyes, the other EMT felt for her carotid heartbeat beside her neck. He immediately discovered her slit throat. They each confirmed to one another that she was dead. I could have told them that already.

After a quick call to their dispatcher, they turned their attentions to me. One fellow took me by the arm and led me along the ambulance, then coaxed me to climb up through the sliding door. Inside the lighted ambulance, I saw that I had puked upwind and the vomit came back and hit me all over. I searched for my handkerchief to wipe my mouth and face, when an EMT took my arm, and then handed several paper towels to me from the dispenser in the ambulance. He helped clean me up. He did not say much, except, "I'll help you get through this. The investigators will be here soon. Are you injured? Do you hurt?" He was very reassuring and comforting as he wiped me clean.

Twenty minutes or more passed; while I sipped extra-sweetened black hot coffee, offered to me by the EMT and watched outside as many flashing lights arrived at the scene. Suddenly the back door flew open with a huge gust of cold wind. An unshaven man, who identified himself as a police detective sergeant, told me to get out and go with him. I reluctantly followed him as ordered. He led me back to the body. I stood there several minutes freezing my tail off, while men photographed the body and scene. A rubber sheet was then placed over the girl. A man told the detective he was uncertain how long she was dead.

"She might not have been here very long, because there have been heavy snows all day and there's relatively little snow upon her. According to the under body collections, her blood loss was somewhere else…she was murdered and then dumped here. Rigor mortis isn't present, yet, but beginning," one masked man dressed in a green doctor's smock related to the detective.

"I'll of course need that vaginal swab sent off to the lab right away. Have them search for some sort of sucrose present, okay?" Gray explicitly requested of him. "I'm afraid it may be another one of those, again," he mysteriously added, as if the forensic man knew.

The area around the body, cordoned off with yellow plastic tape, read "Police lines…do not cross", so I stopped short.

"My guess…less than five hours," one investigator related. "We'll get her temperature now and another swab with hairs at the coroner's office."

"Step closer...yes, you...over the tape. Watch your step, eh. You say you found her this way. Is this your first experience?" the detective questioned of me.

I put my hand over my mouth trying not to vomit, again, when seeing her head turned sideways, dangling from a piece of meat, and nearly cut off. Her gaping slit throat exposed more closely now, I gasped to speak an answer.

"Ohhhh...hell...yes!" I spouted.

The forensic people covered her up after removing most of her clothes. They were evidence and stuffed into separate paper evidence bags. As they completed their routine, Gray pulled the rubber sheet back away from her body. I felt my knees buckling, but leaned against a tree trunk.

All the investigators had stayed away from trampling the immediate area around the scene to maintain its integrity. They each followed one path onto the scene. The visible footprints leading up to her body in the snow were mine. Thus, I became a suspect immediately, though it was I, who had used my cell phone to summon authorities, as soon as I spotted her lying there. If my car had not overheated and broken down a half-mile down the road, she might have laid there unnoticed, covered in snow, until the spring thaw in May.

Detective-sergeant Nigel Gray summoned me even closer to his side and asked me if I knew her.

I responded, "I do...or did, sort of...I had read her bio for weeks when she was hoping to find a new romance with her personal ad. When the ads halted in my personals' column, I thought she had met someone special this time. Her name is Meredith Monroe, a first year, first grade teacher in one of our local grade schools. Now she lays there obviously raped, murdered...slaughtered would be more like it. Oh my, God...look at her!"

Gray replaced the rubber sheet upon her, and then took me by the arm leading me to his unmarked cruiser. He stopped at his side in the blowing snow and motioned for me to go around and sit in the front passenger's side. His ass was cold too. I leaned against the squad and eased around the back to get to the other side where snow had heaped up and it was a challenge to continue. However, I finally opened the stuck passenger's side door and caught it as it blew wide open. Gray's papers flew in all directions inside and he cussed in disgust as he caught them before they flew outside. I quickly sat down inside and slammed the door shut. It creaked for lack of lubricant.

"God damn, it is cold tonight," he moaned, while flipping the heater's blower switch all the way up, and then began rubbing his hands together after removing his gloves. After he flexed them to get circulation going, he reached for a pen from inside his top coat.

"Now, what's your full name and address…got a driver's license handy?" he asked, himself beginning to shiver. His teeth rattled as he reacted as though the cold had totally chilled him through and through.

"Burrrrr!" he sounded out loudly, as he continued to shake and shiver, which made me feel even colder. His trench coat emitted coldness next to me, which I felt on my neck and face, as I watched him fumble around with his clipboard and papers trying to manipulate his stiffened fingers.

As I reached for my back pocket, I found that I was sitting upon a gooey French fry with ketchup on it. There would be a stain. I was pissed since I did my own laundry. I handed my license to him and then he quickly jotted down all my personal information on a "Police Investigator's Preliminary Form", it read. As he filled out the form scribbling frantically, he turned to me and asked me if I was gay.

"Hey, screw you! No, I'm not!" I yelled in aggravation for him asking me such a stupid question.

"Look, bud, cool it…I must have struck a sore spot, eh? I have to ask you all these kinds of questions, so watch your temper or I'll make you wish you had behaved," he said, with a stern voice and looking directly at me frowning like he was going to punch me hard if I continued my discord.

I settled down when he displayed the form, which showed that specific question for him to ask me. Nevertheless, I was not happy to say the least.

The seat was also filthy with cigarette ashes and there were chewing gum wrappers all over on the floor. His police radio's microphone, positioned between us, looked as dirty and worn out as the wrinkles in Gray's forehead. Guessing, I figured he was about forty-five, but actually looked sixty. I suppose the job had gotten to him. He immediately got inside the glove box and reached for a bottle of Tums. After downing a half-dozen, he turned to me again and stared at me as if to intimidate me into confessing something I had not done.

"Okay, let me have it," Gray commanded. "Start from the beginning and if you don't mind, speak into this microphone using your normal voice, got it? I am recording everything you tell me. I am not very good at taking notes while freezing my ass off at this time of night. You know your rights?" he grumbled.

"Yes, but am I under arrest, for God's sake?"

"Not yet…it depends how well you explain being out here on Ames Road this late at night. Well, start talking, bub. How old are you?"

"It tells you on my license," I advised him.

He turned to me with that evil eye and frowned as if I was about to get my due from him. I felt like belting him up along side his stupid head and calling a lawyer on my cell phone, but I remembered its battery was dead. Nevertheless, I took a deep breath, looked him straight in the eye, and began rather nervously.

"I am almost twenty-nine…I work at CMEN as a personals' column writer. My job name is Gerry Loveletter…ever read my stuff?"

He looked up at me and cringed negatively.

"Anyway, my real name is Jerry David, with a "J", my address and everything else is on my driver's license, there, if you can't see through those dirty glasses," I said, as I pointed at it for him.

He then looked hard through those rather smudged reading glasses and decided he wasn't going blind after all.

"Continue, Mr. David," he said as he took off those filthy reading glasses and tried to clean them on his scarf, "Continue."

"I do love letter ads in my columns to help bring the opposite sex together. Meredith was once a user of my column, while searching for a friend. That's how I met her…about six months ago. I remember that she said she had forgotten to mail in her love letter ad piece and came into my office to make the paper's weekend deadline. That's how I first met her."

"What do you mean, first…met her?"

"Well, we ended up having a date that very night. She was very pretty and I thought she might be that hidden diamond in the rough. She wore sexy jeans and cowgirl boots, but that's really not my type.

However, she was so vivacious; I just asked her to dinner that night and a movie. She said yes."

"Did you do her that night?"

"What the hell kind of question is that? Is that on that form?"

"Don't get uptight; no, I just want to know if she was easy. Here, it is part of another question on the form, but it asks if the deceased was promiscuous. I need to know something about her moral character. If she was easy...well, maybe she was a loose character and dated just anyone, or maybe even a prostitute," he tried to substantiate his cause.

"No, no, I didn't get in her pants...ever. She was a decent girl; a grade school teacher, remember? We just didn't have anything in common and after the date I took her straight home."

"Why would a beautiful young thing like that have to search for someone to love her?" he asked disgustedly.

"I don't know, I just don't know. But I can tell you this...there's a bunch of wonderful women out there that do the same...I just don't understand it," I explained.

"I think it's because young guys today are horses' asses that take after their horse ass fathers...that's what I think. They don't grow any real men anymore. They all have to show their womanly side, whatever that is...just to show their tenderness. They are all becoming wusses. Now, where'd she live?" he asked quickly to change the subject.

"Near Canada One, overlooking the Bow, in Cochrane...in a duplex with some other college girls."

"What other college girls, from where?"

"I don't know...never met any of them...she mentioned Calgary, Calgary University, I think. She was getting her masters...ah..."

"How'd this happen?" he asked interrupting me abruptly, looking out towards the crime scene.

"Her...I don't know...my car overheated because my anti-freeze was low, I guess. It's still sitting down that way smoking, I hope," I explained.

"I started hoofing it up this way using my flashlight, because only one car passed and I just happened to see her next to the road. I called you immediately."

"What time was that? What car?"

"Umm, I left work late at five thirty…caught a bite at the Roller Deli watching some cute skaters and left about ten thirty. I found her about eleven, I think. I was almost run over by a yellowish or light greenish colored Hummer as I walked this way through the darkness. It came right at me and then veered hard…took out the ditch. "

"That's it?"

"Yes, that's all I know about this horrible thing. You think that Hummer had anything to do with this?"

He looked me in the eyes and told me he would catch up with the sons-of-bitches who did this. His eyes dwelled deep into mine, and then he said,

"Okay, I believe you. Got any hot chicks on the string at work?"

I could have died when he asked that, but I lied.

"Hey, I get three hundred letters a month. Want me to set you up?"

"Yeah, fix me up with a sexy young thing…ha…but, only if you ask my old lady, first. She gets real pissed when I do things like that."

He leaned over smiling, pulled on the stuck passenger door's handle, and then said, "Kick!"

I bumped the door with my knee and it flew open.

"Well, could you give me a lift to get help?" I asked, standing outside in the freezing cold.

"No, your ride is right over there," he said, as he pointed to my car up on a hook. "I called Gino's wrecker right away when I almost hit your Jeep sitting back there partially on the road. I have to get to the morgue right away to see the coroner. I will contact you at your workplace, if I need you. Thanks, mate!"

Then he left me standing in the roadway as his spinning tires spit snow up at me…soon he was gone.

Gino's Garage from Red Deer, it read on the door panel, had my car in tow. Old Gino was a nice fellow. I had never ridden in a wrecker before. We were up high and it was bouncy inside the cab. After we arrived at his garage, he poured me a hot cup of coffee and let me stand in his office by his oil-burning furnace's blower to thaw out. Gino skillfully put on a new hose and refilled my car's radiator with anti-freeze. When it started right up, he hit me up for seventy-five dollars for his services and twenty-five for the hose and installation.

I went home feeling very sick. Thank goodness, it was Friday. I could sleep late in the morning. The hideous situation was so tiring, I almost slept the whole weekend, off and on, except for the nightmare Sunday night, where I dreamed I touched her, and she came to life and sat up. That scared the hell out of me. I took a whiz and tried to go back to sleep. I still felt exhausted.

It was Monday, seven in the morning; I had an hour to get to my desk. I looked and felt like hell, but I made it anyway. I grabbed the mailbag and a mug of java, and then sat down at my computer desk and started sorting through my mail of nearly a hundred ad pieces, mostly from women, but not all of them.

At $30 per personal ad, which included a nice picture, I was making money for the paper, I imagined. I never really figured it out, but I knew I was earning my own salary and making the company a profit.

Before coming to Canada, I was a B.A. journalism major, South Dakota State College graduate, and steadfastly searching for a position anywhere. My life took shape across the U.S. border into Canada when I followed up on a local Rapid City newspaper's ad for Canadian employment near Calgary.

I was impressed upon meeting the editor of our paper. It was something new, he wanted…a special place for people to meet each other in his paper, he told me. I was the first, and my own boss, he explained. He wanted my best…he got it. I got the job as an intern on probation seven years ago. I called Mom and Pop and told them the money they spent on my education was not in vain…they were thrilled. I began from scratch.

Women, women, women…it seems like I have gotten to know them all. Anyway, through all these years of searching for the right one for myself, I have learned from many desperate women, their wants, needs, their passions, desires, and vulnerabilities, inside and out. So far, I have struck out for myself, because there are so many lovely peaches waiting to be picked. I am a bit confused, because sometimes I imagine that I love them all and each has a hidden key and a secret I must unlock before anything develops between us.

On my job, I read thousands of love letters. Mostly, they are requested ads from women and some men who all want listings with their made-up bio particulars in my personals' column.

I find that women get very serious, starting about age eighteen when their biological clock starts ticking. They learn to quit trying to get laid every night, because they have been through it all; stood up, jilted, forgotten at the alter, and divorced usually. They have decided to share and receive love of their treasures with only one lucky person. Something with someone, they could not have before. Some have kids, some want to have kids, but all want to share everything with just one special person that they cannot seem to find by themselves out in public.

For women, it's not quite the same kind of loin yearning, passionate, lusty, love that men expect to have. For most women, it is not in the same magnitude of instantaneous, burning lusty desires; although I've seen a few of those also. Women dream of a loftier type of long lasting, forever, never-ending, entirely devoted, totally secure, romance and love.

It is that "knight in shining armor" syndrome that mother told them about, but failed herself to seize. Most people never find "that special one" and settle for second or third best. That's when they finally realize it's not supposed to happen with them and settle for what they have. Love grows in time and time heals all wounds.

On the other hand, for men, love means a temporary sexual gratification fix. It's a relationship mostly of lust, where they can jump from one exploit to another, until they find the one they cannot just drag into bed for a one night's stand. If they do succeed, they feel like they have conquered her and eventually press forward to their next quest.

If she fails to put out, his ego is twisted. He may stick around, still expecting, very hopeful, but then leave anyway if she does not eventually do it. Unless, of course, using her womanly ways, she hooks him by other feminine means. She treats him like a king, feeds him like a gourmet chef, and pampers him completely. This lasts until the ring goes on and a firm commitment made. Then, he's a goner...sells his toys, gets a full time job, hears wedding bells, and signs a mortgage. All of a sudden, he wants kids and a dog or cat. Soon afterwards, he wonders what happened to all the pampering he got before the vows. It's a woman's gimmick to success.

Whenever a man or woman lose their loved one, or want to find their first true love, they sometimes write to me, Gerry Loveletter. That moniker, my interested party, is my workplace's column name. You see, I just might have the best job in the world for an ever-searching bachelor. I am the infamous daily personals columnist-writer for the CMEN, sometimes affectionately referred to as man's CMEN, correctly known though as The Canadian Morning Express Newspaper. That is where I play Cupid, as a matchmaker for lonesome lovers. Yes, it has been an interesting job for seven years now, especially since Nigel Gray came into my life investigating the death of Meredith Monroe.

CHAPTER 2

Two long weeks had passed since my horrible experience and I became very busy at my desk. The endless requests for personal ads, screened only by me, seemed as though they had doubled nearing Christmas. I could not put some ads in my column because they were down right raunchy…like, "I'm easy", "I'm horny" or "I've got a really big one for you".

Nope, there has to be more to dating than lust, although lust plays a big part with a personal picture attached. You must think you have some physical attraction to go along with your ad to get noticed. On the other hand, maybe your personal job description lures a talent-seeking individual or moneygrubber. Each submitter has to decide that before they give that info out. Often it ends in heartbreak.

I get some nasty poses, too, mostly by women, that I have to request a more "not so revealing" or less sexually explicit picture, which usually comes from first timers who have not submitted before. Most ads are full of lofty ideals, often inflated, but all touched with a dire need of love.

I also write a short article preceding the column with suggestions for dating and the current hot spots for lovers in the area, which offer relaxed, adult entertainment. Sometimes, because thousands read my columns, businesses who advertise and some noted restaurants often donate coupons for discount dining or free. I can give them out to help get these lonely people into their establishments. That I like a lot because it somehow gives my column some merit throughout the Calgary area. The advice I give, of course, is where to dine, then go dancing, and enjoy a current romantic movie.

I sometimes get to give out theater tickets also. These are only my personal suggestions, however. I always include the starting times for the Stampeders and Flames games for those sports-minded individuals. Women will go anywhere for a good date. Football and hockey games fill the air this time of the season and it is a nice first rendezvous' starting point, to meet a stranger…in a crowded place for one's safety.

Actually, I like my job. I like to think I am helping the lonely hearted people find some happiness.

I leaned back in my chair to sip a now cold cup of coffee. I noticed my old ashtray still sitting there on my desk, so I slid it off into the trashcan, then got up and wiped it off and put it back. I might need to smoke again someday, if it legalized, and where could I dump my ashes without starting a fire? Legally, I guess we employees are not supposed to be smoking in this building. Nope, I pitched it back into the trashcan and set the receptacle outside my door to be picked up later by Joe, our custodian. That way, I would not have to look at it. I was still weak having just quit three weeks prior. Every now and then, a coffee and a cigarette seemed so right-on. I sat back down, and then started reaching for more letters and ads to read.

My mind suddenly drifted back to Meredith Monroe. Her obituary had been in our paper and I kept that picture hanging on a thumbtack, up on my bulletin board. When my telephone buzzed, it startled me so much that I fumbled, and then dropped the damned receiver.

"Hello, this is Jerry David speaking," I shouted.

"Hi, Mister David…is everything okay there? This is Detective Gray. I need you to come down to our headquarters and talk with us today. Can you make four o'clock?"

"Why, I've told you the truth and everything I knew about the Monroe girl. Do you think I did it?"

"No, no, no, I need you to look at some pictures. I thought you might have known some of them. It seems there has been another murder of a young co-ed. Can I depend on you at four?"

I took a deep breath, wanted to deny him, but thought of my own honest integrity and then committed to his request, "Yes, I can make it there at four."

The rest of my Friday seemed to fly by, until I noticed it was a quarter till three. I called my managing editor, Freddie Upshaw, and told him I had to leave early to meet with the cops.

"Hey, that's okay. We need more cop shoptalk in our paper. See if you can find a scoop down there. I will expect something on my desk Tuesday morning, Jerry. If you come up with something, ol' buddy, I might even give you that beat and you can get off that gravy job I'm paying too much for…ha!"

"Why that's not…"

He hung up laughing loudly before I could get my two cents in. I knew he was probably kidding, so I hurriedly gathered my things and headed to my car.

The sky had cleared nicely, but the unbending cold north wind blew briskly. I tightened my scarf and then pulled my hat down. I raised the collar of my trench coat, leaned against the big door, and took my planned upright exit. A gust of wind, which always follows the lined up rows of city street buildings, caught me as I scooted along to my Jeep. I liked my old Cherokee. It seemed to always crank right over in the cold and bust through the deepest snow banks with gusto when I got silly and wanted to play in the snow. I would forever remember to check the anti-freeze though.

The new police headquarters resembled a modern prison as I slipped into a parking space. I could not believe there were parking meters and I had to slip some coins in the slot and turn the handle. I wondered if the illustrious sergeant would reimburse me if I asked for my money back.

I dropped the thought and headed across the parking lot when I saw several cars headed my way. The drivers and passengers looked creepy. They must be visiting one or more of the prisoners, I imagined. They looked like they might belong in there themselves. I ignored their honk to expedite and made it safely. I glanced back and saw one passenger holding a pistol, who shoved it inside the glove box. I pretended not to see and headed inside. I looked at the floor menu and saw in bold letters, "Investigations" with an arrow pointing down the hall.

I found the door wide-open and Detective-sergeant Gray sitting in a swivel chair with his feet propped up on the windowsill. He had his back to me while talking loudly on the phone, so I remained standing quietly in the doorway.

"Look, you little fart blossom…I'll spank your butt black and blue if I have to see you in the woodshed, I don't care how big you are. Don't you dare pull anything like that again. Hey, I don't care if the other guys did it also. I expect more than that from you…got it? You're nineteen, for God's sake, grow up!

"Tell your mother I love her and I will be a little late. Get your homework done before you go out tonight and be home before the eleven o'clock curfew. I will definitely look at your homework when I get home. Love ya, son."

Boy was I glad I was not his kid. Actually, what he said was threatening, but had merit. This cop must really be a human being after all, I thought for the first time.

"Knock, knock!" I summoned.

"Oh, there you are…come in, Mister David…have a seat," he nicely responded.

He turned, and then reached to his intercom system and requested that the photographs be brought in from the morgue and The Peppermint File.

The Peppermint File? Humm, what was this all about, I wondered immediately.

"Cup of coffee, Jerry…I may call you, Jerry, eh?" he asked, as he grabbed an empty cup off its hanger on the wall that read, 'Arrest and Conviction' in script.

"Cream and sugar," he suggested.

"Yes, thanks…two lumps and a touch of creamer," I replied.

I was beginning to get comfortable with my first sip, when this young, gorgeous, dark-haired goddess of a woman wearing a star on her humongous chest came in through the door. She accidentally dropped some of the big paper file upon the floor near me. My heart fluttered and I raced to bend down to help her. As we rose up together, I gave her the papers that I gathered and we were face to face. Her eyes were dark, as was her skin. Surely, she was not from around here or she spent a lot of time inside a tanning bed.

Looking closely, I assumed it was the latter. In addition, when she bent over in front of me to pick up an additional lone flyer, I nearly stumbled over the chair backwards, seeing her hourglass shape of her rear. I think it was instantaneous love, but I could not even muster hello. All I could think of is, "Arrest me!"

She giggled, smiling widely. Her perfectly aligned white teeth accentuated her perfect lips of red. I am afraid I just stood there dazed and stared at her like a fool. I had never felt that way before, never. I became embarrassed, but did not move, as if a deer blinded in the headlights.

The lovely woman eased up to me, looked me straight in the eyes, winked, and then smiled a smile I could never forget.

"Do you mind, sir? May I get by?" she spoke.

It was somewhat sassy, maybe playful, but enough information to know she was way out of my class and there was no place in her heart for me.

Holy cow, I thought. Could she be a cop? My eyes focused on her like magnets and I felt a twinge in my loins. Her perfume crossed my senses and it was wonderful. I watched as she exited, until suddenly Gray got my attention back.

"Ah hem!" he coughed loudly, as he cleared his throat to regain my attention. "I have some pictures I'd like you to look at...these are six co-eds that have been murdered in our province over a five year period...two earlier this year," he informed me, as he handed them to me one by one for my review.

"Two are definitely related, because of their kinds of death-method. Of course, I say they are all college girls. These others are older murders and missing persons that are all about the same age. This covers five years, with no arrest made or information on any of them. Some just disappeared into thin air. Seems to be spread out, but maybe our killer likes to travel, eh?"

The first one, I immediately recognized, because it was the nude body of Meredith Monroe taken at the coroner's office. I could not believe he would hand me that picture. It was so cold with no respect for the naked dead. The rest of the photos did not cause me to know any of them. However, all were very pretty young women, I then told him. Therefore, I was afraid I could not be of any usefulness.

"Hold on a minute. Do you keep the photos of those girls who write to you?"

"Yes, they are filed alphabetically, unless they send a self-addressed envelope to have them returned. Some run week after week. I hand them off to a secretary, not as beautiful as yours, I must say."

He looked rather peeved and frowned hard at me, as if I just flirted with his wife, so I carefully continued.

"Ah hem…she files them someplace. You want me to have her send them over to you?"

"No, Mister David…I'm coming to you. I personally want to go over each and every one of those ads and pictures with you. I need you to tell me as much as possible, if you can, about your operation and those you've come across several times."

"Why?"

Then Gray handed me a folder with a picture of a nude dead woman's body in it.

"See that girl you didn't recognize? This was in her purse at the scene of her death."

He leaned over his desk and handed me an envelope with a handwritten note inside for an ad request, addressed to me, Gerry Loveletter, CMEN Newspaper. I was astonished.

I gulped, "So, someone is murdering my clients, huh?"

"That's actually very perceptive, Mister David. You might make a good detective. Now you know why I want to go through all those pictures and ads. We might discover something that could help you to remember… something that connects them and maybe be a big help in solving these crimes. I believe we have a serial killer out there."

"All right…I'll do everything I can. When is a good time?"

"No, when is it good for you? I get paid, you don't," he said rather seriously, but smiling.

I knew I was cutting into my recreational life, but I suggested that the only time I had free was my own on weekends.

"Can you take those pictures to your house?"

"Yes, but I live in a one bedroom apartment near Didsbury, west of Canada 2. I'd like to move closer, but it's so beautiful and peaceful there."

"Great! This has to remain top secret with us, no leaks. If we do have a serial killer, we don't want any investigative news to get to him before we nail that son-a-bitch. If you don't mind, I'll be there Saturday, eh?…that's tomorrow morning…can't delay or waste one minute."

"Well, I don't know if I can get the entire info ready by tomorrow. The office will be closed. I can still get in though with my keys. I'll call you tonight if I get them, okay?"

"You must get it done for those girls, eh, Jerry. We have to do our best before something like this happens again."

Then he handed back Meredith's picture.

"I want you to keep this…I know, I know, you don't want it…but it will give you guidance, inspiration to follow through on this."

Without looking at it, I put it in my coat pocket, shook his extended hand, then left.

"Oh yeah, what's your telephone number?" I asked.

"775-3200…that's my home phone…and, I hope you will be interrupting one of my wonderful meals which are prepared solely by my daughter, at six," he said, excessively loudly, as if he wanted someone else to hear his compliments. "She's a wonderful gourmet… look at my waistline," he laughed. "She went to cooking school, among others. Spent all my money, too, on colleges…I am still paying for her fun. But, she pays me back, meal by meal," he continued very loudly, still with a glimmer in his eyes.

He was actually very fit and trim…no "done-lapped-over disease" there. When I left, the beautiful secretary was gone. I felt a bit cheated by having to stay past her quitting time.

I headed for my office, hoping I might catch, Jill, Mr. Upshaw's secretary, still overworked, and staying after hours, as she often did; especially lately sometimes. She had been with the paper nearly twenty years and was always very faithful to Mr. Upshaw's requests.

The parking lot was empty. On Fridays, while the printer personnel started rolling out the papers, the writers and columnists scurried away to cash their checks and hit the grocery stores. I was no different, but today I did not receive my check, because I left early. Maybe it was left on my desk, I thought, or Jill still had it. I would head there first. The janitor did not get there until five thirty, so my office was locked.

Jill's office door was still open as I headed there. However, some kind of unfamiliar noise was coming from somewhere, so I stopped short to listen. There was a bumping noise, which undoubtedly generated from the boss's office. Maybe he had left that damned coffee pot of his on again and it was jiggling empty. Yep, that is exactly what it was, I thought. I hurried as fast as I could.

It could also be a fire starting up, I imagined, so I burst through the unlocked door. Oops! The boss had Jill on the couch, punching a hole in her, with a bump, bump, bump rhythm, pounding against the coffee table next to it. I saw more of them both than I ever wanted to and tried to sneak back out, but... "Shit! It's Jerry, get off!" Jill screamed to a very feverish Freddie.

When the boss rolled off and stood up, he showed his sweat and had a big frown... "Get the hell out of here, you son-of-a-bitch!" he hollered.

I skedaddled and I mean quickly. Nevertheless, Jill came running out of the office door behind me, completely frustrated, hanging onto my arm and begging me not to tell a soul.

"I didn't see a thing, Jill. What you and the boss do is your business...you are my friend remember? I'm just looking for my check and the cops want all the pictures and files from my personal ads."

"Your check is on your desk...I'll bring those files to your apartment on my way home, I promise. Please, don't tell anyone, please!" Jill begged.

I took her by the shoulders and looked her straight in the eyes.

"Now I'll say this once more...you are my friend. Why, heck, you are a very beautiful woman. I have even thought of being with you that way myself. However, I knew better. It cannot happen in the workplace. Why wouldn't the boss, or any man for that matter, not look at you as a very attractive woman? You definitely are. You are also a wonderful person, Jill. You have always been more than kind to me. When your husband passed, I felt so sorry for you. I know you are lonely. I am too. Now, forget it. I appreciate the files being brought to my apartment, because I'm starving and if I don't get something in my gut, I'll faint. Are you sure it's not too much to ask?"

"Yes, I mean, no, it's fine…I know where everything is and when Joe the janitor gets here I'll have him load them in my trunk. He won't mind if I ask him," she assured me smiling.

I then wondered if she did it with Joe, too.

"Thanks…go back to what you were doing…I'm a personal love-ad guy, remember?" I said smiling.

I turned away and tried not to look back. I wondered if she would actually go back, so I peeked around and saw the boss's door closing slowly. Oh well, who cares…I desperately need sustenance. I left, but my thoughts went to what I saw. I would never wonder what Jill's body looked like again. However, I just might dream about seeing it now and then.

CHAPTER 3

I hit Hardee's and the place was jumping with teenyboppers. I was one of them not so long ago, I reminded myself, as this young stud started hitting on some cute little thing right in front of me. The line was so long, ten deep, so I looked outside and saw the drive-thru lane was moving along fine. I hustled out to my Jeep and drove into the car lane. "Out of order" the sign read attached to the outside speaker. "Order inside only". No wonder everyone was inside standing in line. I pulled out and decided a nearby homemade pizza place would be good with a cold mug of Molson's. There was not much of a crowd yet, so I got served quickly. I ate, and then headed for the nearest Safeway.

I decided to BBQ a big rib eye steak on my patio grill, with a nice-sized baked potato, with some fresh salad greens for tomorrow's dinner. The Stampeders were playing the B.C. Lions at noon, and I did not want to miss that, but then I remembered Detective-sergeant Gray was coming. I also picked up some instant Folgers and a half-gallon of 2% milk, then grabbed up another steak just in case Gray stayed too long and was hungry. I cashed my payroll check at the checkout and then headed home.

As I drove down Canada 2, I could not help thinking of Jill coming later. I had to hurry, because as a bachelor, I kind of let things slide. I had not dusted, washed this week's dishes nor did any laundry. In other words, my apartment was a real mess. I would be very embarrassed if Jill saw it that way.

I drove into my apartment's parking space, gathered up my grub sacks and work satchel, then headed through my walk-in patio door. I immediately put away the groceries and grabbed up all the newspapers I left on the floor by my favorite chair. I quickly changed into my house clothes, shorts, socks and a tee shirt and cranked up the sound system to hear the beat when "Tall Cool Woman in a Black Dress" came on blaring. I then gyrated and guided the vacuum around the living room and kitchen. It was the weekend and I was dancing around happily.

I took out the week's garbage, grabbed up all my dirty socks, towels, the clothes off the bathroom floor, and shoved them all into the washing machine. I could sort them and wash them tomorrow. I looked around and the place was neater, so I hit the remote and put my feet up in my recliner to watch the news. I began reading today's CMEN, especially my column to check for errors. There were at least seventy lonely searchers-for-love ads, and many sounded just like the next. All were desperately seeking romance.

Apparently, I dozed off, but jumped straight up when the doorbell rang. It was Jill, with a very embarrassed look on her face. I just ignored her look and went straight out to her vehicle to get the picture-files. I had to make two trips. Jill waited patiently then she tugged at my arm.

"Jerry, don't look at me that way," she suddenly spoke.

"What way? I'm just freezing my butt off, that's all. Care for some fresh instant?"

"Might as well. I have nothing to go home to, remember?"

I immediately felt sorry for this lovely woman. She wasn't a slut or anything close to that. She was my friend, so I put my arms around her to give her a big hug. We embraced a little too long, I guess, and then found each other looking closely into one another's eyes. Instinctively, I kissed her and she kissed me back. Then she turned away and told me she was sorry.

"Sorry for what? We are both adults and we don't ever have to forgive anything to each other. We are friends and friends hug and kiss, as much as needed. I thought we both needed a kiss to clear the air.

Now, how about I get you that hot cup of coffee, Jill, eh? Besides, I'll need you to go over these files with me, if that's okay?"

"I guess so. As I said, I have nothing else to do tonight."

I didn't even mention "What about Freddie?" He was married and probably dining with his wife at a nice restaurant. He sometimes stole my columns' better restaurant coupons and used them himself… cheapskate!

Jill helped me to figure out her files and we tried to get the duplicates together. We had them spread out everywhere.

Suddenly, it was eleven. I peeked out on the lighted parking lot, and all the cars seemed smothered in a blowing, fresh 10" snow. It was then I realized that Jill might have to spend the night.

Now that's not too unacceptable. In Canada, everyone eventually finds himself or herself stranded somewhere, because of sudden blizzards and blowing, deep snowdrifts…that is common. Complete strangers often take in stranded persons and offer temporary shelter for the night. Therefore, I asked her to stay. She looked outside, saw the deep snow, and then said she would appreciate that. Yes, maybe there was more than a friendship going here, but it was the logical thing to do.

We searched through more of the older love ads when I found Meredith Monroe's first request, then six more, which spanned three years. Her last was nearly six months ago. According to her pictures, she was not always blond but very attractive. I read her bio and discovered that she once worked as a health spa's aerobics instructor and attended only part-time at Calgary University. She was majoring in primary education with a minor in psychology.

The wind started howling outside and when I peeked out the patio curtain, I noticed ice forming on the bottom of the sliding doors. There must have been an air leak, so I went to the washer and grabbed several used towels to place against the draft. It seemed to help. I noticed snow had drifted over two feet high on the doors, unlike any time I could remember. After all, I leased this apartment because the windows faced the south.

That worried me, so I turned the TV to the weather channel and learned a big Norther was blowing in a blizzard across the Rockies and onto the Alberta plains. I had not paid enough attention. My first thought was of the big football game being delayed, or postponed. That thought was aggravation enough, but the lights started flickering and in moments, we were in complete darkness.

I had but one scented candle that was in the bathroom, so I fumbled around in the darkness to get it. Jill had a cigarette lighter in her purse, which surprised me. We lit the candle and sat it down on the coffee table next to us on the sofa. It soon got chilly, so I went to a closet and got two extra blankets and a pillow. Jill rolled up into a ball with one blanket and asked if the water was still warm in the pipes for a pot of coffee. I got up, turned on the hot water at the kitchen sink, and then thought of the fondue set that was in the rear of the cabinets. I got it out. It was clean, never used, and had a little silver pot that could heat more water by candle if we needed it later.

I brought over the instant coffee, with some milk from the fridge and poured each a refill. It was then I noticed how quiet everything seemed, except for voices from within the apartment complex, when one man shouted out into the hallway inquiring if anyone had extra candles, batteries, or a lantern. Footsteps went pitter-patter across the upstairs floor. I had never paid much attention to those noises before.

I turned to Jill and asked, "What's next?"

"What do you mean?"

"You can have my bed, but I haven't changed the sheets for awhile, I must warn you. I'm not a dirty person or anything like that, it's just it might be nicer on the sofa."

"This sofa is just fine…please don't leave me just yet, eh? This coffee will keep me awake for hours and I hate to be alone in a strange home. I need to shower and use your john right about now. Think there's any hot water left?"

"Hum…I thought about that. I think everything is on natural gas, which means there should be hot water for a while, right?"

"You'd think so," she hoped.

"Okay, the clean towels are next to the shower and the new soap, oops, I don't think I bought any, sorry. However, I have body wash and shampoo on the shower hanger. Let me put the candle back in there for you to see."

She followed me into the bath and then said, "Aren't you going to shower?"

"Well, no, under these circumstances I'll wait until tomorrow, I guess."

"Don't be silly. In this dark, we can both shower at once. Give me a minute to tinkle, and then you can find the shampoo and body wash for me. I do not see very well in the dark. I'll hold the candle while you wash and vice versa," she said, as she slipped past me and closed the bathroom door.

Hold the candle…now how was she going to do that? I guess she was just nervous. Nevertheless, we did shower together, as friends no less. She scrubbed my back as I did hers…that is it. We giggled a lot. There wasn't any fondling or anything…not any that we intentionally thought about. The shower was small so we touched here and there a lot. It was close quarters, but manageable. I had placed the candle on the toilet lid so there wasn't much light going on.

Our shower was cut short, because halfway through, the water suddenly went cold, which quickly broke our mounting tensions. We hurriedly rinsed, danced in the chilling stream, then hopped out and toweled off. We laughed hardily at each other's body shivering actions as we bumped into one another.

"We would look awfully silly if the lights came on," I mentioned.

Jill asked to borrow something to sleep in. We headed for my bedroom closet. Jill followed, holding onto my waist. Feeling around in the dark closet for a long shirt to wear, she selected my favorite football jersey of the Stampeders. She slid it over her head and it fit fine. I no-looked it to my dresser drawers like a blind man and put on my underwear, as usual, and then grabbed the shorts I always slept in.

"Who says two friends can't have fun on a cold winter's night?" Jill suddenly spouted, still shivering, while shaking her hair loose from a towel wrapped around it.

"Let's get back to the sofa and under a cover…I'm freezing," she said, teeth chattering.

My eyes had adjusted somewhat to the darkness and I could actually see how bright, and how white her teeth looked shining in the candlelight when she smiled. It rather gave me inner warmth, because I knew this antic in the darkness made her happy. Ours was a rekindling of an old friendship.

I really enjoyed Jill's company, always did. She was always there at work with a compliment and a smile when she delivered my mail or paycheck to my desk. She always dressed nicely and had a great body, too, for a forty-ish something woman, almost twenty years my senior.

As we sat on the sofa, she seemed to go off in a dream world that included telling me about the first time she came to work for the paper when her husband got hurt in a hockey game. Jill continued telling me how she met Turner, her now deceased husband. They both were attending Calgary University, he a senior on a scholarship for hockey, she just a sophomore. After Turner's graduation, they married when the Flames selected Turner and signed him with a huge bonus.

Unfortunately, when he right away broke his ankle, he did not end up making the team, and was eventually released. They lived high off his big bonus money for a while, until he later became a professional and star player with the Alberta Stars, an amateur league. Jill had quit school before Turner had lost his first paycheck.

Jill had worked summers for the Calgary Sun during school, but they had hired someone else after she left to get married. That is when she came to work for CMEN to support them both. Turner later became a well-paid oil rig worker in the vast fields around Calgary. Jill stayed on anyway at CMEN. They never had children.

I fell asleep listening to her soft voice still reminiscing. I also overheard my upstairs neighbors trying hard to make a baby, but it did not excite me this time. There was no extended, deep moaning, as many times before. It only lasted two minutes with a loud "Damn it… sorry!" I guess they needed some warmth, too.

We both apparently had fallen asleep, balled up in our covers at each end of the sofa to stay warm. We were rudely awakened about 2 a.m., when the electric suddenly popped back on. All of the electrical appliances made noises. The electronic digital clock faces flashed and I felt the heat begin to blow from the furnace. The TV was off its station and crackling loudly, so without much said I got up, turned off the TV, lights, and headed for bed.

I was very thankful the power company men were out doing their jobs. Jill got up too and followed me into my bedroom. She then lay down quietly on one side of the bed with her back to me and pulled the covers over her. I guess she was sleepwalking. I hoped she would not wake up screaming in the morning when she saw I was in bed with her. Oh well, nothing happened.

Ours was not at all like a new romantic relationship. After all, I had known her for all the years I had been with CMEN, but never thought of her as anyone other than the boss's secretary. Tonight in the darkness, I saw the light, I guess. It's funny, I thought. There is much more to some people than we ever realize, unless we spend time with them. That thought would be in my next column, I decided. However, tonight, exhausted by all the tension of trying to do too much too quickly, I fell asleep very easily.

CHAPTER 4

The loud scraping outside of the highway snowplow was annoying. I knew his job was necessary, but not as annoying as the pounding on my door. I peeked at the nightstand clock and it read 5:37a.m. I then realized Jill was beside me sleeping, but arousing also from all the pounding.

I hurriedly got up, still in my shorts and tee, and asked whom it was?

The quick responsive voice was jovial as he spoke, "It's your favorite donut delivery man!"

I recognized the voice as Detective-sergeant Gray. I unlocked the door wondering if he were nuts or something, coming to my door this early.

"Good morning, Mister David…got any hot coffee to go with these Dunkin' Donuts?" he gleefully sounded.

"It's kind of early, don't you think?"

He looked at his wristwatch and advised it was nine-thirty, "Too late to be sleeping in when we have so much to accomplish today," he rattled off.

Then I realized the electric had been off and I had forgotten to correct the clocks, so I stepped aside to let him enter. He immediately slipped out of his snow-covered boots and put them inside my closest trashcan. I guess he did that at home, but I had never thought of that. I always left them outside the door.

"Had a big one last night, eh? I followed that big snowplow right past your door. I guess we must have gotten a foot. There were abandoned empty cars on the streets all the way here. It must have caught a lot of people off guard, eh," he advised me as he took off his coat, hat, and scarf, and then went straight into the kitchen to start up the coffee pot.

"Where's your coffee?"

"I only drink instant, sorry. I only use the pot to heat up water. Here, let me get that."

"Nonsense…you get dressed and I'll break open this box of donuts…oh, you have a guest…sorry."

He was looking at Jill who was still scantily dressed in my Stampeders jersey, stretching, and yawning in the bedroom doorway.

"Oh, I smell fresh donuts," she sounded out, as if that was her delight.

"Jill, this is Detective-sergeant Gray. I told you he was coming, but not this early. Detective-sergeant Gray, this is Jill Burner, our company secretary and my friend. She was trapped here last night when that Norther blew in. Wasn't your electricity out?" I asked.

"Actually, I don't know. I had a callout about ten…haven't been home yet. It was a call to assist Red Deer. They have another unidentified female body going on. It's still mum, so you mustn't give a peep."

Jill looked concerned and moved closer to ask, "Did you see the person?" she asked Gray.

"Lady, I'm a detective…of course I saw her. I saw her throat-slit body lying…"

"That's enough…please…I tried to contact my sister last night, but she never answered. I guess I'm jumping to conclusions that something may have happened to her. She lives in Red Deer also."

"Oh, sorry…but if your sister isn't black; you can rest that idea, eh?"

"Okay, thanks. I will get dressed…those donuts smell scrumptious," Jill told him hoping to get one.

"We'll save ya one, missy," he told her as she quickly went into the bathroom. His eyes followed her every move.

"Well, ol' chap, looks like you've brightened your horizons a bit," he said, moving his eyebrows irregularly up and down to compliment me.

I went into the bedroom, put on my slippers and returned to Gray. He had the pot heating, while nipping at a big chocolate éclair in his hand.

"I see you have those pictures we needed. Find anything unusual?" he questioned.

"Not really. I don't exactly know what you're looking for. I did pull Meredith Monroe's files…there were several picture ads of her over about three years…here they are," I said, handing them to him.

He looked at them briefly, and then put them down to grab another éclair. He then tried to talk with his mouth full.

"She was, ah, wea..rvy pretty, eh?" he spoke, spewing donut bits out and cupping the crumbles that fell from his lips in one hand. He gathered them up in his palm and dumped them back inside his mouth, swallowed them, and then continued. "First black gal in our case…she may have been a prostitute, but then again a real nice dresser and not part of the others. She was in the technical triangular area, so we have to suspect her as another part of the serial killer's victims…especially because her throat was slit like some of the others…like Monroe's," he advised me. "Have some donuts, eh? I haven't chowed-down all night. I decided by the time I went home and changed, I wouldn't be able to keep my eyes open."

Jill came out, then immediately took three coffee mugs from the cabinets, and served up the instant coffee. Her eyes were on the donuts and she helped herself. He had bought two dozen, so we had plenty.

"Thanks for the donuts," I told Gray as I grabbed a very soft glaze.

Then it was dunk and, "Ummm!"…dunk and "Ummm!" We almost finished off the whole box. I ate five.

Gray walked around the room looking at our displayed pictures, picking up one or two at a time, here and there, checking the dates. He must have pulled out a hundred or so. Then he turned to us and said, "Those can be returned. These others are our ammunition. Let's get them spread out on the kitchen table…no, no, on the floor in front of the sofa…that's better…I may have to snooze a bit," he spoke yawning. "I always get dopey after I eat…just a wink, mind you," he said smiling as he flopped down on my sofa and stretched out, talking with his eyes shut. He catnapped for several minutes to our amusement, then snorted and awoke.

Then Gray reached for his briefcase and removed the largest magnifying glass I had ever seen.

"Sometimes you really have to scrutinize a picture to see the whole of it," he added. "All we investigators possess that unique talent," he mused.

We just listened.

"Now, of course, we are concerned mainly with the ladies, but we have to go over all these blokes also. After all, these girls did not do themselves in, did they? Now, since we have all been drawn together so comfy-cozy, you must both call me Nigel, eh? May I call you Jill and Jerry?"

Jill and I voiced our agreement, and then we all started searching through the pictures for anything we thought might be suspect. Jill seemed organized and pulled some peculiar men from the files immediately. After all, she had contact with those pictures before. We did not know exactly what we were searching for, but Nigel said we would be going over each, repeatedly, until we did get a clue, or found nothing. We searched for over an hour before clues began to appear.

"There you go, missy, you have the eye, eh?" spouted Nigel. "This bloke is a fugitive from the law. He has committed several rapist crimes in the past. I sent him up years ago."

"Do you think he's the one?" Jill anxiously inquired.

Nigel smiled that silly smile of his, put the picture back under the paper clip, which attached it to his bio, then said, "Sorry am I for alertin' you, missy. He died last year in prison," as he placed the picture in the dead file he started.

Our search lasted several hours when suddenly Nigel asked me if I had any provisions. Therefore, I looked outside at my snow-covered grill and decided I might broil the two steaks, make some extra hamburgers, and bake the potatoes too, all in the oven.

"Get to it then, Jerry. I feel it's time to get your TV turned onto the big game, eh?"

I was surprised, but yes, I hoped the Stampeders game would be playing. In addition, it was starting as scheduled, to my surprise.

"Here, give me a chance to wash this ink off my fingers and I'll do the cooking, while you blokes sit," Jill said to my relief. I wasn't much at cooking. "Jerry, you might season everything for me, first, please."

The game became a breakaway quickly as, Quarterback Buck Pierce, of the B.C. Lions, hit receiver, Geroy Simon, for a forty-six yard touchdown, on second and three. I got up and went to help Jill. Gray closed his eyes and did not say a peep. The kitchen was warm and the aroma smelled heavenly.

When the steaks finished well done, I set out the tableware, and Jill placed the food on the table. I thought it rude of Gray to pass out on my sofa, but then again, poor dog had been up all night. We decided to let him slumber as we dined. I ate one hamburger to save the best for Jill and Gray. Apparently, the aroma woke up Gray and there he was standing behind us.

"You mean you started without me?" he questioned rather gruffly.

"You were snoring, so we thought it best you got rest before you went home. Jill has your steak in the microwave," I explained nicely.

"Did you make it rare, missy?" he asked Jill as he peeked inside.

"Actually, you didn't say anything, so it's well done," she said rather apologetically.

Gray walked away from the microwave with plate in hands, and then advised her, "I can't eat well done steak. It ruins the whole idea of a well-marbled steak. A steak has to moo back at you when you cut into it. That's the only way to eat one. How about I belly up to one or two of those burgers with one or two of those Molson's I eyed in your fridge, eh?" he suggested as he scooped up four burgers and then opened the fridge to grab two beers. "Anyone else?" Gray motioned with the bottles of beer in hand. "Now, this is what I call hospitality… got horseradish or Grey Poupon mustard?"

"Yes, here, I'll get them for you," I said, as Gray juggled his meal past me and placed it all on the dinner table. He raised his leg up over the back of the chair and slid over and down into the seat.

"Man, I'm hungry," is all he said trying not to nibble a bit off the burger in hand, awaiting my return.

I got the condiments for him and watched as he bowed his head and gave the sign of the cross. Then he slopped on the mustard, covered the hamburgers with horseradish, and then stacked four slices of bread with double-decker burgers. He stuffed potato chips on the other side of his plate with a heaping portion of pork and beans and a few sliced onions and tomatoes he spotted.

"Got a jimmy, eh?" he asked for to open his Molson's.

"Twist off tops!" I told him.

"Oh, imagine that…and all these years I wasted time searching for an opener, ha! How long have they had those?"

"Oh, about twenty years, or so," I advised.

Nigel must have felt pretty dumb, because he kept looking at the bottle top's screw-on cap very strangely. Then he took out his reading glasses.

"Well I'll be damned…never noticed those rings before."

We all had a good laugh.

The football game on TV roared with hometown sounds of excitement when one of the running backs for Calgary hit a hole in the offensive line and tiptoed into the end zone.

Gray got up, took his plate to the coffee table, and then started getting excited in front of the TV. He kicked off his shoes, and then sat down in the middle of the sofa leaving no room for anyone else. When another exciting play occurred, he jumped up and down on my sofa after our Stampeders recovered a fumbled kickoff return by the Lions.

"Come on, girl, show your smile and those white teeth!" he screamed suddenly. "Now kick higher and show the guys your fine legs, woman!" Again, he was yelling.

I peeked over at him and he was prancing like a cheerleader of all things. Jill and I both put our hands over our mouths and about split a gut. He eventually propped his feet upon the coffee table, quickly drank his two beers while cheering the Stampeders on, and then curled up and made himself right at home on my sofa. He continued to hoot and holler, until the game was over, a long three hours later. He missed doing the dishes.

When the game was over, Gray grabbed up dozens of selected photos with bios and told me he had lots of ammunition now, but also told me not to return the others just yet, as they may hold clues or patterns. Jill advised him she must put them back in the files, but they would be available anytime. Gray said he would like to run all the names through NCIC, Interpol and any other RMCP and FBI crime computers available to him and hoped he would get lucky finding some possible suspect.

"See ya, kids…thanks for the meal and the rest. Giss will be frantic if I miss supper at home and don't tell her how great she was today… later!" he spoke, confusing Jill and me, as he put on his shoes, coat, and hat and disappeared out the door into the hallway.

"I must go too, Jerry. Thanks for the good time. I enjoyed being social with you like this after all these years together at work. We will have to do it when it snows again, but next time at my house. It does not matter if the electric goes out there. Turner built our home underground to share the thermo heat down under. It is warm in the winter and cool in the summer. He cherished his idea. That is why I have kept it. Well, see you on Monday," Jill told me as she gathered her things to leave. "Oh yes, one thing, don't mention this to Freddie or he'll give us both troubles at the office. He's a pain as it is."

I watched the lovely woman through the patio curtain as she walked out to her car, dusted off the snow with a big snowbrush, and then drove away.

It was funny, because I had never seen her car before, since she and the boss shared a private garage behind the offices. Who would have expected she drove a big Cadillac? It was an older model Deville, but looked like new. I guess she and Turner had bought it back in his hay day.

I closed the curtains and started gathering the photos to put back in their boxes. I smiled to myself about how we all had come together in such a happy way for such a terrible reason. These boxes of pictures had become part of the Peppermint Files, eh.

CHAPTER 5

The days that followed were hectic. More snow, more new love letters arrived at my desk and more Nigel Gray. Jill was an angel and I could not help but thank her ten times every day for assisting me. We became much closer. She developed a cold and began coughing incessantly. I was worried she had the beginning of pneumonia.

Sometimes, my mind would drift off in the afternoon's bog of paperwork to thoughts of that lovely woman I saw in Nigel's office. I dare not ask him who she was for fear she was his own lady-friend. Little did I know how much she meant to him? He apparently protected her from every advancing male who had anything but police business on his mind.

Nevertheless, I could still dream. I thought of her eyes staring into mine, her smile, which I could never forget. I think I was in love with someone I really did not know, but I was certainly obsessed with thoughts of her.

One evening my phone rang and it was Nigel. He sounded a bit intoxicated. I suspected that he was drinking, because Nigel very politely asked me to look into my love files the next day to see if there was a Kelly Barns in my files. He was more demanding, usually. He advised me that the girl was a brunette, twenty-two, Caucasian, single, young and pretty and unfortunately found murdered near the USA/

Canadian border. She was not a student, but was from the Calgary area. She was stabbed to death like some of the others.

Every reported death of a young woman became treated as part of Nigel's investigation. It had grown month by month, year by year, with no results. Some were feasible serial murder cases, but some were ruled out as highly improbable or unrelated.

In the Barns' case, before I could check my files, Nigel called me at the office, told me the killer was her boyfriend, and police already apprehended him in Montana. Well, not really apprehended him, he was shot and killed by the local sheriff's deputies during a traffic stop. Case closed.

This entire investigative thing was wearing on Jill and me. I guessed it had to be worse for Nigel, since it was his sole responsibility to catch this killer. Therefore, I gave him my every ounce of effort. Then I goofed.

After I finished with several folders one Friday, I inadvertently left them open on my desk for Jill to put into our files. However, unknown to me, Jill had left earlier than usual for personal reasons. She finally had a doctor's appointment for the cough, which I continually suggested she see a doctor for help. I guess she finally had scheduled that appointment. She never had done that before on company time. Unfortunately, Mr. Upshaw came into my office after I had left and started snooping.

Upon reading the files on my desk, Mr. Upshaw decided to open all of the locked files and on his whim, after reading about Nigel's investigation, developed a story of his own about the terrible murders, including some of the victims' names. He had asked me several times if I had found any cop-related news, but I kept putting him off and telling him that I was still working on it. He decided to finish my work, I guess.

It was our paper's front-page news and he had divulged the murders as a serial killer on the loose. In his own editorial column, which he sometimes wrote as managing editor, he named Nigel Gray as the sergeant-detective in charge. Upshaw described the killings and gave away pertinent information only the detectives should have known. It was a breach of my agreement with Nigel, which I had made to maintain the secrecy and integrity of his investigation. That agreement was blown sky high now.

When I saw it in the Saturday's paper, I almost barfed. Then my phone rang…it was a very angry Nigel Gray. I could not explain fast enough for him as he accused me of disclosing pertinent information, which may help the killer to escape capture or change his mode of mutilation to make it impossible to determine his pattern. He slammed his receiver down.

I grumbled to myself thinking why Nigel got off on me. I was only partially at fault and I could not chew out the boss, Mr. Upshaw, as Nigel did me. I turned on the TV, poured a Molson's, and then sat back down to watch the big game. Football was the only remedy for my now mutilated feelings.

Go Stampeders…rah, rah, rah! Only that certain Outrider cheerleader on the Stampeders' sidelines really looked heavenly. Nevertheless, she hardly ever got any close-ups for those TV shots when I was watching, so one's imagination was then left to surmise. Oh, she was in other close-ups and even TV interviews, but I never seemed to be watching.

When a touchdown scored after a long drive up the field by the Stampeders, a rear shot of that cheerleader seemed much too familiar. Now was that one of my love letter girls, I thought to myself…no, but her butt sure looked familiar…hummm. The Molson's put me at ease and I dozed off to the constant hum from the noise emitted by the 43,000 fans screaming and blowing their horns. However, the constant ringing of my telephone, which I finally realized was not coming from the TV, disrupted my needed rest.

"Hello, this is Jerry," I answered, still drowsy.

"Jerry…Nigel here…sorry about the riot act…I was taken aback by the loss of our pact of secrecy. I still need your cooperation and Jill's also. Do I have that, Jerry?"

"Sure, if you go holler at my boss like you're doing at me…no, strike that, he'll only fire me…forget that," I spoke into the receiver. "Yes, I'll still do my part and I'll try to rectify what has happened," I told him, loudly, as if he couldn't hear me. "Where are you anyway? The background noise sounds as if you're in a drunken barroom brawl."

"Got free tickets to the Stamps…we just scored on the Rough Riders and the tally is 27-10…aren't you watching the game?"

"Yes, but I fell asleep somehow," I whispered, just to annoy his delight.

"What? Can't understand you? Well good…now that I have allowed myself to stop seeing red and actually considered the consequences, it might be a gift after all. Nothing has deterred the murderer yet, so maybe knowing now he is being hunted will force him to do something we can trace…anyway, sorry about that tirade thing," he shouted out and then I lost him.

Damn, damn, damn, I wanted to get away from all this. Subconsciously, I really hoped this miscue had been bad enough to have Nigel expel us from all this misery. I would never make a homicide detective. It is just too gruesome and demanding. I guess Nigel was a good candidate because murders never seemed to bother him too much. Getting his man was his only concern, not the deceased, nor their mutilated conditions, I figured.

The Stampeders scored once more…rah, rah, rah! I looked hard to see Nigel sitting somewhere in the crowded Calgary Stadium to no avail. Now that was senseless…no just plain stupid, I realized finally. Then I saw that girl again along the sidelines and wished I had bought a season pass.

CHAPTER 6

On Monday, Jill had not reported to work. I was shocked to see a new secretary handling her desk duties, so I went to her and inquired why.

"Pardon me, who are you and where is Jill Burner?" I needed to know.

"I'm Rita Tory, a temp worker. I do not know anyone here, except Mr. Upshaw, of course. Who are you, and what do you do here, may I ask?"

"Loveletter," I told her ignoring her question, as I bolted to Mr. Upshaw's office. I found him with his feet propped up on his desk while reading yesterday's news from the Calgary Sun Newspaper.

"Pardon me, Mr. Upshaw...what happened to Jill?"

"She went to the doctor Friday for her cold and then got tested. Her doctor advised her that she must not get out in the cold and stay in bed for at least a week. Some sort of lung congestion problem, she mentioned."

He said it so nonchalantly that I almost cussed him for not telling me.

"Did you send flowers?"

"No, didn't think of that. Maybe it would be a good gesture, huh... after all, she has been here so long. I doubt that girl over there in her office will make out like Jill has."

That did it. I was really pissed at the man. He was so low…it was he who took advantage of his secretary. Now when she was in need of physical and possibly mental support, he apparently abandoned her.

"Look, I'm driving over to her home right now, looking to see if she needs anything. Want to go along?"

"No, I've got a business to run, remember? I might call her later today, after you take her a big bunch of roses from us all. Tell her to take the entire time off that she needs. She's still on the payroll and her insurance will cover everything."

How cold and so business-like of him; I dare not cuss him aloud, but if he could read my mind, he might realize what an ass I thought he was. I left on the run. I just knew it was more than a simple cold affecting Jill…I just knew.

When I had locked my office, I told the new secretary, Rita, to call the florist and have four dozen roses ready for me to pick up and charge them to Upshaw. She was impressed.

At least she got that right because the flowers were just being brought out of the chiller as I arrived. I signed for the flowers and had trouble getting them to stand up in the passenger's seat of my car while I drove, so I stopped and put the seat belt snugly about them. It was a half hour drive to Jill's place. I had not been there before, but seeing that immense underground home up on the side of a wooded hill led me up the long drive. It was really fancy and a real showplace. I never knew it was that big even though Jill had told me in her night-over.

When Jill answered the doorbell at ten, still dressed in a bra and her panties, covered up very loosely by her partially opened housecoat and puffing a cigarette, I was shocked. However, seeing her hair up in curlers and mudpack on her face about blew my mind. She looked like Aunt Jemima, only much thinner. I stared as she said, "You come by here for that coffee?"

I handed her the roses and intended to kiss her on the cheek, but the mudpack was everywhere, except on her lips. I planted a sincere kiss that I hoped showed everyone missed her. She laughed at the brown mustache I got kissing her lips. She wiped it off immediately with her robe and exposed her fine legs. Then she took the flowers, and said, "Sorry, with this cold thing, I couldn't smell them even if I wanted…

but they sure look pretty and brighten my day…thanks, Jerry," she told me as she placed the vase on a doily on top of her grand piano.

"You play?" I asked.

Jill sat down and sprang a 'Hello, my baby, hello, my lover, hello, my rag time guy", then stopped while coughing. She played effortlessly without as much as a peek at the ivory keys. Her voice sounded a little raspy, but very, very sexy.

"Wow!" was all I could say.

"Turner bought it for me when he hit the big time. I've always played the piano, since I was about four or five," Jill told me as she swung around with her arms extended.

"Come here, big boy. I need a big hug…just got a call from the doctor and I have to go in for some more tests and chest x-rays tomorrow…it seems there is more to this cold than a bad cough. I'm afraid of what they might find."

"Did he also tell you that smoking was bad for your health?" I demanded.

"A hundred times…but I didn't listen. I guess you reap what you sow, huh?"

"I never knew you smoked or I would have made you quit."

"Now tell me, love, just how you were going to do that?" she said smiling, her voice slurring just a bit.

"I'd grab you up and shake some sense into you…that's how."

She looked at me, took my hand, and then pulled me closer to her.

"You know, there's not much time in one's life. You pass up opportunities to make your life nicer and no one can say why. I guess its pride or stupidity."

I could then smell alcoholic beverage on her breath and saw an empty bottle of Crown Royal behind her on the kitchen table…a tall glass next to it had just a shot left in it. Jill had been drinking heavily and now her morals were slipping. She drew me even closer and kissed my lips very hard as if we had been lovers all along. I returned the kiss and it was long, but she backed away to cough several times, and then saw another mustache she left on my lips.

"About took my breath away…sorry," as she reached for me again to wipe off my face.

When her housecoat opened, I felt the warmth of her body next to mine but when she turned to lead me to her bedroom, I balked.

"I don't know…will it hurt you?"

"Boy, I certainly hope so. But if it's about you catching this cold… it ain't contagious, baby," she said, very sexy-like and in a voice I hadn't heard from her before.

I always wrote in my columns about that lust. It was a burning desire type of lust, which I had never actually experienced. We undressed, and then she saw herself in the vanity mirror and shouted, "Oh God, I forgot about that!" she freaked out, seeing that smeared up mudpack still on her face.

Jill dashed into her bathroom and I heard the shower begin. After a minute or so, she called to me.

"Okay, guy, I'm clean now… this time we'll share my shower, don't you think?"

I should not have done it, but I undressed, and then quickly hopped into Jill's shower. It was huge, much larger than mine was, and there was a big sitting bench. Jill grabbed a towel and placed it on the marble top. Then she turned on a huge spray of undirected water mist from the showerhead and lay back on the towel. The hot water enveloped us in a warm mist, as we came together. It was about to get very uncomfortable when Jill could not stand the pressure of my body on top of hers. The marble was just too hard. For a brief moment, I thought she had reconsidered our union, but instead she again took my hand and led me to her king-sized bed. She flopped down, spread out, and I slid down into her.

We locked in a vigorous, driving madness, which first-timers usually share. I missed her and that was uncomfortable for both. Then everything seemed to get into rhythm and I was pumping her with burning desire. Jill was good, but I was better. She bucked hard and then came in a burst of emotions, which caused her to cling to me, clawing my back, and then pulled me even closer. Jill gasped and moaned soulfully and that turned me on. She was completely satisfied.

"You can go in me," she whispered. "I'm sterile, they told me long ago…haven't reached that old lady menopause yet, so I want to please you fully, now."

It was like a hurricane. Jill got out from under me and pushed me back, flat on my back. She mounted me very strategically and when she came down on me, she bent over, grabbed onto my shoulders, and began rocking her pelvis hard. I was in heaven, but not very long. Her breasts were tickling me as they swirled gently against my chest while she gyrated. Then I, too, burst into orgasm and reached the fullest pleasure I had ever known. We kissed hard until we both were able to safely separate. Jill hurried to the bathroom and cleaned herself up. When she came out, she had a big smile on her face.

"Ah, ready for that cup of java now, lover?" she asked, still naked and started singing to me while searching her dresser for undies and a bra.

"What a day this had been…what a rare mood I'm in, why it's…" Jill stopped short to answer the phone.

The phone stopped, then rang again. It was Mr. Upshaw inquiring if I was still there. I heard her say, "Yes, he's here…do you want to talk to him?"

Apparently, not, because she turned her back on me and whispered. Then she hung up and poured that cup of coffee.

"I think you made him very jealous."

"Oh no, what did he say?"

"I told him you were hung like a Missouri mule and twice as stubborn."

"Not really…did you really say that?"

"Nah, but I was thinkin' it, mate!" she said beginning to laugh at my worried face. "I told him you were here with the maid, but he doesn't know I fired the maid two years ago, ha! I use that excuse to keep him from coming over to this house."

"Why then, did you let me in?"

"You're different, much different. Besides, you brought me flowers," she said as she again kissed me. "Thanks for everything!" she told me.

"It was wonderful for me, too, Jill."

"I have to leave to go to my parents' house outside of Calgary. They live only blocks from Calgary General and I can stay overnight there. They are expecting me by two. It's after one, so I have to let you go now, okay? Thanks for giving me something to look forward to on our next secret rendezvous, eh!"

Again, we kissed, but this time it was more of a peck. I left thinking how I would worry if something ever happened to Jill. I did not know then that it was our one and only intimate rendezvous. Yet, never in my lifetime will I ever forget that brief, but precious time together. Jill never returned to her work or her lovely home.

After just one week, Jill sent word through her parents that she had contracted a vicious-spreading sarcoma cancer. Her lymph glands had allowed it to spread too far. It was in stage five, no return, or cure. She would die in only two weeks, the doctors advised. Even sedated with morphine, she still experienced much pain and suffering.

I was able to visit Jill in the hospital only twice; the second time, however, she did not know it.

"Well, how's my girl today?" I asked while reaching to hold her hand. When that was uncomfortable for her, I let go and just moved a chair next to her bed.

"Push the black button to raise me up. I want to see you when we talk."

I pushed the bed-raising button until I noticed her wince.

"Is that too much?"

"No, just let me look at you. I have to tell you first we will not be having that second rendezvous. I guess you've figured it out yourself or Mom…"

"Yes, I'm so sorry. Your mom filled me in and asked me to be with you since she and your father are plum worn out with all the family coming in to see you. I came early and asked a nurse I know if I could see you before they all crowded in. You have a very loving family and they'll all miss you…but not as much as I will, Sweetheart," I said, trying to show my affection and deep concern.

"I wanted to tell you a couple of weeks ago, after our up close and personal get together at my house…I wanted to tell you how wonderful you made me feel again. I thank you for that," she whispered lowly as not to be heard by anyone but us. "You were damn good then, buster… the best ever!" she said with a jovial louder voice.

"You were terrific…my first," I said timidly.

"Well hallelujah…I always dreamed of makin' out with a virgin," she giggled.

"I always dreamed about making it with you," I said to keep her happy.

"Okay, you love birds…I heard that. Sorry, Jerry, Jill gets more medication now and she won't be able to see or hear your pretty words after that. Kiss and say your good-byes," ordered the floor nurse.

I looked into Jill's eyes and saw the fear as I bent down to kiss her good-bye.

"Hey, did you hear that?" I asked while looking up.

"No, not a darn thing, but food trays rattling down the hall as always."

"I never knew Turner, but I distinctly heard someone say 'Get away from my girl!'…I really did. I bet he's anxious to greet you…think?"

"Oh, you little fool…I know what you're doing. Nevertheless, it worked. I have something wonderful to look forward to, don't I?" she said with a smile.

"Get now; I have others to attend to that also need my help," the nurse spoke loudly.

With that, I winked at Jill and walked away.

A few days later, Jill's mom asked if I could visit Jill again, because that last visit changed her whole outlook. However, when I got to her room, she was breathing through an air hose placed down her throat and IVs were in several places. I stood there telling her I would miss her and then whispered, "I love you, Jill."

It just seemed the only thing to say for the last time, as she slept so peacefully. I kissed her good-bye, and then left her there in her hospital room, still unconscious.

That afternoon, while her family stayed, Jill passed. She died at four in the afternoon, just as the gray clouds opened up and the sun gently poked through. Maybe, I thought, it was her beloved Turner opening his arms to greet her. There was sudden warmth then, as rays beamed down from that opening. I would like to think that is exactly what happened.

I sent numerous flowers, as did CMEN to Jill's wake. I was one of those she chose, before she passed, to be one of her pallbearers. We laid Jill to rest in a personal plot upon Turner and Jill's dream property, beyond the hillside, under an old tall-standing white oak tree. There was a big, bold, hand carved stone, with a double-written and inscribed epitaph, dedicated to the lives of them both.

It read only these few words, "Together in life, together in Heaven… Jillian and Turner Burner…Forever and Ever, Amen".

It was one of the saddest days of my life. Her sudden illness and subsequent death occurred so quickly, my time for mourning came afterwards. I returned to work and realized how much she meant to us all.

Mr. Upshaw flew to Montreal for a weeklong newspaper editors' gathering. Freddie usually never attended those. He called me when he got there and told me to watch the shop and keep the paper on keel. That really shocked me because I was just a columnist, not his partner. Suddenly, I realized that he, too, needed Jill's touch and went away to grieve his loss.

I lowered the receiver slowly, not finding any words to offer him. I just felt very disturbed God had let this fine lady pass, as she had, in pain and suffering, when she spent her time always trying to make it easier for her fellow workers…I was depressed.

Rita the temp-secretary came into my office. I was surprised that she was still there at Jill's desk. She came over to me, and then softly placed her hand upon my shoulder and patted it.

"I know you are feeling really bad now. I can never replace Jill Burner, but I am willing to try. This is my first job experience out of CU and I was just supposed to be a temporary worker…but Mr. Upshaw hired me full time yesterday. I hope you will give me a chance to learn the ins and outs here. He told me I would be assisting you, also. It might take a while, but I promise I'll try my best."

Her young face seemed saddened also. I looked up at her and told her she would do just fine and we would work together.

"How old are you, Miss Tory?" I asked, only wanting to associate her hiring age compared to mine.

"Well, a girl never tells that, but for you, I'm twenty-one."

"I know how hard it is to get used to a new job. I came right out of South Dakota State College searching for a journalist's position when Mr. Upshaw gave me that chance that he is now giving you. I have been here seven years now, I think…anyway, you show up everyday on time, always look busy, even if you're not, and make sure the Folger's

Coffee pot is fresh and plugged in at Fred's office…I like mine black and sweet, by the way…do all that and you'll have a great start. He'll let you know right away what his needs are…just don't stay late after work," I quipped.

She looked surprised at that suggestion and said, "Well, okay there!"

Then Miss Tory left and brought in two hot cups of coffee.

"Hey, I only need one cup," I mentioned.

"I know, the other, it's mine. Now tell me more, since the boss is away. I want to be really good when he comes back…fill me in more, please," she replied while beginning to sip her java with a big bright smile.

We discussed every little detail I could think of, and then, I asked her if she could definitely keep a secret.

"What, you're going to tell me you want me bad, but you're married, or something?" she spit out giggling.

I guess she felt I wasn't much older than she was nor a threat, but her lack of respect wasn't what I expected. Nevertheless, then again, she was a young vibrant college graduate on her first venture into a workplace and she was asking me for help.

I told her, "No, not exactly. This is really important and top secret."

She then took her index finger and swore her "cross-my-heart" pledge of honor that, "Mum's the word."

When I began telling Rita about the murders which were happening to co-eds near and around Calgary, and we'd be working together with police, she immediately replied, "Yes, I know, my ex-roommate, Meredith Monroe, a really lovely girl, was murdered and they still haven't found out who did it. I told her not to move in with the creep that she had started dating. I bet he did it." I about fell off my chair and then took Rita by her shoulders to tell her,

"That is the big secret I needed to speak to you about in confidence. I am working with the police to help find clues about Meredith's death. You just might have helped us more than you'll ever know!"

Unfortunately, I learned from Rita that Meredith had moved from her apartment more than two months before she met her demise and there was not much more than what she originally first told me. Except, the creep she started dating had bleached blond hair and picked her up in a big SUV.

I immediately grabbed up the cup to sip my coffee and began dialing Nigel Gray's office. That beautiful voice answered and I almost forgot my important breaking news.

"Ahhh, this is Gerry Loveletter, may I please speak with Detective-sergeant Gray…please?" I almost begged her.

My heart started pounding. Boy, what she did to me was not funny!

"Oh hello, Mr. Loveletter…the old detective is away for a week in British Columbia…he's attending a re-training class as an instructor. He will not be back until next Friday evening. May I take a message?"

"Oh, darn, excuse me…I guess it can wait until he returns…but please leave a note for him to call me as soon as he returns. It's rather important."

"Done…anything else?"

I wanted to ask her right then what her bust size was, because she was stacked. However, I withheld my burning desire to know her better and said, "No, that's all, thank you."

I hung up hating myself. After all, I could have gone right to his office and talked to her without that ogre boss listening and giving me the evil eye. As important as it was, I let Rita go back to her desk and I started daydreaming of that gorgeous woman. The rest of the week was going to be very dull I began to realize.

For several days, I did not write much. My thoughts each afternoon went to her, and then Nigel Gray called, again.

"Hello, Jerry…sorry to hear about Jill's death. I was away for cadet training at the police academy these past eight days. I found out there are two other weirdos operating within our sovereign borders. When I told the other investigators there of our ongoing investigation together, using your column to assist getting suspects, it seems everyone thought it was a marvelous idea, except they were leery of leaks in evidence. I assured them it was different with you. I hope this does not change your desire to help me apprehend this killer we're after. Have you had time to collect any new weirdos?"

"Yes, did you get my message?"

"Not yet, I'm on my way to my office right now. Did you catch the murderer while I was gone or find any other weirdos?"

"No, Detective-sergeant Gray, only you," I said unwittingly to a then very silent listener. "Oh, hell, I almost forgot the most important information. My new secretary knew Meredith Monroe and saw the creep she was newly dating…get this…he had bleached blond hair and drove a big SUV. Remember, I almost got run over by one before I found Meredith's body?"

I heard a car's horn honk and other street noises coming from the background of Nigel's cell phone as he apparently was digesting what I had said. I could imagine him turning the steering wheel making turns for he grunted slightly and I heard the sounds of his trench coat rubbing together, as one might hear, imagining what that sound was. Finally, I spoke to see if he was still there. I thought he might have laid the phone down on the car seat without turning it off. I heard a voice say, "Go!"

"Helloooo!" I yelled into the receiver to get a response. It might have been at the wrong time, I guess. There was a rustling sound of sorts, again, then a hard breathing as Nigel spoke.

"I'll call back…when I'm not trying to avoid other traffic, Mr. Loveletter. That's great news. I…have not been to my office yet…I am on the move with my cell. I am sure I have a truckload of paperwork before me there. Again, I am very sorry for Jill's sudden demise. I thought she was an excellent person…well, good-bye."

Then I overheard a woman scream, "Lookout!"

I heard background sounds emitted from the still open phone. There was an extremely loud, but muffled-sounding thump. The phone went dead and the busy signal sounded.

That certainly shook me up from my trance as I tried desperately to find Nigel's business card with his cell phone number in my desk drawer. After I found it, I hesitated, wondering if I should call back. When I did, there was a pickup to leave a message saying Nigel would return my call as soon as possible. I sat back in my chair with the thoughts that he must have been in a terrible accident and might be injured. I called his headquarters' phone. The desk sergeant already knew of Nigel's plight, but would not give out any information, except they had traffic cops and emergency personnel alerted and on their way. I hung up.

CHAPTER 7

In less than an hour, the news was out that the infamous Detective-sergeant Nigel Gray had been involved in an unusual accident. Apparently, he was uninjured, but the victim died at the scene. It seems as though a two-ton bull moose, with an immense sixty-five inch antler spread, had darted onto the roadway and Nigel whacked him good. All of Canada's moose were experiencing the yearly rutting season and during that confusing time, the animals acted just like lusty humans, as the males pursued the females with reckless abandon. It was their time for love.

Thus, this one huge trophy bull moose became Nigel's Mercedes Benz hood ornament. Apparently, the rut accelerated because of the sudden rise in temperature brought about by the Chinook Winds that blow in off the Pacific Ocean. A Chinook is a continuous phenomenon when warm air transverses the Rockies to settle onto the plains of the Calgary area. It sets the animal instincts into becoming amorous.

There would be extra meat for the food pantries, and the providence would have to afford Nigel a new means of transportation. He had permitted personal use of the vehicle, he drove it home as a benefit, but also that same transportation gave him immediate accessibility when summoned on a homicide scene, 24/7. The totaled unmarked Mercedes was Nigel's pride.

Nevertheless, Nigel requested to have the big spread of antlers sent to a taxidermist for display above his home's big fireplace. No, he had not hunted it, but he could always relate that he killed it.

I was relieved to hear the otherwise humorous news, as long as only the moose suffered the ill-fated demise. Every dendrite in my body relaxed and I committed myself to return to my columns to update the love letter messages. So, I asked for Rita's assistance to type in the newest personal ads.

"Here are a few new love ads I need you to insert into my column and send to the printer. Here goes number one…reduce her (3) two by two inch pictures' sizes to one inch square to fit. The message is as follows; Sun bunny, 29, Calgary AB, Canada, seeking men 25 to 32. Here is the flow…

'I am a calm, laid-back city girl who loves the excitement of the city lights at nighttime. However, I sometimes enjoy male company on casual outings into the woods or traveling the world. I enjoy carefree spontaneous get-togethers. I am a gourmet cook.' I think that will suffice."

"Number two…reduce picture of subject on couch, nude? Oops, never noticed that…return it…but first let us cut this one down and see if we can make her presentable. Blow it up only to her face and ad some color to her cheeks…she looks drunk or death warmed over… these desperate women!" I spouted.

"I think you are too judgmental on these girls," Rita suddenly quipped. "They are just trying to meet some nice guys, and since there aren't any in this world, they get impatient…that's all," she told me with a passion.

"Now that seems strange coming from you. You're not one of those girls, are you?" I inquired.

"Well, I wouldn't write something like that in a column. I would go to a singles' bar or check out a church pew. It's really tough to find a decent guy these days," Rita said rather listlessly.

"You mean a good-looking girl like you has trouble?"

"It's not easy…that's all I'm saying."

"Think about it…how would you find a decent guy in a singles' bar? He would probably be a heavy drinker. Why not a sporting event, the beach, or…or…gosh, I guess there aren't many other places except the Calgary Stampeders and that's in the spring…humm, I guess there are few places. I know! Join the RCMP!" I gleefully teased.

Rita really wanted to get off on me then, but she just said, "Next, please," with a bit of sarcasm attached to her voice.

I swung my chair around to look at this girl. I saw her concerned, puckered brow, but I could not believe that she, too, had difficulty getting any guy. Rita was a very nice looking girl…very wholesome-looking and had a decent figure. I imagined though if she just let her hair down, got rid of her big black-rimmed glasses, and maybe went to laser surgery or using contacts; it would be a big improvement.

I continued reading aloud another ad request. I was now seeing Rita in a different light and peeked up at her occasionally to visualize what she might become with a cosmetologist's help. She just might need ol' Gerry Loveletter's help, too, I thought.

"Ready? Here goes another… 'Boogiebabe…28…also Calgary, AB, Canada…seeking gentlemen 29 to 55'. Hummm, her picture isn't very strong…she must be hiding something here to need a guy who is twenty years older…I'll have to help this one…let's see…'like veggies to keep my figure going…love to cook, BBQ in the summer, and drink Molson's'…no, scratch that drinking part. Put down instead… 'will imbibe with the right guy for an evening of pleasurable laughter and romance'…how's that?" I asked Rita.

"That's not at all what she said."

"I know…I have to assist them for saying the right things that guys want to hear and also what they don't want to hear."

"But that's not what she really said. What she wrote was what she actually felt, I think."

"Nope, nope, nope…who's Gerry Loveletter, huh? Me, that's who… they all need this proper overwriting to make them more attractive… don't you see that?"

"That's not what she wrote is all I am saying."

"Well, little Miss Smarty Pants, tell me…how you would describe yourself for one of my ads, huh…tell me in as few words as you can."

She took a deep breath, and then hit the keys on the file computer.

"Okay, buster…here goes… 'Attractive, sexy, virgin woman, 21, seeking a real working man who knows who he is and where he's going. Must be trustworthy, loyal, helpful around the house, reverent, make me laugh and want children. In return, you'll get a vivacious, responsible, outgoing, and supportive mate and a very passionate lover for life.'"

That sent chills down my spine, but I was not going to let on to her.

"Sounds like you want a Boy Scout…eh, some old businessman will read that and think you're older than you look…very used, and very demanding. He'll write back and ask you if you will feed his Irish Setter or milk the cows," I told her laughing.

"Yeah, right! I bet you thought it was really good, didn't you?"

"I guess so. You're very different than I expected you'd be. You're not a girl…you're a real woman with your head on straight. I like that."

Rita smiled, and then turned back to the computer keys…"Next!"

We entered seven new names with pictures to the "Women Seeking Men" column. Then I encountered an ad for one woman, seeking another woman. Now these always caused me moral trouble, but the law of the land held discrimination a felony and I had to include everyone, even objectionable people.

"Hey, here's one for you to write. Let's see what you can do for her," I requested.

"Hey, to you back…I'm not trying to take over your job, here. I'm the helper, remember?"

"Okay, please…will you HELP me with this one?" I accentuated the help part. "She's a lesbian and I don't know really what to say to help her. She's 35, from Red Deer."

"Let me see…'I'm alone. No man has ever pleased me nor wanted to because I have different desires. Help me find love!' "

"That's very perceptive…I think I'll use that in whole…thank you. You are really schooled well, Rita. I believe, or I hope, we will have a long continuous office relationship here at CMEN."

She looked into my eyes, and then said, "I do too, Mr. Loveletter."

That seemed to brighten her smile, but suddenly she became very formal. Maybe Rita thought I would hit on her and she wanted to

keep our relationship strictly business-like…never crossed my mind…
well maybe a little. My ego was damaged somewhat by that, but then
there was that female cop in Nigel's office who diverted all my amorous
attentions.

We finished the only male request with a short but sweet ad.

"Here's Harry, again. He renews his ad…must be ten years old."

"Isn't that illegal…a ten year old boy shouldn't be listing in an adult
personal love column."

"Duh! He's over fifty and has been searching for a woman who will
cook and clean for him…a maid is what he really wants. He's been
sending in these ads a long time."

"Oh, of course…I knew that!" she replied, trying not to be
embarrassed.

"That's it for today. Want to go for lunch?" I asked.

"Sorry, I'm brown-bagging it. I need a paycheck before I start
wasting my hard-earned cash on fast food."

"Oh, well in that case…accompany me on my expense account.
I think we need to talk some more about you assisting my column…
really!" I said, trying to convince her.

Her sudden wide-eyed look was as if she thought I was enticing
her for an afternoon seduction. Bearing in mind the dubious concern
showing in her eyes, I quickly reached inside my desk and found one
coupon that was for a free "seven course, meal-for-two". I had not
used it for any of my columns, but saved it for the most deserving
love letter ads, and one Freddie Upshaw had not gotten his hands
upon to use.

"See this?" I held it out to her so she could read it. "This is
business. I have to check out every dining gratuity that restaurants
send us for advertising and sample their cuisine personally, just so I
can recommend them. They beg me to come dine. I think that is safe
enough, do you not? But, I'll let you drive us…then you can dump me
if I get too fresh," I laughed. I knew she was leery.

Cramped up a little with my very long legs inside her very small
compact Ford Focus, I did not complain, because surprisingly, it was
such a smooth and quiet ride to Eloe's.

Told that, "Eloe's is an exclusively fine dining restaurant, which
requires formal attire at all times to maintain our dignity, including a

tie, sir," even I could not convince the maître dei that I was only there to review the establishment.

"So much for celebrity perks, huh?" I curtly quipped to Rita looking the maître dei straight in the eyes.

We decided to do McDonald's instead. I think I ate crow.

CHAPTER 8

Mr. Upshaw returned from his gallivanting and asked for my presence in his office.

"Sit down, my boy…have a cigar."

"I thought smoking was illegal in our building," I replied.

"You know what's illegal?" he questioned.

"Ah, I guess not, sir," I said, somewhat expecting an abusive remark by his tone.

"Illegal, illegal…that's a sick bird…ha, ha, he, he, he!" he joked with more brightened laughter than I had ever seen at any time working for him. "Relax, Jerry…I need your input. What do you think of the new secretary, Rita Tory? I think I have to let her go."

"Oh, I think she's very bright and will be a real asset to me…I mean our entire company. I have already used one of her quotes in my column and she is very easy to work with…I like her. I think she's bright…fresh and new. Of course, no one could ever replace our Jill."

"Maybe I'm just used to Jill's refinement. This new gal makes me feel so old with her young talk and ways. She even talks back at me. I let her be because she is always right. Ha, I am old, of course, but I don't want to think so. I've got it…son, you take her…she can move into your office…and I'll make another choice, okay?"

"Well, you're the boss, boss…whatever you say goes. However, I don't have enough room for her desk and all those files we have to keep."

"Oh yes, I never thought about that…hummm…my nephew owns his own construction company. I will see what he can do on remodeling your office…make it bigger and better. I learned last week that we all can get bigger and better around here," he said with zest. He seemed different, much different.

"Sir, was that trip to Montreal that informative?" I meekly questioned.

Mr. Upshaw leaned across his desk and giggled, whispering as if someone might overhear…"Son, I didn't go to Montreal. When Jill passed, it broke my heart. I loved that girl. I took a walkabout to Mexico, senor!" he spoke with that same zesty, new tone in his voice using a little Spanish. "Do you know what puta` means in Spanish, son? No, no, of course you would not…I will tell you, son…it means more fun than a barrel of monkeys and a woman who loves you for your money. I spent so little and got so much in return, I think all my old golf buddies need to visit there twice a year. Nevertheless, without question, my wife must never find out. She, too, thinks I flew to Montreal. Why if she ever found out, she'd have me castrated and feed my balls to the wolves," he told me very convincingly.

"You went to a whore house in Mexico?" I asked disgustedly.

"Now, boy, not so loud…you'll understand when you get my age."

"No, no, I will never understand how you could be unfaithful to Mrs. Upshaw. She is a fine lady. You should be very ashamed of doing such a thing. Why I ought to call her right now and tell her what a heel you have been…especially remembering that tryst with Jill. I think I am still upset with that. If it were not for Jill asking me to maintain silence, I would call Claire right now…but, but I won't since I always keep my promises. But then again Jill's not here now, is she?" I fumed.

"Son, son, slow down, here…I never suspected you would respond this way…why I told you, I'll never know…I needed to tell someone, but I guess I picked the wrong person to divulge my personal happiness. Mrs. Wonderful Wife is not the kind lady you describe…she's frigid, selfish, and unyielding to my advances almost always. I know she just married me for my money. Why else would a former Miss Canada look at me? Just understand, son, if you go to her, I will be ruined…then you will lose your position…maybe everyone working here will, also. You know she never comes here. Her relatives are horse people. She wanted long ago to sell this paper and move to a ranch in California. Please, son, reconsider!" he begged, then searched for water and some aspirins.

His mood had done a three-sixty. I really did not want that. I realized by his shaken demeanor that he was horribly afraid of a loose tongue. Nevertheless, why did he pick me? He must have thought of me as a close confidant, I guess. I began to cool off and saw the situation more clearly.

Now, I thought, I had that proverbial "Little Black Book" entry that someday would serve me well, just in case ol' lover boy, here, decided to fire my ass…sort of like blackmail. However, I never would consider that. Nevertheless, I might use it to my advantage if I ever become desperate.

"Now, getting back to remodeling my new office," I reminded him. "How about a carpet on the floor and new wallpaper, a water fountain…no, coffee espressos bar instead?" I suggested.

"You're going to hold this against me, aren't you? You think I've confided in you a little too much, eh? I trusted you! Well, I'll tell you this, sonny," he spoke loudly with distain. Then after he thought some…"Ah, ah, oh, oh, oh yes…just what kind of carpet do you want?" he spoke and then began smiling, realizing I would keep my mouth shut after all.

I guess Mr. Upshaw felt better about confiding in me. He knew I wasn't demanding too much of him for my silence, because he had already planned that expansion with Rita Tory moving in on me.

Yes, I liked it also that he had opened up to me. He was happier now than he had been in a long time. Mischievous ol' Freddie Upshaw decided also to promote me on the spot, yes promote me, and to his assistant editor, no less…imagine that? He figured, I'm certain, it was in his best interests as he imagined now he would be free to go to more of those business meetings in "Montreal" . Freddie needed someone he could trust to stay behind in charge and keep things running. He must have had one hell of a time!

That very afternoon, Mr. Upshaw brought his nephew by my office and he and his nephew took measurements. After looking at Jill's files, which were actually mine, too, he suggested huge expansion…a hundred thousand dollars worth. Mr. Upshaw did not bat an eye…well; he did wink at me with a big smile. I guess things were looking up for me. Then Nigel Gray called.

"Hello, Jerry…I guess you heard of my ridiculous accident, eh? I have a note from my secretary here that reads you need to speak with me ASAP. What's up?"

"To make a long story short, a couple of days ago I may have found a possible clue in Meredith Monroe's murder."

"Great God, why didn't you call me sooner?" he demanded.

"I did…you were away, remember…anyway, my new secretary, Rita, actually saw Meredith's live-in boyfriend. She can identify him, I'm certain. Apparently, he was a real odd ball. She even said she thought he was a creep and could have done it."

"What's his name…maybe I've crossed his path before?" he said with excitement.

"I don't know if she knows that, or not," I told him reluctantly.

"I'll need to talk to her privately. I'll come over now, if that's okay?"

I was about to say, "Sure," but quickly thinking of only myself, I then thought about seeing his beautiful secretary again. Maybe we could swap meeting places…"Ah, no, I'll drive her over. We are about to have carpenters and such doing remodeling here. Name the time."

"In an hour…is that too inconvenient?" he asked.

"You got it…we'll be there within the hour. I just have to tell the boss it's official police business. Bye!"

"Wait…if you have any new leads, like love ads, bring them, too."

"Got it, Sarge!" I said happily, as I hung up.

My heart leaped when I thought I was going to actually get a chance to talk with, with, with…my God, I did not even know that beautiful woman's name. What a real dummy I am, I thought. Well, I will get it this time. I'll have Rita go into Nigel's office, so I can be alone with…

what's her name…hummm. I went up to Mr. Upshaw's office but he had left with his nephew to go somewhere, Rita told me.

"Come, get your coat…you're going with me to see a very important friend of mine, Detective-sergeant Gray. Get our newest photos and bios, too. I want you to tell him what you told me and I'm certain he will have more questions than I asked…he's a real pro," I told her.

She quickly turned off her computer, left a penned note to Freddie about her whereabouts and laid it on his desk, put her work down and then hopped up to get her jacket from the coat tree. I helped her with her jacket, as a gentleman should, but she was jumpy about that. She turned to me and had a serious look of concern upon her face, as if she was now untrusting of me. Nevertheless, she did come along.

Again, I searched for a parking place in the police lot, and again I found one far away from Nigel's office, but the stroll in the new warmer sun felt nice. I wished it were spring, for love was in the air.

"Hello, we're here to see Detective-sergeant Nigel Gray," I told Nigel's beautiful secretary. This time I noticed a name on a plate upon her desk, which identified her as 'Special Officer' G.M. Gray.

"Oh, come in, Dad's expecting you, Mr. Loveletter."

My heart sank. She, the dream of my life, was actually Nigel's daughter. I was stupefied, as she led Rita and me into Nigel's office. How misdirected could I be?

Nigel introduced himself to Rita, and then had the audacity to ask me to leave them alone and have a cup of coffee with his secretary, Giselle. Her name fit her to a tee. However, knowing her dad was Nigel pulled the proverbial rug from under my feet. I was now cautious, timid, and afraid I might say something out of line to her. Nevertheless, I managed to say, "Hello, again…it's nice to see you, again. My real name is Jerry David. Loveletter is my columnist moniker."

What a dork, I bet she thought I was. If she only could see past my crude behavior, hear and feel my heart pounding, and know I truly had a thing for her; she might just let me down easy…so I could go commit suicide somewhere.

"Hey, Dad says you two are in cahoots on this serial killer thing. How's your girlfriend involved in the case?" she curiously wanted to know.

"Oh, Rita…she's definitely not my girlfriend…she's just my new secretary…that's all," I managed to inform her.

"Good, I thought a tall, dark handsome guy like you would have been married. Are you dating anyone?"

"Handsome, huh…hey…I'm Gerry Loveletter…you know, the CMEN personal love ads columnist? No, I guess as unbelievable as it might be, I haven't found that right one, yet…how about you?"

"I'm not sure…what are you doing Saturday night?"

"Oh not much, usually just…oh, you mean me, as far as a date… with you?" I almost peed my pants. Giselle was a woman who came to the point quickly.

"You did just vaguely ask me if I was interested, didn't you?"

"I did? I mean, yes, yes, sure I did!"

"Then Saturday night is the usual time for a date, isn't it?"

"Why yes, got any ideas where to have fun or do you want me to suggest somewhere?"

She looked at me with a big smile, and then said, "Let me surprise you!"

"Okay, when and where should I pick you up?" I asked.

"You'll just have to meet me. I have a second job that starts about eight. Can you buy that?"

"Sure, whatever it takes to make you happy. How shall I dress… casual or you want me in a tux?"

She laughed, and then looked very suspiciously at me. "Why don't you wear whatever you would wear to a Stampeders' game? I work part time for the Calgary Stampeders."

"You do? Oh, well, I will like that option…I love the Stampeders…I have my Stampeders jersey, will that do? And, I especially like their caramel popcorn…I'll order some, maybe ten, just from you," I thought she was a vendor. Then I thought what if she sells beer? "Oh, but not ten beers," I told her while chuckling. "I don't really drink. I would be stone dead from ten."

Still looking at me, but now seriously frowning somewhat, Giselle reached into her desk drawer and got out a brightly-colored red, white, and black ticket to the next Stampeders vs. B.C. Lions home game. I was flabbergasted, because I could not even get one through my office to that game. It was a playoff game for a chance to go to the Grey Cup. I think she saw my delight and smiled.

"That seat is also right behind where the Outrider cheerleaders usually perform, so don't get too overly friendly with them," she jested.

Then Nigel summoned Giselle. She grabbed her dictation pad and winked at me as she left. "See you Saturday night, come early, about six," she told me.

I sat back down to thank God and the Calgary Stampeders. I thought right now, at this moment, I am truly blessed. My heart was zooming.

Rita came through the door and closed it. She said she had finished with Nigel, but that was all. Through the closed door, I heard a little loud discussion going on. I think Giselle told Nigel we had that upcoming date at the football game and he was not at all happy. I guess he wanted someone else much better than he wanted Gerry Loveletter as a son-in-law. We left to go back to CMEN. Maybe she will call and cancel our date. That thought saddened me.

CHAPTER 9

Mr. Upshaw kept his word. Friday morning, before I arrived, his nephew's construction company truck parked in my parking space. I had to park down under an elm where birds crapped all over the cars. My car needed a wash job anyway, so I just ignored the wings above me fluttering when I slammed the driver's door. Up went the starlings and down came their purple poop. It was like a hailstorm. One feces hit my shoulder and splattered on my clean shirt. What a mess! My car looked like the Barrow Gang had shot it up with machine guns. I left looking back in disgust at my Jeep all speckled with poop droppings.

When I got to my office, there were too many men with sledgehammers pounding and raising drywall dust while knocking out walls. The room furniture was emptied somewhere. Where was my desk and everything else? I looked for Rita or the boss. Neither was around, so when I found Norman, Mr. Upshaw's nephew, I asked him if his uncle had mentioned removing the big elm out by the parking lot. He told me he would have some of his men take care of it that afternoon or as soon as he could. What a gullible, but nice person Norman was, I thought. Wish I had told him to put in a bowling lane, or two, ha!

With absolutely nothing to do, I decided to go to the florist and have a single red rose made ready for me to pick up on Saturday. I put in a special love note that I admit I got the words from my column, and wrote them on the card. "One rose date leads to another. I hope to send you dozens!"

Then, I decided I could not stand the sight of my dirty car anymore and drove to the carwash. I zoomed through it in five minutes, tipped the detail person a buck, and just took off towards downtown.

Why I dialed up Giselle at her office on my cell, not even knowing what to say, I did not know why. When she answered, I lied, and told her I was sorry and that I had found a number in my shirt pocket and could not remember to whom it belonged.

"Well, now you know, don't you?"

"Ah, ah, is ah, ah our date still on?" my words stumbled out of my mouth on top of one another expecting a 'No, sorry, I can't go now, something unexpectedly came up' type of reply.

"Yes, can't you make it?" she asked. I was stunned.

"To tell you the truth, Giselle…I called just to hear your voice."

"Well, that's certainly sweet, but everyone will hear your voice, too, it's being recorded," she advised. "We get murder calls on here and sometimes confessions to crimes. That's why it's always being recorded," Giselle told me rather business-like.

"Oh, sorry…see you Saturday night!" I told her and quickly hung up.

"Now she knows you are a jerk, dummy," I spoke out loudly to myself.

Well, anyway I found out the date was still on and that perked my ego, so I just drove around with happiness I had not felt before. I felt like a king.

The streets were not crowded as I passed the big Chevy dealership. I spotted the red Corvette in the display window that had been there quite a while, so I thought I would check it out, even if I could never afford it.

"Hi, Mr. Loveletter…how's your car running since our mechanics worked on it?" a man asked.

"Oh, that's right…it's just running fine, fine. I have been looking at that Vette sitting there so long that I thought I would finally stop and look…emphasis on look, ha!"

"Yeah, it's wasting away there. The battery is getting low…needs to run…are you interested, by chance?" he said worriedly, as if I wasn't buying, his salary was shot for the month.

"Sorry, I wish I could afford it. I did just get a promotion, but I don't think there's a raise involved. Nevertheless, I do not have that kind of position where I work. I could never afford a dream car like that."

"Whoa, whoa, whoa, Mr. Loveletter…you are talkin' to the wheeler-dealer here. I can put you in that shiny red pussy-getter, oops, ex-cuseee me! I mean that girl-getter for practically nothing down and small monthly payments anyone can afford."

"Would you rent it out for a weekend to test drive it, with no strings attached? Now, that I might be able to swing," I chuckled.

"Hell, Mr. Loveletter, for you, it will be free. Just tell everyone where you got it…hell, I mean heck, who knows, someone might see you in it and want one just like it. When would you want it?"

"Really? That would be fabulous. You see, I have a hot date with a really great girl and if it impressed her, I'd make you my best man at my wedding someday," I told him.

"Okay, it's a deal. Pick it up…when?"

"Saturday, after two."

"All right, she's yours. I will have it sitting outside and you leave your car in its place. We'll park it inside…need any work done on it?"

I knew there might be a hidden catch here somewhere, but I needed that car.

"Four new tires would be good…aligned and balanced."

"Wonderful…see, I scratch your back, you scratch mine!"

I walked over to the Vette and slid behind the wheel. The leather smell, the newness, the gauges, the feel, it all started growing on me. I now wished more than ever that I could own it.

"Boy, that's a once in a lifetime car, isn't it?" I told him, looking back at it after I got from behind the wheel.

"Yes, sir…and you look good in it, too, by the way. Wait until you feel the ride, the power, and the way everyone stares at you when you drive by. Why hell, I mean, heck, I took it out to charge the battery and four chicks tried to climb in…but of course their boyfriends held them back, then pulled guns, so I stepped on it and left them in the dust, pronto. Can you just imagine your girl…what's her name?"

"Giselle," I said sort of dreamy-eyed.

"I bet Giselle, what's her name, would put out if she knew you drove this, don't you think?" He said enticing my dreams to the limits.

"I'll buy it!" I burst out.

"Well, let me get the little info I need to run a credit check and draw up your contract. What's CMEN's telephone number, so I can put it down on the app?"

"Here's my business card…everything's there. I'll write my DOB and social security number down, too, for you, here," I said handing it to him.

"Well, I'll jump to it and call you in the morning when I find out everything's hunky-dory."

He quickly took my card. He was already on the phone and waved wildly to me, while smiling broadly, as I left. My senses began to seep back into my brain, as I realized there was no way I could even make the payments. I headed back to my now under construction office.

The first thing I noticed pulling into the parking lot was a big tandem dump truck with two people picking up tree branches and leaves. A shredder had already made nil of the tree menace. That starlings' tree haven home was history and I was pleased with Norman's initiative. I parked elsewhere and went inside.

"Where have you been, Jerry?" asked Mr. Upshaw. "I received a call from some guy at Miller's Chevrolet wanting to know your salary. What is going on, Jerry…are you planning to leave me, now, for a car sales representative's job? You cannot do this to me, Jerry. I need you, son."

"What did you tell that guy my salary was?"

"Well, I just figured you should at least make a hundred thousand, don't you? Hell, two hundred employees work here for me. How in the hell would I know what someone makes, unless they come to me for a raise?"

"Just send that figure plus twenty percent to the bursar tonight before payday and I'll stay," I happily responded. "By the way, can I use you for a GM's loan reference?"

Mr. Upshaw looked at me hard, realizing my leaving was not the case, but just a car loan. Frowning a bit, his eyebrows high-arched, but he took a long deep breath before he spoke very calmly.

"Certainly, Jerry…you're like the son I never had, and I sure don't want you talking with your foster mother," he said amusingly.

Then he took out his handkerchief and wiped his brow.

"Boy, I thought you were seriously going to blackmail me."

"Like the TV advertisements say, 'What goes on in Las Vegas or Warrez, stays in Las Vegas or Warrez!'" I joyfully told him. "Adios, amigo," I said smiling brightly.

Then he turned and walked the stairs to his new office, because he decided to remodel his own office also. The only available space left was in the printer's office or the storage room on top. My things must be up there somewhere, also, I imagined. It was not bad up there. We all needed the exercise walking stairs as the rest of the desk set did.

My locked office door had a sign attached by duct tape that read "Under construction…completion date approximately October 24th", which was in only six days, and right before Canada's Thanksgiving. In the USA, November was the traditional Thanksgiving month, but the actual day date changes each year. In Canada, the Thanksgiving is a month earlier because that is when autumn begins.

Being from South Dakota, my body should have been used to this cold, but I do not think I was born to northerners. My parents must have adopted me. I used to tell them that all the time, because I love the warmer climates. Yet, when I had the opportunity to head anywhere I wanted in search of a job, I migrated north…go figure.

Therefore, without an office, I decided to gather all my paperwork, drag my new ads along home with me for the next few days, and call my ads into Rita. Of course, some time during the workday I would have to come in to get my mail. I could not avoid that, but the weekend was here and that job was left for Monday, as I would just work from home.

Hey, the boss said I was his assistant, so I had to be responsible for keeping abreast of my work, I imagined. I also decided to take the rest of this day off. After every year of my being way behind and scurrying to find last minute gifts, this year I promised myself to do some advance "get it done now" Christmas shopping. I also decided

I would definitely buy some new shoes and jeans for my date with Gorgeous. It was a very good day, so far.

I shopped for just about everyone on my last year's Christmas list; Mom, Pop, Uncle Willy and Aunt Ivy. Humm, wonder what can I get for my sister Tracey and her new twins Karen and Kate? I got it! I would give her that jogging, twin stroller I saw in Bergmann's store. She is a health nut anyway and I could touch all of them. She needs to get outside, now that her husband Gary left for Iraq with his army transportation unit. They activated so suddenly and then shipped out.

Then I saw a note I had written last year for me as a reminder. It read that I must remember to get Jill something extra special next year. That made me sad. Last year we had such a great office party with togetherness and spiked eggnog. Jill put up decorations and I helped put the angel on the top of the tree. Everyone was so joyful and merry.

Oh, what a difference a year makes. Jill gave me such a nice gift. It was a new watch. Jill happily announced it was actually a gift to her, because I was always asking her for the correct time. It was much more than the twenty-dollar gift allowance limit we all said we would stick to on gifts.

Unfortunately, I only had a bottle of inexpensive perfume to give her. I felt diminutive and cheap then, so I wrote that note to myself here on my name list. I remembered her kind act of opening the perfume, dabbing some on her wrists and neck and then telling me, it smelled so wonderful. She kissed me and gave me a hug then. Oh, if I could only have her back here now, I thought. Remembering her painful struggle through her illness made me sick to my stomach. Yes, I thought to myself, you don't know or appreciate some of your loved ones until they're gone.

My Jeep was full of presents when I stopped by the Dollar Store to get wrapping paper. Then I drove home and put everything on my bed to wrap later. I slipped on my new jeans and Nike shoes to see if they fit. I removed the store tags, and then threw the jeans in the washer when they seemed baggy in the behind.

The shoes were very comfortable, so I laid them in my closet and pulled out my Stampeders jersey. I had just hung it up when Jill last used it and had not worn it since. Unbelievably, her perfume fragrance was still there. I held it close and decided I would go buy another in the morning. Then I realized since the big game was here, the jerseys might all be sold out. Reluctantly, I placed the jersey in with my jeans and washed them together on permanent press, just so the jeans shrank some and the jersey was clean. I had to make certain I was ready for Gorgeous.

I called to Rita's apartment to see if she had gotten home yet. There was no answer. I then called our office phone. Rita was working overtime already.

"Rita, are you still there?" I asked her.

"Yes, this darn copy machine is so slow; I think I'll just take it all to Staples and let them do it, think?"

"No, I'm sorry but you can't. Those duplicates represent personal files and they must be kept secure."

"Well what can I do if the darn thing doesn't work?" she moaned.

"Write a little note saying 'out of order' and go home…that's an order. I'll come in to work in the morning and jimmy it around a bit til it works. Sometimes a swift kick works. Jill always knew what to do," I said, before I thought of what I said.

"Oh, well, let me try," she said, before I could tell her to forget it.

I heard the thump of her kicking the copier, then the buzz of the machine cycling.

"That worked alright!" her voice echoed away from the phone. "She's spittin' those files out at 90 miles an hour, now. I'll be done in ten minutes. Boy that was easy after I've wasted two whole hours thinking I did something wrong. Why didn't you mention that, first, when I came to work here? I was about to cry."

"Awe, I'm sorry, Rita. Look, I will make it up to you, sometime. Now go home and come in late on Monday morning to compensate for my mistake, okay?"

"Yeah, right…then I'll have more to do than this," she spoke realistically.

"Okay, then, we'll work something out. I'll order you a new copier in the morning…now go home!" I demanded.

"Tomorrow is Saturday. Did you forget?"

"No, I have to get all the letter ads opened and checked for accuracy that I didn't get done today."

"I already did that for you. I figured you would be very busy with your shopping. Got a date with that secretary at the cop shop, huh?"

I was awestruck. This girl had done what Jill had done for me for years without asking. "Gosh, I didn't expect that, thank you very much! Yes, I do have a date with her."

"Are you going to use those complementary dining coupons on your date?"

"Hardly…I'm meeting her at the Stampeders game."

"Oh, she doesn't trust you and wants to be in a public place, huh?" she said giggling, just to taunt me, I think for not telling her about kicking the copier.

"What makes you think that?"

"That's what you write about in your columns, remember? Quote…'If you are unsure of your date, meet them in public to be safe,' unquote!"

"Giselle part-times there…that's why," I assured her. "However I never knew you read my column."

"That shows you how much you know. I sent in three ads last year. I never got one bite," she told me somewhat sarcastically.

"I'm sure you must have sent in a bad picture with your ad. Why any guy who took a good look at you would know you're a real babe," I said to appease her.

"Really…you think so? Gee, I appreciate that. I have a new dress and a cheap date with my roommate's brother. He's a college guy, nice, but not a prospect…just a date."

"Well that settles it; you just go to my desk and take those dining tickets to Eloe's. But remember, your guy has to have a suit and tie."

"Oh, that would be great, thanks! When I saw it, I thought I would like to dine there someday…much appreciated. I feel much better about working overtime for that old copier now. I'll gladly accept those tickets and head for the barn. That copier just finished. See ya Monday and good luck with your date," she told me.

"Same to you…now go home before the boss comes in and catches you."

"Ha, he's already left. The Missus called earlier and she wants him home pronto…bye now!"

"Bye now, to you, too," I repeated, and then finally hung up.

I could not help thinking that Rita and I were in for a great workplace relationship. Anyway, she was off on the right foot.

After hearing the washer's buzzer go off, I put my jeans and jersey in fluff dry and let them tumble. I headed for the fridge and took out some tuna I had made. I spread it on some rye bread with some lettuce and Colby cheese. Then I poured a glass of skim milk, grabbed the Calgary Sun, hit the TV remote for the evening news, and then lay down on my couch. At last my mind could rest. I fell asleep for several hours.

When I awoke, my sandwich was stale, the milk was warm, and the TV sports announcers were on with a review of the next day's big football event. I was certain to be there. I took a bite, checked my jeans and jersey, and hung them dry on hangers. I came back, gulped down the milk, and put the glass in the sink. I overheard a voice I thought sounded familiar. It was one of those Stampeders cheerleaders telling how they had planned to perform something special for tomorrow's big game. However, as I peeked from the kitchen, a darn commercial came on and I missed it.

I was going to be in a predicament tomorrow at the game. That cheerleader, who I worshipped from afar, only able to see distantly, or close-up from her backside, always, would have to take second fiddle to Giselle. Nevertheless, at least I would be near enough to see her up close and personal for the first time. My anxiety was mounting. It was like getting a double-dipper ice cream cone. I was very tired and slept all night.

CHAPTER 10

I pulled my pillows over my head when the rising sun shone through a crack in my bedroom curtains and hit me directly upon my closed eyelids. No matter how I tried to go back to sleep then, I could not. I began to hear the pitter patting of footsteps upstairs, pipes rattling, showers utilized, and toilets flushing. It was so extra-unusually noisy that I decided to get up.

Hesitantly, I elected to take my leisure in the bathroom with the Calgary Sun I had not quite finished. I flushed the toilet just to hear screams from above when the water got excessively hot for them. I chuckled to my own amusement for them waking me up with all their clatter. It was seven on Saturday morning.

The phone rang, but I was still indisposed, and let it ring. When Nigel Gray's voice left a message, it said, "Jerry, just wanted to tell you I'll be seated next to you at the game. Don't let anyone take my seat, if I'm late. See you there."

"What!" I yelled out loudly, still sitting on the throne. "No way," I spoke to myself…"This couldn't be happening to me." I ended my conversation to myself when the upstairs voices began to laugh at me. I guess they thought they had flushed when I was in the shower for revenge.

The illustrious detective is an overly protective father, I surmised… so taken with his daughter, he cannot even let her go to a football game in a crowded arena? I just could not believe it. I finished my paperwork and regained my thoughts of what I must do. Then at eight, the phone rang again.

"Gooood morning, Mr. David!" the happy voice greeted.

I almost told the guy to go to hell, but he then said, "Your financing is done and your Corvette is being serviced right now."

I realized then it was the car dealership and Virgil Perkle, the sales representative I talked to was speaking.

"Hey, I thought it was a prank call. Good morning to you…what time do you go to work?" I asked.

"I'm always here to see to it my customers are satisfied. I had to call to see if you like the deal and if you'll take nine thousand for your Jeep."

"Oh, I didn't want to trade in my Jeep. I need it for the winter," I advised him. "What's the payment?"

"I think I'll have to refigure that…humm, no trade-in, huh…you'll have to come up with ten grand down then."

"I don't have ten grand in the bank to spare…now what?"

"Come in and we'll talk. You can still use the Vette tonight for your date."

"I might be interested in a new Tahoe, though," I said to brighten his day. I saw that white one sitting in your showroom. Does it have leather?"

"You betcha! It's a great choice and it's ready to roll out of here."

"Then let's figure my Jeep as a trade-in and we can talk turkey. I'll take that instead of the Vette. My insurance won't change much and I really like my four wheel drive."

"Great! I'll snap to it immediately. What time will you get here?"

"I'm up and I'll drive in about two."

"Super! You see, we can work anything out if two heads get together and cooperate…see you at two," he said, sounding relieved his paperwork was not in vain.

Yes, I liked my old wheels, but being four years old in Canada's inclement weather caused me concerns to rethink how long it would last. Only lately, pushing a hundred thousand miles, had parts begun to wear out. Knowing I needed four tires on my ride, it helped steer me towards buying that $45,000 white beast. I was satisfied that new Tahoe was the more sensible selection.

I showered and shaved. Then, like saying good-bye to an old friend, I emptied out my glove box and rear mats that were not even a year old yet. I would use those if there weren't any in the new one.

Then I headed to the carwash. I read that cleaner cars got better trade-in prices. I thought about the game as the pre-washers took my car from me into the washing line. People with rags and loud sounding vacuums zipped through it with speed as the Jeep's wheels were hand soap-sprayed, while slowly advancing down the rails, to the big whirling brushes. It shined nicely after the rinse cycle. I tipped the detailers and off I drove to the car dealer. The new car spray they used helped a lot.

I met Virgil in his office right at two. He asked me to come in and sit while we dickered on price. He reminded me how wonderful his Tahoe was and how worn out my Jeep was. He only offered $5,500 this time and my down payment was $3,000.

"The vehicle you chose has every accessory available, except hot and cold running babes…you'll have to provide that, Mr. David," he laughed.

"You mean you called me down here and that's the best you can offer? I guess I bit off more than I can chew, eh? I saw a nice little red Jeep Cherokee sitting at your competitors. I guess I'll have to go over there, sorry," I said, as I rose up and told him, "No thanks."

"All right, you pinned me to the mat. I need your sale more than you know. The boss told me he thinks you driving one of our vehicles might raise our sales. Let me refigure this with a sharper pencil… hummm…I will allow you $9,500 and skip the down payment. Mind you, I'm not making enough to buy my lunch on this deal…what say you?"

"I say you throw in a full tank of gas, new matching mats, and the deal's done!"

"You drive a hard bargain, Mr. David," he told me reaching out to shake my hand to confirm the deal.

"And you have a silver tongue of a high pressure salesman, but I like you anyway. Here are my keys, where's yours?" I said smiling broadly, as I looked over to my new ride. She was a beauty. I was going into debt.

After I signed all the bank papers, Virgil ordered a worker to fill the gas tank and place the luxury floor mats inside. I saw the new dealership decal they placed on the Tahoe's rear bumper and knew I would have to get rid of that right away before it dried. I always knew thieves looked for out of state dealer bumper decals to help them select to pilfer or steal the vehicles.

The papers on the floorboards were pristine and I didn't want one bit of dirt to be tracked in by my shoes before my big date. The leather smell made me feel rich and a windshield so clean allowed me to see the highway like never before. I was a proud owner and imagined everyone I passed was looking at my ride. Then I hit a pothole filled with salty water and it splashed up upon my passenger side windows. I cussed, and then pulled over to get out my handkerchief to wipe the crud off I thought would be there. Surprisingly, it did not show at all after I looked. White was a great color choice I found out. It hid the dirt. I got back inside my new Tahoe and drove home a more than satisfied customer.

Before I got home, I stopped by to pick up the rose I had ordered for Giselle. The florist assured me my gift would last for many hours in this temperate weather, if left inside the small presentation box. It looked fresh and I was pleased. I made it home without hitting another pothole.

I showered and shaved, put on my new duds, and then tried to pump the last drop out of my Canoe cologne. The spray bottle was empty, so I tried out my new spray bottle of Nautica. Now that should get a warm response in a tight embrace, I hoped.

I took one last look at my face, brushed my teeth for the second time, and then decided I had done all I could do to myself. The rest would be up to my charm. I put on my tan trench coat and alpine hat because the wind was chilling in McMahon Stadium, unless you imbibed until you were too numb to notice. I would not, because I had a special date. Therefore, I would freeze, especially with Nigel seated next to me. Oh, what a dreadful thought. Nevertheless, his daughter's beauty was my sole desire and the thought of her near me warmed the cockles of my everything! You might say I would be intoxicated with the warmth of love.

A bit early, I headed out in my new ride for The University of Calgary. Several sports teams also use their McMahon Stadium, including our Calgary Stampeders. The stadium, overcrowded with the extra end zone seats they put in temporarily for events like this, would push the mass to about 45,000 fans. The noise would sound much too loud, but the excitement could not be matched anywhere on a cold Canadian Saturday night. My anxiety was running high with thoughts of that gorgeous woman beside me later, after Giselle got off work. Then a horrible thought crossed my mind. What if Nigel comes along home…nah…not even he would be that ridiculous.

University Drive was at a standstill, so I cut over to Cowchild Trail. I caught a courteous driver in traffic that let me in and I was only a minute away from getting into the parking lot. Then a student assigned to direct traffic stepped out right in front of me and motioned for me to turn into an adjacent field, where excess vehicles were forced to park when the concrete lots were filled. It was sloppy-muddy from the daytime thaw and my white Tahoe suffered her first mud bath, as several young exuberant drivers spun up mud all over my windshield and the exterior finding their spaces. I could have died. My new ride looked like an old mud buggy. I locked up the Tahoe with the remote. The sudden chirping bird resonance was neat.

The sound of the college band playing the Canadian anthem, Oh Canada, made me hustle. I found my wallet and the ticket Giselle had given me, and then handed it to the ticket taker. It was a glorious sight inside, as our black, red and white adorned team was already out doing stretches, warming up, and sprinting.

Four quarterbacks were passing back and forth to receivers. I immediately noticed the Stampeders' Outriders cheerleaders across the Field Turf playing area talking with the B.C. Lion cheerleaders. Then a roar began as the Outriders began their high kicks and dancing at the center of the arena. I saw that girl I liked so much doing her thing. She was built like ah, ah, well, you know.

I searched for my seat and it was indeed a great front row seat. No Nigel Gray there yet, so I stripped off my coat, put my hat in my coat sleeve, and then wadded it up to sit. It was warmer than I imagined. A vendor selling Molson's stepped past me to deliver brews to several seated fans next to me. They looked like underage college kids and some like really older folk. The unusual mixtures of fans were that way all about me. This crowd had apparently gotten their tickets as gifts as I did, because we bunched up closely, while much other seating around us had not yet filled.

I looked to the field as the crowd roared when all the Stampeders football players left the field, headed for their locker room, as did the Lions at the other end. Then my heart raced as both teams' cheerleaders rushed out together to put on a special performance at the 60-yard centerline. Seated at the forty-yard marker, only twenty yards from midfield, I saw that gorgeous cheerleader I had secretly been in love with for several years. She was standing at attention ready to perform. When the music's beat sounded, I stood up, not only thrilled, but also unexpectedly stunned. That special lady out on the field was none other than Giselle, my date and Nigel's daughter.

My eyes never left her. My heart could not stop pounding with pride. I became almost teary-eyed when each girl did the splits one by one at the finale of the entire rendition. Giselle brought the most applause. Everyone adored her…at least all the men did. Their performance brought the enormous crowd to their feet cheering and blowing horns.

One exuberant fan seated directly behind me stuck a long plastic horn near my ears and blew it repeatedly. Reacting to the pain, I grabbed that horn and flung it out onto the field in disgust. The guy said some few choice words, then brought out his drum and pounded it at me in spite. I reached back to sock that smart-ass, when suddenly someone caught my arm. It was Detective-sergeant Nigel Gray, he told the rowdy fan while showing his badge, who then reluctantly sat down and shut up.

"Hey, Jerry, don't hit the quarterback's younger brother," Nigel told me. "Dean, this is Giselle's date, Jerry David the CMEN columnist. Shake hands and let's watch the game, eh?" Nigel ordered us.

We shook hands, both apologized, and then I turned around.

"Hey, Handsome…surprised?" Giselle shouted over a big noisy crowd.

Every guy in the stands pushed to get closer to her, so she backed off and winked at me. Some wanted her autograph, but the security came and held them away from her.

"Daddy, I have to go to work, love ya! Take care of Jerry for me and keep him entertained, until I get done," she shouted out. "Jerry, thanks for coming and see you after the game, okay?" she called out, as she ran to her spot on the entry lane, where the football players soon came bursting out to their Stampeders fight song. Then the kick off and all hell broke loose.

I still hadn't taken my eyes off Giselle. I quickly realized how fortunate I was just to have her talk to me. Guys would send a beer to me as a result of them knowing I was her date. I don't know if it was friendly, or they wanted me to pass out so they'd have their chance with her. I was the envy of all the other men needless to say, but I gave their offerings to Nigel.

Repeatedly, each team would pass us running down the field, as they worked their ways to the end zone. Nigel was the recipient of an errant pass and his souvenir was the football. He was so thrilled he knocked me over.

Her moves were every man's dream. I began to look at Nigel and noticed he was always looking at me. He didn't say a word, but stared hard as if I was his criminal arrestee. I was somewhat uncomfortable, but deep inside the feeling I experienced seeing Giselle in her Outriders' attire constantly pried into my imagination of making love forever to this woman.

Nigel became concerned with the fourth quarter score tied 18 all. He actually got up, turned around to the crowd, and started up a highly exciting roar each time the Lions entered the red zone. The noise caused the Lions' linemen to jump off sides, for a five-yard penalty, three consecutive times. The twelfth man was doing well. The Lions had to settle for a successful forty-yard field goal, but took the lead 21-18, with only one minute to go.

Sixty seconds left, it was all on our quarterback's shoulders. The resounding roar at the Lions' failed on-side kick became deafening. Who would ever think they would try a stunt like that? Old Coach Burns had many tricks up his sleeve he had pulled off successfully in the past, but no one leading with under a minute left would consider an on-side kick…but that is exactly what happened.

Our special teams grabbed up the slow-bouncing football and smothered it on the Lions' twenty. Now, our Stampeders could score, or tie the score, with a field goal. It was a game of chess.

A time out by the Stampeders with just 43 seconds left on the clock created a stir in the huge crowd. What play would get them a win, everyone tried to guess? Everyone wondered, would it be a pass, a run up the middle, or a sprint around the end, what?

The Stampeders' big fullback, took a handoff, but was tackled behind the line of scrimmage for a two-yard loss. Then, the Lions' defense bull-rushed, as every defensive back came after the quarterback, and chased him out of the pocket. They sacked him for another loss. It was third and twenty-seven with 11 ticks left on the clock. The Stampeders called time out. When the two minutes were up and the refs blew their whistles, the Stampeders field goal unit ran onto the field to the hometown fans' disapproval. They wanted it all.

The move took the Lions by surprise and Burns called for a time out to get his specialists onto the field. Then, as the Stampeders set up for a field goal try, and just when the center was about to snap the ball, wise old Coach Burns again called a time out, his last. He wanted to distract the kicker.

There were eleven seconds remaining, third down, and twenty-seven yards to goal, when the Stampeders linemen all went into their stance. The ball snapped quickly to the holder, as both sides of the Stampeders linemen collapsed.

Instead of tying the game, the holder flipped the ball back over his shoulder to the fullback, who was in high gear passing him from behind, and headed around the left side. The crowd was stunned, but roared with a deafening cheer when the fullback scored untouched, as time ran out. The horn sounded and the game was history. Calgary won the game 24-21. What a game! Everyone went nuts!

Nigel pounded on my shoulder like a lunatic. He jumped up on his seat to raise more hell. People were throwing beer and confetti at the same time. It was the most excitement I ever had. Then came Giselle with a player draped all over her. I was jealous instantly, but tried not to show it.

"Jerry, this is my cousin, Bryan LaBowe," Giselle yelled to me. "We all have to go inside for some public relations pictures, and then I'll be back out," she said, with a worried look at my distraught face. "It's okay, I'll be back in ten minutes…I promise. Better yet, warm up your car and I'll meet you at gate six, okay?"

Then another cheerleader and player grabbed them in joy and they all hustled back down the tunnel. There I was stuck looking at Nigel.

"Nice kid, Bryan…sister's kid…takes after his grandfather. My dad played for the Eskimos back in the fifties. He was an All-Canadian player out of Vancouver. Art is his size, too."

"Sweet, did you play?"

"Nope, I was the smart one of my family. I became a police officer and my body does not hurt on cold nights like this, as much as those old players with arthritis do, after they got banged up in sports. Well, let's go to your car, eh? I'm getting hungry and the chill is getting to me now that everyone is leaving."

Honestly, I could have just died when he said he was actually going along home with us. I looked again at him to see if he were kidding… he was not.

"Say, that Rita is something, eh? She identified that guy who dated Monroe. He was not Monroe's live-in…I checked it out. He was just a no-good from north of Red Deer. He has left the area, according to his family. I think he is a prime suspect…good thinking, getting Rita involved."

"She never confided in me what you two spoke about."

"That's another reason I like her…she's trustworthy and can keep a secret when told."

"That sounded like an insinuation to me. I never gave that info to the writers and pressmen, my boss did, remember?"

"You should have secured it better, I think, eh?"

"There's just one thing that sticks in my mind about Meredith. The night of the murder, you asked the coroner's assistant to check her vaginal area to see if there was sucrose present. Sucrose is like sugar, right? Why would that come out in a vaginal swab?" I questioned.

"Can I now confide in you knowing this piece of evidence is secure with you?"

"I said, I didn't let the cat out of the bag…it was Mr. Upshaw snooping in my drawer," I spoke without a reply from Nigel.

I just shut up as we finally beat the crowd to my car. He apparently wasn't going to confide in me again. The remote opened the doors and Nigel jumped in with muddy shoes. The mud splattered everywhere. I did not say a word. I drove through the muck slowly, until I got on the dry pavement. Then I punched the accelerator, which spun off all the goop on my tires. Nigel was not impressed to say the least.

"You don't always drive like this?" he questioned, as he repositioned himself in the bucket seat after he was thrown around when the Tahoe fishtailed a bit too much.

"Where's gate six?" I asked moving slowly in traffic, trying hard not to run over a pedestrian.

"Keep going, it's around on the other side on University Drive… nearer my car. I had to park almost a mile away. Pick up Giss, and then drop me off," he told me. "It's sugar found on several of the victims' pubic area. The murderer must be eating a peppermint stick or sucker as he seduces his victim…strange, but not all that uncommon, as far as psychos go. Psychos do lots of self-satisfying things," he suddenly spoke, then became silent again about it.

I was relieved he brought his car and then sighed a little bit too loud.

"What'd you think…I was going on your date?" he said, starting to laugh.

"Maybe…I was wondering if you trusted me at all with your lovely daughter. Thanks for trusting me."

"Oh my daughter is a black belt. She can take care of any situation. Taught her most of it myself," he then bragged.

"No, not that…I'd never hurt Giselle. I meant about the sucrose thing."

He smiled and eased back in his seat. We watched numerous people exit, but my gorgeous date, and Nigel's daughter, did not quickly show. We waited a half hour for Giselle to come out. When she did, there were many young guys there trying to ask her for a date. I think she about turned around when she saw my filthy Tahoe, but Nigel jumped out quickly, took her by the arm, and led her away from the throng. When she hopped up into the front seat next to me, she leaned over and gave me a peck on the cheek. My heart raced.

"Gosh, it's a lot cleaner in here than on the outside," she hinted.

"Now, Giss, Jerry had this baby all shined up for you, until he was forced to park in that old football field off Cowchild. Besides, it's pretty sporty, don't you think?" Nigel explained. "By the way, Jerry, where the hell you taking my daughter?" he asked too aggressively.

"Actually, I have a single room at the Calgary Sheraton…which way is that anyway, from here?" I said, to annoy his fatherly nosiness.

"Yeah, right…you want a big funeral, or be cremated?" he jested.

"I think I'll ask the lady of her desires. However, I can get us in at Luigi's," I told Nigel.

"Well, that's a great place for dining. Are you sure you don't want me there? I'll pay the bill," he coaxed grinning.

"Now, Daddy, stop your fooling around or I'll tell Jerry to drop you right here."

"Stop here! That's a good idea…that hayride is going my way," Nigel said, as he opened the door, jumped out of the rear, and with a burst of speed caught up with, and hopped aboard a wagon load of happy fans who were enjoying a hayride. He waved back as the tractor pulling the two big wagons turned the corner and picked up speed. They were all celebrating, singing and playing guitars, fiddles and banjos. Everyone was excited about going to the Grey Cup.

"Hey, you! What's this?" Giselle said, looking at the rose box on the center console, which I planned to give her for our first date.

She pulled open the ribbon and removed the rose. "I hope this was for me…how sweet," Giselle spoke in a soft voice after she read my note. Then she pulled me to her breast, which blew my mind and gave me a deep, wet, kiss, while we were stopped in traffic. "Hope that starts us off on the right foot," she whispered.

My heart was pounding and I think I was dizzy when I asked her, "Do you wanna dine or have sex?" It just slipped out and I was outrageously embarrassed.

Giselle leaned back in her seat, "Whoa there, tiger. I didn't see that coming!" she said loudly.

"Neither did I…I'm sorry, your overwhelming beauty must have warped my mind…I'm sorry, I'm really sorry," I repeated sincerely.

"Okay…let's have sex, then," she said, laughing, completely wrecking my mind.

"You're kidding, right…and you forgive me? Please say so, Giselle. You won't know this, but for years I have been avidly watching you on TV, not knowing who you were, and unable to see your face clearly. I have dreamed about you many times. I didn't know Nigel was your father either, nor you were that cheerleader of my dreams, honest. Seeing you in his office caused me tremendous anxiety as to which woman I really liked most…you or, or you, ha! Seeing you now, live, up close and personal, has been overwhelming. Can you understand that?"

"No…I'm just an ordinary girl with ordinary needs and desires. Right now, I want you to take me to Luigi's. I'm starved, and then maybe we'll see about that single at the Sheraton," she told me smiling sheepishly, very unconvincingly.

Luigi greeted me on sight and led us to a secluded table for two. He held the chair for Giselle and told me, "Mr. David, yousa escort a very lovely lady tonight," as he seated her.

"Luigi's has the best Italian cuisine in Calgary," I mentioned to Giselle thinking she had not been there before.

"You always bring your dates here?" she inquired, seemingly somewhat jealous that I might.

"No, you're the first and I hope the last," I told her.

"Jerry, slow down. We've just known each other for a few minutes. Let's ease into this relationship. I do like you, but looks aren't all I want from a man, IF, I was looking for someone special," she accentuated.

"I'm ready when you are," I just wanted her to realize.

"Okay, that's nice…let's eat before I embarrass you and grab that guy's t-bone over there."

When Luigi suddenly appeared to take our order, he suggested mozzarella garlic bread sticks, red wine, along with huge plates of his famous spaghetti and meatballs. Giselle thought that was super and told him she was starving.

"I will'a serve'a yousa very quickly, my beautiful little princess. Let'a Luigi hurry, please," he said to her in his most complimentary Italian accent. He turned to hustle away through the kitchen swinging doors.

Then, we rekindled our conversation, but diverted to the game and her wonderful performance. I got lost in her lovely hazel eyes and watching her lips. Man, I had it bad. She told me of all her physical activities, practicing, lifting weights, and occasionally cross-country jogging. Then she enjoyed ice-skating at the community lakes in the fall and winter, she told me.

"I just enjoy watching one certain, really stacked, Outriders' cheerleader on TV, doing her thing for the Stampeders. My mental gymnastics go totally hog wild. I bet I burn a lot of calories…no fat here, see," I said, while lifting my jacket open. "Tell me, Giselle…how is it being the daughter of such a dominant man like your father?" I asked her, just to change the subject because I never worked out very much.

"Daddy…he's a pussy cat. He loves his family…might be a little protective of his girls…but, all in all, he's just a pussy cat," she said cheerfully as Luigi returned with a basket of bread sticks and a bottle of his choice wine in a silver cooler. He popped the cork and asked me to taste it. I sipped the nectar, swirled it gently on my pallet and announced to Luigi it was superb. Then he poured Giselle a glass and she quickly sipped and said, too, it was superb. Giselle could hardly control her hunger and dipped a bread stick in the cheese dip dish, then the hot sauce dish. Her eyes began to water and she suddenly gulped her wine glass and extended her arm with the glass for more.

"Hurry, I'm on fire!" she moaned, trying not to spit it out on her napkin.

"Slowly, there…let it linger. If air hits your tongue, it will burn. Now put your lips together like this," I showed her, puckering.

Then I kissed her lips softly out of shear necessity.

"Your lips told me they needed to be kissed…feel better?" I asked afterward.

"You're a very different guy, Mister David…very nice…I like your taste in cuisine…and yes, your lips feel very, very, nice, too."

Then Luigi's servers came quickly with our spaghetti plates and we both delved into the wonderful meal. Giselle had a second serving with more wine and that made Luigi very happy. She was an athlete and needed her carbs, I guess. He sent around his violinist to play a lovely Italian love song. In the dim candlelight, our love blossomed.

"Just to get things straight, you mentioned your father is very protective of his girls, plural…are there more like you at home?"

"Yep…Michelle is the youngest…she's thirteen. Diana is sixteen and gives Daddy fits…then Artie is Dad's favorite, I think. He is at Cambria studying to become a lawyer. Daddy hates lawyers, so he prays he changes his mind or flunks out and becomes a police officer or joins the Royal Navy or Royal Air Force. Anything but a lawyer," she giggled.

"Then, Momma, she is the real boss of the family and always tells Daddy what to do…they work very well together, but seem lost without the other's help…we affectionately call her Queenie, just because she was once Canada's entry in the Miss World competition…placed in the top ten, but some girl from Brazil actually won Miss World. When we quarrel, I call her Queen Anne for being so demanding sometimes. Like tonight, she told me to act like the lady she raised and not be so wild and spontaneous. She says it's all my father's breeding background. His people were rugged, very tough mountain men…fur trappers way back in history. Mom says that's why his instincts are so good at tracking down those criminals."

"So that's where your beauty derives, huh? I would love to meet her some day. I bet you're just like her."

"Pretty much so, except she's much prettier…looks more like my big sister and keeps physically fit for Daddy. Dad lived near Red Deer all his life, but Mom moved there when she was in high school. She fell for his silver-tongued love message, and has been head over heels for him ever since they were seventeen at Montclair High School, where I also attended…they're like two young inseparable lovers. Now, you know all about me, how about your personal history; it's your turn, eh?"

"Simple…Mom and Dad are grain farmers down in South Dakota, where I grew up with my very independent sister, Tracey. I like to hunt and fish when the ice and snow are all gone. I graduated from SDSC with a bachelor in journalism. Tracey married a derelict named Gary who Dad hates. I think he is going on active duty with his army reserve unit to the war soon. Tracey and Gary fight constantly. If he leaves, Tracey will stay with Mom and Dad. Oh, I've been at CMEN, now, going on seven years, I think. That's my whole story and I'm stickin' to it!" I told her smiling. "Oops! How could I forget…then I met you!" I added hoping she liked that.

She did, but I had to tell her about my past girlfriends from kindergarten on. I told her I only remembered one, which was my first grade teacher, Missus Hall. After her, no other girl has ever measured up, "Until you," I explained. I think she thought I was hiding a bunch of girls in my past, but gave up asking.

We ate, and then drank another bottle of Luigi's expensive wine, as the conversation seemed to flow well between us. We found out we shared many common interests, especially when it came to sports. She, of course, knew every Stamp player well. She dated a few, but they were jocks and their talk was only of their abilities or their future playing time. Most were narcissistic, very egotistical, she told me.

"Wanna dance?" I suggested to Giselle to stop my talking about me, hoping to hold her in my anxious arms.

"I like the wine and the violin music, it's very romantic, but I don't see a dance floor."

"Tell you what…kick off your shoes and we'll slow dance right here. Luigi likes to promote romance, believe me…he'll suggest it pretty soon anyway…that's his style and why he sent the violinist…he really approves of you."

She hesitantly looked around not seeing anyone else there dancing, so I took her hand and gently eased her up to me then embraced her. The four glasses of wine she already drank much too fast made her a little tipsy and she more or less fell into my arms. When she put her arms around me, I was in heaven.

We slow danced, embracing each other closely for a long while. We stopped to sit and have more wine, and then she spoke. "I have an idea…ever been to that all night indoor spa?"

"No, never heard of it."

"Well, I haven't been there either but I heard there's one at the Calgary Sheraton," she said with a twinkle in her eyes.

It was getting late. The game was over at ten and now it was well after midnight and Luigi was closing up. I suspected the wine was talking and she was affectionate only because of the music and the atmosphere. I had to have the better judgment tonight, but it sure was hard not to say let's go.

I congratulated Luigi for his fine cuisine and tipped the waiters and the violinist who stayed too late, just for us. It was a very good choice for romantic dining I would later write in one of my columns, I thought…a very special place.

The cold fresh air did not help Giselle's inebriated condition at all. She suddenly felt sick and then threw up on Luigi's decorative bushes outside. I held her up, gave her my handkerchief to wipe her mouth, and led her to my Tahoe. She was very embarrassed, but just could not help herself. She fell into my arms too closely so I could not resist the temptation. We then kissed hard. The taste of her lips had changed to a whiff of a Dom Perignon flavor. Giselle was losing all sense of stability and I had to literally pick her up and seat her in the passenger's side. I asked her if she was all right and thought six or seven glasses of Luigi's fine wine was just a little too much.

"Geeez, I do not…know, Mis…ter Da…vid, sirrrr, it tas..ted glow slood," her almost incoherent voice slurred. "I neber drank al..cloholic berveragers before," she mumbled, sometimes giggling as she spoke. "Daddy floorbids that! Wait'll I till I tell ol' Daddyo you got me drunk as a skunk and sleeduced me," she giggled trying to tug at my tie.

Oh my God! I totally ruined this woman's integrity, I thought.

I did not have to wait very long to see what this beautiful non-drinker did when she got loaded for the first time. First, her judgment and balance left her, next her morals, and finally, her ability to stay awake. My gorgeous lady eased back in the passenger's seat, closed her eyes and went sound to sleep. I buckled her up snuggly in her seatbelt so she would not get hurt if I had to stop quickly. Having bucket seats and a console between us made it difficult to remain close.

"Now what?" I said aloud to myself as I started the engine and drove off wondering what to do next. I couldn't take her home in this condition. I certainly wasn't going to the Calgary Sheraton with her. Nigel already, more or less, said he would kill me if anything happened to his daughter. I had no choice. I headed for my apartment. Maybe, I thought, she would sleep it off in a few hours, and then, even though it was late, I would take her home.

I shook Giselle gently, after I had parked in my apartment parking lot. She would not wake up, so I put her arms around my neck. I was lucky that I lived on the first floor, because I had to carry Giselle in my arms, open the sliding patio door, and get her inside. If anyone saw me, they'd surely call the cops on me. Giselle was as loosey-goosey as could be. She looked dead and flopped down on my bed face first and just lay there after I put her down.

Oh my, I thought. What the heck do I do now? I removed her high heels and put them next to the bed. Turning her onto her side, I pulled off her coat and laid it on the back of a chair. I rolled her over gently with her head upon a pillow, and I pulled the covers over her. Her breath was sour smelling when I touched her lips to mine to kiss her good night. I was very worried.

I went straight to the phone and dialed Nigel. I feared he was going to explode. However, Queenie answered my phone call.

"Hello, Missus Gray…this is Jerry David, Giselle's date. May I speak with your husband, please?"

"Nigel was called out on police business. What's wrong…is something wrong?" she asked very worried.

"No, Missus Gray, please believe me. I picked up Giselle after the football game and we danced and dined at Luigi's in Calgary. I am afraid she drank wine and got sick. She is at my apartment now, sleeping in my bed. I thought I had better tell you both before you worried about her. Do you want me to bring her home as soon as she awakens, or let her sleep it off until morning? I promise you nothing bad has happened and I'm an honorable person. She did not tell me until she drank four glasses that she never drank before. I'm afraid she's drunk. We talked and she told me all about you."

"I believe you. She is an impetuous girl, willing to try anything once. I assure you she has never done anything like this before. I guess it was in celebration of the victory," she confided. "You sound very sober and intelligent enough to know we would be sick with worry had you not called us with the new girl incident near campus.

"I am relieved, but after all, she is twenty-six and an adult. Nigel told me you were a decent person, so I guess I can trust you. Let her rest. I was certain that after her performance tonight and the Stampeders winning, that she would celebrate to some excess. I will have to tell Nigel she stayed over at your place for honorable reasons. He might be angry, at first, but certainly not with you. Unless she gets home before him, Giss will get an ear full in the morning. Thank you, Mr. David, for calling. Please see to it Giselle is safely sleeping it off. If she had just four, she being a non-drinker, she will be sick sometime tonight. Call if there's a problem, okay?"

"Absolutely, but I think she will be fine in a few hours…thank you for understanding. I am glad I called. I look forward to meeting you in person…good night, ma'am."

I had lied about Giselle's intake, it was actually six or seven, but I hung up knowing it was the proper thing to do. I hoped this did not hurt my future with Giselle. I looked in on her and she was still sleeping soundly. I left the light on in the john so if she woke up in a strange place she could at least see the bathroom. I grabbed a pillow and a cover from the closet and headed to the couch. I prayed this would turn out better than I felt it might.

When I lay down on the couch, I flipped on the TV. The news was bad. The anchor stated that a co-ed's body, found near the Calgary campus, brought fear into the community of a vicious serial killer. They reported that the assistant coroner divulged details of the mutilated body, which brought an all out search underway by authorities to apprehend the murderer. I knew Nigel was the detective called to that scene. He might never know of Giselle's date details, if he remained long enough for Giselle to regain her wits, I hoped. I got four hours sleep, and then I heard Giselle.

"Oh my God, where am I?" I heard the moaning voice of Miss Sleeping Beauty cry out.

I went to the cracked-open bedroom door, knocked, and then went in. Giselle was sitting up on my bed, holding up the covers about her, looking very confused. She looked much disheveled from apparently tossing and turning in her inebriated state. Giselle's long black hair was twisted and swirled into a bird's nest appearance. Her new look not only seemed extremely sexy, just like a porn star's appearance might, but she also had the appearance of a girl who had just become a woman. Her eyes blinked repeatedly as she tried to rub her watery eyes to see more clearly. She was looking to me, trying to find answers in my face about her being in my bed. Then she saw herself in my dresser's mirror and assumed she had lost her virginity.

"Oh my God…what did I do?" she said, aimlessly looking up to the ceiling. "Did we do it? I cannot believe this. Oh my God!" she disgustedly repeated, as I then started to snicker. "I don't remember what happened past Luigi's," she continued.

"What, wasn't it good enough to remember?" I asked jokingly.

She squinted with her swollen eyelids, trying to focus on me.

"I thought I could trust you," she quipped. Then she did an immediate assessment of her being. "We did do it, didn't we? Funny, I don't feel any different, except I have this horrible headache."

"That should be your first and last experience with ol' John Barley Corn," I mused. "I'll get some Bromo to help you out. I'm not an expert on hangovers, but you sure did too much last night."

"What did I do?" she sadly asked, as I went to the bathroom and got a Bromo packet for her.

"Well, you drank too much of Luigi's good wine. You were really hungry, too, and very, very thirsty. Of course, you are an athlete and after that performance you needed something."

"What performance?" she wanted to know, looking at me with a very leery eye that was focused on my lips for the answer.

I turned away, went to the kitchen for a glass of water, and then returned. Giselle had lifted the bed covers from her, which revealed she still was fully clothed.

"What...you did me and didn't even remove my clothes?" she asked somewhat sarcastically.

"Here, take this," I said, as I opened the Bromo packet and dumped the white contents into the water glass. It immediately began to fizzle up. I handed it to Giselle, but she was reluctant to drink it.

"Go ahead, it might help your throbbing brain," I advised.

Giselle then downed the entire drink and suddenly belched.

"Oh," she said as she shivered, shaking all over in disgust. "That's some horrible stuff! Burp! Excuse me!" she said, while expelling gases and being very embarrassed at the same time. "Burp!" again the Bromo was causing her discomfort.

"Ohhhhhhhh," she suddenly gasped, as she got up to make a mad dash to the john. She threw up hard, so I went in to flush the toilet, get a washcloth, and a clean towel out for her. She remained bent over the bowl with the dry heaves. It hurt me more than her to see the girl in such misery.

When she became unsteady, I held her up as she blew up once more. She paused her performance and reached back blindly for the wet washcloth. I handed Giselle the washcloth, which she held to her face, then wiped her mouth. I grabbed the towel and blotted her face dry when she turned around. Boy was she sorry she ever went to Luigi's with me, she told me.

"Did you give me a ring, or just a good time, which I must tell you I can't remember," she said suddenly more collectively.

"I hope it was just a good time, because we never 'did it'," I assured her. "Your mother said you are very impetuous and she expected you'd kick up your heels after the Stampeders won."

"You talked to my mother, when?"

"After you passed out in my arms and I laid you, ah, ah, placed you softly on my bed and covered you up. You might notice your clothes are still untorn, buttoned, and except for the wrinkles, they are just like they were when you put them on. But, I must say, it was very hard for me not to touch you in your condition, even though you were more than willing, I must add."

"I was? Oh, yes, I was, I think. I am still very confused. You mean I'm still a virgin, eh?"

"Yes, and someday I hope I'm the lucky guy who takes you into womanhood. But for now, you still have choices and all your self respect."

She looked up at me, obviously feeling much better. "Thanks… thanks," she repeated whispering with a much-relieved look.

"It's eight; I bet my daddy is fuming."

"Not necessarily. I called your mother at two and told her everything. I knew your parents would be worried, but I didn't want them to see you drunk out of your gourd."

"What did Queenie say, then?"

"Well, as I said before, she knew you were a very impetuous girl and thought I was a perfect gentleman for calling. She told me to let you sober up, then bring you home before your daddy gets back, more or less."

"What…he got a call-out?"

"Fortunately, for you, but not for some poor co-ed found murdered after the game near campus."

"Oh, my God, no, not another!" she slowly lamented. "Well, you'd better take me home…sorry I made accusations."

"I hope this doesn't ruin our friendship. I really enjoyed everything… just being near you was enough," I pleaded.

Giselle smiled, then wiped her mouth with the towel, looked into the bathroom mirror, squeezed out some Crest toothpaste on her finger from my toothbrush holder, then rubbed it on her teeth and spit in the sink. She quickly fluffed her long hair with my brush that was sitting on the vanity and then turned back to me.

"I guess if a guy like you can see me this way and still want to be friends; I'd say we have a start of something good here. Don't you agree?" she said, as she then planted her lips on mine softly.

After the kiss, Giselle scurried to the bedroom and tried to straighten up the covers.

"I'll get that later. Let's try to beat Nigel home," I suggested.

"Right, let's went, Poncho," she jested, as we both grabbed up our coats and headed out my patio door.

It was a very clear morning, and everyone was off the streets. I sped just a little, but it was worth the effort. Giselle spotted Nigel gassing up his unmarked car at a nearby BP station, so we were in the clear. I was able to quickly kiss Giselle good morning and still get her home before Nigel arrived.

"Call me," Giselle yelled as she made her way through the front door and past an awaiting Queenie. Queenie was still in her nightgown, so I dare not go up to greet her. Instead, I waved after I backed onto the street and drove away. She waved back.

The Sunday streets were vacant, as was the car wash I usually used. I found a little three-bay operation, and decided to zip into it for a quick clean up job on my new Tahoe. I could not help but notice the steam rising from one bay where someone was washing their big SUV. I could see gobs of mud splattered over it and huge hunks of mud lying on the concrete that apparently had fallen from under the rig. It was a jacked-up SUV, with wide, oversized, deep-cleated tires. It was probably some kid's ride, I thought as I put my dollar bill in the slot for the soap cycle to begin.

Often with my old Jeep, I could get the wash job done with two dollars and a good rinse if I hustled. However, the crud I picked up from the football field on my new one had frozen over night and the pressure could not touch it. I used up five bucks and it was so streaked I had to go to the moneychanger for more ones. It was then I saw this creepy-looking dude who turned his back on me when I looked at him. I got my change and returned to washing my Tahoe.

Suddenly, the driver of the vehicle in that next stall raced his SUVs motor. The SUV zoomed out of the stall, still dripping water from the rinse cycle. I watched the exit. That young driver put the pedal to the metal as the SUV's motor roared loudly. Its wheels spun fast on the hard pavement, until traction was made and rubber met the road. Tires squealed, laying smoking black rubber down as it disappeared out of sight.

At first, I wasn't impressed by the performance, until I stopped short to think. That SUV was actually a lime colored one after the mud came off. It might be the same color of that big SUV, which almost nailed me the night of Meredith Monroe's murder, and here I didn't even get a good look at him or his vehicle. I think it was a four door Hummer…with Alberta plates, I surmised with a memory flash. What a dunce I was. I could never catch him now, I thought. Nevertheless, I might!

I dropped the wand of the washer. It danced wildly out of control, and then jetted itself beneath my Tahoe. It actually was doing a good job underneath before I started up and sped out of the car wash after the Hummer. The last I saw of the dancing wand, it had stuck itself up on the garage door, but was still spraying hard.

Maybe, I thought, he would hit some red lights and have to stop, so I could catch up. All I wanted was his license plate number and maybe a good look at him, also. I disregarded two red lights, another turning from yellow to red, and then saw the unit turn right, just two blocks ahead of me. I accelerated the Tahoe and she answered my request as I slid around the corner after the Hummer. The Hummer was at a standstill at a red light. In addition, there was a cop coming the other way who stopped. I eased up and saw the Alberta plate number. I had no pencil or pen so I had to try to remember it. 7AB65-12, it read. I used spit on my finger to write it on my clean dash. I hoped I could retrieve it. The old Jeep would have had dust on it.

Still easing up, I drove along the inside lane to get a look at the driver. He took one quick look my way, and then suddenly made an immediate right turn on red. I'm not sure he looked at me, maybe it was the squad car. I only saw him for a second. He was an unshaven person, maybe my age. Seated, I could not tell how tall he was. The only outstanding feature I saw on his grizzly face was an earring of the devil hanging from his right, no left ear; I summated from my brain's sight retention. My occipital lobe was straining to feed my gray matter.

I was unfortunately in a left turn only lane, and the green arrow came on for me to go left. I eased around past the police officer and saw him looking at the Hummer. It had turned with the driver not using its right turn signal, why didn't that cop go after him, instead of me…not me…oh, no, not me!

I saw his squad car's red lights flash on and heard the siren's short burst. I put on my turn signal and actually pulled into another car wash, which had real people working. They all made fun of my predicament, pointing their fingers at me and stopped washing to watch the proceedings.

"Sir, you didn't use your turn signal to turn left and I noticed your registration missing, though I now see your application on the passenger side windshield. May I please see your driver's license and insurance? Is this Tahoe yours?" he questioned. God, he was a giant of a man, literally.

"Yes, sir, I just purchased it at Miller's yesterday. It is brand new," I replied as I reached for the console to get my wallet.

"Easy there…do it slowly," he ordered.

I guess he thought that I might be armed, so he put his hand upon the handle of his Smith & Wesson.

"Officer, I haven't had time yet to get a new insurance card…here's my driver's license, the sales slip, and my insurance to my previous Jeep that I traded in," explaining what I had for him. "By the way…did you notice that big SUV beside me over there. I was trying to get a good look at the driver and get his license plate number."

"Why, did he do something to you?"

"No, sir, it's just he might have been near a killing I was at?" I recklessly spoke.

"Okay, buster, now get out of your car and come back here."

I knew he was aware of the earlier murder on campus, because he was leery.

The hoots and hollers coming from the car wash were chaotic until the huge officer rose up and advised the workers he would come over to see them next for obstructing his arrest procedures. They quickly shut up and spoke whispering to each other with all their heads down.

"What murders and where?" he demanded with one raised eyebrow.

"Do you know Detective-sergeant Nigel Gray?" I asked.

"Yes, what's he got to do with you?" he wanted to know.

"We're, ah, ah, well, you'd better ask that question of him. He may not know me after today," I told him after rethinking my promise to Nigel to maintain secrecy about the cases and him possibly finding out about Giselle's date with me.

"What'd you do to Nigel? Are you his informant?"

"Nothing, nothing, like that, I swear. Okay, I only had a date last night with his daughter and we stayed out a little too late, that's all."

"How late is too late?" he eased up closer, face to face, as if he had to be told the truth and very intimidating.

"Ah, she got sick and stayed at my apartment all night. I just dropped her off…but what's that to you?"

"Holy shit, you got into Giss' pants, didn't you, sonny?" he said snidely.

"Never said that at all…she's a fine girl…we had a date last night at Luigi's and we danced too late, that's it!" I loudly blurted out.

"Wait till I tease Nigel someone stole his little girl's virginity. He'll shit!" he declared.

"Why would you ever say that…it's a lie…don't you dare or I'll, I'll…oh shit, I'm a dead man," I halfway begged.

The cop could not stop laughing at me. I guess it was the frightened look on my face, but it was very unprofessional and rude of him. He got to me.

"What's your badge number, officer?" I demanded. "I work at CMEN and I don't like the way I'm being tormented by your insulting insinuation."

"It'll be on the bottom of the ticket you receive if you get to be a wise guy...CMEN, huh? The pen is mightier than the sword...I know...I have several I use daily on traffic violators, ha! Look, I'm joshing ya, sonny. Nigel is my best friend and I am Giss' Godfather. I am glad you were upset, because I was just testing you. I was waiting for you to say something derogatory about her and then you might have tripped and busted your head open. Here, you get off with my verbal warning to use your turn signals. And...good luck with Giss... you seem like a decent fellow...she's really special to us all."

He smiled, handed back my license, and then yelled violently to the washers as he returned to his squad car.

"Let's see those green cards, you heathens!" he bellowed.

The workers were scared half to death and took off running fast down the street, but in all directions. He just screamed out loudly, "Calaboose!"

He started laughing again, then got in his squad, and motioned for me to ease up, so he could drive away. I did drive forward, as I sat putting my things back in my wallet to the hoots and hollering of the car washing proletariat who suddenly popped back out peeking from behind houses and buildings. I shook my head in frustration and just drove towards home. Disappointed in my own detective work, I noticed the spit had dried on my dash and I could not see the license plate number I smeared on it anymore.

CHAPTER 11

"Let's see, Rita…help me with this one, will you, please?" I asked my secretary seated in our new office, which placed her within earshot. "And would you please pour us each an espresso latte…isn't this nice?" I gleefully inquired. "Look at all those file cabinets so handy, yet out of the way. And there's a water fountain…and it's clean!"

"It's simply wonderful, but what you did to get the boss to do all this, I would certainly like to know. I bet you have something on him, don't you?" she wisely concluded.

I smiled at her wryly, but ignored her inquisitive character and set about my work while admiring our new surroundings. After a week of calling in my columns, we finally were invited back into our new office. It was amazingly swank looking. The adornments were plush carpet, dark oak desks with glass tops and pads, and new great florescent lighting above, as well as two comfortable office chairs and two new computers.

Ol' Freddie had even hired a tech to transfer the files from our old system so we would not lose any data. Yes, not a dime was spared on remodeling and I felt like an executive. Now I would have to improve my column accordingly, I knew.

"These are five new ones…they're all winners. Listen to this one, 'Rockymountaingirl…attractive, outgoing, young 65, W/F…widowed recently with lots of money left by stingy hubby…seeking intimate good times with gentlemen 35-45, no older'. Geeez, what next… okay, ready, here goes nothing…lead with age and particulars, then 'attractive; wealthy babe seeks romance with mature gentlemen for possible long lasting relationship'…how's that?"

"How long lasting can any relationship be starting at age 65?" Rita deduced.

"Oh, she might be a vegetarian, or something, who knows. Next!"

"You must fade out her picture or she'll never get a contact."

"Forget that; add financially sound, that gets them…again, next!"

Just then, the office intercom system in the ceiling buzzed. "Miss Tory, would you please come to Mr. Upshaw's office?" the female voice spoke rather lustfully.

"Who in the hell is that?" I asked of Rita.

"Mr. Upshaw's new secretary, Victoria Secret, believe it or not."

"Who?"

"Not really…she was a model for lingerie. Her name is Veronica Stone."

"I've got to see this gal…let me take those finished reports on office expenditures to her," I quickly suggested.

"Sorry, I did that earlier and she asked for me, not you. Go if you want, but it will be my ass in trouble, if you go and Mr. Upshaw expects me…I will introduce you two later. But you'd better not notice her blond hair, long legs and big boobs or Freddie will get awfully ticked…I can guarantee you that, boss."

Rita was taking charge of my office as taught in school. She quickly left, so I tried to review the other new love ads.

My mind wandered a bit to thoughts of Giselle and what she might be doing, thinking. I had not called her, even though she asked me to on the run when I left her. I figured she really could not be with me again if daddy found out about us. Nigel probably would stay away from me, also, so I would keep away from his daughter. I felt some pity for myself, because I tried my best to impress her and the situation failed us both. I missed her badly, but I was afraid to call her, because I figured her cop Godfather had squealed on me and Nigel was just waiting to get his paws on me.

Rita came back and told me the new girl could not even work the copier in her office. Rita had to show her twice, she told me giggling.

"Blonds…you know the jokes," I quipped to her delight. "Well, you ready for another?"

"Shoot, boss!" Rita replied.

"Missingoutonlove…45, b/f…slim but pleasantly endowed…good with kids…seeks honorable, religious man for moral support."

"Now that gal tried to tell it like it is. I bet she is probably saddled with 10 kids and needs financial help. She's probably unemployed… let's see. Hummm…says here in her bio she is a teacher! I guess I was wrong, humm…so much for pre-judging people. Nice clear picture… good looking too…that will fly as is…bet she gets a guy quickly. Next!"

We worked until noon and took off for lunch. Mom called right as I was leaving. She asked me if I was coming home for Christmas as everyone was going to be there. She wanted to know if I wanted turkey, pheasant, or ham. If it was pheasant, she advised, I had to shoot some first, because Dad had been down with the gout in his big toe and had not been out hunting lately. Mom and Dad had a nice grain and cattle farm in South Dakota where mule deer and pheasant hunting were a way of life when it came to hunting and dining. There were flocks of geese and ducks galore, but I thought they were too greasy being all dark meat. Nevertheless, everyone else loved them and they were fun to decoy in and shoot.

"I can do that. Did Dad get any deer tags?" I asked.

"Sure, doesn't Dad always? He was a little miffed last year because you stayed up there. He did not hunt at all. He misses his huntin' buddy. Your dad will get well very quickly knowing you are coming home. He has to get away from the twins anyway because they get on his nerves after a while. They jump on his lap and though he laughs he has his pains."

"Okay, great, Mom, I have to head out to lunch now…oh, I didn't tell you…you should see my new office with my new secretary…she's a beauty!"

"You can tell me all about everything when we talk at Christmas. Calling across the border costs too much. Bye, sweetie…Momma loves you!" she told her little baby boy.

"Love you, too, Mom. Tell Dad the same. See you all at Christmas and tell Pop to oil up our shotguns and buy some extra number 6

Federal Black Cloud shotgun shells for our pheasants…I might take him out for some Canadian honkers, too, this time, if they're down there…bye!"

I looked up and was surprised Rita was standing in the doorway listening. She was waiting on me, I guess. Though I was telling Mom how beautiful my new office was, Rita overheard me say, "She's a beauty", and mistook it, thinking that I thought she was the beauty. Her smile told me so. I hung up and kept my eyes on her. She began looking devilishly innocent, as if she knew I held a secret thing for her. I think it was just the other way around, which I was surprised to learn later.

"Let's go eat!" I told her.

When Rita saw my new Tahoe, she asked to take a ride in it to get lunch.

I told her, "Better yet, you drive. Where shall we eat…I'm buying."

"In that case, how about some pizza at the Hut?" she decided.

"Lead on, you're driving," I directed her.

She drove sensibly, but adjusted the seat closer as she drove in traffic. A horn honked at us. I guess she crossed the line.

"Please stay in your lane. There are cops all around mid-city, you know," I warned her.

She drove fine after that and easily parked in the Hut's lot and left room for me to get out.

"Hey, pretty good…you split the parking slot right down the middle. Let's get inside before the crowd gets here."

We ordered deep pan crust supreme pizza and the server said it would be twenty minutes. Therefore, we sat sipping our drinks and chatting.

"Hey, were you talking about pheasant and duck hunting to your mom?"

"Sure did. She's a safari guide in Zimbabwe," I teased.

"Really…that must be dangerous, eh?"

"She's the Great White Lady Hunter, the natives call her," I continued.

"Oh my, aren't you afraid for her?"

"No, she was a Navy Seal, a rodeo bareback bull rider and used to be a paratrooper, also."

"Hey...you think you're pretty smart and I'm pretty dumb, don't you? You're full of it, I think!"

"Sorry," I chuckled. "My mom and dad live in South Dakota, where I went to school. They have a big cattle and grain farm in the Black Hills area," I confessed.

"So, that's where you hunt pheasants. I used to hunt them around Pincher Creek area. That is until they tried to make me surrender my Citori."

"You owned a Citori...a Browning Citori?" I could not believe this girl.

"Sure, I had a Gattling Gun for geese though. I filled a Chevy pickup truck's bed with white spots once."

"Nahhh, really, you shot geese with a Gattling machine gun?"

"Touché!" she said smiling.

"Oh, you got me back, eh? I deserved that, I guess."

"But I still have that Citori. I put it in some oily rags and buried it in a capped PCV pipe, right in my dad's backyard," she told me.

"Still, digging, huh?"

"No, really...I grew up with three brothers and a father who told me he didn't know how to teach girl things, so if I wanted to be with him I'd have to learn to hunt."

"What about your mom?"

"Never knew her. She died at my birth. I have felt the weight of that on my shoulders each time I look into my brothers' eyes...Dad's too. Nevertheless, they don't hold that against me. It's all in my head."

"Sorry, I didn't know. It must have been hard on you not having a mother to go to when you needed an answer to your girl questions, eh?"

"Hey, I made out all right. I am not complaining. Except, this damn country seized all the other guns here. Soon, we will have favorable ministers back in rule and I can go hunting again. I heard the reverse, back to registered guns, is coming soon with the new prime minister."

"Sweet! Let's eat!" I said as I served Rita a slice of heavenly pizza. We ate and finished quickly and headed back to the office. I drove and Rita examined all the cup holders, glove box and cranked up the stereo.

"You should have gotten a better sound system, dude."

"Dude...where did that come from?" I questioned.

"Actually, I say that to my brothers and it just slipped out, sorry."

"That's okay, I guess that fits,eh"

We got back to the office and I wrote out my column for the paper. Gerry Loveletter was straight to the point. "Do not drink on first dates," is what I wrote. I advised the misfortunes that may develop, when your judgment and then morals slip. You could lose that special person...the love of your life," I wrote with a bit of anxiety.

When Rita answered the ringing phone and said that Nigel wanted to talk to me, I almost told her to tell him I was out. However, she had already informed him I was there. After she managed to punch the right transfer button, I received his transferred call.

"Hello, Jerry...busy?" he asked.

"No, I expected you'd call sooner than later. Go ahead."

"What the heck's wrong, Jerry? You sound rather belligerent today."

"I expect you're going to let me have it for being so late bringing Giselle home. I can explain everything."

"Ha! That is your worry? I know a traffic cop who thinks the world of you and a little girl who is very crabby, because you haven't called her."

"Really... I thought you would scold me like a kid."

"Jerry, how old are you?"

"I am going on twenty-nine this coming February."

"I would think a guy with your knowledge would know a girl has her own ways come eighteen and daddy and momma let go of her. She has to make her bed and sleep in it, too. I trust Giselle explicitly. When and what she does is strictly her business. I'm glad you respected her...I'm glad, son."

I had never heard him so humble. He was telling me, basically, that he approved of me to date Giselle.

"May I speak with her?"

"That's just it. She has gone to Vancouver with the cheerleaders. The Grey Cup's schedule is there this Saturday against Montreal. She called twice to ask if you had called the office yet. Now can you see my concern? I think she really likes you…why…I'll never know!" he chuckled. "Got any more clues?"

"Well, I saw this young guy in a light green Hummer that I thought might be that big SUV that almost hit me at Meredith Monroe's scene."

"Did you get a license plate number?"

"I tried, but I had to write the number using my spit on my finger, and then write it on the dash. I have that new Tahoe and after it dried it disappeared."

"Have you cleaned the dash yet?"

"No, didn't touch it."

"I'll be over with one of the techs in an hour. Listen; here is Giss' cell number. If you have time tonight, please just call her. I know she's dying to talk to you."

"Thanks, I'll call after work. Are they on Pacific time?"

"Oh, that's right. I called her at six this morning before I got up for work. I guess it was five there."

"Okay, see you in an hour. I parked in the front lot near the entrance. It's a new white Tahoe."

"Oh, that's nice. Must be a good paying job there, eh?"

"Yep…just got a raise, then I bought the SUV for the date, remember? You rode in it Saturday night, remember?"

"Damn, I was called out that night after the game…I'm blank on remembering that," he told me.

We agreed to meet in an hour and Rita looked concerned about my interest in a woman. She asked if Giselle was the cop's daughter.

"Yes, I just had a great date with her. I think she's the one," I told her.

"No wrath so terrible than that of a jealous woman," I once wrote in one of my columns. I do not remember the author, just those words.

Rita became quiet and began a "Yes, Mr. David, sir, no, Mr. David, sir," thing. Caught in a perplexing situation, because she was a nice person, my secretary, and a new friend, I felt trapped. I had to handle this carefully. She was twenty-one, but reared by a widowed father. She did not realize everything about the pursuit of a man. Therefore, she began her way, the only way she knew.

When Nigel arrived, Rita got up and followed me out to the Tahoe. I could not just tell her to get back to work. Nigel had a young woman forensic tech with him, who asked me just where I tried to write down the license number. I pointed to the area. She opened her case, pulled out a green liquid spray bottle, and sprayed just a fine mist there. Soon, after several more sprays, the number was quite prevalent.

She took a photo of it and jotted the number down on a pad, then handed it to Nigel.

"Looks local...I'll call it in. Thanks, Jerry. We have to get back... don't forget to call Giselle, okay?" he reminded me.

Nigel was insistent, I thought. I wondered what Giselle said to him? I hoped she felt the same about me as I did her. I was happy that I could assist in the investigations, but more delighted that Giselle wanted me to call her. I returned to the office where Rita had beaten me back somehow and was typing the last of my column before she sent it to print.

"Almost done...did they find your spit?" she giggled. "Maybe they wanted your DNA for a paternity test," she snidely remarked.

"Now that's not nice. I don't pry into your romantic life, do I? Giselle isn't that type of girl."

"What type of pedestal does she stand on anyway...tell me, please?" she asked somewhat mockingly.

"First of all, it's private. But I can tell you she is very refined and beautiful."

"Oh, you two did it, huh?"

I think Rita sounded more like a guy talking than a lady. I could feel her jealousy beginning, so I decided to ease her mind. "Look, Rita...you're a very nice looking woman and if I thought you liked me like that we might have been closer. I think I am in love with Giselle. I have been for years, I guess."

"Like I said...you guys did it and now you're in love, ha!"

I grimaced at her and just turned away. I wasn't prepared to hear her next thoughts.

"Would you like to go to bed with me?"

I didn't even turn around to look at her. "No, you're not my type, sorry, but let's still be friends, okay?" I said as nonchalantly as I possibly could, just to show her that those words did not shock me, but they did. I continued to ignore her, took out a pencil, and began to jot down notes on my next column.

"I'm sorry…really I am. I somehow thought you cared for me," Rita said having come up from behind me closely. I felt her hand on my shoulder, which caused me to spin around, knocking her off her feet, right into my lap.

"Hey!" I yelled, trying to keep Rita from hitting the floor.

She regained her balance and got off me. I am afraid I liked the feel of her body next to me breathing, much too much. Her figure was very nice, but I never wanted to be the boss who did exactly what Freddie did with Jill.

"Sorry, now let's get back to our work," I strongly suggested.

Rita sighed, and then reluctantly went back to her desk. I looked up at her and I thought I saw a tear. Maybe, I thought, she might grow on me and I would have different feelings for her eventually. After all, she was intelligent, pretty, not gorgeous, and so far, we both enjoyed hunting. That was my mistake.

"Hey, sometime we will have to go out pheasant hunting at my parents' place. I'd like to see you use that Citori," I said to liven up her bent ego.

There was no answer, but when I looked up at her, it was like rekindling her desire. She was silent; however, she stared hard across the room at me and seemed to be in a trance. I think she was plotting something, or teed off in anger. It was weird.

"Quittin' time!" I told Rita, as I headed to turn off the lights and adjusted the thermostat down. "Be safe going home…see ya tomorrow, same time same place," I told her smiling. I held Rita's coat out for her to slide into, then we walked out, and I turned to lock the office door. When I turned around, Rita had gone.

Mr. Upshaw allowed his office personnel to always leave ten minutes earlier; sooner than any other employees. This was to avoid the mass exit out into the parking lot. The other employees punched time clocks and clogged the hallway, while others would be punching in. Therefore, I rarely met the other workers of the pressroom.

I looked for Rita, until I saw her small car exiting the parking lot ahead of me. I hoped everything was all right with her. If not, I was in for a bad office relationship. I headed to the grocery for the essentials to replenish my little food needs at home. My thoughts ran to hearing Giselle's voice. I imagined her saying, "I love you, too, Jerry!"

On that Wednesday evening, I tried to call Giselle, but I received a recording. I left several messages. After that, my calls transferred to voice mail, but I never received her return call. I suppose she was too busy, or really did not want to talk to me after all. I got a little pissed, then I stopped calling. I guess Nigel did not know his daughter's desires as well as he thought.

I tossed and turned all night, because between Giselle not returning my calls and Rita showing her fangs, I went to sleep with too much thinking on my mind. I woke up from a dream. I dreamt that I was hunting pheasants out in the fields of my parents' farm with both Giselle and Rita. When a pheasant burst into the air cackling, someone yelled, "Rooster!" and both Giselle and Rita shot me. I jumped up in bed sweating. It was surreal.

My workweek was concluding on a rather even keel with Rita. She lightened up her being much too forward and I kept from saying anything to provoke her further interest in me. Then on Friday at lunch, she did not want to go to lunch with me. That was all right, but she purposely had a new person that she left with, making certain as we left the building I would see him. I imagined it was her attempt to make me jealous, but I told myself not to be so vain. She had probably met someone working here who was more receptive to her and that was fine. I smiled at them both, went to my Tahoe, and drove away.

Then, as I pulled into Sarah Selby's Cafeteria, a home-style smorgasbord, which also catered to the CMEN workers and the business people in the area, I noticed Rita and her new friend in the parking lot getting out of a car. Just to avoid further confrontations with her annoying, gnome looking smiles, I waited until they entered and drove off to Burger King to do the drive-thru.

So much for Sarah's great vegetable beef stew, I thought. Sarah was the owner and did all the cooking; her soups could be considered a delicacy in most establishments. I often suggested her place to young couples dating on a dime.

I ate my lunch in the Burger King's parking lot and beat Rita back to the office. A carrier arrived and delivered a stack of mail that was much larger than most times. There were bunches of personal love ads, so I set the other mail on Rita's desk and went to mine to open the personal love ads.

Apparently, my words of wisdom were having a great social enhancement on our community. After all, I had built up my subscribers and most were repeaters. I began opening the envelopes and placing them on a pile. I heard footsteps behind me and assumed it was Rita returning to her desk.

"Ah, hem!" sounded a voice. It was Mr. Upshaw. "Jerry, how involved are you in this police business regarding the serial killer?"

"Oh, hello there, Mr. Upshaw…I thought I'd never see you again to thank you for this fine office, after you got that new secretary. I must say she's a looker, eh?"

Freddie did not speak; he just looked at me waiting for the answer to his question. "Oh, the serial thing…well, I'm working on it a little with Detective-sergeant Gray…why?"

"My secretary, Miss Stone, lost her sister to that monster the night of the game. I have been consoling her since. What do you know about that one?"

"Nothing…I wasn't privy to that investigation. I might ask though. I cannot guarantee Nigel Gray will tell me anything. It seems people just tell him clues and he follows up on them without telling anyone if their info was useful or not."

"Veronica's so upset…see if you can get out of them what's going on."

"If I did, they would make me promise not to say a word."

"Do what you can and let me know something by Monday, alright?" he ordered.

"Do my best, but Nigel is very touchy on letting things out of the bag, if you remember what I mean," I reminded him.

"Right…well, enjoy your new office…where's your secretary today?"

"Oh, she went out to lunch late. I told her to take her time and not to gulp her food. She's a very hard worker and you missed out on a great secretary there, boss."

I had not noticed it, but Rita was standing in the doorway listening again. She had her coat in her hands and tried to act undaunted by her lateness. She put her coat away and then asked Mr. Upshaw if there was anything she could do for him. She apologized for eating past the normal return time from lunch.

"Jerry already explained how you worked past your noon hour. No need to say anything to me...he's your sole boss now. However, could you please get closer to Veronica? She thinks the women here are talking about her behind her back."

"What would you have me do?" Rita asked.

"Well, take her under your wing and help her get started. Everything seems to be difficult for her. Well, Jerry, get that info for me by Monday, will you?" he said turning and then walking out.

She waited until ol' Freddie was out of earshot then said, "What... he wants me to show her how to douche, too?" she remarked angrily.

"What's that all about?" I asked.

"Oh, nothing...where'd you go to lunch?"

"Burger King, and you?" I inquired knowing her answer.

"I saw you drive out of the lot at Sarah Selby's...why?"

"Changed my mind...a big Whopper seemed to fit my hunger pangs."

"Oh, I thought you didn't like Harold. He's a pressman here. Did you ever meet him?"

"No, can't say I have. Did he need to send in a love ad to get a girl with all that red hair?" I jested.

Rita stared hard at me for my demeaning remark.

"She's his whore!" she suddenly spoke out.

"Who is whose whore?" I questioned, somewhat taken aback.

"Veronica...she stays past quitting time quite regularly. You know what they say that bitch makes?" she blurted out.

"Hey..." I said, trying to stop her vicious tirade, but Rita continued her wrath being fiery mad.

"That bitch pulls down a hundred grand...a hundred grand...and he asks me, me...I have to help her and I make twenty-five. That really pisses me off and every other competent secretary here, also...that's all!" she said fuming, stamping her foot.

I spun around and quit looking at her madness. Then I got up and closed the office door before the boss heard her. "Now stop! I do not like to hear this. I have enough to worry me about with you. I sure don't want to have you committed," I said smiling, but maybe serious, also.

"Why would you be worrying about me?" she coyly asked.

"God, I only want to be good friends with you and maybe even best friends. You are confusing my mind, because I subconsciously would like to ask you out. But, now there's Harold, so forget that," I told her, wondering what I just told her. Boy did she have me confused.

"So, you do like me after all, don't you? Forget Harold…I told him I'd buy him lunch if he went where I wanted to eat. I did it to make you jealous."

"I know, I know…but there's Giselle…what about Giselle?" I asked her.

"Date me and you'll throw rocks at her…guarantee it!" she said so full of passion.

Just then, my cellular buzzed. That did not happen very often, so I assumed it was Mom.

"Hello, Mother dear!" I greeted without checking the caller ID.

"I'm not your mother, but I might be your girlfriend."

It was Giselle, and I was very embarrassed, especially with Rita standing there closely and after I had just expressed my deeper feelings to her. Quickly, I asked Rita for privacy. She scowled then abruptly turned and went to the espresso machine. She hastily put in the ingredients and made the deafening blender whirl on high speed.

"What's that noise?" Giselle asked.

"It's only my secretary taking a coffee break…why haven't you returned any of my calls?" I asked rather pitifully.

"Well, my cell phone wouldn't pick up here…darned thing! I got a call from Daddy wanting to know if you called…go figure. He must really like you…almost as much as me," Giselle told me.

I took a deep breath and had difficulty with my words. I dreamed of Giselle saying she really liked me. "Where are you now?"

"I'm in the BC's Place Dome down on my keester. I have my legs in the air, bicycling, and down upon the dome floor, warming up for our performance at tomorrow night's big game. Are you gonna watch?" Giselle asked rather breathlessly.

"Let's get something straight, Giselle, I really miss you and wish I could hold you right now. I am relieved you called, because I was getting these angry feelings within myself that you might have just been too upset with me and our date to ever want to see me again."

"There's one thing about alcohol I learned, besides never to do that again," she began. "You cannot remember anything, but the good times...that's exactly what I remember...I want to be with you...how about you?" she puffed out.

"That's all I want to hear you say. When are you coming back?"

"We'll party afterwards, win, or lose, then fly home from Abbotsford Sunday morning on a chartered flight aboard Borek Air to Calgary International. You wanna meet me there?" she asked.

"Do I! Wild horses could not keep me away. What time is your flight?"

"Usually about one, depending on the players...some get lost or zonked and we have to find them before we can take off."

I was worried about her being with all those jocks. Nevertheless, what could I say? "Call me tonight, if you can. Or, at least tomorrow before you fly out," I told her.

"Okay, hear that music? I have to get up and go practice now...love ya!"

My heart skipped a beat. Giselle said she loved me, I think.

"Love you more," I spoke, too late, as the line went dead.

"Shit!" I let out with my disgust.

"What's wrong now...your gorgeous sleeping beauty turned up again?" Rita said looking dishonored.

After all, I just said I would like to date her. Now what, you big mouth genius? I thought about myself, and this new turn of events. I believed I was only trying to be kind, but I sure had bad timing.

"Rita, I'm sorry for our clumsy relationship. I am much too old for you. You deserve a much nicer guy than me, really."

"I gotcha...eight years is an awful lot...I just came in second, huh?"

"She's just got seniority on you, and that's all. Besides, you are a real babe in your own right. I do want us to be best friends though. I write in my columns never to say that very same thing 'Let's stay best friends' after a date...it's just now I mean it...and we will be here working together for a long time, I hope. Did you just say that bitch gets a hundred thousand dollars?" I suddenly realized. "I think you definitely need a big raise!" I shouted out to try to break the somber moment, appease Rita's ego, and get out of my stupid rhetoric. We went back to work.

"Here's a new one! Oh, by the way, I want you to tally the total checks, which come in because of this column. I want to show that amount to Mr. Upshaw to prove that our work counts here on the income. Now, ready…here's a winner."

We processed several women's personal ads, and then I stopped dead in my tracks. "That's the guy!" I told Rita. "He's the guy I was after in that Hummer!" I shouted.

"What guy in what Hummer?" she said confused by my sudden reaction.

"Oh, crap…I can't tell you, but he may be involved with the serial killings…I just don't know for certain. Let's say he's the only candidate I have found," I related to Rita.

I soon found Rita looking over my shoulder at the picture.

"That's him, alright!" she said loudly, which surprised me. "Look, I know about all this stuff, remember? I was with Nigel while you romanced his daughter. That guy is the same guy who Meredith left with the last time I saw her. He's the creepy one," she avowed.

"That guy? Well maybe we do have something here. I best call Nigel and give him this info."

I dialed up Nigel and he answered directly.

"Rita identified the creep that was last seen with Meredith Monroe. He submitted a personal love ad. It's lengthy. You best come over and get this," I suggested.

"I'll be over within the hour. By the way, did you ever get hold of Giss? I think she has phone problems out there, or something."

"Yes, thank goodness. I'm picking her up Sunday at International."

"Oh, well, I usually do that, but okay. We have a big meal planned for her return and celebration if the Stampeders win. Can you come out to the house and join us?" Nigel asked, so pleasantly I could not believe my ears. "You'll get to meet the whole family," he advised.

"Sure, thanks…see you in an hour."

I hung up to further read the ad. Rita was right over my shoulder breathing on my collar very hard, like she was really upset.

"Hey, run a copy off, no two, one for Nigel and one for you so you can read it yourself."

"Well, the appreciation I get for being so alert. I should have been a Royal Mounty…at least they would have shown some appreciation… more money, too," she grumbled.

Now where did that come from, I wondered. I guess she thought I was being arrogant. I handed Rita the copy and she quickly scanned everything, then handed the original back to me.

"Wonder if Veronica, who makes four times what you do, can do that…better teach her," I said, to aggravate her just a bit.

"Maybe I should ask Mr. Upshaw if he wants a real secretary and have him give you Veronica. For a hundred grand, I could stay over," she said in spite.

Rita was pissed. She then sat at her desk and began closely scrutinizing the ad. "Yep, that's him all right!" she added.

"His distinctly long red hair, mustache, and goatee remind me of pictures of General Custer," I told Rita.

"Huh, reminds me of Manson," she quipped. "Look at those eyes…they look like a zombie's. That stare…what woman would ever go for a guy who looked like that?" she questioned openly.

"Meredith Monroe," I reminded her.

We both had a grim feeling about him.

Within the hour, Nigel came to my office.

"Wow! Things are really looking up here, eh!" he said of our new office amenities.

"Come in, sir," I greeted him.

"Nigel…it's just Nigel…is that so hard to remember, son?" he asked.

"Just trying to show respect for our Jon dorm, that's all," I told Nigel.

"What ya got for me?" Nigel quickly said while reaching for the ad. "I get the original, you get the copy. Prints…you apparently touched this, eh?" he asked somewhat dismayed.

"We didn't have an idea he might be the guy, until we opened it and saw everything he's written," I tried to explain.

"Only he opened it…I didn't touch it…shoot him!" was Rita's helpful suggestion.

"I might have to print you later if forensics finds any prints. I don't think he would be that careless, if this is our perpetrator. Damn, maybe this address is valid though. That's the name of the character that matches the license plate number you retrieved, but it's expired over five years. He must be stealing the registration stickers off other units and reapplying them over his old one. Otherwise, traffic would have gotten him by now. He must be behaving himself locally…traffic-wise anyway. Nevertheless, we haven't found a legitimate residence on him, yet. We have three dozen detectives working on this now. It's our only real live lead left. Everything else is stone cold. Mind you, this may be a dry lead also, who knows, but we have to search it out to its end, eh. Now, Miss Tory, you identified this photo as the man you saw Meredith Monroe with the last time you saw her alive?" he questioned Rita.

"I'm sure of it. Who could forget a creep like that?" she reconfirmed.

"You two deserve a medal for this, even if it's the wrong guy."

"Oh, can I speak with you in private just a moment, Detective… ah, Nigel?" I requested.

I looked at Rita's frown and so did Nigel.

"If it is about this case, Rita is privy, I think. She has been a wonderful help to us so far. Okay with you?" he asked.

Rita quickly scooted over to us.

"It seems I need some info on the last murder out there on campus. Mr. Upshaw's new secretary wants to know what they've found out so far. She is her sister, or something."

"Oh, Veronica…well, I feel for the family, they're very close knit. I've talked to the family and they are being kept abreast of this. I think I cannot trust your boss to keep his mouth shut."

"Why don't you feed him some false info, like 'cops are on the heels of the killer' or 'new evidence opens up case', to roust him out… or…" Rita blurted, but then Nigel cut her short.

"Might be a good idea at that…let me think…if Mr. Upshaw spills anything good, it will damage any case we develop. Humm…why don't you let out to him what you know about the suspect's vehicle. The owner will probably try to dump it. If he doesn't burn it, we might get lucky with some prints, or physical evidence, like blood. Sometimes…

most times, the names criminals use are fictitious anyway. We might be searching forever if we just relied on names, but not always."

"Wait a minute…that guy was using the car wash that morning of the murder. He might have been trying to wash out some blood!" I surmised.

"I already guessed that when you first told me. Our forensics have been to the car wash and gathered the mud they could to run tests for any DNA that could be related to any of the cases."

"Wow! They can do that?" I asked.

"There's a lot they can do. They just need a place to start. If that mud has any blood, hair, any cloth, string, fabrics, from any of the victims they will tag it to the crimes if there's a match. Now we need that suspect and he's our sole survivor, so to speak. Have to run. See you Sunday, Jerry?" Nigel asked.

"Wouldn't miss it for the world," I replied happily.

As soon as Nigel left, Rita said, "Wouldn't miss it for the world, huh?" she mused puckering and making a silly face.

I did not reply knowing she was hurting somewhat. Then, to our surprise, Nigel poked his head back inside the door and asked, "Miss Tory, are you busy Sunday? My son, Art, is coming home from school and there needs to be some young blood for him to socialize with…I would certainly appreciate this as a favor, if you would dine with us. Besides, it's going to be a huge meal. My wife and mother are great cooks, like my daughter Giss' cooking. You know those Scandinavians, eh."

Rita looked at me, then said, "Why, I'd like that, Nigel…thank you…I'll be there," she accepted looking to me for my approval, yet somewhat arrogantly.

Nigel said, "Good!" then left and we sat looking at our suspect. He was very creepy looking. Little did I know that Rita had ideas of her own. She went back to typing out the ads on her computer, and then got up.

"Going to see Veronica before quitting time. I will confide in her and show my sympathy. I actually never knew it was her sister. I will also tell Mr. Upshaw about the news, so he lets it out in print. I will just tell him I overheard you and Nigel talking to get you off the hook.

Then he'll be satisfied…sort of like killing two birds with one stone," she expounded walking out the door. The girl was confusing me.

An hour passed and Rita had not returned. I needed some Scotch tape, so I opened her locked desk drawer with my key. It was identical to my desk's lock. I was amazed at the contents. Nevertheless, the picture of me from one of my columns was in there also. I laughed, because she had taken her pen to it and put on big dark sunglasses, arching eyebrows, a mustache, and cigarette burning in my mouth. I looked like Ozzy Osbourne with a doobie hanging from my mouth. I could not see any tape…it was on top of the desk under a newspaper and in a dispenser. I closed and locked the drawer, and then I retrieved a sliver of tape. I took it over to tape the suspect's picture onto my computer. I wanted to look at it when I needed to remember his ugly mug.

Rita suddenly appeared with tears in her eyes. "Poor, Veronica," she moaned listlessly. "She was really close to her sister…who has been in my desk!" she suddenly exclaimed.

"I needed your tape," I tried to explain. "You know, he does resemble Manson," I told Rita.

"Who, the killer?" she asked.

"Nope, my picture…looks like either Manson or Ozzy Osbourne," I chuckled.

"I did that art work two days ago. I should have burned the evidence," she quipped.

"I guess you had cause, I forgive you," I jested.

"What do you mean 'had'?" she emphasized.

"No worse wrath than that of a jealous woman," I spoke out. "Wrote that last week in my column," I continued.

"Maybe I'm over it. You really are not that hot. I might like Nigel's son, then what?" she said scornfully.

"Then, my dear, Miss Tory, everything will be hunky-dory, don't you think?" I said with delight.

She slammed her desk drawer shut, and then took out a key from her purse and locked it.

"Now, stay out of my private drawers, Mr. David," she ordered.

"I intend to stay as far as I can away from your private drawers, Miss Tory," I said using her own subject.

She stopped short to think about what I said and then frowned. "You would say that, wouldn't you?"

I could not win so I changed the subject. "Did you say anything to Mr. Upshaw about the murders?"

"Well, if someone wants to know, he fell hook, line, and sinker. I saw him jotting down my every word. You know that old guy can take down shorthand?" she mused.

"He started out as a cub reporter for the Calgary Sun. He is a swift paper man. That's why he's the boss," I told her. "He's a self made man. Actually, he's a very rich, self made man," I repeated.

We settled down, going through the rest of the ads together without any further derogatory comments; reworking most, and only rejecting just a few for their lewd photos. My eyes kept going to the picture of the creep. I wanted to remember that face if I saw him again in public.

"Did you read what that creep wrote?" I then asked Rita.

"Yes, how could I forget?"

"It seems so apropos when he says he seeks women 23-37, doesn't it? You get a gist of what he is actually saying. He is somehow stating his needs…like prefer dark haired babes, trim, prefer her to have some college, ready for passionate encounter…encounter! Who but a killer would say encounter? It is right here on his app…as if he wants us to find him, really. See here, he says, 'need a woman who won't quit on him like the others'…now what the hell does that mean?" I yielded politely to Rita's younger vocabulary.

"Well, if you're asking me, it might mean he wants a woman who can handle his…ah, endowed-ness…he thinks he's a real hung mule… just a guess. I've heard that before in the singles' bars from guys who try to impress a girl saying something like that, even though they have a sock in their shorts, ha!"

"Are you a crotch watcher?" I asked jokingly.

"Are you a boob and booty watcher?"

What could I say? "Yes, I guess I am…I'm guilty," I confessed.

"Enough said," she responded mockingly.

"Touché!" I admitted.

CHAPTER 12

Hump day was here before I knew it. Rita suddenly became busy on the telephone, unlike her usual self. She knew personal calls were to be kept at a minimum, but someone began calling her repeatedly. As long as she maintained her proficiency, I did not mind, it kept her mind off hating me.

I watched as she became giddy and often looked embarrassed at the words whomever was speaking to her was saying and turned her back on me. Sometimes, she seemed mysterious and I did not understand her at all. Was she still insistent on being my girl and trying to incite my jealousy?

We did our daily ad requests and I wrote my column as usual. When there was a lull between Rita and me, she was quick to go back and await the call from that special someone.

When her phone rang, with no one to answer it, because she was with Veronica, I picked it up.

"Hello!"

"Who is this?" a young female voice asked.

"Well, I picked up Rita's desk phone, but she's away. Whom may I say has called?" I asked just as I had heard Rita answer many times.

"This is Sherry. Just tell Rita I called, please?"

"Okay, is this Sherry Jackson?" I asked to trick her into giving me her last name.

"No, it's Sherry Buckley…she's got my number. Have her call me please. I have an address for her."

"Oh, you mean about her new boyfriend?"

"Hardly…say, you ask too many questions. Who are you anyway the janitor, or someone?" she said annoyed.

"No, just another employee friend of hers, that's all. I'll tell her as soon as she returns, bye."

I reached for Rita's desk phone again. I pushed her reference dialer, which conveniently showed the callout numbers. Evidently, Sherry was a college student on campus at Calgary. She probably had info on that creep, because his address was near campus. I became concerned that Rita might be taking on more than we knew. I jotted down Sherry's address for some unknown reason, possibly the devil in me thought I might use it to rouse Rita some other time. I heard Rita's high heels clicking and obviously heading towards the office, so I quickly skipped back over and sat down at my desk.

"I saw you! Were you in my desk again?" she accused, then jiggled the drawer to see if it remained locked.

"Oh, no…you still don't trust me? I answered your phone because it kept ringing."

She looked down and saw that she had not set it to her answering machine. "So, who was it?"

"Some girl named Sherry."

Rita's eyes grew wide. "What did she want…what did she say?" Rita spoke loudly and frustrated.

I played it cool saying, "Oh, she just said to call her back…you have her number."

"How do you know that?" Rita quickly questioned, as if it were a secret.

"She told me so. Now let me get back to work. I have to write my column for this week. Don't thank me for the inconvenience I went through to help you make contact."

"Contact…what contact?" she again said very intimidated.

"With her, silly…let me alone, please!" I begged, which seemed to ease her mind. "I think I'll write about avoidance of annoying office people," I told her.

"Thanks," she whispered lowly, then went to her phone and dialed Sherry.

"What's up, girl? Good, give it to me. Are you sure? That's in the back there in the low rent district behind the stadium, isn't it? Sorry, I know you come from there, no problem. Fits him, right? Call you later…thanks much, sister, bye."

I guess my little office girl was going slumming. Maybe she was looking for someone she recently met. No more calls came from Sherry before Rita and I headed home.

I didn't know where she lived, so I just decided to snoop. I waited until she left the parking lot and followed far enough behind she would not spot me. Her turn signal light came on and she actually entered the police parking lot. I made a "U" and headed home. I guess she had business with Nigel. I suppose she could not, or would not, tell me.

Saturday approached quickly. I left the office and that somewhat over zealous, and often irritating, Rita, after work Friday night still yakking on the phone. I guess she was going on a date. I left her behind in my mind, also.

After a very pleasant night's rest, I surprisingly woke up just before eleven and the kickoff of the Montreal Alouettes was just about ready to happen. I thought the game started later. The damn camera did not focus on the cheerleaders at all and it was much too far from the field. Of course, they had close-ups of the coaches, huddles, and field goal attempts, but the big field was too much for their planning.

I grew anxious to see Giselle out there cheering. When I did not see her after the entire first quarter of one team going three downs, then punting to the other, I went to the fridge and grabbed a cold Molson's beer and a glass. Then, I grabbed two, so I wouldn't have to return, because the first beer always slid down so quickly. I returned to the couch and the announcers were reviewing the first quarter.

In the background, I could barely see the Outriders cheerleaders performing a short skit at center field. Then the TV channel went to commercial, just as I know I saw a close-up of Giselle's bare legs running up to her black panties, under her short skirt. I almost fell over trying to follow the camera up. Then the screen went black and popped back on.

"Enjoying the game, well grab up a cold bottle of Molson's and really enjoy it."

"Blah, blah, blah!" I interrupted, as I mimicked him and then chugged down a full glass of beer. I quickly poured the second. The narrator continued speaking out about the brew, so I flopped down and shoved a cushion under my head.

I watched as our Stampeders corralled the Montréal's quarterback and sacked him on the first play from scrimmage of the second quarter; then something changed.

When I finally opened my eyes, I heard cheering and confetti was falling from above, blown up into the air by machines, onto the winning Stampeders team. There were the Outriders cheerleaders hugged by many of the players and I was certain the one getting a big long hug was Giselle. I sat up as the commentators said, "We bid you adieu from the Grey Cup in Vancouver…the final score…Montreal 13…Calgary 21…until next season, so long for now."

My God, I missed the whole game, practically, I thought to myself. What am I going to tell Giselle, for God's sake, if she asks if I watched it?

I'll just have to fake it, I guess. Maybe there is a re-run, I hoped. I looked at the Sun's TV guide. I found a re-run program scheduled for 2 a.m. I will have to watch that, I told myself.

I dumped the empty beer bottles in the trash, rinsed the now smelly beer glass in the sink, and dried it. I looked around my empty apartment and for the first time, I felt lonely. I bet Giselle is in the arms of one of those jocks and she will be too busy to call, I imagined. I bet she changes her mind and does not call at all, unless to tell me to forget tomorrow. I was becoming paranoid.

I went to the john to relieve the beer and looked into the mirror. I wasn't ugly, not really handsome, I thought, but still I had all of my hair, no wrinkles and all-in-all I was fit and trim. I pulled up my shirt and looked at my six-pack abdomen. Yep, it was still going strong there, but my waistline had widened, I thought, as I stood sideways and then backed up to see myself. I stumbled, and then fell backwards into the tub.

I cracked my head on the tile and lay sprawled out inside. I saw blood as I tried to get out. When I did, I took a washcloth and ran cold water on it to cool it, and then put it on the back of my head.

"What a dumb ass you are!" I spoke to myself. It was just a small bump, but it sure was sore to the touch. I cleaned up the blood off the tile, rinsed the cloth, and threw it in the hamper wet. Then I pulled it back out and hung it on the shower door towel hooks. I began to get a headache, so I took two aspirin. "Boy, you're a dumb butt," I repeated to myself as I lay down on the couch to collect my feelings.

I had so many questions addressed to myself. Does Giselle really like me, or not? Will Giselle have so much fun with the jocks that she will forget to call…hell, forget I even exist? Disenchanted, I mourned her absence and needed her to tell me now, once more, that she wanted me.

I dozed off and was in a dream. I dreamt that Giselle came off the plane and jumped into my arms and kissed me hard. Then she held out her hand to exhibit her new engagement ring and then flaunted it in my face. It was huge, must have been ten karats. I asked her what about us. She simply said, "I was just using you! I really wanted a rich football player. That's him over there signing autographs," she pointed. When I looked, my God, it was Freddie Upshaw.

I must have rolled off the sofa during the night when a luggage hauler on a tractor about ran me down in my dream. He was ringing a bell to have me get out of his way. He must have been doing a hundred miles an hour, because when I finally awoke in the morning about eight, I was on the floor, trapped between the coffee table and the couch. My telephone was ringing off the hook also, as I struggled to get up and finally reached the phone on its last ring. No one was there.

My head was pounding and I returned to the bathroom to get more aspirin. Then the phone started ringing again. I made a mad dash and grabbed the receiver, but it flew off the hook and banged against the refrigerator. I quickly picked it up and put it to my ear…"Hello!" I shouted.

"Gee, you seem excited! I just called before but no answer." It was Giselle.

"Giselle!" I blurted. "I had a little mishap and bumped my head hard. I'm a little slow answering the phone, sorry."

"Wellllll?" she quickly questioned, completely disregarding my head wound story, as if she was expecting me to say something. "Well, did you enjoy the game and see my performance, or not?" she wanted to know.

"Oh, yes…you were great! I especially liked it when the camera guy ran his camera up under your skirt," I chuckled. "You have super fine legs, and I love your black panties, I might add. Those were black panties, weren't they? "

"You saw all that? I didn't know he was shooting me that close up!" she complained.

"Back in South Dakota, we used to call that 'shooting squirrels'… ah, without a shotgun, no less," I continued to tease her. "But I never saw anything like those gorgeous legs before, believe me."

"I think you're a nut," she said giggling.

"Really? I think you're the most beautiful girl in the world and… and…I think I love you, Giselle," I hesitantly said in fear of ruining our new relationship. However, I was met with a sweet reply.

"Isn't it funny how two people get together…complete strangers… then their eyes meet and you know instantly they're the one…that very special one," she then told me.

"You don't know how great that makes me feel, Giselle. If I told you I was in love with you from so far away, for so long…well, I just did, but God must have his hand in this. Don't you think?"

"He must have. I love you, Jerry. I honestly do," she whispered.

"I'll always say that I love you more, Giselle. I can't wait to see you."

"Well, in about four hours we can be together. You can pick me up at International…flight comes in at one forty."

"You can count on it…did you get some sleep last night? I thought I saw all the players lining up to give you a hug."

"Nope, not me…I went with Joann after the game…she's my away roommate…and she's very married. We both spent our time in the hotel room while she consoled her three-year old over the phone who just happened to be giving his daddy a fit. Ro, that's Joann's husband, is a hockey player…plays for the Flames. He couldn't go along because he's in training."

"Not Roman Leflorea, by chance?" I asked.

"I guess so, she's Joann Leflorea."

"Gosh, he's a big star. By the way, your dad invited my secretary, Rita, to dinner today with me. Is there anything I should bring?"

"All your love for me…that's enough, I believe. Yes, your secretary has been a big help to Daddy. He thinks she would be a good police officer…even a detective. Anyway, she sure impressed Daddy with her initiative to catch your creepy person. Think he's the one?"

"I don't know, but he really is creepy-looking enough. If it's him, I hope we can stop him," I told her.

"Hey, my phone is needed by a very worried mom. See you later, love…kisses…see ya!" Giselle said with a voice that curled my toes.

"Good-bye, love you more my love, loveya…bye!"

I was dancing on the couch, coffee table, hitting the walls and screaming, "Oh happy day!" very loudly. "Giselle said she loved me!"

Then that familiar pounding upstairs started, which I knew were gyrations from my upstairs lovebugs. It was an "early morning delight" and I embarrassed myself by yelling out, "Sock it to her!"

The noise suddenly stopped. It became very quiet upstairs. I think they finally realized I could hear them. I hope I had not ruined any future unions of theirs. Nevertheless, it was very quiet all morning long.

I shined my shoes, brushed my trench coat, took my sport coat and Dockers out of the plastic cleaner's covering, and then tied my tie in the vanity mirror. I had a date to pick up my angel, who by now was flying in the clouds from Vancouver. I was flying high, too.

The bump on my noggin was gone, but still hurt when I brushed my hair. Should have gotten a trim, I thought, so I took out my barber scissors and trimmed around my ears. There! Looks decent, I thought. I took one more swipe through my hair and headed out the patio door to the Tahoe.

As I shoved in the key and turned on the ignition, the radio blared out. I thought about what music Giselle liked and I tried to find a smooth jazz station. I did and hoped that was favorable. I got on Canada 2, the big highway headed north to Calgary. My thoughts went to Giselle and I imagined the ring I might get sometime soon at the jewelers. She would have to be sure before I asked her. I was sure anyway.

It was deja vu. I saw Gisele's plane come in and I walked past everyone to the tarmac. All the cheerleaders came off first. Suddenly, when the wind caught Giselle's coat it blew it open. Her legs were then exposed, and she looked like Miss Canada coming down from one of those big staircases they always use. She was gorgeous.

Giselle saw me and rushed into my arms. She kissed me as she had never kissed me before. The lip lock brought hoots and hollers from the players as they passed and one told Giselle I was a shrimp. I looked up and gave him the evil eye, because I know he was jealous. I was somewhat dwarfed by the linemen, but the slot back was just my size and the quarterbacks were actually much smaller than I imagined. Overall, they were a nice bunch of fellows and went on their way past us to their wives and kids and awaiting girlfriends. I was not small, just not an overly huge person.

"Let me have your grip and let's go meet your relatives," I told Giselle.

The drive south to her home near Red Deer was filled with looks of love at each other as Giselle snuggled up close beside me. She was sitting on the console without her seatbelt, so I told her I wanted her securely seated in the bucket seat and strapped in. Reluctantly, she concurred.

"I'm not sure I like a console in cars. Momma always sat right next to Daddy, still does and that's how I want to be with you…up close and personal," she said.

Those words sent thoughts of lovemaking through my loins. I had a very hard time taking my eyes off her magnificent figure, especially her long legs she stretched out. I was certainly in heaven.

Giselle directed my turns and we took a shortcut to her home. There were several cars parked in the drive so I stopped out on the country roadway. It was as if Nigel's home was a Christmas card's picture. The snow was untouched across the yard, except for the driveway and glistening icicles that hung from the gutters all across the front. A freshly made sign above the front door read, "Welcome home Champions!" I guess Giselle was a champion also.

As I took Giselle's luggage, I noticed a small red Ford Focus parked in the drive. It was Rita's ride. I wondered if she brought her Harold with her. Proud Momma Queenie and Daddy Detective greeted us at the front door. They enveloped Giselle with hugs and kisses, and then Giselle introduced me to Queenie and everyone there seated about a huge burning fireplace. I nodded to Rita, but she ignored my smiling salutation. Seated next to her was a very handsome fella with his arm behind her on the leather couch. It was Giselle's brother, Artie. He was a strapping young man, looked not too much younger than I was, but he could have been one of those linemen getting off the plane at International.

"What's that wonderful aroma?" I could not help asking Queenie.

She smiled, and then told us it was our dinner getting cold and she invited everyone, "Please come to the table!"

There were several kids, who were cousins, and then I met Giselle's sibling sisters, Michelle and Diana. Everyone greeted me with a handshake, but had to hug Giselle. Some aunts even told her I was very good looking. Those compliments made me feel good, and not so intimidated by Nigel's arm through mine. He took Giselle's luggage from me, and then my coat and set them down. Nigel led me to the table to sit next to Grandma Martha Bacon, who was Queenie's seventy-nine year old mother. I think that was fore-planned.

When everyone sat down, with some of the children sitting at an adjacent table set up just for them, Nigel asked that we pray. He was eloquent with his words as he blessed us all and gave thanks for the bounty before him. Then he stood up and took out a carving knife, "Turkey or ham?" he gleefully asked each of us, striking the fork against the knife.

It was quite a feast. I cannot remember eating so much, as did Giselle, but only at her mother's urging.

Grandma Bacon was an exceedingly gentile lady. I could see the strong heritage passed on to Queenie and Giselle. They were all beautiful women.

Martha wanted to know all about me. She asked just too many questions about all sorts of worldly things, and listened intently to my answers. If I had not known differently, I would have thought I was in the prescreening mode for TV's Jeopardy.

However, Martha was so sweet about it and always seemed to agree with me, and then she would add something to substantiate my opinions. Martha often took my arm and liked squeezing my bicep muscle, and then she would ask me another question each time. I think she approved of me and eventually told Giselle that I was a "good one" for her.

"He's got acumen!" she told Giselle politely…whatever that meant. I guess it was a family thing. I hoped she did not mean a disease! I vowed to myself to look that one up in my pocket Webster's.

Artie was a very nice person and loved his sisters. He liked being with Rita also, except Nigel took her into his study and I overheard him ask her if she were sure that she wanted to go through with something. I had no clue nor did Nigel say anything when they emerged from his study. Rita walked right past me and straight to Artie. They really seemed to hit it off, just like Giselle and me. A sudden thought occurred to me if the romances continued their course; one day Rita might not only be my secretary, but also my sister-in-law. Maybe I was overly presumptuous, because Artie had to return to his college the next day and might not have liked Rita as much as I thought.

I was shocked when Nigel got out a very large acoustic guitar and began to tune and strum the strings. Martha told him to play "Greensleeves" which about blew my mind when he began the overture. It takes a lot of string manipulation to play that song, but his sudden baritone voice sang out like an English choirboy. It was an absolute pleasure. I was somewhat awestruck, and then Giselle did a duet with him of Amazing Grace. Spellbound by it all, I watched her lips breathing in air, which made her large bosom rise. Her voice was as beautiful as her being. I had a treasure and I had so much to be thankful for on this day.

My thoughts quickly hastened my decision to ask her to become my bride. I had to withhold my obvious need to kiss her hard and just gave her a quick peck on her cheek after the duet ended.

"Don't I get a kiss, also?" joked Nigel.

"Nigel, you are so full of talent it overwhelms me. You should consider making a recording, you're that great. You both are!" I told him, then turned to Giselle.

Giselle returned the peck and asked if I wanted to shoot pool against Artie and Rita in the rec room. I told her I had not played since my college days.

"But that was how I paid for part of my college courses," I chuckled.

"First, I'll help do the dishes and then I'll be with you. If you coax the kids into there, we'll be able to work faster," she concluded.

"At my house on holidays, everyone helps," I spoke loudly. "All you guys grab your dishes and put them in the sink," I ordered the children. To Giselle's surprise, the kids jumped up, and took them just as I said.

"Good, now who wants to play twenty questions?" I asked. Not one raised their hand.

"There's a new Ninja movie in the DVD player. Who wants to see that one?" Giselle asked them.

"Me! Me! Me!," the children spouted out while each made a mad dash to the big open room with a huge screen TV sitting conveniently against one wall. Giselle took the remote and turned it on. They all bunched up on the big couch and became quiet as little mice when it began.

"There's two hours of entertainment," she told me smiling. Then she gave me another peck and asked, "Twenty questions?" She grimaced, as she was leaving me to go to the kitchen.

"Can I help?" I asked.

"No, thank you...I don't want a guy with dishpan hands," she giggled. "Besides, it will only take a few minutes and Grandma wants to confide in me about you...I'm sure," she told me smiling.

Rita and Artie started shooting pool, so I sat and watched their friendship grow. Rita was good and beat him three straight in eight ball. I guess her brothers had taught her. Anyway, Artie was amazed at her skills, especially when she shot the eight ball three in the side, and in, like a pro.

"Next!" Artie yelled.

I looked around and knew he meant me. I searched for Giselle but she was in an apron bending over the sink talking with her mom and Martha. Therefore, I took the challenge and selected a pool cue from the rack. Nigel had disappeared or I might have asked him to play some tavern music and sing a ballad to get the feel of past environments when my stick was lightning. Rita broke, and then ran the whole table.

She stopped, looked over at me, then said, "You rack…bank ball, this time!" she demanded with the kind of a belligerent tone that drew my ire, as if she was getting revenge on me.

I decided to take her to the cleaners with my own expertise. When she finally missed a shot, I took my turn.

The cue ball, hidden behind the eight ball, made for a difficult shot. I knew she planned it especially for me that way…behind the eight ball. All I could see was a desperate "Four corners in the left corner pocket with the three," I spouted out. Then I hit it four rails and the three ball dropped. The little gathering applauded my efforts, which brought Giselle, Queenie, and Martha to the couch. Someone then turned off the DVD, as the kids got more interested in the competition than the Ninjas.

Tensions grew as I, too, ran the table playing bank pool. When I missed halfway through the second rack, Rita took over. The family began to gather about the table as Rita and I took each challenge as a threat. I think the football set call it "Trash talking".

"Combination, six-ten in the side," Rita advised as she leaned out on the table and placed her fingers spread upon the felt so eloquently. She stood back up, and then took the chalk and used it on the end of her stick. She could not quite figure the angle of her shot. She walked around to see if the balls were touching. Then she leaned over once again, recalled the shot, and hit it. The six grazed the ten, but it hit the nipple and careened off.

"Feeling the pressure?" I said to get into her psyche.

She had left everything on the table and I made quick work of the rest of my shots and won my second.

"Tied up at two apiece…this for all the marbles?" I asked Rita.

"Go for it, hot shot," she quipped, putting more chalk on her stick and then shook baby powder on it to make it slide through her long fingers.

"Tally for break?" I asked.

Rita then walked up beside me and placed a ball down on the felt.

We then each hit a ball slowly forward, rolling from one end of the table to the other, which was to decide who broke the rack. We struck our chosen ball at the same time; each ball bounced off the far rail, winner was whose ball halted closest to that rail. Rita edged me out.

"Hey, are we betting on this one?" I asked Rita.

"Call it, hot shot," she again addressed me, knowing it was her break and she had the advantage.

"Lunch for a week on the other," I suggested.

"You're on, mister!" Rita said, while shooting hard, sending the cue ball crashing into the wooden setup rack, just as I raised it.

"Watch your cookies there, mister!" she blurted out, which raised every adults eyebrows, including Artie's and Queenie's.

Martha yelled out, "You go there, girl!" kicking up her heels on the couch and laughing. The kids just took her words in stride.

Rita was embarrassed and actually turned flushed red. "Oops, sorry...I played pool with my brothers a lot," she said apologizing.

"We understand, Rita," Artie told her. "Just do him in," he encouraged.

I looked at him and knew he was falling for her. I had to use prudence, not to derail his attentions from her. When Rita left an open shot after a miscued attempt, she quickly went to the chalk. I could see her fading confidence and decided I could boost our friendship, if I, too, miscued. So I did. My miscued shot left the table wide open. I winked at Giselle, who saw through my plan.

"Now don't be too forgiving there, Jerry," Giselle called out to me. Giselle only knew winning.

"Tips must be worn a bit," I suggested, as I took the chalk in hand and used it, to a delighted Rita.

That was all Rita needed to run the table. She made her shots, and then laid her cue aside. "See you for lunch, boss," she quipped smiling brightly to Artie's delight also.

They embraced and I felt good about my deed. I felt better when Giselle got up and challenged Rita and Artie to a match. We won four straight, then it was time to go. Martha ventured off to bed and I never saw Nigel anywhere.

"Where's your pop? I haven't seen him since the songs," I wanted to know.

"He got a callout up at Medicine Hat Creek. Someone found a body under the ice, he mentioned as he left."

"My God, is he the only detective in this providence?" I questioned.

"I'm afraid he's the best and when a department needs expertise to process a crime scene, the department sends him. He does not mind. His accumulated overtime is more than his salary, much more, in fact, and the cities who call him out usually pay for it," Giselle explained.

"Gosh, I wouldn't leave the family like this," I criticized.

"In our family that's what the man does…he sacrifices for his loved ones. Besides, Daddy enjoys his position as being the best there is in the north."

I could tell she was testing me. She wanted to see if I was so committed.

"Good thing my job is nine to five, eh?" I related, hoping she found that acceptable.

We sat discussing everything including my family. She seemed very pleased I would think so well of them as she did of hers.

"I guess we'll alternate going to each other's parents, eh?" she surmised.

"Yes, and we'll never have to cook a holiday meal," I laughed.

"No, we'd better just stay home with the babies and I'll do the cooking. We'll invite everyone to our home," she bequeathed in advance.

It was after eight. Therefore, I got my coat and kissed Giselle long and hard out in the parlor. As we kissed, I saw a glimpse of Rita and Artie through the blinds of the rec room doing the same.

"Boy, I had the best time," I told my girl.

"Maybe we can make a habit of this," Giselle suggested. "Call me at the office. I will be back tomorrow."

A quick hug, and off I went to clear the ice off my windshield. Apparently a light sleet had fallen. I had an aerosol vapor, anti-icing spray, which instantly melted the ice, so I sprayed Rita's windshield, also, front, and back. I hoped she appreciated it. As I sat starting up my Tahoe, Rita came out, looked confused at her cleared windows, and then turned my way. She waved briefly, knowing it was my doing.

It was a step in reconciliation, I thought, as I smiled and waved back. Rita backed out and I waited for her to get moving forward. She headed my way at first, as I followed her out of the country towards Canada 2 highway. Rita began speeding and I lost sight of her. I assumed she lived south of Calgary, not north, which confused me as

I spotted her little red Ford headed northbound. I guess she was going to visit relatives. I eased back and set my mind to Giselle as I headed southbound.

I headed towards my Didsbury apartment with a great feeling inside of me, as I envisioned thoughts of a glorious life ahead with Giselle. I decided to go get that ring before she got away.

CHAPTER 13

As I pulled into my parking place at my apartment, I swore I saw Rita's little red Ford zip around a corner just out of sight. Whom she knew out here in the suburbs, made me wonder. Maybe, just maybe, she wanted to see for herself where I lived, I thought. On the other hand, more probably, it was just another person's car like hers. I guess she was on my mind.

The patio door was icy and I realized I had not completely shut the sliding door to cause the inside icing. In this weather, doors as well as windows, often suffered warping, so it was necessary to secure them tightly. My hardwood floors remained unharmed, although ice had melted into a small water puddle. I quickly grabbed up some paper towels and blotted up the mess. There was no harm done. Then my phone rang.

"Hello, darling…I just called to see if you made it home safely," Giselle's voice spoke.

"Gee, that's nice to know you would worry, sweetheart. I had no problem getting here and I'm planning our future in my mind, right now."

"You are! Is it a surprise?"

"It might be. But I hope you will say yes to it."

"If you're asking me for marriage, you know that answer…yes."

"Well how about that…I received my answer via public service… that might be a first time Guinness book entry," I told her. "Giselle, officially, will you please be my wife? I promise to love and care for you forever."

"Didn't you hear…I just said YES!" she repeated loudly to make certain I heard her.

"I should have asked you today, while I could have looked into your big brown eyes…"

"Hazel, get it right!" she jested.

"I'm ecstatic, Giselle…I'm overwhelmed that a babe like you could see something in me, and accept my proposal over the phone… unbelievable. I need to hold you now, but you are thirty miles away."

"We have the rest of our lives, lover. Let's make a weekday date to discuss what comes next."

"Okay, I'll pick you up after work."

"Better yet, I'll follow you back to your apartment. I forgot how to get there. Is there a nice restaurant close?" she asked.

"I'll find something."

We talked back and forth for hours and it was a thorough planning. Giselle was as in love with me as I with her. We were made for each other, we both agreed. When we finally said goodnight, it was two in the morning. I heard her say, "Hello, Daddy!"

"You mean your dad was out all this time?"

"Yes, poor man. Wait until I spring the news. He will be thrilled. He looks much worn out, so he kissed me and went to bed. He told me to open his office and make sure I call Rita and tell her the word is, 'Go'."

"That's strange, I think I saw Rita's car near my home. I wonder what's going on."

"Daddy won't tell me either. I asked him and he said it was just too important. I think Rita is in the middle of Daddy's investigation…I'm not certain though."

"Hey, we have to say goodnight because we can't be dragging in the morning. Goodnight, sweetheart…I love you," I said, then hung up after she repeated those words back to me.

I tossed and turned. It was either too much excitement for one day or my worry for Rita. The alarm went off and I had not even closed my eyes. I got up, grabbed a towel, and then eased into the water for a long, hot wakeup shower.

I drove from my apartment's parking lot and got to work ten minutes early. My door was blocked open with a wedge, so I kicked the piece out from under the door. I did not like the outside air coming into my office in winter. I was surprised to find Veronica Stone at Rita's desk and asked her why.

"Rita is on temporary assignment. I'm here to assist you, authority Mr. Upshaw," she quickly advised.

"Temporary assignment…since when are secretaries used as reporters around here?"

"Since my sister was murdered," she softly spoke.

"Oh, I see. I am sorry about your sister. Was she a student?"

"Yes, she was young, beautiful, vibrant, the academic genius of our whole family. She was majoring in international relations and communications. She wanted to become a news anchorperson on TV," Veronica said with a bit of detected animosity in her voice, as if she wanted revenge on the murderer.

"Again, please accept my sincere condolences," I told her.

I knew Veronica was not going to be much help, because Rita had not left her a desk key. Therefore, I left it that way. I asked Veronica if she would get the mail and an espresso for each of us, before we started with the personal ads.

"I'm not here as your servant. If you need some computer work, Mr. Upshaw says I am to do that. But you'll have to get your own coffee…I drink bottled water and I have my drink," she let me know right away.

Boy, what a help she was? I did not know how to work the machine, so I searched and found an instant Old Judge packet and used the heated water from the espresso pot to make a cup. I thought Miss Prissy could just go back up to Mr. Upshaw. He actually did not like his secretary's qualifications either, except for her big boobs. He called for a temporary worker to replace her. I suppose he was tired of Veronica.

"How long will Rita be gone?" I inquired.

"As long as it takes," she responded.

"Where's Mr. Upshaw?"

"He had a business trip to Montreal. He said you would understand, whatever that meant," she coldly related. "You're supposed to be in charge until he returns, is what he told me."

"Oh, in that case, please feel free to return to your desk and send that temp over here. I have too much work for a high caliber secretary like you," I said with authority.

"Mr. Upshaw said I was to stay with you."

"Well, Freddie isn't here, is he? I'm second in command and I say go tell the temp I need her. I bet she makes coffee," I said to insult her.

Veronica picked up her things, and in a huff, she left. Several minutes later, a young girl knocked at my door.

"Come in…are you the temp?" I asked.

"Yes, sir," she politely replied.

"Do you know how to operate an espresso machine?" I inquired first of her skills.

"Yes, sir."

"While you're here with me, please address me as Jerry…and can you type? What's your name?"

She looked at me somewhat inquisitively, then said, "Better than Miss Stone," she smiled. "I'm Eleanor Bigglebottom," she said with a straight face, so I knew she was serious.

"Are you from the notorious Edmonton Bigglebottoms?" I joked, trying hard not to burst out laughing.

With her skinny frame, no name could have fit her more appropriately. She had absolutely no bottom at all.

Eleanor winced; I knew she was trying hard to hold back showing dissatisfaction of my making fun of her last name. She quickly went directly to the espresso and started it loudly churning. She then poured out a finished mug of foamy brew. Eleanor then came over, set the steaming mug down, and removed the Old Judge instant I had made for myself. I knew she was going to be much better than Veronica Stone was.

"Eleanor, I think we'll get along just fine," I told her.

The day went very well and quickly, also, as Eleanor just seemed to take charge as Rita had and after a while, I became impressed with her. She handled every request of secretarial performance as well as sitting down and giving me help with developing my personal ads. She asked why I had the long red haired guy taped to my computer and asked me if he was a relative or if I was just queer. It was so direct that I knew she meant it.

"If you are one of those misfits, then this is my last day. I am an ordinary girl and do not want that kind of person around me. I go to church," she retorted with authority.

Eleanor's face was so wrinkled in disgust that I had to simply spit out the coffee in my mouth and start yelping in laughter. I envisioned her in a hair net and saying, 'One ringy-dingy, two ringy-dingies' as Lilly Tomlin did on the old "Laugh-In" rerun shows. Now my new secretary gave that distinct look towards me, exactly. She even looked like Lilly. I could not stop bellowing, one of the biggest and longest laughs I could ever remember.

After I kept laughing, she started laughing at my laughing, and we went absolutely nuts with exuberance of each other's inability to stop laughing. She was laughing at me, and vice versa. We both ended up wiping the tears from our eyes and when she grabbed a Kleenex to blow her nose, she honked like a Canadian goose and it started all over again. I eventually stopped when several other office personnel from upstairs peered into my office to see what was going on.

"Hey, where's the party!" Craig from advertising yelled out from my doorway.

Miss Bigglebottom looked at me, I back at her, and the laughter between us started all over again. When we finally stopped, she got up and said, "Oops, I think all this laughter made me pee my pants!"

Yes, it was spontaneous reaction and I asked her to please leave and go to the ladies' room as my stomach hurt and our workday, too. When she did go, I took several deep breaths to simmer down, and then took a Kleenex to wipe up the mess I made on my new desk from spitting out my espresso.

"Queer, huh? Lady, you don't know my fiancée, do you?" I said to an already vacated office secretary.

The phone rang right before noon and it was my Rita. She was free to meet me at Sarah Selby's Cafeteria. She quickly told me she was collecting her bet and would explain everything about her absence. Just to get her goat, I invited Miss Bigglebottom along. The poor kid did not have lunch money and was just going to eat a half of a peanut butter sandwich.

"Come with me for lunch, Eleanor, it's my treat," I more or less ordered. She grabbed her well-worn, flimsy jacket, and followed behind like a little puppy. "We'll have to do something about that jacket, also," I told her, feeling sorry for her obvious impoverished situation.

Rita was seated in her car waiting when Eleanor and I got to Sarah's. She looked disappointed at my bringing Eleanor along.

"I can't tell you what's going on in front of that girl," she spoke whispering.

It was very chilly, so we hustled inside. I told Eleanor to fill her plate full from the long line of choices. She did, somewhat, mostly choosing salad fixings and a big slice of apple pie. I picked up the girls' tabs and we all searched for an open booth. Sarah's was very popular.

"You never treated me this well," Rita then bumped me, still whispering.

"She makes me laugh," I related, as we all sat at a booth.

Everyone was hungry. The only conversation came from Eleanor, directed to Rita, when she asked of her certain secretarial duties and where certain things were. Rita was nice to her and explained some of my needs and I just listened to how hard it was to be my secretary. I just sat by as if I were a picture on the wall.

After we ate, Rita asked if I would sit in her car to talk, so I flipped the keys to my Tahoe to Eleanor and told her to warm it up.

"This is the scoop," Rita began. "I've made contact for a date with the creep you saw in the picture to see if I can find out anything. I called his number and he said he could not meet me very soon, because his professor is giving finals and he has to grade them for 200 students from four classes. I took his address from the app, saw where he lives, and told Nigel. Nigel said I would never see him following me, but he would tail me wherever I went with the creep, after I called him first to get clearance. Check this out; he is a graduate assistant in mathematics at the university. The more I learn about him the more I feel he is the murderer. Anyway, Nigel has me deputized through the providence attorney's office as a special investigator. I have complete arrest powers, if necessary."

I sat amazed, pleased Rita would confide in me.

"But what if he tries something? Did you consider that?" I questioned of her safety.

Rita lifted her sweater, and behold, there was a Lady Smith .357 magnum revolver in her waistband.

"I can use this and I know how to use it, too, if necessary, believe me. I told you before I grew up in a hunting family. By the way, do you miss me?"

"What makes you think I would miss you? Miss Bigglebottom is quite the accomplished secretary," I said to get to her ego.

"Good! If I do well, Nigel is getting me into the police academy. Just so you know I might not come back, make good with…what's her name?" she began to laugh.

"Oh, oh, don't start me laughing. I can't take that anymore," I said trying not to start yelping once more.

"Sounds to me as if you and young miss ol' what's her name are doing fine…good!" she blurted, as I detected some jealousy.

"Rita, I don't know what made you do this…ah…I admire your initiative…but please be safe, okay?" I said with sincerity.

"Oh, so you do care for me, eh?" she said more jubilantly.

"I can tell you this…if something happens to you, I'll have one hell of a time getting another secretary like you," I assured her.

"Well, I hoped you'd actually miss me, personally," Rita spoke.

"I have Giselle, remember? She's the one and I'm planning on marrying her."

"I know. She just told me an hour ago at Nigel's office. She was expecting your call then already. You had better skedaddle and call her when you get back to the office. She is a nice person and much prettier than I am, I guess," she coyly suggested.

"You know…if it wasn't for Giselle…well, you know," I reminded her.

"Get…I have to try to get a date scheduled with a professor's assistant…see ya, boss!" Rita said with a start of moisture building in her eyes.

I never wanted to hurt her, never. Rita quickly left as I went to my Tahoe.

Eleanor had apparently fallen in love with my stereo and I could hear and feel the vibrations emitted from the speakers out on the parking lot asphalt. She was blasting, I think she called it aloud to me, when I told her to turn it down and drive us back to the office. She was happily bouncing her little butt in my seat and enjoying the ride all the way. Kids these days, I thought.

No more laughs during the workday as I finished very early. I dialed up Giselle and thought we would chat some, but she was dialed up on another line. When I realized she was too busy and further love chatter between us would be futile, I told her I loved her and I would call her that night.

Eleanor had completed her work also. As I glanced up, I saw her horrible jacket again upon a hook.

"Hey, I have to go buy some things. Why don't we hit the mall and see the shops. It helps me stay in touch with reality and the people who want my learned opinion," I said to her, whatever that meant. I made it up to take her shopping.

She acted confused.

"Grab your jacket and come along now, quickly!" I told her.

I drove to the mall and headed directly for Sears, because Sears always had women's coats galore. I told Eleanor I was buying one for my sister, needed her opinion and asked her to select a good one. When she finally selected a warm multi-layered parka, very bright, and sharp looking, with a hood on it and lots of down, I asked her to try it on.

"What size is she?" Eleanor asked looking inside for the label.

"Well, I'd say she's just your size," I told her.

"Six regular?"

"Yep, try it on," I ordered.

"Oh, this is heavenly…your sister will kiss you for this one. It feels so light and comfy," she said dreamy-eyed.

"Okay, let's go to the cashier, no wait, here are some Isotoner gloves. She needs them also. Try those on, too," I insisted.

"Fits me perfectly," Eleanor said.

"May I have my jacket back, please," Eleanor shyly spoke trying to take off the new parka and gloves.

I ignored her, checked the pockets of Eleanor's jacket for contents, and then pitched it in the trash receptacle next to the cashier, who then looked at me strangely, however, not as surprised as Eleanor was.

"My jacket…that's all I have!" she let me know reaching into the trash.

I grabbed her arm, told the cashier to ring up the parka and gloves, and then said to Eleanor, "Merry Christmas, early! It's yours, Miss Bigglebottom."

"Really! Oh, thank you," she said, while hurriedly putting the parka back on. "I don't know how to thank you," she insisted.

I spread my arms and suggested a hug. Then she whispered, "I guess you're not gay after all, eh?"

"No, I'm not. I'm engaged to the most beautiful girl in the world."

"Rita?" she suddenly deduced.

"No, not Rita…I'll explain all this after I pay my bill here."

I used my Sears' card, which I had not done for some time. As I looked at the $200.10 charge, I knew it was worth it. Eleanor was worth it, too. She was a nice person, very congenial to be around, and a wonderful secretary.

On the way back to the office parking lot, I told Eleanor I would see to it she was hired at CMEN. If Rita did not come back, she would be my permanent secretary. Little did I know then how unambiguous my words would turn out to be.

As it turned out, I learned that Eleanor walked to work from a rented apartment only a few blocks from CMEN. I dropped her off there. The way Eleanor admired that new coat, she reminded me of Little Orphan Annie. She was warm again, and so was I.

I went back to the office to make certain I had the office locked, but found Herman, the new janitor, vacuuming the floor and he had dusted already. I said thanks, and went back to my Tahoe with a good feeling in my heart. After all, Christmas was just a few weeks away and I planned to buy Giselle that ring and take her home to Mom and Dad.

CHAPTER 14

With Eleanor at home and Rita out and about being a detective, I decided to make the big move. I drove to one of our advertising jewelers at CMEN, DeBlanc's. There were not many diamond shoppers, so Mr. DeBlanc was very happy to serve me. When I told him I was intending to get married, he immediately drew me to a magnificent tray of diamonds.

"About what karat size do you desire, Monsieur?"

"As big as I can afford," I jested.

"And that is?" he hinted.

"Show me a good quality diamond, flawless and very bright," I suggested.

"You will find all of our loose diamonds are SI-one, our best, Monsieur," he spoke in a French accent.

"Well, show them to me, please!" I became antsy.

He started at $80,000 with an unset seven-carat gem.

"More like ten grand," I suggested.

He had to walk all the way down to nearly the end of his huge display to find a three carat that sparkled as much as the $80,000 diamond.

"I really like the shape and luster of that one," I pointed out.

"Monsieur, you have excellent taste. That is a baguette-cut diamond bouquet that will enhance any selected setting. See," he said, picking up a yet-to-be-filled, double-ring, with no stones. It looked very fancy and just what I thought I might be able to afford.

"What is your name, sir?" he asked not recognizing me.

"My name is Jerry David. I write a column in CMEN as Gerry Loveletter," I advised, hoping he now knew of me.

"Oh, Monsieur Loveletter, a`ha...I know you now. I read your column occasionally, oui oui! In that case...for you this or any other selection is half price. My wife says you bring more lovers in here than honey draws flies. We thank you!"

"That's very nice of you, thank you," acknowledging his generosity. "I had been told once, but not so eloquently, that my column drew flies like ah-hem out in the cow pasture!" I said jesting.

This is what seven years of writing could develop, I surmised.

"Mr. DeBlanc, sir...if I chose one and my fiancée isn't happy with my taste, could I bring it back for an exchange?"

"Oui, Monsieur Loveletter, ah, I mean, Monsieur David."

"The girl I am giving this to will be showing it off on TV. It's got to be sensational," I told him.

His eyebrows rose into an arched position. He turned around, and then walked back to the opposite end to where he displayed the high-priced diamonds. I followed him as he cautiously looked outside his front door. Then he hit a button that locked all doors...I heard them snap.

He pulled on his watch fob chain and a watch with a key dangling next to it came out of his watch pocket. He took that golden key, stuck it in a hole, and twisted it around and around, until a panel door popped open. He turned his back on me and opened a secret panel by turning a combination lock. Out from a vault he brought a large tray of completed wedding and cocktail rings...the very best he had.

"I have to be very discrete, Monsieur," he said with a gleam in his eyes, as he watched my eyes widen and stare at all the magnificent radiance. It was a king's treasure.

"Your choice...$25,000 ," he told me. "Each is insured for $180,000," Monsieur. Any of these could certainly embrace a queen's finger."

"Wow, I don't know…how I could ever choose one over the other? They're all so breathtaking…heavenly…whoever designed those must be an angel themselves," I whispered.

Mr. DeBlanc smiled from ear to ear. "It was I, who mastered their beautiful settings. Each has the equivalent of fifteen carats. Choose any, if your darling does not like it, come get another," he cheerfully told me.

"You mean get another girl, never!"

"No, no, no, no, no…you come back and select another setting, Monsieur David…with her beside you."

"Will you take my thanks and my check and hold it until Friday?" I asked.

"I will hold your check for six weeks," he agreed.

"No, no, no, no, no…will you please hold this beautiful ring?" I reached down and touched my choice. "My check today is good, I assure you. Thank you very, very much. I now will have firsthand knowledge of DeBlanc's to tell my readers."

I told him also I would pledge my future efforts to be his store's champion.

"Is this all satisfactory, sir?" I questioned.

"Certainly…then you mean that you will be bringing back your lovely lady for me to see, oui?"

"Oui! Oui!" I said.

Mr. DeBlanc took the ring and buffed it with a silicon-looking cloth, then tagged it before he put it back and then reversed all of his procedures to lock his treasures back into their secret vault.

I wrote out the check, feeling lucky I had just that, $25,000 in my savings account, which I had always intended for purchase of a snowmobile or a jet boat to ski behind on summer weekends. This is what God intended, I told myself. This will knock the socks off my gorgeous woman, I imagined…maybe more, I hoped. I left DeBlanc Jeweler's with a smile so big on my face that everyone who saw me must have thought I was goofy.

I stopped off at my church, since I was so close. The lights were on in the rectory, so I hoped my pastor was there. He was, so I asked him to sit with me and help me decide if I was really worthy of Giselle.

I told him of my infatuation of her physical appearance for years, not knowing who she was. Nevertheless, I had a feeling that made me excited to see her each time I saw her on TV. Now, since I had met Giselle, I just knew I loved her and she loved me.

After I spilled my guts out to him for almost an hour, I waited for his divine advice. Pastor Romero had these words of wisdom.

"I once heard of a man who looked for a bargain on a car. He set the particulars and a price he would be satisfied to pay. He searched for a long, long time for that special car, but no one had one like it. Upon entering one dealership, he saw the exact car, with the right color and a better price than he imagined. He heehawed around with the sales clerk, still trying to get a better price. While he was dickering, another fellow got the same deal on that same car and bought it out from under him. The man was sick because there was no other car like it anywhere. He lost his only chance. Do you understand?"

I told the kind pastor that I thought so.

"Well, are you ready to close your deal?" he so intelligently asked me.

"You're right, Pastor. I need not search any further, eh?"

"Trusting your heart will not lead you astray, Jerry."

"Remind me Sunday to put something extra in the offering," I said smiling.

He looked at me smiling back, and then said, "Jerry, I would just like to see you more often on Sundays. That would be reward enough."

"Touché, Pastor," I said, acknowledging to him of my recent absences.

We shook hands and I asked him if he was willing to unite Giselle and me someday. He said I should not wait too long for the day.

I drove home and immediately called Giselle at her home. We spoke of our mutual loving admiration and then we both became impatient when I told her I had bought the ring. She was so excited that she told Queenie right then.

"I hope you will like it. I wanted to give it to you at a special time, Darling, but every moment with you is special to me," I said trying to mask the fact that it would not be a surprise.

"It's very sudden, but I feel just as you. Whatever this thing called love is, it's our first step toward being together forever, and I don't care if it's just a cigar wrapper…well, yes I do…because that would mean you're exceptionally cheap!" she burst into laughter. "Anything more than that will show me you really, truly, love me."

I asked to see her yet that night. She was tired, but not that tired, she told me. I called Mr. DeBlanc at his jewelers and told him I was coming in with my lady and asked if he would be there. He said he knew I would, and, yes, he would wait until ten.

"A young man's fancy always accelerates after he has decided to make his move. I already have that ring in a beautiful presentation holder and a very nice display setting. What took you so long?" he jested.

I then drove to Giselle's home to pick her up at seven. Nigel and Queenie were all smiles, thinking I was going to pop the question. Giselle had told them something. They were overly friendly, but I enjoyed that.

Then Giselle's sixteen-year-old sister, Diana, asked Giselle loudly if she was knocked up. That totally embarrassed Giselle and I looked at Nigel and said, "Trust me, we haven't!" Those words were met with his approving smile.

Queenie on the other hand, swatted Diana on her behind with a newspaper and told her she was to go to her room and that her father and she were going to send her to a girls' school. Diana stomped out, then shouted out, "I hate you, I hate you!" before she slammed her bedroom door.

"You'll have to ignore Diana, son, because she is confused and will someday grow out of this adolescent rebellious stage; however, I hope it is soon. She drives us loony! She's angry because Nigel won't let her date yet, until she's more responsible," Queenie explained to me laughing. "Nigel was the same with Giselle, so you are getting a very good girl here," she told me, while putting her arm around us both and squeezing.

"I know that it's sudden, Mrs. Gray. I truly love your daughter and I plan to make her happy the rest of our lives."

Queenie hugged and squeezed me some more and again called me son. Nigel extended his hand, held mine firmly, then said, "Giselle has to be home tonight by ten. It's a week night and Giselle has to work tomorrow!"

However, he then smiled and winked at me, as we left together.

DeBlanc's Jewelers had several lookers inside as we entered and Mr. DeBlanc made certain to compliment Giselle by telling me, "Your lady is every bit as beautiful as you told me, Monsieur David. I will be with you both in a moment. And if you please, sit down or look around."

A very young couple stood over one array of diamond rings, trying to choose her engagement ring. The poor guy kept saying, "Too much, too much, too much!" to each of her selections, until they got to the end of the counter and there were no more. Then they decided to go to Wal-Mart. As she turned sideways, it was obvious she was at least six months in term with a pregnancy. We looked the other way as they passed. They looked embarrassed. It was a little too late to become embarrassed, I thought.

Mr. DeBlanc came to the front, looked outside briefly, and then looked at his watch, apparently deciding it was closing time. He set the security systems locking device. The window blinds slowly rolled down mechanically and the door latch snapped shut, locking us in and anyone else, of course, out.

"Now, Jerry, introduce me to this lovely lady," he said, smiling at Giselle. "Say, aren't you that fabulous Outriders cheerleader they interview on TV sometimes at the pregame festivities, before Stampeders games…yes, I know it's you. I must say you create a lot of interest in football," he laughed.

"Thank you so much, and yes, I do get interviewed a lot," she confirmed, extending and then shaking his hand.

Giselle had that affect on lots of men, especially me. After Mr. DeBlanc got over his obvious excitement, he told us to follow him. He led us to a fancy room away from the main room, which predominately exposed a special pedestal that held the ring, displayed under a spotlight on red satin. The light brought out its fabulous colors of the gold mounting and its multi-faceted diamonds' sparkles. We both were wowed.

"I find that offering gems this special way will allow the procurer the opportunity to see the work of art more clearly," he told us, while then presenting Giselle's ring with a hand sweeping gesture pointing to it.

"Oui, Oui!" I let out, as we stepped up closer.

Giselle's eyes grew wide. Her mouth dropped open, as she stared at me, then the ring, and back at me again in amazement. She was awestruck, as if she could not believe or say anything.

Quickly, Mr. DeBlanc took only the engagement ring off from its pedestal and handed it to me to place upon Giselle's finger. It was a perfect ring, which left Giselle simply speechless.

"Will you marry me, Giselle?" I asked formally.

Giselle just stared at it and could not speak; she was still looking at me for answers from questions she could not express.

"Don't you like it?" I jested, seeing her happiness, as I slipped the ring on her wedding finger.

"My heavens, gosh, it's simply gorgeous! It must have cost a fortune…it is so beautifully perfect…I…I…I love you, Jerry!" Giselle finally blurted out in a single breath.

Her red lips were inviting my kiss as her large breasts rose and fell with each deep breath against my chest, which was so very captivating, in her excitement.

Then Giselle hugged me hard and kissed me gently. She looked at Mr. DeBlanc, did not want to forget him, so she hugged him, too. He was proud as a peacock, but so was I. Mission accomplished, I told myself.

We hurried from DeBlanc's and got inside the Tahoe. Giselle had her arm extended, looking at her hand. She turned on the interior mirror light above the visor to get a better look. Though the ring was exquisite, Giselle was also. She scooted over onto the console next to me and kissed me as we never kissed before. She knocked my socks off, right out in front of DeBlanc's.

Our passion grew so quickly, we headed to my apartment at Giselle's insistence. She wanted to show her love was as great as my gift to her. I guess they call it quid pro quo. Whatever they called our emotions, by all means, I was a willing participant. I was burning inside, barely keeping the Tahoe between the white lines when we kissed repeatedly. One word that described us both was…HOT!

We rushed through my patio doors, into my living room, lip-locked in an embrace, each with fumbling fingers, unbuttoning the other's buttons, while disrobing one garment with each step, as fast as humanly possible.

Our clothing trail led to my bedroom, but Gisele said she wanted to shower first, so we hurried into the bathroom in our underwear. When she turned around and asked me to unhook her bra in the front, the beauty I unleashed remained round; they were so huge, and exquisitely firm. Her breasts were large and the nipples stuck straight out, but at slight outwardly angles. I was so enamored that I did not notice my penis had protruded out of my boxer shorts and was against Giselle's thigh. It throbbed and my brain and heart both raced along to it when she put her hand there.

"Is that a huge pistol or are you just happy to see me?" she jested, as she then massaged it against her black hairs of her pussy. That destroyed my mind.

We backed into the shower as I tried to control my anxiety. I had to back away when the water was too hot, then we came together kissing hard under the flow of a warm pleasant stream.

"Do you have a condom?" Giselle asked before I could enter.

"Shit! I never dreamed of this happening. Can we just do it and I'll jerk it out right before I'm coming?" I begged.

"No, go to the pharmacy and get some protection. I will be waiting for you on the bed. Besides, we can't do it in here anyway."

"Yes we could, climb up on me," I begged, while trying to lift her leg up to me desperately.

"No, I won't like that. Either get the rubber, or oral sex," she suggested.

"Well, I'm all wet and it's cold outside. I would probably get pneumonia," I said still as hard as a rock. "Okay, now what?"

"What do you mean, now what?" Giselle asked, as she seemed concerned I did not know anything about oral sex.

"I mean, want me to scrub you, and you me?" I smiled.

We managed to control ourselves, even though my elongated penis kept poking Giselle.

"You know why cheerleaders wear short skirts?" Giselle suddenly asked me.

After eliminating all the obvious reasons, I said, "No, tell me."

"It makes the boys root harder!" she said laughing, and then reached out to me.

She took soap and washed my penis, as I did the same slowly and deliberately against her clitoris. It was a mutual confirmation that it was time to stop the shower and get on top of my bed. I think Giselle had lost control of her senses, too. Overcome by desire, she flopped down on her back with her legs spread and I followed her lead. I forced my penis into her wet pussy.

"Ohhhh!" she yelled out, grasping me tighter with a murderous look on her face, but still pulling me to her. Giselle arched her back, moved her hips, and seemed to be trying to find comfort.

The shower and soap had taken away some of her moisture and she felt dry, she told me. Therefore, I slowed down and let Mother Nature renew her juices, as I slid down on her and attacked her clitoris with my tongue. The view I had was wonderful and Giselle quickly decided I was doing it just right. Her bristles felt silky and curly to my tongue. Her clit was hot and she flinched with each flick of my lizard-like tongue and finger manipulations.

I gently eased her vulva apart, which exposed her clitoris to the tip of my tongue. Giselle began to move around on the sheet and moan loudly. I knew I was doing her good. As my hands found her butt cheeks, her hands found my hair; she held my head against her, but never pulled on it. I think she wanted to though. She took a lock in her fingers, swirled it, and then let it loose before it hurt. She continued as I kept the pressure against her and felt her clitoris growing hard like my penis.

Suddenly, Giselle yelled, "Oh shit!" Overcome by wild desire, she desperately disregarded her concerns of getting pregnant and decided to pull me up to her, as she reached for my penis and frantically directed it into her vagina. I did not resist one bit and entered her deep. At first, I saw her watery eyes looking at mine. Then I felt the warm, moist, roughness of her inside against my rigid penis. I was in heaven and returned to finishing what I had started.

We were locked up in love's madness; I on her, pumping my brains out; Giselle wild-eyed, lying back, exposing her beautiful body completely to me, her arms flailing about, feet up in the air, toes curled, as I continued to pound her long and hard.

The bed was bouncing and rocking faster and harder. There was no feeling like this before, for each of us was out of control, helping the other to achieve an orgasm of tremendous sensations.

My bed started to pound against the wall and I could not stop it, even though I held the headboard steady with one hand. Giselle did not want me to stop it; I guess she liked the rhythmic thumping sound we were making and all the fiery lust was oozing from us. It only lasted twenty minutes, or so, until Giselle absolutely lost it and hugged me like a rug to a floor. I could not pull away from her and unloaded my best, deep inside of her. Suddenly, we fell apart exhausted, but both very satisfied by our union.

"I went inside of you," I told her.

"You don't think I know," she laughed, showing me a creamy-slimy mess running down about her vagina. "Hand me a Kleenex," she told me, trying not to allow it all to drip onto my sheets.

"Don't you care?" I questioned of my going inside of her.

"Hey, I couldn't stop either. I think we have something going here. I'm all for trying to do it better, until we do it right. How about you?" she said easing back up to kiss my neck and fondle my penis. "After all, I heard you don't get pregnant on the first time, anyway, so why stop now?"

My penis grew harder right in her hand and she laid back for seconds, thirds, and fourths. Unbelievably, with just moments of replenishing our air, energy, and a trip to the sink for a glass of water, we locked up again, and again, and again.

Boy, those Outriders cheerleader workouts were very beneficial. Giselle gave to me in movement as much as I did her. We slapped together like two sides of prime beef. There might have been more, but we were so sore, we decided the pain was worse than the pleasures. Besides, I had hit the alarm clock button long before when it was time to get up for work and we continued past our workplace starting time. It was truly a night to remember.

"Do you feel cheated about this?" I asked Giselle, because what we did was what I expected we would do on a honeymoon night.

"I look at it this way. I love you…you love me…so it was bound to happen sooner than later. I had one hell of a time and you are so good!" she let me know out-and-out, which caused me to lay back next to her and tell her she was my dream-girl come true, the best, and I would always love her that way, I told her. We kissed, and yes, that led to another encounter. This time, we were interrupted rudely, by the pounding from upstairs. A female's voice hollered out, "You're disturbing our sleep! Get a motel!"

"Of all the nerve," I said, knowing she had kept me awake many a night.

Then I began more slowly, much more tenderly, as I worshiped her gift. She took no time to come to a climax and I let the cards fall where they may.

"Buy your breakfast after we shower?"

"I have a better idea. Let's both shower, I'll prepare breakfast, and you call Daddy and tell him he doesn't have to come with his gun. I think we need to fly off to Reno, although I'm tired of airports, and make this legal before I get knocked up. I do not think I can look Mom in the eyes without buckling. I have to tell her we are married. She'll get over it, but Daddy wanted to walk me down the aisle."

"We're adults…you're right. I will call your dad right now and my office. I have never missed a day of work without calling in."

I decided I would call my office first.

"Hello, Eleanor…this is Jerry. I won't be in today, so you may lock up and go home also."

"Why? I have some of the letters already opened and filed. Mr. Upshaw wanted you, but left. He is in a good mood. He said thanks for straightening out Veronica. I told him I had nothing to do with it. He said she quit and isn't coming back and that I could be his secretary permanently, if Rita returns."

"Good! Tell Freddie I'm happy for him and I'm getting married this weekend in Reno, I think," I gleefully told her. "Tell him I'm taking three weeks vacation and you'll handle everything."

"May I call you if I'm in a bind?"

"Certainly you may, but only during business hours. I am reserving every moment extra for my bride."

"Well, okay, boss! Congratulations, I'll do my best," Eleanor assured me. "May I write the columns, also?"

"Why not...just shoot 'em by me first and let me hear their content. Be inventive. Well, call me if there is a problem. Anybody but you and I would say no. But I think you have the makings of a great secretary...see ya!"

Then I did the dreaded, "Hi Nigel...Giselle is fine. I asked her last night to marry me, Giselle said yes, and I gave her an engagement ring," I spoke nervously.

Nigel was quiet.

"Giselle!" I yelled to her. "Here's Giselle," I chickened out and told Nigel that Giselle wanted to talk to him.

He never said a word, which freaked me out. I didn't know it, but Nigel was eating a breakfast biscuit and was choking. I became alarmed at Giselle's sudden worry.

"Daddy, are you all right?" she repeatedly asked, with no answer. We both thought his reaction signaled his rejection and a heart attack beginning.

"For God's sake, you scared me!" she suddenly spoke to Nigel who finally got his wind back and explained his silence.

"Here...he wants to speak to you, first," Giselle said with a frown-like expression on her lips.

"Yes, sir...I can explain," I led my greeting with a bright enthusiasm.

I was very wrong and blown away by Nigel's first words.

"Jerry, my new son-in-law to be...congratulations...Giselle has made her mother and me very happy. When and where will the wedding be?" he quickly wanted to know.

"We both decided that a small wedding in Reno could be good, for now. We might just drive there. Giselle is tired of all the flying and airport holdups," I told Nigel, while looking at Giselle for approval. She nodded yes.

"Okay...I always wanted to walk my daughter down the aisle, but circumstances with my work disrupt everything. That might be best... yes...its fine...Queenie thinks so, too. When will you two elope?"

"Elope? That is when you sneak off, is it not? We are calling in advance for your blessing and are heading out as soon as we can make arrangements. We will call you guys as soon as we get there."

"Giselle has always been her own boss. I am certain she goes along with this. Again, I am very pleased to welcome you to the family, Jerry. May I talk to my Giselle?"

"Hi, Daddy…I'm very happy with this," Giselle immediately assured Nigel, which heightened my love for her, if that was possible.

"Honey, I'm going to miss my little girl, but it's time to make a nest for your family and make me a grandpa. As long as you are sure, your mother and I give you our wholehearted blessing, eh? Mother wants to say something, bye."

Giselle whispered that Nigel was sobbing, and then Queenie talked.

"Giselle, remember what I taught you. A man should never hurt you. If he does and you remain, then you're a dumb woman."

"Whoa, Mother! I am a black belt and Jerry outweighs me only by fifty pounds. That will never happen, because he loves me, honest, I know. You will just die when you see the ring he got me. It's more beautiful than beyond belief."

"I'm sorry, I'm just overly tired, dearest…you know your father and I love you. Nevertheless, that might not be enough with him just loving you nowadays. The papers are full of divorces, more than marriages. It is easier to divorce when times get tough."

"Mom! Mom! We went through that when I was twenty-one; remember…I am twenty-six, in love with a wonderful man, who really loves me, Mom. I thought you would be the first to understand and give your blessing."

"Oh, I am…I know how spontaneous you have always been…it's just that a caring mother has to remind a daughter she loves. You have to work hard to make your marriage a success. Remember that…and always remember too, we love you, honey. Bye, and enjoy your life together like Pop and me."

Giselle turned away from the phone with a tear in her eye. "Mom made it sound so gloomy, so final, like I was never coming back. I always thought she and Daddy were that special couple. She talked about divorce before we're even married," Giselle mourned.

"Hey, pretty faces shouldn't be frowning. I will make sure Queenie never has reason to doubt your decision to be my bride. Now, cheer up. We can be off in an hour to Reno, Nevada. It will be a great trip; we will bask in sunshine and much warmer weather. In a few days, we will be Mr. and Mrs. David and I can love you forever and ever, amen," I said trying to relieve her sadness.

"You're right! I guess all moms tell their daughters this before they leave the nest. Nevertheless, we have not discussed much. I still want to work with Daddy and still want to be with the Outriders cheerleaders."

"Well, I think that's great, if you aren't knocked up and can take care of our fifteen kids," I jested.

"Fifteen!" Giselle exclaimed.

"Give or take a few. A woman like you will make a wonderful mother and with a body like yours, what man would ever lose his desire to make passionate love as often as the sun rises? I know I always will…I feel that way, right now."

Giselle smiled, kissed me for making her feel better. "Come here, big boy, Momma has something good for you," she told me, pulling me to her with a very sexy voice. She started my engine again.

Giselle took my hand, and then led me into the bedroom, where, yes, we made love again. Practice makes perfect, they say, and our lovemaking was skirting the impossible dream of perfection.

CHAPTER 15

We left our apartment driving the Tahoe on a very unplanned route to Reno, but fully packed for a two week honeymoon, first staying in Reno, then a look-see trip through the northwestern part of the USA. Giselle said she wanted to meet my family, so I also remembered to get out those Christmas presents to give relatives then, just in case I could not get back for Christmas like last year.

I drove south, then west over to Vancouver. Late that night we stayed in Seattle after having crossed quickly at the USA border. Giselle was enjoying the west coast scenery towards that late afternoon and suggested that she wanted to "Drive through America", she requested, while seated next to me.

"I don't think we can do all that, but we could see the place where I grew up...and along the way, we can share each other's love. Mom especially wants to meet you. We can make it there from Reno, after we're hitched, in a few days. If we see something interesting along the way, well, we'll stop and look-see, okay?" I explained to a bright-eyed Giselle, who looked like a little girl who was all excited getting a new bike.

She kept looking at her ring and only took her eyes off it while we rode through the state of Washington and drove past beautiful Mount Rainier. Then we stopped in Portland for noon sustenance at Arby's. Our drive through the big sequoias was intimidating, but wonderful.

Everywhere was more beautiful with Giselle beside me. We found a Holiday Inn Express along Interstate 5, near Grant's Pass and Crater Lake National Park and stayed there overnight.

There was only a kiss good night, without that uncontrollable lovemaking this time. Giselle subtly hinted she wanted a license first. We missed seeing the sites though because it poured down raining, therefore we drove on all day and evening to Reno, and arrived at 3 a.m., exhausted.

Surprisingly, everyone and everything was jumping, except us. After we checked into the hotel, we showered and virtually passed out as soon as our heads hit our pillows. I began to get amorous feelings with my lovely sweetheart lying there beside me.

Giselle suddenly asked, "Please, not tonight, Honey…save this for tomorrow night after we get through the ceremony, okay?" I was so tired I could not have done anything, anyway, nodded yes, and then closed my eyes.

Nevertheless, in the early morning hours, I awoke to the fragrance of Giselle's perfume lingering on my senses and fought off the urge to wake her. Finally, it was almost noon and the house cleaning service woke us both up, because I had not put the "Do not disturb" sign on our door.

At two, we were dressed in our best; Giselle surprised me wearing a new white chiffon dress and a small lacy veil that caused me to swoon. I questioned her spike heels, and if she would be able to walk in them. She was happy to tell me she was glad I was tall so she could wear them. My heart was pounding looking at her beauty.

"Oh, Giselle, you look like an angel from heaven, this day is the second best day of my life," I told her easing up to kiss her gently.

"Well, what was your best day?" she said, seemingly disenchanted.

"The day I first saw you…I don't care how long I live, but I'm grateful for that day, because it was love eternal. And today proves it, for you are about to make me the happiest man in this big world," I told her sincerely. "Are you ready?" I asked.

"Let's went, Poncho, you're making me horny!" she jested.

I took her hand in mine and we began our trek out to find a place to get married.

When he saw us all decked out, the hotel desk clerk gave directions to me where to go get a marriage license downtown, and then find a preacher at one of those pay-as-you-leave little chapels. We passed so many lovely chapels out there, Giselle finally just said, "That's the one!"

By seven that night, Mr. and Mrs. David called home to our parents to tell them the news. Of course, my mom and dad knew nothing of my sudden plans, or anything about their new daughter-in-law. Mom was anxious to meet her.

"When will you bring Giselle home to meet us?" she asked.

"Maybe it might be sooner than you think, Mom. We are in Reno, with a few weeks of vacation. If we can, we will drive there in a few days. Giselle is Canadian and has never really been through the Bad Lands, or seen Mount Rushmore. We're not making reservations, just going where the road leads us."

"Well, you just better let that road lead you home. Pop has your guns cleaned and is itching to pull the trigger on a pheasant. He is feeling much better and just wait until I tell him this. He will be at the kitchen window looking down the lane day and night. Best call right after you leave Rapid City, to give me a chance to get the house straightened up and some groceries in the refrigerator."

"Okay, Mom, tell Dad to practice up on his shooting, because I'm challenging him to a big pheasant hunt competition."

"I'll do that and tell Giselle we can't wait to meet her…bye!"

So, that's how our lives began together as one. Giselle made me the happiest man alive and I planned to return the pleasure. We took the Tahoe to the Reno strip and I found out I was more than a lucky man. Giselle hit it big on twenty-one, but found the crap table irresistible. The management wanted to send her home. When she thought she had enough, she had eighty thousand dollars in their chips. She took their cashier's check, because it is obviously safer and easier taken back into Canada, and then cashed, once we crossed the Canadian border.

We had three luxurious days in the sun there when suddenly a wisp of a cold weather front blew in from the Pacific. We lay up in the casinos and got bored of winning all that money. I hit the slots and Giselle hit the jackpots. She was the second luckiest person there, I was the first having her as my wife.

"How far is it to your parents' home in South Dakota?" Giselle suddenly asked, while seated at the writing desk in our hotel room.

"Oh, probably three days, taking it easy," I told her.

She was sending postcards to Nigel's office and I asked her to send one to Freddie, Rita, and Eleanor, if she could.

"I did that already, see," Giselle said while lifting up three completed and separately addressed 'Reno's City Lights' pictured postcards.

She was already the little wife taking care of her husband's work. My love for her, and my respect continued to grow.

We made love past midnight after I ordered up our meals and an ice bucket with a bottle of expensive champagne. We ate lightly, and then I popped the cork and poured each of us a glass of '96 Dom Perignon.

Giselle just sipped a tiny sip, and then said, "I remember the morning after from the last time. Let's you and I swear off alcohol forever. It isn't good for you and you feel so darn lousy the next day and sorry for what you have done and don't know what you did," she said rather confused. "Yes, that's right!" she toasted the rest, and then said, "No more, please."

Therefore, I unfortunately drank the remainder of the champagne and became overly desirous of my wife's body. I do not remember what I did, but I woke up wearing Giselle's bra and her panties. When she was still sleeping soundly, I got up feeling crummy, like she said. I looked into the room's vanity mirror.

"Oh, my God!" I yelled, waking up Giselle. "What did I do to you?" I urged.

"Nothing…it was the worst night of sex we've ever had…see, I told you not to drink anymore," she said, rolling over and pulling a pillow over her head.

"What a horrible thing to have happened to us…and on our honeymoon, no less," I spouted out angry at myself.

Without thinking, fuming at my ignorance, I forgot to remove Giselle's lingerie. I took the empty bottle, melted ice bucket, soiled plates, and shoved the cart out the door in anger. Unfortunately, I tripped over the doorsill and landed on my face into the hallway. The cart rolled forward, smashing against the opposite room's door, as I lay there very exposed in Giselle's bikini panties somewhat dazed. The door slammed shut behind me as people began to walk down the hall, and then turned around.

"Creep! Pervert!" screamed an elderly woman walking past, when my bare derriere was open for all to see. She kicked at me then ran away.

"You look pretty stupid lying out there…are you going to go for a stroll in my undies or get dressed?" Giselle scolded from our room's open doorway. "I was supposed to find these things out before I married you!"

I quickly tiptoed into our room with no further confrontations. Giselle started laughing, but I did not see anything about which to laugh. I was totally embarrassed.

"I guess this really screws up our relationship, huh? Do you want a divorce?" I humbly asked.

"Whoa! I have to tell you the truth, now, before you commit hari-kari. The truth is I was hoping to convince you not to ever drink again, when I realized you passed out cold last night from drinking that bottle of booze. While you were out, I got a little carried away doing it, and I dressed you up in my underwear, thinking you would act just this way…embarrassed as I was on our first date. I never knew you would run out into the hallway though…sorry, sweetie!"

"Oh, that hurts me…deep. I only drank the champagne so as not to waste it. I guess I should have pitched it, eh? I am so sorry. You saying our lovemaking was terrible really hurts…it hurts bad," I repeated, with too much emotion.

"Oh, my baby…we never did it. You went to sleep as soon as your head hit the pillow. I did too. I was glad to get some rest. We have been going strong for four days straight. I guess we both crashed."

"Whew! You were kidding about everything?" I questioned.

"Yes, but not the drinking part. I want you to promise me you'll never touch liquor again."

"Are you kidding? I only got the stuff because I figured you partied with all those jocks and I wanted our celebration to be as good, that's all. I do not drink, well one or two Molson's, watching you perform on the field. Boy, did I learn my lesson! When you said you did not like my lovemaking, I died inside, believe me. I really did, Giselle."

She looked at me pitifully and came to me, then whispered, "Take off my panties and we'll try again for real this time."

It was instantaneous. My pecker grew inside her black bikini panties, it bent, and I thought I broke it until it popped loose up to my belly button. Then it got very serious. Giselle burst out laughing, until we lay down. That is the affect Giselle had on me…instantaneous hard-on. I frantically stripped off the panties from both of us, took her to the bed and we frolicked, or something like that.

I promised I would never ever drink alcohol again. She could not complain about me now, because I showed her my best. I was getting good at pushing the right buttons…so was Giselle.

Before the hotel's noon checkout time, we packed our luggage in the Tahoe and headed out towards South Dakota. To the west, it was cloudy, to the east, it was "Big Sky Country," I told Giselle.

I turned the radio on to the local weather station and heard the forecaster tell of advancing rain off the coastal region. I knew what I had to do. I stopped at the nearest Sears store and shopped with Giselle for some new boots for her. As we walked around the mall window-shopping, my Tahoe was at their garage, up on a rack for new snow tire chains being fitted.

"It's so nice here. Why the new snow chains?"

"I want us to be safe crossing through the deep passes in the Rockies. Here, police officers fine you if you are stuck and have no chains or snow tires. These chains have more bite, which I will have to remove on dryer pavement, or they skid too easily."

"Suddenly, a few punk juveniles started following us. They turned away when we looked back, but inevitably stayed up with us.

"I wonder if they spotted that ring you keep flaunting as we pass a window so you can see how it shines on your finger. It's nice, but they might decide they want to steal it. You got a gun?" I asked jesting.

"Yes, in my small vanity luggage…in a holster. I have a Canadian gun permit as a police officer. It isn't good here," she said to my complete surprise.

"Well mine is, it's called self-defense. Look, I don't want to sound paranoid, but things happen around malls this time of year. They may try to carjack my new Tahoe, who knows…that's an easy $40,000 day's work."

After an hour of attempting to lose the jerks in the mall who were following us, I told Giselle to slip her pistol, a Glock 9mm auto, into the console, just as soon as we left the Sears garage. We left the lot and headed east on I-80 towards Salt Lake City, all the way across the state, into Utah's capital.

The little thugs must have gotten tired or changed their minds for we made it halfway to Salt Lake and stopped near Battle Mountain without incident.

We grew tired, so we found a nice motel and ate our first meal of the day very late in the afternoon, and four hundred and fifty miles driven. We had restroom stops at rest areas and station pit stops for gas. The Tahoe was not a gas saver, but gas savers would not get us across the snowy passes either.

After a nice healthy meal, Giselle asked if I was going to the gym with her. She was feeling bloated and constipated, she embarrassingly admitted. It was nice to share our little secrets.

"Exercise is a must. I think I just gained several pounds."

"You can't get fat living on love, my dear. I will love you if you get up to four hundred pounds, so relax."

" No, you will not and I will not want you looking like that either. I packed some extra workout stuff. You can borrow it, its unisex. Let's went, Poncho. I need the exercise."

Surprisingly, Giselle's Under Armor shorts and jersey were nice and fit me comfortably. We jogged down to the gym and found it empty. There were several treadmills and a Bowflex. I guess that is all anyone ever needed. Giselle began to stretch out and I could not take my eyes off her dexterity, and all her other obvious qualities.

"Here, put your arms up against the wall and step back and push with your whole body. That is isometrics and it tightens the muscles."

After I thought that was enough trying to move the building, we hit the treadmill. Giselle immediately began running and I almost got dizzy watching her boobs flopping up and down. I was still on my honeymoon, even if she was not. Someday, I would not be as interested...man I was only fooling myself. That day would never come. We finished jogging; Giselle logged five miles in no time. I quit running at one, puffing hard and feeling like I was dying.

When no one was looking, we snuck over and jumped in the heated pool naked. To our surprise, the wise-ass desk clerk asked over the loudspeaker if he could sell us swimsuits. We ducked under then came up searching for that camera.

We searched and finally spotted a hidden camera above us. I leaned over the side of the pool and grabbed our workout clothes and we had one heck of a time trying to get them back on in the pool, so we helped each other. Then we made a mad dash to the exit door and that smartass said, "Hope to see you all again!" I gave him the bird.

We started laughing hard as we closed the door to our room and our phone rang. I picked it up and it was the desk clerk, who apologized and told me he did not see much, as the cameras pointed mostly at the deep end. I told him it was our fault and apologized for shooting him the bird.

"Hey, you kids heading east, by chance?" he asked.

"Yes, in the morning," I told him.

"Big snowstorms headed for the Rockies…better have chains and get out early."

"I have chains, thanks!"

He wished us no hard feelings and goodnight. Now that was decent.

We slept well that night and at six in the morning, we dined at a pancake house near the I-80 junction. We headed east again feeling better for having worked out. I pulled onto an empty parking lot and as I laid down the chains, Giselle drove forward and I hooked them up.

"Better to be safe than sorry, eh? Look at those dark clouds behind us," I pointed out to Giselle. "Think you can stand a little longer driving today? I like Utah…some of the unusual rocks are intriguing. Nevertheless, there is a great place in Rock Springs, Wyoming called Flaming Gorge, which really is pretty this time of year. We can get there in about six hours. Is that too much driving time? Look at those flakes coming down. They're as big as quarters."

"Well, if you let me drive once in a while, I'd enjoy that. If you get tired, slide over and I'll take the wheel," Giselle suggested.

"Gotcha!" I said, as we began to make good time. In two hours, we had passed up Salt Lake City, and breezed through the by-pass in heavy traffic still headed east on I-80.

When we got to Rock Springs, the hotels were filled, so we decided to make it home by morning. Giselle drove when I tired and I only awoke when I heard the tinkling of a gas pump next to me. I looked up, Giselle was gassing up the Tahoe at a truck stop, and ice and snow had mounted on the windshield.

She went inside and came back out with some hot coffee, and some cat calls from two truck drivers. I must have looked rough, because when I looked at them they quickened their steps inside. I looked in the mirror and yes, I looked almost insane with my long hair standing on end like Don King. I ran my hands through my hair and sat up straight for Giselle to hand me both coffees.

Within an hour, I felt refreshed; we changed drivers and we began singing to the tunes on the radio. Giselle had a great voice and sang to Madonna's, "Like a Virgin" when it came on. I told her it was a little too late now, which brought a punch to my arm and a big kiss right after. We enjoyed the scenery and then came the mountains.

When we started to ascend the Rockies, in only a few minutes we both felt pressure in our ears. I asked Giselle if she had some gum and she did. We chewed and relieved the pain mounting in our ears from the pressure. It became darker and darker as we traveled. Suddenly there was heavier snow on the roadway and shortly thereafter, it really snowed hard. It reminded me of the night when I found Meredith Monroe, I mentioned to Giselle. She turned up the heat when fog began to form inside and the snow became ice on the windshield.

"Speed zone ahead 25 M.P.H." Giselle informed me so I slowed down. Visibility was good, and the Tahoe was doing what I demanded and expected. I was very satisfied we would traverse the mountains safely.

Then ahead there was a family in an old station wagon with lots of snow on top. They were all thumbing a ride. I put on the emergency flashers and eased up to them on the emergency lane, then put down my driver side window to speak to the man.

"Oh, thank God, you stopped," he said. "My kids and wife are freezing…can they please sit in there and warm up?" he begged looking like a cold, wet pup himself.

I said, "Sure," and unlocked the rear to allow them to get inside on the third seat. They all squeezed in and their horrible smell about took our breaths away.

"Their dirty faces looked as though they had not bathed in days, maybe weeks. They rubbed their red fingers together and really caused the windows to fog up. I turned up the heat to max, including the rear defroster and wiper.

"What happened to your car?" I asked.

"Out of gas! We've been sitting here for four hours," he quickly told me.

"Can I take you to a station?"

"No money either," he advised. We were stuck with them.

"Got an Arkansas gas pump?" Giselle then asked.

"Yep, but someone stole our gas can."

"I have an idea. Is your tank on the right or left?"

"Ah, right side, I think," he said trying to look over my shoulder.

"Got her in four wheel drive, Mr. David?" she asked like an informed service wrecker operator.

"Yes," I replied.

"Mister, we're going to push you up that hill. Stop halfway down the other side. How long is your hose?"

"About six or seven feet."

"Find it, and we'll back up behind you and drain some gas into your tank."

"Hey, that's smart. I would have sat here until the road service came," I told her.

"I used to go with traffic once in a while to assist. They did that all the time in the Rockies west of Calgary," Giselle explained.

The man got out and jumped in behind the steering wheel of his station wagon. I eased up behind him and bumped him gently. The kids' weight helped give traction and the Tahoe and the chains did the rest.

We made it to the top of the next hill and I backed off to let him roll to a stop. I swung around and backed up to the station wagon. The father had a long hose in his hands.

"Whoa! Just made it," Giselle said looking from along the outside, then opening the gas fill door and putting in the hose.

"I thought you weren't supposed to be able to do that on these new SUVs," I told Giselle.

"It's a secret," she told me. "If I told you I'd have to kill you," she informed me smiling. "Watch your gas gauge…give him a quarter tank, okay?"

Boy could that person suck! I thought he was going to die when he stood up gagging, then spitting out raw gasoline. He had swallowed some but got drenched with more gas than he anticipated coming through the end of the siphoning hose. I had forty-two gallons from my last fill up. It took twenty minutes, but finally Giselle lifted the hose out, held it up, and then bent it into a "u" shape to hold some fuel back.

"Open your hood, bud…take off the air cleaner, then hop in, and start her," she directed him.

Then she went forward and let the rest of the gas she saved in the "u" of the hose flow into the carburetor.

"Crank it!" Giselle hollered.

The engine started instantly and the rest of his family jumped from mine into theirs.

The grateful man came back, thanked me, and shook my hand. I felt good when he opened his hand and discovered he had a fifty-dollar bill, which I had slipped him.

"God bless you and your wife, sir. She gave me fifty, also…God bless you both. I think this will get us to Ft. Collins. I have a job waiting for me there if I can make it."

"Wait," I told him, handing him another one hundred. "Help the next guy you find out of gas," I told him with a smile, as Giselle said goodbye to his wife and kids.

"I won't ever forget your kindness this day. We can eat now, I think."

Then he hustled back to his running car and sped away. I laughed to myself. Giselle slid back inside and I spun the Tahoe completely around to head east. Giselle smelled like gas, but I did not mind. I knew she was kind and had a heart of gold.

We drove over the Rockies and soon after it began to rain and I could hear the chained tires begin to sing against dryer pavement. They would wear down quickly if I did not remove them, so I found a late-night garage, only found in the Midwest. The owner of the small garage and his son took my Tahoe in immediately. He and his son removed them and serviced a needed oil change in an hour. It was ten. I thought we could just drive on through to my parents' place, but I discovered my cellular was dead.

"Hummm, I forgot to bring my car charger and my cell phone is dead. I wonder if anyone has tried to call. I best call Eleanor in the morning to see if she is okay. I told her to call me and let me hear her column. I hope she did not need me. I guess one week can't hurt anything," I told a sleeping Giselle.

She looked so beautiful there beside me. I filled the gas tank and drove out of Cheyenne east, then north up 385 into Nebraska and at 3 a.m., we entered South Dakota. I knew the campground at Custer's National Park had a hotel and would not be full, so I registered and woke Giselle up to go inside our room. She sleepwalked in and I more or less had to undress her. The long trip had finally gotten to her.

We slept past ten and a housekeeper woke us up rattling the door, then spoke that she would return later. It was Friday, and I immediately called from our hotel room phone to Eleanor. She answered and told me she had tried to call several times, but gave up. However, when she could not get in touch, she looked at an old article I had written, and then put that in the column instead of hers.

"Smart thinking, Eleanor…you're a good girl and very good secretary. We are in the Rapid City area and will be at my parents' home after today for several days before we head home. I'll have to call you from there."

"Okay, boss…everything's going good here now, except Mrs. Upshaw is filing for divorce and Mr. Upshaw hasn't come in for two days. Everything is still going strong. However, I called his office and there is no secretary there either. I went over there and the office is locked. I'm the only person in the editor's department, but it's easy, so far."

"I'm sorry, Eleanor. I should be there. You just have to handle this; I'll see that you get a big Christmas bonus."

"Now you're talking my language, boss. I will do my best. Gerard Business College taught me well. I have not come up with anything except, Mrs. Upshaw, that I cannot handle."

"What's her problem, now?"

"She's really P O'd because evidently, she found credit card bills from Warrez, Mexico, when Mr. Upshaw was supposed to be in Montreal. She put two and two together, she told me, and had him tailed by a private eye. Apparently, that investigator did his job and got some nasty pictures. She told me over the phone she might close this place down. But then immediately after, said she might be our new boss after she fires 'Freddie the poop head', were her exact words."

"Oh my, I don't like this at all. Maybe I have to come back."

"Relax, boss. Just stay near your phone, so I can get your help. If I don't call, you call me. The weekend is here so our work is finished until Monday. Enjoy your honeymoon while you can."

"Thank you ever so much. I cannot believe a temp girl comes in to CMEN and can take over the whole show after three days. I guess I'm not as important as I thought," I surmised.

"Yes, you are…just wait until Mrs. Upshaw comes in personally and starts her tirade. Oops, Mr. Upshaw is calling on line two, hang on," Eleanor spoke. I waited for two minutes.

"Hello, boss…Mr. Upshaw says he'll be back in an hour. I will let you know what happens. Nothing you can do. If I definitely need you here, I'll call. But until then, enjoy your honeymoon and get what you can," she quipped giggling, and then hung up before she got my parents' number.

"You look worried. Is something wrong at your office?" Giselle asked still groggy and under the covers.

"It's nothing we can do. You want to call your parents and ask them how Rita is, if Nigel knows? She was so secretive I just hope she does not get too involved and gets in over her head. I'll dial it for you," I said, handing the phone to Giselle.

I noticed she was sleeping in the nude. I must have not seen her get up, but then I saw her clothes hanging on a chair, so I motioned at them.

"They smelled like gasoline. I had to shed them and I was too bushed to put them away in the luggage and make noise and wake you up. I think I'll...Hello, Mom!" she stopped short to talk to Queenie.

Her face looked worried, as she did not let me in on the conversation. Giselle kept holding her hand up for me to remain calm and quiet so she could hear. Then she hung up, just saying, "I'll tell him." It was a one-sided call.

"Mom says Daddy is out looking for Rita. She did not answer her phone and didn't say she was going out. He is worried, but there is nothing we can do, Mom said. I gave her your mom's number and she will call if they find Rita. Let's go see your parents before the world comes to an end," Giselle suggested.

CHAPTER 16

I called Mom and told her we were near Rapid City, headed out their way in a few hours. She was excited and told me to be careful driving. As Giselle showered, I shaved, and as I packed the luggage in the Tahoe, Giselle returned our room key. We were off again. It was dry and windy, something I was used to in South Dakota. It was much better than six feet deep snow drifts.

When Giselle saw the Custer's State Park sign, she turned around in her seat trying to see Mt. Rushmore. Therefore, I figured 'what the hay' and turned into the park to give her a quick look-see with my personal drive-thru. I had been there bunches of times and I knew just where to go. She marveled at the bison that crossed the road in front of us and stared straight up at the towering stacks of rock mountains.

I drove into the Mt. Rushmore parking lot and we went in through the facility, then out again, in a fifteen-minute self-tour, and grabbed brochures to answer her questions about its development. Then we finally headed up 85 from Spearfish into the rolling plains.

I turned off the main road onto our farm's long five-mile lane. It was unpaved and very narrow and dusty. After several minutes of concern, Giselle asked when we would get there.

"We're here!" I told her looking over at her confusion.

"Where?" she questioned.

"When I turned off the hard road, it was the beginning of my parents' farm. During summer, those bare fields have rows of golden wheat and barley waving in the wind…it's a beautiful sight."

"Are those their cows?"

"No, hey…they're some pretty awesome mule deer out there. I count about seventeen. There are some big antlers out there, also," I said stopping for a moment.

When I stopped, the deer all looked our way, then bounded off in their hopping, loping jaunts to hide. Others got up from unseen locations and stood eyes-fixed on my white Tahoe.

"I'm glad you spotted them, because I want to take Dad out hunting while we are here."

"Great! May I go, too?" she asked.

"Yes, I guess you may…you can shoot, so I'll have to go get you a permit."

"Oh, I don't want to come between you and your dad. I know how much he means to you…your mom, too," Giselle spoke softly.

"Well, I thought you just might impress my mom with some of your recipes that Nigel raves about. As far as getting a permit, Dad gets several landowner permits and they are free. It's just you need an out of state hunting license…ha…I do too…I forgot about that. Anyway, yes, Dad will be thrilled to have you hunt with us, especially…look over there…see those pheasants?"

"Holy cow, there must be a thousand bunched up…look at them all get up!" Giselle shouted. "Stop! That flock…they're flying straight at us…duck!"

Thump!

"A cock pheasant flew into the side of our Tahoe…our Tahoe…that sounded so good!" I told Giselle, who was wide-eyed and very excited as I opened my door, and grabbed a dead broken-necked pheasant and then held it up.

"Oh, poor bird…it's so beautiful," she moaned.

"You know what we South Dakotans say about a bird like this bird?" I asked her.

"Dead bird?"

"Nope! Supper!" I laughed as I put the pheasant on the floorboard under my driver's seat. "No shotgun pellets in this one," I boasted.

I could see them standing out by the picket fence in front of the old weather clapboard house almost a mile away. They were standing side-by-side and Dad had his arm around Mom's waist waving, in great anticipation of our arrival.

When I pulled into the yard, Dad looked old and tired, more than I remembered. Mom's hair was up in her usual bun and seemed grayer. Giselle seemed awed by the big tractors, plows, and combines sitting in a row under a long lean-to. There was a half-million worth of farm equipment sitting there, I told Giselle.

"Who drives them?"

"I used to, but mostly Pop and sometimes Mom disks."

"How could you leave this beautiful place?" she asked.

"Grass is always greener in other pastures, I guess. Anyway, if I hadn't, I might never have found you."

Giselle thought that was sweet and gave me a peck, trying to hide it from Mom and Dad.

Mom and Dad rushed to our Tahoe and Mom was the first to open my door and hug me. She then looked across at Giselle still seated and strapped in her seatbelt.

"Oh, my! She is absolutely beautiful, Jerry. Is she really your Missus?" Mom asked, then hurrying around to open Giselle's door and hug her, too.

"Welcome, daughter. This is the place your husband grew up on and was too happy to leave," she said, giving Giselle a big, long embrace, then a peck on the cheek. "Dad, come look at Giselle…she's a beauty queen," she said, as Dad leaned in and whispered, "Boy, they sure grow fancy women up there in Canada, huh, son. No wonder you never come home hunting anymore. Welcome home, boy, I've missed you," he laughed, added with a long embrace, patting me hard on my back.

"You look great, Pop. Are you up to hunting these birds? Look here," I said, as I picked up the pheasant from the floor board. "Dang thing got up in a flock and flew into the side of my truck. How many times has that happened?" I asked.

"To tell you the truth…every time I ran out of shells and was too poor to buy more and my family was very hungry, I would speed old Betsy down field road, then honk. They would get up scared, fly up by the millions and head right for me. Got two or three at a time, sometimes…kept the freezer full. I don't think they see well after they get up for some reason," Dad said taking hold of the big cock, shaking it up and down, feeling how heavy it was.

"Giselle spotted some mule deer a mile off in the stubble fields. Must have been two, or three, big-antlered bucks in that group. Dad, this is Giselle," I said, when she and Mom came around to us; Mom was holding Giselle's hand.

Dad removed his cowboy hat of a million years old, his favorite; sweat- stained headband, and all. Then he placed it over his heart to speak.

"Giselle, I'm your new father-in-law and I'm proud to make your acquaintance. How my son was able to find such a beautiful girl to marry him as you is beyond me, but I'm glad he did…welcome to our home," he graciously told Giselle as he offered a hug. Instead, Giselle put the smack down on his lips that made him very happy.

"Well it's very easy to see where Jerry got his good looks. I don't know which is prettier, you, or Mrs. David," she said looking at Dad, then Mom.

"Why thank you, dear…call him Pop and me Mom…although our Christian names are Marilyn and Joseph. Our local friends call me Mercy and him Doc, because Pop gets calls from the area cattle farmers in the middle of a winter's deep freezing snowstorms, usually wanting to have him look at their down, sick cattle. I get calls, too. However, mine are to help with births, usually in the winter when doctors cannot come and they cannot get to a hospital in Rapid City. It's our closest hospital for help," Mom told Giselle looking up at her.

Mom was five feet two. Giselle was five ten and just a few inches shorter than pop at six three. I could see over them all.

"Please, Giselle, come in and eat. I bet you both are starved of good home cooking on your honeymoon," she requested.

"Mom, Giselle is a gourmet cook," I bragged.

"Oh, son, I won't hold that against her," she laughed, teasing.

Mom's spread was unbelievable. She must have cleaned, baked pies and cakes, and cooked fresh vegetables from the big cold frame for days to get that table fare. Giselle was caught up in the wonderful fresh bread aromas as much as I was and after Pop said a prayer of thanks, we dug in.

Giselle ate like a starving woman, which made Mom happy and kept saying "Oh, that's so good!" to each, and every one of Mom's dishes.

Finally, we all were full to the brim, we thought, until Mom brought out her big four-layered German chocolate cake. Giselle could not stop raving over how good it was, and it was. Giselle ate two slices.

"Jerry, get your jogging clothes on. After this meal, I know I gained ten pounds. As soon as we do the dishes, I'll meet you outside by that big shed with the farm machinery in it. I want to look at them close up. Gosh, then show me around the farm so I can run off the calories," Giselle ordered.

Pop looked at Mom as if she was surely kidding, so I had to explain.

"Dad…think back two or three years ago. I was home and we watched the Calgary Stampeders football team playing somebody, I forget who? Anyway, we both said they should show that one cheerleader more often because she was better than the game."

Dad looked embarrassingly at Mom, and then said, "Vaguely."

I nodded my head towards Giselle and shook my head yes. Dad looked at Giselle and said, "By God, I thought I had seen you before… yes…she's the one all right!" he said excitedly. "Boy, son you sure know how to pick 'em!"

"Hey…I'm a chip off the old block, wouldn't you say?" I said to compliment Mom.

"Now I have to agree with you on that one, cause Mom will conk me with her frying pan, if I don't," he jested.

Mom and Giselle both giggled.

"You must not worry about the dishes, Giselle. Go with your man and see the farm. Dad will help me."

"Absolutely not…I want to jaw your ear about your son. I want to know everything about him and you both, also. Jerry and I did not date very long and I am a little ashamed to admit it was just a little over two weeks, if that, until we married. It was love at first sight and we could not help ourselves. I love your son and he loves me," Giselle told my smiling mom.

"Just like Pop and I did…only he was seventeen and I just turned fifteen. Boy did my dad cuss. We lived here with Mom and Pop David, until his pop died and mom then too. His dad left him this farm after Doc was twenty-five, and had successfully worked the ground. Then Pop bought more and more ground on credit, when we got a little bit ahead, until it is as big as today."

"How big is this farm? I noticed it was five miles just off the highway to the house."

"How many, Pop?" Mom asked.

"Well, there's six miles in each direction paid for, about thirty-two thousand acres, give, or take a few. In addition, I recently bought the Miller spread, but will not get it, until after the next year's crops are in. It's rented out to a Chinese conglomerate or corporation of some kind. Darnest thing how they ship it all the way to China. Pretty soon, those Chinese people are going to own America and Canada, too. Then they will probably find a way to drill a hole right through the middle of the Earth and ship it that way, who knows?" Dad said with a little disgust.

Giselle immediately saw my dad's concern, stood up, and started helping Mom. I took all the dishes to the sink and put covers on the leftovers.

"Hey, son, come here!" Dad shouted from his bedroom. "Looky here…it's your new Savage .375 caliber H & H magnum I bought you for last Christmas. Now you get this as your Christmas gift, this year, ha! Let's go out to the range and tune it in on some targets. It's supposed to be on target right out of the box."

I thanked Dad and we took out the rifle and two shotguns with the trap thrower and clay birds and three boxes of AA #7 skeet shells. My dad and I used to do that all the time when I was growing up and he loved to beat me. We set up a target out in a pasture about two hundred yards away. I got down in a seated position and fired off three consecutive rounds. Then we walked together back to the target and my Savage was truly accurate as could be.

"Dad, I'm as happy as I've ever been in my life. What do you think of Giselle?"

"What can I say? She is a prize. She is a very nice woman, son. You'd better take good care of her."

We shot some clay pigeons until Mom and Giselle came out.

"Okay, Giselle, pick your poison and load it up. Grab up a Browning auto or a Remington 870 pump…one's as good as the other. No time like the present to learn how to shoot," Dad spoke, not knowing Giselle could already shoot.

"Pull!" Giselle hollered to Dad, who looked very surprised the clay bird quickly turned into dust. She hit every clay bird Dad could launch, including two at a time, five times in a row, which used up all his clay pigeons.

"Man…ain't never, never seen shootin' like that before, missy!"

"Dad, Mom, Giselle is also a cop. She is part of the police department where we live."

"Imagine the frisk she can give ya!" Dad chuckled.

"Now, Pop…behave yourself. Let us all walk out to the cemetery. I want to show Giselle our heritage," Mom spoke.

That cemetery was about a mile away on a dirt road. On the side of a rolling hillside grew a lone oak the size of a Calgary building. Its main trunk was twelve feet circumferenced and must have been there when Christopher Columbus arrived. It was a humongous acorn tree, with curving branches, which touched the ground, shading the graves. It was picturesque, Giselle told my mom.

Dad removed his hat and bent down to pull weeds around his parents' stone. The others were distant relatives dating back to the early 1800s. One was a Dakota Indian named Totowa, who took his white squaw named Birdonwing captive before he became civilized, in the early 1800s. Mom showed Giselle where she and Pop were to rest, and then said she hoped someday we would take the farm, because my sister was too reckless with her money.

"I don't know," Giselle started out. "I'm Canadian through and through. My family is there. I just cannot say yes, not now anyway. This place is beautiful, but as I said, I'm Canadian."

"I said the same thing too. I was from Davenport, Iowa. Let time pass and you'll see a difference."

We spent the day back at the house then the big cowherd started mooing.

"Do I hear cows?" Giselle asked suddenly.

"Oh, do you hear cows?" my dad said. "Come looky here, Giselle," he beckoned.

Dad called her to the east side of the house and pulled back the curtain.

"Coming over that rolling hill is 700 hundred prime Angus beef cattle; feeding out on my good brome grass, until they get shipped," he told her. "When the price is right, they're ready," he added. "Otherwise, they get very cold out in our weather…they sometimes just freeze to death standing up, if they winter out here. We get as cold as you in Canada, but the snow drifts get six feet high sometimes."

"That's when Doc and I get most of our calls," Mom told Giselle standing beside them.

"How in the world can you ever get anywhere with six feet snow drifts?" she questioned.

"If it's an ordinary house call, we take a big tractor. If it's do or die, baby alert, I take the big Bombardier."

"What's a Bombardier?"

"It's our snowmobile, honey. I drive it right through those big drifts like a hot knife through butter," Mom bragged.

"I don't believe you…really?"

"Been doin it for as long as I can remember," she gloated.

Darkness came soon after and everyone went to bed early, too, because TV reception was horrible. Nevertheless, daylight was "getting up time" on the farm. I grew up thinking all TVs had constant snow and vertical flipping.

We said good night as Giselle and I headed upstairs to my old bedroom. Mom gave Giselle her handmade quilt that she had designed herself, just for this day, she told her. It was extravagantly beautiful and Giselle was thrilled as I was for her. It was warm, too, not that we needed it.

"What's that noise?" Giselle asked.

"I think you excited my pop and now he's very affectionate with Mom. I'm used to it," I teased. "That noise they make. Someday our kids will talk behind our backs like this, I hope."

"Well, it is too early for me to go to sleep…let's give them a little noise competition, eh?" Giselle said poking me, then reaching here and there.

My bed was never that squeaky before and we made their noises sound miniscule. There is no place like home, I assure you.

"Giselle, Giselle!" I said, shaking her gently, trying to awaken her to come to Mom's breakfast table and later plan our hunting trip into our fields. She finally awoke and slid into some of my hunting garb. The heavy plaid flannel shirt looked great, but the jeans were breathtaking on her. She filled them like a tight sausage, I told her. I do not think she thought that was a good compliment though.

Dad was having coffee and had driven down to the mailbox for a new paper. Mom had fresh-baked and sliced bread, fried eggs, bacon, sausage, and ham to choose. It was the typical farm breakfast in the Midwest, certainly our house. There were her fresh jars of strawberry preserves on the table, and her special peach, too, which I absolutely cherished. I heaped them both up on top of the warm bread with the melting real-churned butter squares, all to my delight. Boy was that good!

After I gave Giselle a taste of mine, she sighed, "I'm going to gain twenty pounds." Then she ate three slices herself.

"Son, there's frost on the pumpkin, better have Giselle wear some long johns. She got boots?" he asked.

"All set...you should see her in those long johns, Dad...wow!" I whispered.

"Son, don't ever stop feeling like that or telling her so...women need that, trust me," Dad so lovingly advised.

"Head 'em up, move 'em out!" Dad cried out, so happy to be going into the field.

We all loaded up in Dad's old truck after he said mine would get all cruddy, and took off towards the rising sun. That was so we would have the sun to our backs as we returned walking. I had the shotguns and my Christmas rifle in its case behind the seat.

We bounced and slid, and after driving for ten miles on the dusty road and past freshly chopped silage fields, we came to a twenty-five acre field, situated on the corners of four fields. Each had a different crop on them, which Dad left standing for the wildlife and our hunting. Humans did not hunt it only coyotes traveled here. We shot those on sight.

The birds were tight sitting as we spread out to hunt pheasants. Dad said it did not matter one bit that Giselle had no license. Charley McFarlane was his friend, and the only game warden in twenty-two counties. Charley was in Rapid City Hospital from a foot infection, which he allowed to fester too long. He would be there for a few days, anyway, Dad said.

Dad on the left, me on the right and Giselle walking down the middle; we took off searching for birds. In seconds, Dad said to Giselle there was a bird running out in front of her on the ground.

"Make sure it's a cock pheasant you shoot at, honey. We don't shoot hens, if we can help it," he advised.

"How do I tell?"

"A cock will take off cackling loudly. You will see his long tail, too. Hens are light brownish, kind of dull looking, short tail. You'll see."

No sooner than the words came out of Dad's mouth than that pheasant sprang up into flight, cackling like a mad chicken, and bee lining it down the field in front of Giselle. She raised her shotgun and knocked the bird out of the air like a seasoned hunter. We had no dogs so we just walked up on them and put them in our game pocket holders of our hunting coats. Before a few steps were advanced, more pheasants flew up,

"Hens!" Dad hollered.

That went on for an hour. Giselle was having so much fun; she did not want to stop, even though she shot ten. I let her shoot my five birds and carried half of hers; at ten, we were limited out. We never violated the limits.

"Oh, oh," Dad whispered. "Here comes a game warden. Unload your guns."

"Giselle, switch coats with me, quickly," he ordered, as the government SUV was throwing up lots of dust, headed our way. We were trapped.

"Charley! How the heck are you, boy!" Dad greeted him. "You remember junior here, and this is his lovely new wife, Giselle."

"How do you do, Giselle? Hi, Jerry, long time no see," he cordially greeted us. "Sorry, got to check your licenses, new regulations, and you have to sign that you've been checked out. I will give you all a bright florescent tag to wear, so the next warden will be able to see you're already checked out, without disturbing you again. I watched you through the field glasses. I figured it was you."

"Heck, Charley, you're the only warden in the southern twenty-two counties. You know me," Dad said beginning to realize we were about to be ticketed. Besides Giselle and I being Canadian, without licenses, and Dad possessing one too many birds and no plug in his gun, Charley grunted as he bent over the laid out birds to assess the total fine coming.

Dad was cool, "Charley, I know you are just doing your job. I am sorry I put our friendship before the law. I have not been hunting with Jerry for two years and when he finally comes home this happens. It is my entire fault. Can't you just give me all the tickets, please?"

Charley started grinning, and then said, "Gotchha! Remember when we were kids and you told Mom it was me, not you, who ate her pie that she had cooling on the kitchen windowsill? Gotchha, back, ol' buddy," he said letting out a big belly laugh. "You should have seen your face," he said tormenting Dad.

Then Dad got him in a headlock and told him it was a cheap trick and he was going to get even, even if it took until the day he died. They grasped each other's hands and turned to us.

"Say, there's several big mulies out there lying down in those tall grasses. The wind is right. At least you have one of those free landowner tags, don't you…if not I can sell you one from the vehicle."

"Say, I know you, don't I? You were at that football game, as a cheerleader on TV for Calgary, right? I never forget a face, especially one like yours," he told Giselle.

"Better look out, she's darn good with a gun and she's not only a Outriders cheerleader, she's a real cop in Canada," Dad proudly stated.

After the scare was over and we all were relieved, we bid farewell to Charley.

"Giselle, you wanna go shoot a mulie?" Dad asked. It seemed Dad forgot about me and his attentions went to pleasing his new daughter-in-law.

Giselle looked at me and I told her I had three antler racks tacked to the machine shed already; she might as well try.

So with Dad as her guide, Giselle, and he snuck up on several big mulies to one hundred and fifty yards, was my guess. I envied Dad's view crawling behind Giselle. It took thirty minutes or more.

They could see only their huge antlers and the grass hid the rest of their bodies. They had to wait until one stood up. It seemed like they bedded down for the rest of the night, when I decided to honk the truck's horn. Dad looked at me startled, and then the bucks stood up locked in on the truck and me. Before I knew, or Dad also, Giselle pulled the trigger on an exceptionally big mule buck. He jumped high into the air, ran twenty yards, stopped, started wobbling, and then plopped over dead. A direct hit through the heart was his demise.

I drove the truck lickety-split right up to the buck and Giselle. Dad was motioning it had a wide spread with his hands as I approached. He hollered as I got out of the truck, "It's the biggest booger we ever took off the range…has to weigh three fifty plus…it's a five by six… what a shot she made!" Dad spoke out and voiced his learned hunting expertise opinion.

Giselle was smiling ear to ear. I was so proud of her, too, and so was my dad. I pulled out my cellular and snapped several pictures. I did not know then if they took or not, only after I could recharge the batteries. However, it flashed on the first two.

Dad told Giselle to watch him gut the mulie so the next time she would be able to do her own. He pulled a skinning knife out of the truck glove box and removed the dorsal glands on his legs first, then split him down the middle and pulled out his intestines. He examined the liver closely for signs of disease, and then pronounced his operation a success. The deer was healthy. "Next time this duty is yours, Giselle," Dad told her.

"I hope there is a next time. I have never had so much fun," she stated.

Dad and I loaded the beast onto the truck bed. Dad found an old jug of water behind the seat that he kept there and asked Giselle to pour water over his hands to let him wash them. After that, we drove off home. On the way, Giselle asked if we did this all the time.

"Only in season, once a year," Dad said. "But there's geese flyin' aplenty by the millions that should be down any day now from up in your neck of the woods. There are walleye below Garrison Dam and in the Missouri. Neighbors raise bison on their farms and they get hunters who pay. I do not think I would like guiding paying hunters, but I've thought of getting a few bison cows and crossing them with our big herd bull. Moreover, you can ATV and snowmobile to your heart's content on the fields after picking season. There is lots of stone arrowheads and relics lying out in the open fields after plowing in some places where the Indians made their villages long ago. There's a lot to do here, besides drive those gas guzzling tractors day and night," he told a very attentive Giselle.

I saw the look of respect in Giselle's eyes for my father and I liked that. She learned just a bit of this South Dakotan life and it was growing on her.

CHAPTER 17

Mom was out to meet us with a worried look and a message from Nigel.

"Your father called, Giselle. He is a very nice man and asked me to tell you, son, that there is an all out search for Rita Tory. Is she your secretary?" Mom asked.

"Yes, she's a young girl who wants to be a policeman more, I guess."

"We'll have to head home yet tonight," I told my parents and looked at Giselle's sadness. "Sorry, sweetheart. I know it's not a very long honeymoon, but I have to get back and help find Rita. She might be in danger."

"I realize that, honey. I hope she has not met with the fate of the others, that is my worry, Jerry. I had a wonderful honeymoon and we have the rest of our lives together. Ha! How many girls can say they dropped a big buck on their honeymoon?" she jested.

I helped Dad hang the deer in the farm's big cooler, while Giselle showered and packed our things. The buck would be in there hanging to cure out for a few days, and then Dad would butcher it as he did some steers.

I showered and put on fresh clothes. Giselle thanked my parents for their love and hospitality. Then I gave them the presents I brought and told them not to open them until Christmas. The double stroller caused dad some concern; he thought I had bought him a shooting seat to sight in guns.

"Sorry, Pop, that's for Tracey and her kids. How is she anyway?"

Mom looked at Pop, Pop looked back at Mom…"Don't ask!" they both chimed at once, and then laughed.

I kissed Mom good-bye and we left. There was a melancholy feeling as we left waving good-bye and drove up our long lane to the pavement. I gassed up in Bowman.

"Gosh your parents made me feel so at home. I really enjoyed this time we spent. Your mom is so sweet and your dad is a prince. You have good heritage, Mr. David," Giselle told me as we headed for the Canadian border.

We crossed the border on 85 and were vehicle searched. Giselle showed her identification and her weapon and permit to carry card, which did not mean a thing to the young officer. When he ran it for stolen and found it legally registered to our police department, he permitted us to continue.

It was pushing daylight when we turned off Canadian Highway One at Calgary and drove north to our home in Didsbury. It was good to be home with my new bride. I set about getting the luggage as Giselle stood near the patio door stretching against the building. I opened the sliding door, and swept my darling off her feet and then carried her through the threshold.

"Now, old lady, that the honeymoon's over, I need some breakfast from you while I put these things away," I jested.

"I get the dresser, you get the closet and shelves, Mr. David…move it, buster!" Giselle ordered with a smile that caused me to kiss her and squeeze her tightly.

"Thank you for loving me, sweetheart. I am the luckiest man in the world. I think though, it's time to consider moving from my bachelor apartment to a real place for us, don't you?"

"Good idea. Nevertheless, I can stand this place until we do. It has memories, remember?" Giselle told me as she kissed me hard.

I carried the luggage into the bedroom and sat down on the bed to listen to my phone messages, when I saw there were ten, and the flashing number was irritating. The first message was from Rita. She said she would call back as several more messages were the same. Then

on the last call, she quickly told me that she was going on campus to
see a math professor's graduate student. "He's the guy in your column,
boss. His name is Benjamin Dorr. He's got a new address, other than I
gave Nigel. Call Nigel when you get this and tell him. I did not get to
tell him because he was out on a case, or something. It is eight, and I
am headed out. Wish me luck."

That was it. Giselle stood in the bedroom doorway looking very
concerned.

"Oh, God! Dad will have a fit. I know he told her not to do anything
without telling him first. If it was leading to meeting someone, he
was going to be there in the shadows. I know he is just sick about
this…darn, why did she do this? She might be in great danger," Giselle
mourned.

"See if you can get hold of your mom and Nigel. Tell him I'm
going into my office to search for an address off Rita's caller ID. I think
I saw his number there by accident. I should have put two and two
together then, but she was angry for my snooping in her desk one day.
I'll be back…here, would you plug my phone into the charger in the
bedroom? I'll skip breakfast; make yourself at home."

"Like heck I will! I'm going with you," Giselle demanded.

I plugged in the cell phone myself. Giselle and I headed out to my
office. Eleanor was busy working on the computer.

"Hi, boss! Didn't expect you back so soon. Everything's good, but
still no Rita," she advised me, while looking at Giselle. "This must
be Mrs. Boss…glad to meet you, I'm Eleanor Bigglebottom, your
husband's temp," she said, rising up to greet Giselle. "Boy, what made
a good looking girl like you fall for a guy like him?" she jested to
compliment Giselle's looks.

"It was that old love at first sight thing going on. I'm delighted to
meet you, Eleanor," Giselle quickly responded.

I looked at the notes left and somehow ran across the number for
Benjamin Dorr. Eleanor had it written down on a piece of paper, and
taped to my desk.

"How did you know that?" I asked Eleanor.

"I got a call from the guy about five days ago. He wanted to speak
to Rita. I told him to call Upshaw's office. No one was there, he said,
so he asked me to tell Rita. I tried to call you after Rita turned up

missing, but there was no answer, so I wrote that note. His address is on the back. It's at a college dorm, I think."

"Did you call Nigel Gray?"

"Who's that?"

"Oh yes, you don't know anything about anything, do you?"

"All I know is what I overheard you say and that's Rita is working as a pigeon or something for the cops. That's the scuttlebutt at the cafeteria anyway."

"How would anyone else know, I wonder? Rita must have told someone. Maybe it was Freddie."

"Giselle, call your office and see if they know where your dad is. I'm headed to the university."

"Are you just going to leave me here?"

"Oh, of course not…ah, time might be important here. Here is some cash for a cab. Go see your mother and wait until I can return," I suggested with a kiss.

"Sorry, Mister David…where you go, I go. We're partners now, remember?"

"She's right, boss. Listen to the little lady," Eleanor said, rather boldly. I guess being the only person in the office gave her new authority; in her mind anyway.

"Alright, but call your mom and tell her we're back and see if she knows where Nigel is."

Giselle used my office phone and dialed up Queenie. Being very certain not to alarm Queenie, Giselle learned from her that Nigel had called and was going to be home there shortly.

"Tell Daddy I'm with Jerry headed to the university's math department."

Queenie asked if it was about Rita.

"Yes, Jerry has an address he wants to check out. It might lead us to Rita's whereabouts."

When Queenie asked about our honeymoon, Giselle told her it was wonderful and she won a small fortune in Reno. Then she said she would fill her in later and hung up.

"Let's went, Poncho!" Giselle's favorite get-up-and-go expression.

We headed out to the university, not knowing if there was any real connection, but I had to find out. I found the office of statistical learning and they directed me to see Professor Grebe. He was the head of that department giving a class to seniors and postgraduates, his secretary told us. We had to wait until his class was over. Then as the students filed out, Giselle and I addressed him.

"Professor Grebe, may we speak with you, sir?" Giselle called out as he was about to exit a side door.

He turned to us and looked over his reading glasses to see who was calling him. He was a man in his fifties, I would guess. His grayish hair resembled Einstein's and he wore a white smock like a doctor. He looked the part of his position.

We asked him if he knew Benjamin Dorr. He spoke rather ambiguously about him.

"The young man has been absent from his duties for almost a week," he began. "I have my doubts he wants to further his education, since he knows I depend upon my assistants to be prompt and help me with the classes. After all, they get remuneration from the college to do so. I am afraid I will have to fail him. Why do you inquire of him?" he asked.

Giselle displayed her badge, which raised his bushy eyebrows, and told him it was official police business. I was as surprised as he apparently was at Giselle's forcefulness.

"I'm not surprised," he spoke. "The young man is a misfit. He hangs out at the bars and mingles with the young innocent underclassmen females too much. He sometimes smells of rotgut. Has he harmed anyone, may I inquire?"

"We just want to talk to him to see if he knows anything about a missing girl. We think he does. Please tell us where you think he is," I told him.

He looked upset and went to his book of postgraduate home addresses.

"He's listed here as living off campus at 501 Whitelaw…that's just off campus by the football stadium," he told us.

We thanked the professor and hurried away to the Tahoe.

"He sure was creepy," Giselle said. "I have a bad feeling about this. The night of the playoffs that girl was found there in that parking lot at the stadium. This really might be the guy we're after."

We stopped at a roadside campus phone and Giselle called her office.

"Daddy! Thank God, you are there. Did Mom tell you what we are doing? Yes, well we have a lead. We talked to Jerry's secretary and she said a guy named Benjamin Dorr called for Rita Tory. He was one of Jerry's love ad requests, so we have his picture and an off-campus university address. We are at a phone near the university library. The creep lives right near the stadium at 501 Whitelaw. Daddy, get over here and we'll talk to the guy." Giselle quickly turned back to me.

"He's coming. Daddy will be here in a half hour with a search warrant. He said stay here."

"How can he get one so fast?"

"That's his secret…I don't know how. He has to have a magistrate's approval and signature first."

We waited for Nigel's arrival at the library. He was prompt. We gave him all our information we had, including a copy of the photo ad taken off my computer, in case he did not have one handy, and the words of Professor Grebe.

"I have to tell you something, Nigel," I began. "Rita called my home phone and left a message on my recorder. She mentioned that she could not get hold of you and called me instead. We were on our honeymoon. Anyway, Rita said she had a date with Dorr, but that message was five days old."

Nigel immediately looked worried and told us to remain there at the library and that he would return after he had talked with the suspect and had searched the premises. A marked squad rolled up with two of the department's uniformed officers, and then another squad rolled up behind that one. Nigel was prepared to go in now, so away they all sped.

"Let's go back to the main office and find out where that Professor Grebe lives. He is just too creepy. You know what they say…birds of a feather flock together," I told Giselle.

On our return to the main office, the secretary gave us the professor's off campus home address, which was in an adjacent high rent district, where most of the teachers resided. His home was a huge Victorian place with great pillars out front and ivy climbing the walls. We expected to see a large family living there, but it was just the professor, as we found out knocking upon his door.

"Oh, it's you two. Did you find my Mr. Dorr?" he asked, as we stepped inside.

We were both overcome by the palatial interior of his home place; it was huge, with high vaulted ceilings and a spiral staircase. There were many ancient artifacts openly displayed, which seemed appropriate for him, corresponding in my mind, anyway, to be part of any college professor's interests.

I could see into his study. There was a huge desk, obviously a Mediterranean burley teakwood. In addition, against a wall there were several miniature African facemasks, painted and decorated native shields and several long African spears. A long curved sheik's scimitar sword was hanging on the wall, also, which looked somewhat uncared for and rusted, unlike the other neatly stationed objects. It seemed out of place.

A multiple gun cabinet held several long guns and many taxidermist-created heads of a variety of beasts hung on his walls.

A huge time clock chimed somewhere in the house, and then another began and another. The sounds echoed as if it came from a deep cavern. It was five o'clock. Giselle stood looking up at a magnificent crystal chandelier, which hung above us. Everything was amazing.

However, when I stared too hard at an unusual piece, a twelve-inch statue of a brown monkey sitting on volumes of books and holding a human skull in its hand, I just had to ask about it. It almost looked like the statue of 'The Thinker', and I wondered about that.

"What an unusual object…it's so very interesting. What does it represent, if I may ask?" I questioned the professor.

"It was a gift from another colleague, Professor Dingle, our distinguished head of the psychology department. It represents man's traverse through this world in reverse, thus the monkey depicted wondering of its humankind's origin. Now tell me, have you found my grad student?"

"Yes, and no, sir…we wanted to ask you some more questions about Mr. Dorr. You see, sir, we suspect him of knowing about all the serial killings going on around here."

Grebe became very nervous and looked like he might be culpable of their knowledge.

"Then you haven't found him, have you? Why must you waste my time?" he waved his hand at us to hustle us out.

It was then I saw the huge ring upon his finger. It was a turquoise stone ring. The stones surrounded a leatherneck sea turtle. I think the shell of the turtle was actually tortoise shell. It was quite a work of art, obviously a very expensive, one of a kind.

The professor became very obnoxious and told us quickly that he knew nothing of his protégé graduate student's off-campus activities other than his drinking, except he probably was the one we were looking for.

"Search for him and you'll find your answers, I am certain."

He said we would have to do investigative work on our own time, not his. Then he advised us that he had guests coming for dinner at eight and asked us to leave, so he could dress. He more or less pushed us out the door.

"That old coot knows something...did you see him flinch? I'm certain of it. It also seems he wants us to find Dorr, for some reason," Giselle told me, which was my exact feeling also.

We decided to go back to the library. When Nigel had not immediately returned, I drove over to 501 Whitelaw and saw red lights flashing from an EMT emergency vehicle that parked out front.

"Oh my God! I hope it's not Daddy," she moaned.

As we approached, an officer directing traffic leaned in my window to tell us the road was closed off temporarily.

"Jim, what happened?" Giselle asked him.

"Giselle! Someone said Nigel's little girl got married. Congratulations...is this here your new hubby, I presume?"

"Yes, Jim Halihan, meet Jerry David. Now, what happened? Daddy was going there."

"Don't know for sure. They just called me for traffic...said there was a suicide in there. Do not know who it is, but he was ripe a few days. Relax, it's not your detective-sergeant," Jim told Giselle.

Then Nigel stepped out on the porch with a mask about his face. He pulled it off and lit up a cigarette. He saw us and motioned for us to approach, so Jim let us through.

"Was it Rita?" I immediately asked.

"No, it's the guy in the photo all right. He was apparently a masochist. Tried to get his cookies off on the stairwell and hung himself by accident. It appears he struggled to get loose before he became helpless and unconscious. I've seen it before. They try going under, with a rope around their neck to choke off their oxygen to get a high of some sort…then get loose right before they climax while masturbating…sounds exciting, eh?" Nigel laughed. "I guess he's not a real live suspect, or as we say, his case is closed."

"They're certain Rita's not in there somewhere?" I asked since I feared the worst.

"No, we searched everything, but they're still in there covering the place. We found many Polaroid-shot porn pictures in his bedroom…no Rita pictures that I saw. There might be something there to implicate him in the murders. I am done here. However, forensics is at work dusting for prints and I could not examine the nasty pictures, without possibly damaging evidence. I could see several nude teenaged girls who looked very young. They sell them on the black market on campuses. Girls pose for college money. He was a real pervert. If nothing else, he will not have any procreation for me to contend with in the near future. Hey…I am simply famished…you guys hungry, too, eh? Mom has a meal going and expects you'll be there, eh?"

I was overjoyed to learn it was not Rita, but saddened to know our one lead was gone that could possibly help locate her, dead or alive. We followed Nigel and drove towards his home. The thought of the rude professor stuck in my craw. I never thought of him as a real suspect, until he acted so weirdly.

"Well, when are we going to put a tail on that creepy professor?" Giselle suddenly asked. "Birds of a feather, remember? I say we find a way to watch his house. I saw a vacant home for sale within eyesight of his front door. Maybe we could rent it and watch him from there."

My Giselle was just like her father. She was cunning and cool, very observant and lovely also. I had quite a girl.

Queenie met us at the front door. She kissed Nigel, hugged him, then hugged Giselle and me.

Her face was lit up with a cheerful welcome smile and I could see she was anxious to ask Giselle all kinds of questions. I wondered if when mothers and daughters got together, if the women asked each other how their husbands performed and if they were hung, but I was not worried. I know I would not discuss with Nigel about my driving his daughter insanely wild with multiple orgasms during sex, so I let that thought vanish with the wonderful aroma of Queenie's heavenly cuisine awaiting our arrival.

We dined and as before, Giselle went off into the kitchen to tell Momma all her secrets. As Nigel could not keep his eyes open for lack of sleep, he crashed in a big leather recliner with the newspaper over his face. The paper rose and fell with each exhausted breath he took. I watched the news with the sound turned down and heard giggles coming from the women in the kitchen.

There was an "Oh no!" from Queenie. I think Giselle was telling her about my stint wearing her underwear and trapped outside our hotel room. Now that was funny. It sure cured my drinking ever again.

When he suddenly snorted loudly and pitched off the newspapers upon his face, Nigel apologized. He was so beat, he said. His team had been beating the bush to no avail and Giselle and I had brought some good results in no time at all. Then Giselle came in with Queenie.

"Daddy, did Jerry tell you of our discussion with the university's head math instructor, Professor Grebe? He was the deceased's mentor at the university. He is a real kook, Daddy. We went to his house while you were at the scene and he acted so queerly. He said Dorr was a misfit and he suspected he did the serial killings. He lives in this big Victorian, dungeon-like home."

"I think all those guys are nuts…and they're teaching our children, too. You know, birds of a feather, '**flock together**'," we all finished his words together in harmony, then laughed.

"Daddy, Jerry has a plan. We are technically still on our honeymoon and Jerry does not have to be back until the twelfth. He suggests that he and I rent, with the department picking up the tab, of course, a house that is for sale right in eyesight of the professor's home."

"It might be just too expensive; I don't know…sounds good," Nigel hinted.

"Tell the higher-ups how much money they will save if they aren't posting overtime. We'll work for almost free, except paying the rent part."

"I'll run that by them. They give me fits because it's providence money…just look at my old squad with over two hundred thousand miles on it I have to drive. I wrecked it hoping to get a new one and they fixed the damn thing!"

"Oh, the moose was on purpose, huh?" I chuckled.

"No, son, it was truly an accident. Looks like it's going to be two-on-one from here on out, doesn't it?" he said with a big grin.

"Why not spend the night? That way we won't loose contact again with each other," Queenie suggested.

"Sorry, if Rita is out there somewhere she might call my home phone. My cell was dead and I could not be reached. There just might be a call back number or something on a voice mail she left. Say…did Giselle mention the huge mulie that she shot at my parents' farm? It might be one of those record-breakers in South Dakota."

"Really, well how about that, Mother?" Nigel sounded out.

"Giselle says Jerry's mother can really cook…maybe just as good as me," she sighed.

"Hey, we have to go. I'll call if anything pops up."

Queenie shouted laughing, "I bet you will!" then put her hand over her mouth embarrassed.

"Mother! We're supposed to act like ladies…keep those big secrets about privates, I, mean, private," Giselle stuttered and made Queenie start yelping in laughter. Then we all did, at my expense, I think. We left feeling very jovial.

Giselle and I started unpacking and discussing our plans of how we were going to spy upon that professor. I checked the phone logs on both the cellular and voice mail, nothing from Rita. That saddened me.

Giselle and I planned that after Nigel's superiors approved our covert operation, we might just move there anyway. It was a very nice home, which had been sitting vacant for nine months and the previous owner was a former discharged teacher. He was in need of the sale, so he was willing to listen to our offer.

We enjoyed each other's company on treks around the college campus just to get the feel of how it might be to live there. College towns were fun, we found out. There was always something entertaining going on for the students. We decided it was a good location for both of us.

CHAPTER 18

Bureaucracy hinders the long arm of the law sometimes. In our case, it took almost a week to find out that Nigel's bosses refused our offer. We were so certain renting that house near Professor Grebe's mansion would eventually lead us to finding Rita that we decided to spend some of Giselle's Reno cash. Giselle had already contacted the realtor who had it for showing and we met Phyllis, the real estate salesperson there. We planned our rendezvous showing, during Professor Grebe's instruction periods, so as not to draw his suspicion.

Our faith of finding Rita alive was dwindling, according to statistics. Nevertheless, being able to watch his home and sometimes his movement was too great of an opportunity to pass. We leased the home anyway, on a three-month lease, at $2000 per month with an option to purchase. We liked the home, but maybe did not like the neighbors as much. It seemed there were more neighbors around like Professor Grebe living in that community. We moved into the home in the middle of the night, which caused our next-door neighbor to summon the police. One officer responding was Officer Jim Halihan.

"Giselle, what's going on?" he said, with his gun drawn. "We received a call there were burglars in this house," he continued while returning his pistol to its holster.

"Jim, I need a favor. We are unofficially code 213 and you need to tell everyone interested that everything's fine. Here are the papers, we leased this."

"Code 213, huh? I best get out of here, gotcha!" he turned, raised up his portable radio and told other officers responding it was a false alarm. He left immediately.

"Code 213, eh? That must mean covert, like undercover stuff. Well, let us begin that part about under the covers stuff. I like that idea," I told my gorgeous wife.

"The bed's not even here yet, just the mattress covered up with boxes of clothes," Giselle told me.

"We have a couch, don't we? Lay down, baby, I think I love ya," I said jokingly, but Giselle seemingly took it the wrong way.

"What? That was crude! You can go sleep in the upstairs tub. Never ever call me baby like that again," she commanded.

Giselle got her personal pillows and blankets from a packing box, put down a sheet, and then curled up on the couch under the covers.

Reluctantly, I believed her, and my heart was broken. How could she not forgive me? It was only a pun. I grabbed my bed-things from a box and began to ascend the staircase. I heard Giselle begin sobbing, so quickly, I turned around to go to her. She had covered her head, so I eased the blanket down. She had this big, shit-eatin' grin and was about to burst into laughter.

"Come to momma, baby," Giselle jested. It was her joke now.

I eased down on her nakedness and asked whispering why she did that.

"Mom says I have to be coy and make you fight for it to keep you interested and the marriage going," she explained, allowing me her secret.

"Never, never…you'll never have to do that unless you really don't want me. Giselle, I will never stop loving you or wanting your love, never."

Giselle opened her arms and in our nearly vacant house, we made passionate love for hours.

"Did you call in to get the water and electric turned on?" I asked.

"No, didn't you?" she said, trying to clean up the aftermath mess of two humongous orgasms, and an almost third one.

Giselle was inventive, took a water bottle up to the upstairs john, and cleaned up. She came down motioning for me and whispered, "Come up here!"

I followed her up to our bedroom and we peeked out of our curtainless window. There was a party going on at the professor's and they were not old fogies. The noise was loud when the front door opened and we could see scantily dressed girls dancing in his rec room.

A kid came out and upchucked on the bushes. Then the professor came out behind him and scolded him, then sent him packing. He began walking towards us, so we watched as he staggered our way. He then turned himself and headed into our next-door neighbor's driveway. We had never met any of them but apparently he was the neighbor kid, locked out, and rang the doorbell hard.

Giselle had gone to the other window.

"Oh my God, look at this," she whispered.

Through that curtain less window, we could see a man and a woman, naked on a bed, who we supposed were our neighbors. They were locked up in copulation. He was on top of her, pounding her, and she was yelling out, holding the bars of their violently rocking brass bed. Though we could not hear her moans, we could hear the doorbell that the kid was pounding on in aggravation. Suddenly, the man must have heard the doorbell and rose up off her, exposing both of them.

Reading the expletive from his lips, I recognized, "Oh shit, it's our kid!" I thought.

He scurried to get his clothes gathered and she a robe. He kissed her quickly and exited the window, butt-naked. That window was above their rec room and it sloped gently to being only a short jump off onto the backyard grass. He leaped off, rolling upon the ground. He must have lost something because a shiny metal object remained behind as he fled.

"Think we should be watching?" I asked Giselle after the fact.

"The eyes cannot trespass, if you have a right to be where you're standing," Giselle quipped, as she opened the window to watch where the guy was headed. "He should have closed the curtains," she concluded.

"Adultery is illegal though," I mentioned to Giselle.

We both watched, giggling, as the man ran across the backyard, desperately trying to put on his underpants and shirt, and then stopped in the alleyway to put on his long pants and shoes. He took off running once again.

"He must be a jogger, too," she said, noticing his Nike iridescent glowing stripes on the sides of his shoes.

"Maybe I misinterpreted his lips, he might have said, 'Oh shit, it's your husband!' because he sure was scared. Either way he was a hoser."

From the open window, we could hear the drunken kid curse his mother as a whore, when she finally let him inside. Then he collapsed and passed out on the floor. She lit a cigarette and just left him. We saw her climb up stairs and peek out a window overlooking her backyard, then close the window and curtain. She turned off the bedroom light and it was then dark. We went back to watching the old professor and his party.

One by one, college-age kids left Grebe's front door. We saw smoke and noticed a big bong and its hoses passed among the willing takers in the circle they formed to share the big puff. Then, we saw the old professor get touchy-feely with one of the co-eds who looked out of it. He took her breasts in his hands and fondled her in her dazed condition. Then, he encouraged everyone to go home, except the girl on the couch, who had now passed out.

"We cannot let this happen," Giselle said when we saw him pick her up and carry her to the upstairs bedroom. He was going to molest her.

"How can we stop him without blowing our cover?" I asked.

The girl's luck was good and so was ours. The drunken kid that the professor expelled from his party, had awakened, crawled out the front door, and staggered over to the professor's entrance. He desperately tried to go back in. The door remained locked; even kicking it did not open it. We watched as he began pounding on the doorbell of the professor's front door and began cussing loudly just as he had at his own home.

Soon the professor came to the door and hollered vehemently at the young man. The young man belted the professor square in the puss and we soon saw them tumbling around on the front yard's grass. Each was at the throat of the other and I thought the kid had the upper hand when sirens sounded out.

Someone may have called the cops, because Officer Halihan returned and arrested them both for disorderly conduct, resisting arrest, and assaulting an officer when the professor took a poke at Jim. Jim handled the situation and had them both cuffed and in the rear of his squad car in a matter of minutes. I did not see anyone go back and lock the door.

It was a miracle. The girl finally came out alone and left, rather dazed. She was walking and not driving, but Giselle ran to our Tahoe, caught up with the girl, and picked her up.

My girl had the makings of a real cop…well; I guess she really was if she carried a badge and a gun. I suppose a longer engagement might have revealed more about her, but I liked everything about her anyway. Nevertheless, I was alone for an hour, until I heard the garage door opening. Giselle came in with quite a load of hearsay evidence.

Under the influence, the girl admitted to Giselle that she had screwed the old professor that semester before for good grades. He was so unbearable to her when sober that she willingly smoked dope to become numb, which allowed him to do his will with her without her gagging. Other girls had followed her lead many times for years.

She said he had parties for his failing students, posted on his bulletin board, once or twice a semester, masquerading pot parties and orgies for tutoring. Often there was group sex, she told Giselle.

When asked if she knew any of the co-eds who were found murdered, she said, "Sure!" She knew Alice Farthing, a girl murdered several years ago who was just a high school student taking advanced math for pre-college credits during summer courses at the university. I had no info on her. The girl was one of the first slain.

Giselle hauled her little ass to DETOX, the drug rehabilitation system, run by the providence, and left her there. She also called Nigel and told him to get a search warrant for the professor's house ASAP. Then she called Jim Halihan and told him to get an extra set of prints and hold the bastard as long as he could, so she could complete a search warrant. She knew we had seventy-two hours, unless he got a sharp attorney. He most likely had done that when processed in the jail.

"What a nice piece of work that was," I told Giselle when we lay back down.

"I think that the girls who entered there and resisted, or changed their minds not to have sex with him, met their fate inside that house. What animal could be worse than the one we just witnessed? He might have perpetrated all those murders," she surmised.

"What about our neighbor's drunken kid? You think he will talk, since he seems to be an invitee to his home. He must have been there before; he lives so close. He might be involved, also…think?" I questioned.

"Later, maybe…we might find out… he was in this somehow," Giselle spoke getting very slow and incoherent.

She was very tired, so I massaged her back and feet, which felt good to her, she whispered. She kissed me, right before she fell asleep in my arms. We slept together on the big couch.

I heard pans clanging and cabinet doors slamming. I looked at my watch and it was seven. I looked toward the noise and there was Giselle putting away our pots and pans. She was dressed in her jogging attire.

"Where are you going, dear?" I asked.

"I have to jog. It's late, but I still might see something, or meet someone in the neighborhood to help us. There are many joggers out there right now, probably other teachers. Besides, I need to hit that confectionary I saw up the street last night and get us some grub. Like Fruit Loops?"

"Really, I'm an eggs and bacon man, but oatmeal will do, please."

Giselle gave me a kiss, and then out the door she ran. I got up and showered.

While in the kitchen, I noticed the female neighbor leaving in her car. I thought about that shiny object left in the grass by her lover, so I went to the back and looked across the fence into her backyard. I spotted the object, checked around to see if anyone was looking, then hopped over, and snatched up the object. A pin stuck my palm and after I leaped back over to my side, I saw it was a police officer's badge.

Humm, that could be traced because upon it were numbers from the police department. I went back in and laid the badge on the kitchen table, just as a marked squad stopped in the alley behind the homes.

Obvious to me, it was the owner of the object for he was without a badge on his chest. He actually took out binoculars first to search for that brown badge, then gave up and left.

I heard the front door squeak and I saw my bride carrying a sack of groceries. She was red-faced and puffing somewhat.

"Hi, honey, it's me!" she shouted, then came into the kitchen. Immediately, as she set the bag down, she questioned the badge being there.

"I retrieved that out of our neighbor's yard after I saw her leave. Her lover that took off last night was a cop, I guess."

"That is a coincidence...I just met our promiscuous neighbor's husband, Mr. Bob Wheeler. He said he works for Pyrex and is a sales representative. He said he is gone a lot, we know that, huh? Nevertheless, he seemed like a nice person. I asked how he got along with the professor and he said he never sees him at all, unless he goes jogging early in the morning. Bob offered to run with me each morning that he is home. I guess he is married to a slut-whore, like their son called her, eh?"

"So its friendly neighbor Bob now, is it? What about this badge?" I asked feeling a bit jealous.

"Don't you dare get silly on me now. I only thought I might find out something from Bob. As far as this badge, whoever he is, I can see if Internal Investigations wants a piece of him. I will have to write a report and appear at his hearing though and he could sue us if he somehow proves it's not him."

"I could just give him a call and tell him I was going to castrate him if he even looked at my wife again, being Bob Wheeler, think?"

"Think you can be convincing? You can't threaten him, or you could go to the slammer, too, if he found out."

"How's this, Giss...'Hello! This is Bob Wheeler. I know you have been fucking my wife! I do not give a shit, but she has a contagious STD and you have to register with the providence health department, before your balls fall off'. How was that?" I sounded out in my deepest voice.

"It might work at that," Giselle said laughing at my antics. "When did you start calling me Giss? My grandmother started calling me that when I went through my terrible-twos," she explained.

"It just seemed like a very personal, warm, loving name, that's all."

"Let's eat, I'm starved!" Giss told me.

We still had no clue about Rita and I began to feel it was too late. Nigel called us during breakfast and told me he came armed with a warrant. His team was already inside, including the forensic personnel, and arrived in a marked plumber's van prior the dawn. He asked us not to come over as they had collected several boxes of physical evidence, which possibly could lead to the professor's involvement.

"Did your people see that goop on that curved sword? I bet that's the murder weapon."

"No, he must have used it for opening a coconut once and didn't clean it. I thought it was blood also, but it tested negative. I am afraid we don't have enough to keep him behind bars. What we need is a witness to come forward and testify against him. By the way, I need you to look at some of those photos with me, Jerry. There's a bunch of nude women who you might be able to ID."

"How many fathers-in-law would ask their new son-in-law to sit with them and look at nude pictures? You have to be the first, I bet," I said jesting.

"I suspect when you get as old as I am, you only hope none of them is anyone you know, eh?" he said wisely.

We arranged for Queenie and Nigel to come for supper and we pretended to be normal neighbors with guests parked in our driveway. Giselle fixed Nigel's favorite dish of lasagna supreme. I thought too much sour cream was used for my tastes, except when Giss mixed it with special spices in the only way Giss knew how; it was heavenly.

After showing my new in-laws our home, Nigel asked if we could use the dining room table to look at the pictures he had brought. I thought there were dozens and dozens, but something had changed. Some detective from another department identified several of the girls' pictures of murders from his venue some years ago, after Nigel sent out a fax sheet on the pictures. They were not even Nigel's responsibility. Nevertheless, he was assisting the other department with their case. Those pictures were everything Nigel had.

I began to look at the pictures, which were very old, and I could not identify any. Then I spotted something peculiar. Spread out naked, showing her all was a woman lying on top of a dark Mediterranean teakwood desk. There in the background was a statue of a monkey holding something white in his hand. It was not that clear, but I was certain that it was the exact statue in the professor's home of a monkey holding a human skull. It was the exact desk, also, that I saw in the professor's home.

"It definitely is, I think," I told Nigel. "Didn't you notice that while you were inside?"

"No, I was upstairs supervising the removal of the sheets off the beds for pubic hairs and DNA. I guess I did not catch that…it was all so extravagant inside we could have searched for days if we actually found any DNA or clothes that might have been identified. The professor's home is basically clean. This turns out to be all we have; few prints, no blood splatters, nothing but these few pictures. The murders took place up by Edmonton, not here."

"Isn't my identification of the desk and statue enough?"

"Did you? Look again…can you swear under oath that this is the exact same desk and that this is the exact same statue?"

"I guess so?"

"Guess so, just doesn't cut it. You have to be proof-positive. You cannot do that. Therefore, all we have are a new lead that once those women were on a desk like that and a statue like that was there, nothing else."

"Damn! I thought we were on the right trail. I failed trying to help Rita. I'll never forgive myself for her safety," I said feeling very dejected.

"Well, we left his place clean. He evidently had a party and he won't know we were inside unless a neighbor saw us and tells him. This guy's a creep and in my venue. I am going after his ass for his deviate behavior. I will nail his ass, I hope, sooner than later. Guys like him should be castrated," Nigel then complained, which reminded me of the badge I found.

"Say, did Giss tell you of our neighbor lady's tryst on her upstairs bed last night?"

"What?"

"We don't have all of our curtains up and Giss looked across into our neighbors' bedroom and they were screwing."

"So?"

"Their kid came from the professor's, drunk as a skunk, and when he rang the doorbell, the guy on top took off lickety-split out the bedroom window. He dropped this when he jumped off the roof," I said handing Nigel the badge.

"Let me have that. I will find out who this officer is. Humm," Nigel sighed.

We continued to watch the professor's house. We later learned he had made bond and returned home the next day, apparently unaware his home had been swept by Nigel and his department's forensics specialists. His lawyer got him off on lesser charges and probation. The university overlooked his misdeed, because of his long tenure. He remained a threat. I grew sick about Rita and it became difficult trying to sleep at nighttime.

Giss suddenly had used up her vacation time and had to return to work. She refused to quit at my request and that was just one of many things we never had time to discuss, because of our quick engagement and marriage. I submitted to her demand, though I made enough for us to live comfortably. Giss wanted to be near her dad and see he was well cared for at his office.

After Nigel told me the name of the police officer who belonged to the badge, I secretly called the jerk at his home and gave him the business.

"I'm sorry! I will never see her again, I promise," he pleaded, after I told him not only was she an AIDS carrier, but a stalker who had mental troubles with other men before and always called their wives. He was shook up. I left it at that.

I did not like being there by my lonesome, so I told Giss I was returning to work. After all the years I worked there at CMEN I had used only some of the extra vacation time for our honeymoon, which I had previously accrued to go hunting. I felt refreshed and invigorated to walk back into my office. I had not called in, nor had Eleanor needed me. She was running the whole show very handily.

"Hello, boss, got one in the hopper yet?" Eleanor quipped, surprising me with her overly forward wit.

"Nope, still happily practicing all I can," I shot back. "Well, how are things going on the home front?" I asked not finding any letters to open and review on my desk.

"Shit hit the fan. Old Lady Upshaw is in and Freddie is on the way out by divorce. He will not fight it because she has the evidence. You are the new big boss, says the missus, if you ever return from where you were on your honeymoon. I did not tell her, mind you. She advised me to have you call her when you arrived. Good luck, kiddo," Eleanor spoke with over enthusiasm.

I stared at Eleanor and wondered where in the hell she came from. I knew she was very efficient, but her off-color manner was a sailor's delight. I was unsure she was sane, maybe she was on drugs or something. She typed on that keyboard at terrific speed and accuracy. I guess protocol was not part of the curriculum at her business college. I just did not know.

"May I please make a request? Please do not curse in front of me. I'm a holy man who forbids those words used in my presence. See to it you take them home with you, Miss Bigglebottom," I directed.

"The proper word is cuss and I heard you say things worse than that, and I was only here one day. Therefore, you gotta be joking that you're a holy man. So, I'll curb my cussing, if you curb yours, boss," she told me with much assertion and seemingly aggravated.

"Eleanor…let's start over. I really appreciate you and how you have taken over…and as boss, ah, how much do you make?"

"I'm still temp, at fourteen-forty, boss."

"As your new big boss, as you say, and if Mrs. Upshaw promotes me, as you say, I'm promoting you to my former position as love ads columnist. I will get you a secretary and I hope she cusses, just as you do, to keep you company. I owe that to you for allowing me the opportunity to be with my lovely wife, mostly undisturbed, thanks to your resourcefulness. Got it?"

"Got it! Now get out of my office, go to yours, and call future Ms. Upshaw, before she comes back and has another conniption fit. Once was enough."

I was totally taken aback by her flippant attitude. I think the future Ms. Upshaw should have made Eleanor the big boss, instead of me. She had this special way of spinning what I said into rubbish, just like Freddie.

I said farewell to Eleanor and my office and told her I would call her, if and when, she could take my words seriously. I went to my new office and noticed there was no secretary for me either. I fumbled through Freddie's old files and found his home phone number. I hoped he would be there. I was not a back-stabber and did not take Eleanor's finality on my promotion either.

Mrs. Upshaw answered with a long agenda ready for me.

"Jerry, I'm placing you as the new supervisor in charge of CMEN operations. You have Freddie's position. He is out and does not give a damn; he is staying across the border in Mexico somewhere and does not intend to ever return. I am divorcing him incommunicado. He says you are the best qualified, so I will expect you to take over completely, as long as the checks come in, otherwise I sell the paper. I will monitor the operations. CMEN has always been a reputable paper, profitable, and discreet. I expect the same of you. You will be totally in charge, as I am finding a place away from here and will call you only if necessary. You might even consider buying this business from me later. I think I have covered everything. Keep a steady hand on the business for me, Jerry, and you can stay there as long as you like. Anything you need?"

"Yes, I'll need your authority to pay the employees and hire and fire those who deserve promotion or dismissal."

"I'm sending Ed Harmon, my attorney, over with the proper papers this afternoon that includes giving you power of attorney. I have always trusted you, Jerry. Do not let me down, please. Ed has everything set up as I requested. Give yourself an appropriate advance raise and put someone in your office…good enough? Bye now…good luck, Jerry."

In a matter of a few minutes, my entire working life took a huge spin. I was the big boss, as Eleanor said. I immediately sat down, called Eleanor, and told her she was now salaried at fifty grand and she should get a secretary. I left room for raises, as needed, since I was making $125,000. I told her to keep up the good work, but clean up her mouth. I hung up before she could insult me again.

I contacted a temp place, told them I had need to hire one fulltime secretary, and one for Eleanor Bigglebottom, our new love ads columnist. The manager was amazed at Eleanor's rapid advancement and assured me she was sending two very qualified women as efficient as Eleanor. I bit my lip and said that would be satisfactory.

"Miss Bigglebottom may decide whom she wants or rejects," I advised the woman.

I used the secretary's broadcast intercom system to summon all the department heads to my office. I met most of them for the very first time. I asked each to submit his or her ideas and requests as soon as possible. I also asked if anyone could give up his or her very efficient secretary, until mine showed up. I got no help there…so much for company unity.

Ed Harmon arrived and was surprised I had no secretary as he needed papers duplicated and thought he could do it here free, I guess. I then did the secretarial duties myself, and after a lengthy informational explanation, I signed my new contract for two hundred and fifty thousand Canadian dollars per year, which Claire had insisted. I took it all in stride, as I was the new big boss.

Ethel Head, my new secretary, arrived just at quitting time, huffing and puffing, for she had gotten lost and finally found the business. I sent her home and told her to return in the morning. My day had just been too full.

Then my mind went to poor Rita.

CHAPTER 19

My work soon became mundane, almost nil, and actually unneeded. There was nothing to do but read the papers, check their content and play free cell on my personal computer. In no time, Ethel Head had already begun to handle all my business here, referring quickly to company policy, which addressed questions from other department heads about procedures.

My day, usually just spent signing off on bills and payments, slowed further when Mrs. Head wanted my best signature written down for making a good rubber stamp, which she said would expedite everything. No wonder Freddie went on so many business trips. This place was getting to me very quickly just sitting around. I welcomed anyone who came through my door, including Eleanor complaining about something.

I did answer some supervisors' operational questions, which took only a yes or no. It was a comfortable job being 'big boss', but very boring. With all of the talented supervisors here, already in their positions, I had nothing to do that I could not handle over my new cellular, which was my best challenge. I had to learn all its operational techniques, texting, and features.

At the end of my second week of being in command, everything was running smoothly, even Eleanor had the love ads column humping with more ads than my best months. I was amazed at her new-blood columns, more in step with the now-crowd, which I really thought were inventive, and from a completely different viewpoint. Eleanor could have been anyone of those lonely hearts seeking friendship and romance, so she knew the futility of the dating scene, much better than I did. She was destined for success.

I wrote a little column and bid everyone adieu. Miss Eleanor Bigglebottom was now replacing Gerry Loveletter as Eleanor's Secrets. She was a hit.

Giselle and I celebrated my two-week-old promotion at Luigi's, but this time we did not order the wine, only Diet Pepsi. Luigi was his usual self and very flattering of my Giselle's beauty. We returned home after a wonderful meal and an evening of slow dancing to romantic violin playing. I could afford to tip much better now, and did so, hoping that when Giselle and I returned, everything and everyone; the food and special treatment would remain.

It felt good that I did not have to review another establishment's cuisine, now it was Eleanor's responsibility. In addition, with her skinny butt, she needed all the nourishment she could find, much more than I did.

We returned to our posh suburban neighborhood sometime after eleven. We noticed all the lights at Professor Grebe's mansion were lit up and he apparently had another party going on. His audacity, only superseded by his overbearing sexual desires, was driving his perverted behavior.

Our new, beautifully decorated home, fully furnished with elegant pieces arranged appropriately by Giselle's special sense of fashioning, beamed of her loving touch. This time we had curtains, but the professor's drapes remained closed tonight. We could only imagine what was going on in there, as young students came and went, one by one, some looking very inebriated, high, or both.

We both sat upstairs in our bedroom watching the professor's place; until Giselle and I could no longer stay awake. It was a Friday night and after two. Just as we fell asleep, we heard a gun shot from nearby. We heard our neighbor yell hysterically, "Oh my God, Brent, what have you done?"

I rushed to the curtain facing the Wheeler residence and saw Bob Wheeler bending over Cindy Wheeler's dead body, which lay sprawled out on the backyard. Apparently, their son had chased her out of the house with the gun. The backyard's security light was shining brightly on them all. The son stood nearby with a pistol in his hand, pointed down, looking wobbly and very drunk.

Giselle quickly started dressing but I forced her back into bed. I was afraid she would rush in on the scene and that drunken kid would shoot her. Instead, I dialed 911 and reported there were shots fired at 602 Benson Place, their address.

I kept my eye on the kid and his gun, until he quickly put the gun to his own head and pulled the trigger. I almost puked when his head exploded like a watermelon from that .357 magnum's discharge. He fell down limply, although his brains looked like hunks of bread scattered everywhere about the yard.

Bob began screaming desperately for someone's help, and I could see he was going into shock. I opened the window and told him I had called 911. Then I rushed down to his side with a blanket from our bedroom and tried to cover his shoulders from the cold, because he was still in his underwear as was Cindy.

I looked up and saw Giselle watching from our upstairs window. The sound of a lone siren broke over the ongoing loud music emitted from the Grebe mansion. They remained undisturbed by the shot. An EMT emergency unit responded to my 911 call.

I looked toward Bob and he had taken the cover off, which I had placed on him, and placed it over Cindy's dead body very slowly, as if he was just pulling her cover up to her chin, as in their bed, to keep her warm. Blood ran from her mouth and it was apparent she suffered major trauma from a direct blast into her chest.

Brent was awful looking and I held Bob away, until the paramedics took him. I told them I was a witness. One of the EMTs recognized me from way back on the night of Meredith Monroe's murder.

Then a police officer arrived looking very familiar. It was that same officer Giselle and I saw screwing Cindy that secretive night. He looked sick, and almost did not come forward. I took Bob over to the emergency unit with the help from the EMTs. We held Bob back when he suddenly did not want to leave his wife.

After Bob was in the emergency vehicle, I stood beside the officer and said, "Look what you have done."

He turned on me confused, said, "What?" and was very agitated.

"See that window up there. That, sir, is Officer David. We saw you screwing Cindy that night. The kid knew it also, when you jumped naked off their roof."

"That's slanderous and I'm going to press charges and sue your ass for that statement," he madly declared.

"Oh yeah…It's not slanderous if it's true. I found that badge you searched for the next day with your number on it. Did you miss it? The only thing you can be thankful for now is that Internal Investigations just lost their prime witnesses to the adultery charge I am sure they were investigating. Do your work, officer. You made this mess," I said vehemently wishing I could have poked him.

Then Jim Halihan suddenly turned up. I asked him if he ever slept and if he was tired of coming out here. He seemed confused.

"Didn't someone just call from around here on a drug overdose?"

"No, this is a homicide-suicide that I personally witnessed. Both parties are deceased."

"No, that's not a teenager overdosed. That is a gunshot. I heard that dispatch called earlier. This is a new dispatch, only moments ago."

Then Giselle hollered out from above to Jim, "Jim, there's trouble over at the professor's mansion! Better check that out!"

Jim left me there alone with a very disillusioned adulterous cop.

"Look, it's over and done with. You made a big mistake, bud, which only God will handle now. May I get you a cup of coffee, while you sit down and I'll explain everything I witnessed?"

He reluctantly followed me inside and Giselle vaguely knew him dressed in uniform, but he knew her and could not look her in the eye, as she poured out a fresh perked cup of black java.

"Thank you…thank you, both. I have made a terrible judgment with this whole thing…and my life. It was you that called my home, eh?" he accused respectfully, looking at me and I acknowledged with a nod yes.

"That wrecked my marriage, because I got scared and went ahead and told Becky, my wife, and she kicked me out. I deserve everything I get. This work is too much for me. You get to know the good and the bad things in life, I've learned…but the bad far outweighs the good and good cops have to steer their lives away from temptations.

"You have to know the dens of inequity, but resist their attractions. Women and money, they say, are the downfall of most officers. I'm another statistic, I guess. I wasn't an angel, I let Cindy use her feminine ways to lure me into her bedroom. It was exciting to sneak in and out when she called me that she was alone…until I lost that badge…it was worse than losing your gun. It had my number on it and it identified me. This is my last official duty call. I am headed in to headquarters and resigning. I can't take this any more," he began to whimper, then sighed, and took a deep breath to reorganize.

The officer completed what he wanted to tell us, and the report as the coroner knocked on our back door.

"Come in, Judd, it's not locked," Giselle yelled to him, and then took another cup from the kitchen cabinet.

She poured a cup for the coroner and introduced us. The cop left after telling the coroner he was submitting his full report at headquarters. I gave the coroner my statement and he asked my opinion of the death.

"It was plain and simple domestic violence. Giselle and I heard the shot shortly after two. I ran to the upstairs window and saw Brent Wheeler standing over his mother's body. Then he put the pistol to his own head…oh, man that was horrible. Bob went berserk, so I called 911 then went to help him. He did not know his wife was unfaithful. He took a cover off his shoulders I had given him and covered her up. She was already dead.

"The kid was a druggie and thought his mother was a whore. He could not tolerate her behavior, and probably felt his own was horrible, too, addicted to something. Now, they are both gone."

The coroner asked me to raise my right hand and swear to the truth, which I did.

"Giselle, will you sign here on the line, as an officer of the law to attest your husband gave this accurate report? I believe there is no reason now for an inquest. We have had just too many costly inquests, you know. My budget is overburdened. I will notify any relatives through my office. Thanks for the assistance, Jerry, and thanks for the coffee, Giselle. Good to see you both, bye now."

The coroner was a nice man and left the same way he came in, through the back door. The lights in the Wheeler home were still on, so Giselle and I did the neighborly thing and went over to lock it up and turn off the lights. I went upstairs when I heard loud music and noticed one room had a light on, but the door was padlocked. I started to leave it that way, but became curious when Giselle also ascended the stairs and saw the padlock.

"It's locked and the light is on," I told her.

Giselle, too, first thought to let it be, but recanted with, "I wonder if that's Brent's room...I bet it is. Someone doesn't want anyone in there."

She kneed the door hard. The screws came out and it popped open.

"What a mess!" Giselle exclaimed.

There, in plain view, were several pictures of a naked girl, tied up, with her mouth duct-taped shut. Upon close examination, we saw it was our Rita.

"My God, it's Rita!" I screamed out in horror.

"Let me see!" Giselle said, while jerking the picture from my hand. "That is her...I'm calling Daddy, now!"

"She's been missing for days...weeks...how could she still be alive?" I asked my police-minded-officer.

"That photo was taken by a cellular camera...see that date there... that's yesterday! Look at that background...it looks somewhat familiar. However, I cannot really say. Maybe Daddy will figure this out. Hurry, you stand-by, while I go to our house and call him...hurry!" Giselle screamed, as she stepped down the stairs quickly as if she was jogging.

The door slammed and I was alone. I tried to see anything of forensic worth to tell Nigel about later. I saw a girl's necklace, but I did not think it was Rita's.

In the partially opened desk drawer, I saw a ransom note addressed to CMEN and Mr. F. Upshaw, scribbled out in pencil. He wanted $25,000. I did not touch it. The clock radio was still playing hard rock, so I turned that crazy music off. It then became deathly quiet inside. I got the shivers when I heard strange noises in the house. It was dark downstairs, because we had turned all but the kitchen light off. I called out for Giselle to see if she had returned, but got no answer.

There I was in a stranger's house, listening to something that sounded a bit like my old upstairs apartment neighbors having sex.

I peeked out of the upstairs curtain and saw the party was still going on at the professor's mansion. I still heard that strange noise, as I descended the stairs, only it got a bit louder. I just could not pinpoint where it was coming from.

I searched all the rooms listening, but was confused, still, about that strange noise. Then, I saw a floor vent and it seemed to be coming from there. I kneeled down, put my ear to the vent, and listened. That noise was coming from the basement. There was no basement, and I did not know anyone in the suburbs that even wanted one, with Canada's tundra-like soils that were often unstable for foundations, much less basements.

I searched for any downstairs door, but could not find one, until I noticed a scuffing on the linoleum, inside a hall closet, which I found cracked open. I turned on the hallway light and tried to see inside if there was a trap door. I pulled out a mop bucket and some cleaning fluid bottles off the floor. Peculiarly, there was sawdust inside there on the linoleum. I pried it up using my fingernails and then removed the floor covering, which exposed a rough, hand-sawn trapdoor. It was pitch black down there and I could not see a thing in the pit, and then assumed it might just be a sump pump down there making that noise. A sickening stench arose from the pit, which caused me to back away.

I almost stopped my search, until I saw a hand mirror lying on the master bedroom's vanity. I got it and came back, tilting the mirror to shine a ray of the hall's light down into the opening.

I was horrified! Skeletal remains lay in a small dugout room with 2x4s bracing up plywood boards that were holding up the sidewalls. The small dungeon, hand dug out to just about ten feet square, was the scene of someone's demise. I knew that immediately, because the body had decayed, with rope still bound around the victim's wrists behind her back. The face was down and it was a woman's clothing, ripped and torn.

I called out to Giselle, but did not hear her response. That is when I heard another strange noise down in there; the stench overwhelmed me. However, I just had to see if it was my Rita lying there, and I quickly whispered a prayer it was not, as I eased down into the horrible pit.

It was so dark; I could not stand up straight without fear of hitting my head, until my eyes adjusted completely. I was about to regurgitate right there when I took a full breath, having held it too long without breathing. I suddenly made out the dead body's image and slowly tried to roll the head over with my foot to see the face. The hair looked just like Rita's. I was aghast and fell backwards, when the head rolled off the corpse and exposed a pus-oozing slime.

I unexpectedly felt another body, which seemed to be standing right behind me. Suddenly, it moved and kicked me. My heart went to my throat and I almost fainted, and frantically tried to dig my way up and out to get the hell out of there, but could not. I grabbed onto a support and it came loose. Dirt fell off the wall. I picked up the 2x4, and raised it up as a club to defend myself from whatever evil lurked in the darkness. I almost struck out blindly to protect myself.

"I'll kill you, you son-of-a-bitch!" I screamed out at the top of my voice.

I heard a whimper, and then suddenly realized it might be a live person, so I extended my hand out slowly into the darkness, seeking to feel any person. First, I felt cloth, and then ran my fingers up, slowly moving them like a human walked, carefully forward, and then I touched human skin.

I pulled back, but realized it was a warm body. I quickly reached out for more and I felt the bosoms of a woman. I eased up and could barely see a woman seated, bound to a chair by ropes and duck-taped completely around her entire head. Only a slither of an opening exposed the mouth area, so I used my finger to open it further. Air came out in a breath-like gasp.

The words she spoke were almost incoherent and very insulting, but the most joyous words I ever heard in my life.

"What...the hell...took...you so... damn long?" she managed to whisper through the hole, as she collapsed into my arms and became silent when I untied a knot that secured her to a heavy chair and set her free. It was my Rita and she was barely alive.

I screamed bloody murder then up the hole's opening, until Giselle and Nigel appeared above me, looking down on me in surprise. I told them I had found our girl and get the EMTs rolling back here pronto!

I eased my hands under Rita and could feel her feces and urine wetness. She smelled all right to me, because I knew that her bodily functions still worked, though she was left there to die in that hole, for how long I could not guess. Rita refused to give up her life willingly, because she was waiting for her boss. I tried to comfort her and held her next to me while kneeling on the ground.

Then an EMT slid in beside me and talked directly to a doctor, via his portable radio. Another came down and I was in their way, as they quickly gave her life supporting assistance, as only they knew how. I was so happy I cried like a baby for her. Then Nigel helped me up and hugged me. He knew how much it meant to me to find her. Giselle put her arms around me and whispered that Rita would be all right.

"She's in good hands now," Giselle whispered,

"Nigel, I know there's others down there, because I accidentally destroyed your forensics' search scene, by knocking off one corpse's head," I grimaced and shook in disgust. "I'm a little sick to my stomach and feel I might upchuck at any time."

Nigel quickly reached into his pants pocket and retrieved a piece of gum. Giselle quickly peeled off the wrapper and put it on my tongue.

"Damn! That's hotter than hell!" I yelled to both Giselle's and Nigel's amusement.

"Been using that gum for thirty years, son, never died from it yet, but it sure takes your mind off that smell, doesn't it?" he chuckled.

Rita had to be carefully lifted from the hole, because the EMTs thought she might have unseen spinal injuries. They had immediately started IVs and when she regained consciousness, they gave her liquid through a tube in her mouth.

We left Nigel when his forensic people crowded inside the hallway and started busting out more flooring to make room to lift Rita gently straight up out of that hole on a scoop-type stretcher. The emergency personnel had her bound tightly onto the scoop, with straps. EMTs had carefully removed all the tape around her head with alcohol, and we could see cuts and bruises there.

Rita, being fed intravenously, passed by Giselle and me on the scoop, and appeared to have gotten much more alert. As she passed, I touched her thin, boney hand, and told her we would see her at the hospital.

We followed Rita alongside the scoop, until the EMTs put her on a gurney and lifted her into the emergency vehicle. The emergency vehicle's run was silent because they had stabilized her condition.

Nigel wanted my report as soon as possible, but he told me to clean up first, because I stank. I told the detective I would as soon as possible. Giselle held me tightly all the way, even though I was filthy and smelled of human carrion. She knew I was very upset, spent, and needed her loving attention to ease my anxiety.

Giselle came inside my warm shower and we both held each other closely, not saying anything, gently, softly washing the other, as the warm spray trickled down upon us. It all had a soothing affect on me. I could not have been more overjoyed, by finally finding Rita, I told Giselle. She had joyous news for me also.

Then Giselle said she had seen her gynecologist and was with child. I had knocked her up and soon there would be midnight runs to that small confectionery up the street for pickles and ice cream, she enlightened me. I hugged her in great surprise and I told her I was thrilled and relieved.

"All this practice we were doing while making this baby was making me a tired old man," I jested. "Hope this kid looks like you. Boy or girl?"

"Don't know yet, but I decided to schedule a sonogram."

"Good, I want to know in advance," I told her.

We kissed, and yes, we kissed again, then again, and soon found ourselves dripping wet upon our bed sheets in heated passion.

"Better get to it…Daddy's coming over after he's finished…you better get it while you can, and I can enjoy it, too. Fourteen more is a lot of down time for sex. You sure you want fifteen?"

"Better see if this kid has my disposition, first. If he, or she, is as impetuous as you are, we'll both have our hands full with just two…a boy for me and a girl for you for certain," I told my wife who was about to enter orgasm.

"Shut up and finish your homework, buster. I'm feeling good, better than ever…I don't have to worry about you knocking me up anymore."

Then her vagina tightened and she drew me to her in steaming lust. She began sucking on my neck and nibbling my ear, whispering repeatedly to me how much she loved me, begged me sighing, pleading for me not to stop. She was really enjoying our union this time. She gave me as much pleasure though, maybe more, as I looked into her wild eyes and forgot all my anxiety of the day. My sweat dripped down on her and we used it to slide together. We both came together again, again, and again…it was 'Heaven on Earth' for twenty minutes with multiple explosions. Then we heard Nigel calling.

"You guys going to take till afternoon?"

"There are ready-made ham sandwiches in the fridge, Daddy, make yourself at home," she yelled down to him.

We unlocked on the bed quietly and I realized she had blown away my cares. Our minds were set free at that special moment. Then as Giselle and I cleaned up and then dressed, I flipped on the TV.

"We have breaking news from Calgary Memorial Hospital…a longtime missing, Calgary woman, feared dead, was delivered there by emergency rescue workers just moments ago. Foul play was suspected before she was found alive this morning after a hideous domestic murder-suicide slaying. The severely emaciated woman had been held, tied up in bondage, and duct-taped, left for dead in a makeshift cave, dug deep beneath a home in one of the more prestigious neighborhoods today, according to authorities.

"Rita Tory, age twenty-one, was discovered by an employee of our CMEN Newspaper, Jerry David, chief editor. Mr. David, formally known in his column as Gerry Loveletter was doing a never-ending search for Tory and accidentally stumbled on her whereabouts next door to his own home and realized only after he removed the tape from her head that she was his kidnapped secretary…much more to follow of this unbelievable event on the late news hour as developments unfold."

"I wish my reporters could write like he speaks," I told Giselle. "He got it right the first time."

"Oh, that's old Ozzie Schulte…he was an information officer and former traffic cop from our division for ten years…he liked report writing better than giving tickets. Eventually, he got his chance and took it, that's all," Giselle told me, as we quickly dressed, prepared to go down to talk to Nigel.

Nigel called upstairs again that he was waiting for us, but was on the phone.

"Coming, Daddy!" Giselle called out.

There was Nigel with mayonnaise on his chops, seated at our kitchen table, sipping a glass of milk, and gobbling down a sandwich, which Giselle had previously made for me. He had his cellular phone up to his ear in his one hand listening, and a pencil working swiftly in the other. His report tablet was out on the table ready to take my statement. I learned he had already jotted down a terrific amount of what Rita was able to tell a police interviewer.

Nigel told us first that he was going to fill us in on what he found out, so he could review and remember what he wrote down. His narrative was what the other detective told him, and used as a time-line for his final report. I noticed his writing was terrible as I got a cup of coffee and sat down next to him at the table.

"Yes, thank you, Deb," he spoke over his cellular, and then folded the cellular and put it away. "Good news, kids, on Rita Tory...she has no broken bones. However, she is very emaciated and dehydrated. She would have died in twenty-four hours, the doctor told Deb. Dreadfully, she has spent almost the entire time kidnapped, tied up, down in that hole where you found her. If that homicide-suicide had not occurred, who would ever have looked there in a hundred years?

"Anyway, Rita reported she was repeatedly raped and sodomized by several different men; therefore, Deb said a birth termination will be performed upon Rita when she is fit. According to tests, Rita is a few weeks pregnant. She will recover fully, thankfully, and is resting now, gaining her strength back, hour by hour, but she requests no visitors, or is not allowed any. She can tell us a lot once her mind is clear. She's under medication.

"According to her statement, so far, Rita witnessed others being murdered, slaughtered, is more like she described them, Deb said, but dead is dead...and then buried, all by Brent Wheeler and once or twice by two other unknown men of different ages...surprisingly, she said the other burials were not the bodies in the Wheeler pit. As I mentioned, she was bound and blindfolded...maybe those times she peeked... makes me wonder if we missed a sub cave at the Dorr place.

"Anyway, there's other bodies buried somewhere, someplace. Who knows, we might never know where, since two of the perpetrators are out of the picture.

"She says Rita can ID both, but, doesn't know either's name. I don't know if I got that straight, or not, my scribbling…I can't make it out…anyway Rita told our female detective, Debra Brantley, she thought she heard one man refer to the other as 'preacher' or 'father'.

"The other person was a longhaired creep. She felt his locks on her bare chest when he molested her…it was not Benjamin Dorr though; she knew his penis size was different from the other guys from before… sorry, that's a fact we have to establish when we catch a creep and his defense attorney asks the victim about that in court. Giselle knows.

"Many a short-petered man has gotten off when the woman says a man raped her with a humongous penis. We even had one guy get up and show his penis size to the jury."

"Must have been a hung jury, huh?" I quipped smiling, but Nigel wasn't impressed.

"I bet the old guy is your neighbor, Professor Grebe, and I am finally going to nail him," Nigel then continued. "Rita was kept bound-up in another place also, at first. Wheeler moved her around from place to place blindfolded and bound up in the back of a big SUV. He liked her a lot and told her he loved her often during sexual intercourse. The other person came to her at someone's house and raped her several times. I bet that was at Dorr's house and his SUV. DNA tests on his SUV still have not returned yet. It might take six weeks."

"My main questions are…how did Bob and Cindy Wheeler not know this was going on?" Nigel theorized. "And, who is the other old guy Rita saw. I guess we can ID him using a picture of the professor."

I, too, wondered how either parent did not know what their son was doing. Maybe they did. Maybe Bob was one of those other people. However, Bob was half-bald, Rita said the rapist had locks…humm…I had to think. They were all very weird people. I was not ready to say, "Case closed", neither was Nigel.

I was sick for Rita and I knew she was going to need psychiatric assistance as weeks passed to help her through this. Rita was an overly strong-willed being and she fought all the way.

Several weeks later at his home, Nigel told us he learned Rita had dug her fingernails deep into the face and back of one man during intercourse with him. Dorr had those types of marks on him at the time of his autopsy.

Countless numbers of DNA evidence had surfaced, including the IDs of five females whose sexually assaulted bodies were dug up; all extricated from the Wheeler pit. Some of them had been listed as missing over fifteen years ago. An additional three more were discovered on a second body search by police cadaver dogs, thanks to finding that Wheeler house pit.

Nevertheless, how, I wondered, did Brent do all this by himself? He wasn't mature enough to rape someone fifteen years ago, at nine years old.

CHAPTER 20

We wanted to move out now and find a place to raise our forthcoming son. Yes, an afternoon's visit to the hospital to get Giselle's sonogram and our first allowed visit to Rita was a joyous reunion. Rita looked great, but not scheduled to be released. I told her I had kept her position open.

After several more weeks of psychiatric evaluations and counseling, Rita remained there beyond expectations for additional hospital time to heal her emotional hate; each day with psychologist's help, she revealed more information.

Daily, the words of our skinny little secretary who was still laid-up in the hospital for many weeks became front-page news, especially in the CMEN. Although most police deduced finally, that the serial murderers had killed themselves, case closed, and everyone was safe. Most believed that theory, except Detective-sergeant Nigel Gray and me. He had not closed his mind for a second and was constantly searching for evidence and that unknown older man. So was I.

On a Sunday drive in the early spring, Giselle and I took a trip up to Red Deer to put flowers on Jill Burner's grave. It was a nice ride into the country and a warm Pacific wind had blown in. Giselle was showing and we needed a permanent place to settle down. When we drove up the lane, Giselle immediately got excited.

"Oh, look at this place!" she shouted. "Look…there's a for sale sign in the yard."

Then she had that look on her face that she wanted it. She got out of the car and ran up to a window to peek in. Then she ran to another and another, until she walked up on top of the house covered with grass. From the top of the roof, she told me that the inside was wonderful.

"I want it, honey. Who could have thought of a more picturesque setting and unique home than this? It is a showplace…it took a lot of planning, and it has the biggest fireplace I have ever seen."

My mind and heart went back to the only time that I was inside there and I felt somewhat guilty remembering. I did not know Giselle then, even though I loved her from afar as a girl on my TV screen. However, Giselle was insistent that this was her choice. We walked the hill to Jill's grave and I noticed it needed mowing. As I put the flowers on her grave, Giselle asked me how long I knew her.

"It's funny you ask that. I saw her everyday at the office for years, but never knew her, really, until I became involved in Meredith Monroe and the others started happening and your dad came to see me for the first time at my apartment. Jill had delivered the love ads that Nigel wanted the night before to my apartment and got snowed-in there.

"Jill absolutely slept in my bed and I on the couch. Nigel came very early…he thought she was my girlfriend. No, she was my friend…she died of cancer in less than a month afterward. I saw her for several years but only got to really know her in that one day.

"There is her famous Turner next to her. He was a hockey pro. That night she stayed over, she talked for hours about her love for him. I hope if I go before you, you'll be as loyal as she was to him and speak of me the way she spoke of Turner," I said, as we then headed back to look once more around the outside of the underground house.

There was no more searching. Giselle took a leave of absence from the department and one day called the realtor and toured the house. She called me from there that she had put an escrow down on it and headed to our banker to get the loan money. The price was $300,000. I was pleased, because six weeks later, after Giselle was really getting fat, she gave birth to our son Nigel Joseph David, named so after his grandfathers.

He had a home…and when he arrived, I immediately nicknamed him, Nidjo, because if you said both Nigel and Joe quickly, it came out Nidjo when I tried it. Thus, the poor little guy could blame me twenty years later for nicknaming him that way.

One afternoon, while at my office with practically nothing to do, I read of the newest police academy's cadet class. I buzzed through the list of names and was simply amazed to find one 'Rita Marie Tory' on that list. I was so surprised I called Giselle at home.

"Oh, I guess I forgot…sorry, honey, I forgot to mention it…she had asked Daddy for a reference soon after she was released from the hospital. I think she was fully herself."

"I thought after she said she wasn't returning here that she was headed out to live with relatives…I forget where she said she lived with her brothers…hummm…I still don't have a secretary…now Ethel quit."

"Buster, you don't need a secretary. What you need it a good jog with me in the mornings. I got my cheerleader's body and weight back. Practice starts in two weeks. Junior is just waiting to be with poppa," she reminded me of my willingness to take care of my Nidjo, while she danced and practiced for the Outriders team.

It was my pre-nuptial promise to let her continue being a cheerleader as long as she could make the team. Giselle liked the camaraderie and I liked her waistline…among her other fine attributes.

Then one afternoon while I was reviewing…snoozing, beneath the morning's paper, someone knocked upon my door. It was Officer Tory in her uniform and I was delighted to see her. I almost did not recognize her all muscled-up and wearing her hat. Nevertheless, that pretty smile of hers gave her away.

"Hi, boss…what's up?" she greeted me.

After the initial shock, I hugged her anyway. She saw my coffeemaker was empty so she set about making a fresh pot as we talked. I learned she had our newspaper on her beat and she was anxious to test out for detective. She wanted to be like Nigel and that made me very happy, but concerned. She had gone through such a horrible experience, but now was going to reclaim her dignity, she told me, by finding the other man that no police departments, including Nigel, could find.

We finally began discussing the case. I was telling Rita about Giselle and my encounter with Professor Grebe. I related that I saw a sword on his wall with rust on the blade, thinking it was the murder weapon. However, after forensics checked it out, the off-color turned out to be only coconut grit.

It was right then that I recalled something important, which I had forgotten. I then told Rita of the peculiar monkey statue in the professor's home. She had never seen anything like that, but told me they murdered the girls with what she recognized as a super-sharp fish-cleaning fillet knife.

"Yes, but now I remember," I told Rita. "The professor told me he got that statue from his colleague, ah…what was his name? It was a funny name…humm…I remember, Dingle! Professor Dingle gave that to him. Oh why didn't I think of that before?"

"Tell me…what's on your mind…you look dazed, boss," a worried Officer Rita spoke.

"Birds of a feather stick together. Remember that, always," I told her. "Maybe this Dingle is your man. Don't do anything until I talk with Nigel," I advised.

"Oh, I can't anyway. I'm on probation for a year and I'm supposed to stay clear of investigations, until I've got the traffic code and felony codes understood out on the road…seasoned is what they meant. Sounds good to me…I have to get out of here now, didn't even get your coffee poured, sorry, boss."

"Keep in touch, Rita. I am so proud of you…I may need you though, ha! I still do not have as good of secretary as you to fill your vacancy. Think you could part time?" I jested.

"Hey, boss, I hate to tell you, but I changed my life plan. I can eventually help more where I am. That is why I joined the force. I will be back, and yes, we can work on this secretly…alone, if we have to."

Then I tried to be serious.

"Rita, I can never give up knowing what those monsters did to you and the others. I know there must be others involved, we just have not yet located their dens…you must not desist either…keep this investigation alive. The investigative crew is back to just one man, Nigel Gray. We have to give him a hand and completely rid this community of the carrion on human life they deal out.

"We'll have to solve this thing ourselves, together, before some other girl ends up like you did. It seems over, but I do not think so. Maybe some of the wheels fell off this terrible machine of death, but this past kind of macabre has somehow rejuvenated themselves over time, even after many years' hiatus. Did you hear the bodies found in the Wheeler pit dated back fifteen years? Those girls were just listed as missing...that's it! No one came for them. I fear it will culture back here and the next time it will be our children in one of those pits. I am sorry if this rekindles your bad thoughts...I'm sorry...I feel obsessed, also very helpless, thinking this is not over, just in limbo," I told her.

"I know, boss. Nigel told me how you were dedicated to helping find me. I might have gone through a lot, but I know I would have been dead without you, thanks," Rita said, kissing my cheek. "Got to go. Rick, my senior partner is waiting for me outside in the squad, see ya later, boss!"

I had renewed spirits about remembering the name of that man Grebe said gave him that statue. So many months had gone by, which might have involved him, too, and I just thought of this now, darn. I remembered Nigel was in Edmonton on police business, so I called my beautiful mother-in-law.

"Duh!" I told myself aloud, while dialing up Queenie to see if she and Nigel were free to dine at Luigi's Friday night. I planned to ask for his advice how to go about checking on this Dingle suspect, but did not want to spoil his meal.

Queenie answered the phone and she said Nigel was expected home by five, and they both needed a night out. I told her I would arrange for us all to dine at Luigi's at seven. Giselle, Nidjo, and I would meet them there. Queenie was delighted.

I had a special thought for my wife and dining at Luigi's, which always acted as an aphrodisiac for Giselle, would prepare her for what was on my mind. Luigi's environment always made her very affectionate afterwards. Giselle's regained sexy figure was bothering me, I thought of her constantly, even as she sometimes bent over the crib to pick up junior. I planned to give him a sister after CFL football season was finished.

I arrived home early at 4 p.m. and my lovely wife was watching "As the World Turns", just one of her 'soapies' she enjoyed when Nidjo slept.

"Hi, honey, how was your day?" Giselle greeted me in her usual way with a big smile, a kiss, and a long hug. It was why I liked coming home most. Then she took me to see Nidjo who was sleeping soundly.

"Guess what, sweetheart? I am feeling as if I will just die, if I cannot eat some of Luigi's wonderful spaghetti. How about you? I called Queenie and she and your dad will meet us at seven there, okay?"

"What about our son?"

"We'll take him along."

"Not a good idea, I'm afraid he would wake up and scream bloody murder and ruin everyone's meal. He will not eat spaghetti; remember…he is on my milk. You wouldn't like me to flop one out in the restaurant, now would you?" she giggled. "However, I know a very responsible person who would be willing to work cheap and can spend the night if she has to."

"Diana?" I seriously questioned, hoping she was not her choice.

"No, her name is Kim Casey, Jill Burner's sister. She just lives fifteen miles away. I met her first when I was at the realtor. She was the executor of Jill's estate and had to be there to accept our counter offer. Kim is a really, really nice person, single, and first grade teacher at Red Deer Elementary…might even be our son's teacher someday. I see her all the time at AG's grocery shopping and she said she loved children and sits babies a lot in the area. She might be booked, unless I call right away…it's Friday night and there are lots of hockey fans in need of sitters."

"Okay, good idea, babe, call her."

As luck would have it, Kim was free and anxious to sit for Nidjo. She would come at six, so Giselle and she could discuss Nidjo's needs. Giselle went inside the bathroom and I heard the breast-pump going. I wanted to watch, but Giselle already said I would think of her as a milk cow thereafter, so she refused me.

I showered, shaved off my five o'clock shadow slick, and put on my best tie and grey, pinstriped, sharkskin suit. I was simply smashing I told Giselle as she came in to get ready.

"Sweetheart...why not wear that low-cut, red, thin-strapped...you look simply smashingly sexy in that...remember our first date?"

"Yeah, I was trying to hook ya then, and I was too darn cold, and, yes, I got smashed, too. Nope, that went to the church charity. I have a new dress I've been saving to wear for you. I bought it just for this occasion," Giselle said with a twinkle in her eyes.

I had to stop and ask myself, "Is this our anniversary?...no!...is this her birthday?...no!...humm...what special date lingers here I've forgotten?"

I just let it ride, hoping I would some how come up with the answer.

Kim Casey was a mirror of her sister, Jill, but thirteen years Jill's junior, at thirty-three. She was very nice and I had to stop myself from calling her Jill. I was pleased she would be our son's sitter. We left Nidjo sleeping in his crib with Giselle's milking efforts in his bottle.

Mother's milk always provided Nidjo with lots of nourishment, but I kidded her she should try to give some chocolate milk occasionally. I had often seen wet spots on Giselle's tee shirts from breast leakage, just before she gave birth.

I left energized, very affectionate, longing to hold Giselle close while dancing, after seeing Giselle's newest dress she wore. It was a dark blue, almost bare shouldered, spaghetti strapped, low-cut creation, which I thought overly exposed all of her wonderful attributes. It was similar to the one I liked best, ha!

Her dark hair fell upon her shoulders. I did not want any other men's eyes wanting her, except mine. Nevertheless, I knew that would be futile. I dare not show my jealousy, because she warned me before. I would walk tall and evil eye any guy with a roving eye. I suppose I just had to be thankful she loved only me and enjoy her nearness.

Queenie and Nigel were at our table and Luigi's was practically empty. He came out and told us the Flames had an important game and he would have gone to the hockey game if he could have. It was the Canadian heritage, Luigi said.

We dined on Luigi's fine cuisine and danced some afterwards. Father and daughter danced and then Queenie became my partner. She was an elegant lady and if I squinted, I could visualize Giselle twenty years from now.

"Is there something in your eye, Jerry?" Queenie asked.

I was caught squinting at her and said, "Your beauty is blinding me, my dear, that's all."

I then tried holding her more tightly, which caused her to extend her arms to keep me distant. She appreciated the compliment, and politely winked.

During some enjoyable prattle and our after-dinner sherbet dessert, I hit Nigel with my new, forgotten information, which I had recalled about Professor Dingle being Professor Grebe's friend. Surprisingly, he was congenial to my trying to help him and was glad for the tip because his superiors were ready to close on the case, since he could not produce any more leads. Giselle listened intently to her father.

"I was by your old rental house," Nigel began. "It's still vacant. I talked to Phyllis, your realtor, and convinced her to give me a key. She said there weren't any lookers and if I should see her pull up with clients, just tell her in front of them that I was interested in putting a bid down. She would explain to them my being there as a potential prospect and I might help her make a sale. I haven't seen much. Bob Wheeler has been back once, and left the next afternoon. I am using infrared surveillance video equipment on both Grebe and Wheeler's homes from upstairs when I am not there at nights…seen nothing… except, old Grebe still jogs in the early morning at six."

I then told Nigel my plan.

"I was thinking of going to Dingle's class and sitting in on one of his lectures, so I could recognize him. However, the doors lock to outsiders; only students on time get inside, and no one after the hour begins. The big hall he lectures in seats three hundred. I do not have a lot of time that I can spend away from my office, but I have to tail him somehow."

"That's simple. It is time I get a few hours credit towards my masters," Giselle broke in. "It would work well, and there is a childcare facility right there on campus. In fact, the college girls that take care of the children might know something about Dingle. They get paid through the school as a form of employment. It's a wonderful thing for mothers, all the workers are screened before they are placed there by our own department. I know, because I usually get the application requests to check for criminal records. It is a law."

"We'll have to discuss this further, my dear. I want Nidjo in safe hands."

"You don't think I'd even suggest that if I didn't know it was safe for certain, would you?"

"Actually, I considered getting you a live-in house maid to eliminate some of the problems we'll have when you start back with the Outriders. I was thinking of a woman who can cook, clean and do diaper changes, better than I do, ha! There are going to be times when I just cannot sit Nidjo…then what?"

"Let's dance and talk about this at home."

"I can think of nothing better, my dear."

We all left Luigi's with Nigel's approval on my ideas. We were all going to sleep on the alternatives…not!

Giselle and I arrived home in a mutual amorous mood. After I saw how Nidjo was well cared for by Kim, I tipped her well. Kim was pleased and so were we when she departed for home at eleven.

"She did a great job," I told Giselle. "I should respect your opinion of people more. You have a gift for knowing people's true character."

"Does that mean you will trust my opinion of the girls that baby sit the children at the university? They do this one on one, with no other children to oversee, but their assigned child."

"We'll see…now I want to supervise the removal of that dress. I cannot stand it any longer. Tonight, my dear, you are, and always have been, the most beautiful woman in the world…I want you now," I said, dropping one thin strap off Giselle's shoulder, then kissing there.

Giselle became putty in my hands as we kissed our way onto the bed. She knew to relax and lay back, for I wanted to be in charge. Skillfully we maneuvered her dress off and I laid it across a chair. I dropped down on her and knew she demanded foreplay, so I undid the snaps of her bra and exposed her breasts, huge and round, still laden with nourishment, so I sampled their taste. It was warm and sweet.

I continued to lip-lock, my flickering tongue on her nipples, and then gently used my fingers to rub them as I walked my licking tongue down the middle of her six-pak abs. I became overanxious and quickly yanked her panties off. I nibbled around and then gouged her navel with my tongue, letting her feel the pressure to simulate a pounding penis searching for the harvest.

However, by then she pressed upon my head to go down to her clitoris. I lifted her legs up and over my shoulders and began to lick harder and harder, pulling back her vulvae and exposing the tip of her clit to the rough flicking of my tongue.

Giselle was hot and ready for passionate love. She always gave me much more than I deserved. She pushed me over and saw I was ready. My hard cock was throbbing and it needed no assistance, but she licked the sides and made me squirm. I pulled her to me and she lay on top of my cock, which she pushed and rolled upon, then eased off to lay on her back. When she spread, she was full of fire and wanted me then.

Giselle had grown into a matured woman after the baby. Her hips widened a bit accentuating her curvatures and she was more able to enjoy longer, hard-driving sex.

She was so fascinating, so sophisticated, so much more than the girl I worshiped before we married. She had become part of my spirit and soul and I loved her.

"You're enjoying this more tonight," I told Giselle, pumping her just the way she told me felt best. Her eyes had that wildness and she began to cling to me tighter and more tightly. She had been working out daily and her movement mirrored my thrusts.

"Uh, uh, uh, oh, oh, oh, Jer…rr…ry…uh, oh, you…are ..goo…o…ing to …be uh, oh, ah, fath…er…uh, uh, aga…in n n n uh, uh, uh, oh, oh God!"

She moaned in pleasure, disrupted and not very understandable. I worked her slow and deep, then fast, and then sunk it deep again, as she became sultry, groaning in pleasure, and rigid from her about to explode feeling of orgasm. She lurched, and then burst into hard gyrations using her hips to satisfy us both.

We held each other tightly, until the emotions of our sexual encounter subsided. We both breathed heavily and laughed together at our playful exuberance. We kissed, less sexually excited now, but in respect.

As my mind cleared, I realized that in her heat of madness Giselle had given me the news. The whispered words Giselle spoke just then really sank in…"What did you just tell me?"

"It's time to call that maid agency and get a good housekeeper. You are about to be a father of two," she told me. Giselle had missed her second period, and that was the special occasion.

Monday, the work temp people sent over four women to interview, who applied for our semi-permanent, baby-sitter/maid position offer of $25,000 plus room and board. Giselle was in charge of their interviews and selected a wonderful woman, a very hardworking German immigrant, who had much previous experience with children, she told Giselle.

Spinster frau, Virginia Cortner, who had gentle ways, was a beautiful woman in her early fifties. She had traversed the Atlantic as a baby with her parents aboard a steamship to come to the free world and stayed. A very smart woman, adept in home domestics, and a gourmet cook we later found out.

Her attributes were many. She was educated, intelligent, reverential, and trustworthy, her letter of reference read. Her German-accent-flavored voice was very pleasant, a bit bold, but very intelligent. Most of all, Nidjo took to her big bosoms like his mother's and easily fell asleep in her loving arms.

She was a perfect fit for our family and Giselle once again proved to be a very good judge of character. Virginia moved into our guest room that day and was thrilled that her room had a fridge and stove, plus a big screen television on satellite. She just loved our huge fireplace, which reminded her of her German home that her parents left behind.

"I will do my best," she told Giselle. "You are a wonderful little family and I will help you grow. This house is the most wonderful home where I have ever been employed. I feel the love inside here. I can see it in your furnishings, your son's face and yours," she told her with a bit of desperation.

Virginia was living out of her suitcase, because her former employer passed, and his spoiled and ungrateful children-heirs made no provisions for her after twenty-five years of service, raising not only those children, but also their longtime invalid father, after their mother had passed in a car accident, which left him paraplegic. She was very grateful to us.

CHAPTER 21

The hustle and bustle of the college kids' techniques, darting harem-scarem, getting to and from their classes on time, is overwhelming. They walk-run, bicycle, scooter, cycle, and ride shuttle buses to each destination for their next class. The rushing is to get there on time, or be late and suffer grade demerit penalties; Lord help those who get in their way. I almost hit three lackadaisical kids stepping out, from who knows where, crossing the street right in front of our Tahoe, none of which watched where they were going, caring not, for they had the right-of-way everywhere on campus.

I drove to the curb and parked in a "students only zone" allowing my wife to get out, dressed in her oh-so-college student look. Giselle entered the registrar's office to sign up for two classes, both taught by Professor Dingle. Her registration was last minute and a bit late. Both advanced postgraduate courses were in the field of psychology.

With Giselle's schedule in hand for her Monday, Wednesday, Friday classes with Dingle, Giselle kissed me through my driver's window and told me she had registered a bit late. Her class was to start in twelve minutes.

"Bye, honey, pick me up at two, right here!" she yelled leaving me, while on the run.

I watched Giselle vanish into a huge auditorium assembly hall named Cook Hall, so named after Captain James Cook, British explorer. Her class with Professor Dingle lasted one hour, however only a half hour into her class, Giselle texted me with a camera cell phone picture of the professor leaning over a young woman and seemed much too close. I got a good look at him.

Later, Giselle leisurely came from class looking somewhat chagrined.

"Well, that didn't take long. That Professor Dingle has already offered to tutor me up to date on the three sessions I missed. He openly said that in front of the class. Some girls actually turned around, and looked at me with disdain. Their sneers were obvious, but I did not understand why, until a girl walked next to me and said, 'Sometimes a girl has to do what a girl has to do to get by'. Then she snickered… they know something…I have to find out. I have two hours until my next class. Honey, I'm going over to the student center and see if I can find some of those faces that scorned me and try to make friends. I will meet you here at seven tonight, after class."

It seemed safe enough. I called Virginia and asked how Nidjo was doing. Virginia told me she was holding Nidjo in her arms right then after a bottle and told me to talk to him over the phone. Nidjo always goo-gooed and gaa-gaaed when he heard my voice. Nevertheless, although I did not understand a word he tried to tell his poppa, he seemed happy, until he accidentally slobbered upon the phone's receiver and Virginia stopped him to wipe it clean. She told me she was afraid that Nidjo might get a shock. I said good-bye.

While killing some time, with nothing to do for several hours, I thought that I would check on things at CMEN. I called Eleanor and asked how her department was doing and if she needed anything. She was too busy to talk to me, told me she had sent all the pertinent data to me already, so I told her she was doing very well, and then hung up. She was her same old demeaning self, but very good at her job. It was amazing how she found her niche in life so early and quickly. Then I wondered again, why they even needed me at all. That feeling was the same I had for Freddie being in charge.

Later, I unintentionally parked in one of those reserved parking places waiting for Giselle. I was still seated in my car, calling Virginia again about Nidjo, when this mail carrier-like scooter pulled along side me and the campus cop started issuing a ticket to my vehicle. The short girl could not reach high enough to pull my big Tahoe's windshield wiper blade up to put the summons under it. Therefore, she finally noticed me through the tinted glass and tapped on my window to roll it down. I did, and she handed me the ticket and just said, "No parking here, sir, without a permit."

That three-dollar ticket she handed to me was in Giselle's name, because I had the Tahoe in Giselle's and my name after we married. Giselle's name was first on the registration and on that ticket. I chuckled to myself, because Giselle would be aggravated. Then I put the ticket in my wallet and sat on it.

I immediately saw Giselle coming as she spotted our Tahoe. Her lovely ponytail bounced rhythmically, as did her big boobs. She hustled her way towards me through a throng of students. A young man, apparently infatuated by her gorgeous looks and swaying hips, moved up quickly beside Giselle to stop her.

Then this young guy ran up to maneuver in front of her, walking backwards and facing Giselle. He stopped out in front of her, and asked her for a date. When she said, "No, thank you," and also shook her head no, then ignored him, he grabbed her shoulder and said something derogatory in rejection.

I immediately headed out to stop him. As I ran, I momentarily lost sight of Giselle in the crowd. When I got there, she had the young man in a reversed arm bar behind his back. He was dancing up on his toes and begging for mercy. The students were heckling the guy who was hollering for clemency. When I almost punched him, Giselle yelled, "Stop! Apologize!" Giselle ordered in such a loud, intimidating, very forceful voice…so I did.

"I'm sorry, honey!" I said very startled by her loud angry shouting.

Giselle grimaced and said, "No, not you, Jerry, for God's sake, him!" she laughed, realizing then I had never heard her raise her voice in anger in a cop's tough manner to effect an order.

After a little more coaxing, and just a little more pressure, the guy finally conceded this girl was too much for him and issued a quick apology. Then he dashed away embarrassed just like a coward, never looking back.

Giselle had dropped her books when she took on the young unrelenting creep and another girl stood by holding them for her.

"Thank you, Margaret. Margaret, this is my husband Jerry. Jerry this is Margaret Thatcher."

"You don't say! You look much younger than on the TV," I mused.

"He's a clown, Margaret. Forgive him, he always wanted to become Clarabelle on the old Howdy Doody reruns," Giselle jested.

"Oh, that's alright...I get that a lot. My parents named me before the real Margaret became prime minister."

"Margaret told me some very interesting things about our new Professor Dingle. He throws wild parties...sound familiar?" Giselle looked at me concerned.

We said good-bye to Margaret and hurried home to see if Nidjo had been a good boy. Virginia had the door deadbolt locked on the inside, so I rang the doorbell. When she answered, she inquired if I had a key. I told her a key would not open a deadbolt. She believed in maintaining top security for our son and we liked her protective attitude. Nidjo was sleeping soundly, so Virginia offered us a few hints.

"You must understand that Nidjo needs lots of sleep while his body grows and grows. When the phone rings every half hour, it disturbs him, as does a ringing doorbell," she told us and that was all she needed to say.

It seems Giselle and I both had called several times keeping Nidjo awake.

The aroma coming from the kitchen smelled different from usual. Virginia had prepared pork sausage, mashed potatoes, and sauerkraut, a German mainstay meal. However, she was keeping it warm, thinking dinner was at six. She suggested that if we were dining later, she would appreciate a notice. Giselle and I sat down to our first meal with Virginia's cooking and devoured it. She was an excellent cook.

"Virginia," Giselle told her, "from now on please dine with us. You are now a part of our family and we want you here. If we have guests, sometimes you might not be able to serve and be here, too. But we intend to treat you better than your previous people had."

Virginia did not know what to say, but a little bitty tear spoke for her. She had eaten, but sat down with us to enjoy a coffee. We all told the other about our heritage and the evening was very pleasant. Later our son sat with us in the living room, by a crackling fire, and it felt like a very close family gathering.

Virginia let us keep Nidjo in our bedroom, instead of his room at night. Nevertheless, she advised strongly that the longer he slept with us, the more attached he would be and later would become distressed by moving into a room by himself. She knew her stuff.

As we lay in our bed, Giselle filled me in with her day in the classes. She said the professor noticed her and began hitting on her almost immediately. When he asked her if she were an athlete at the college, she told him she jogged a lot in the mornings. He hinted he did, also. She said the professor seemed always to have an eye on her the whole hour of class. She had assignments and homework, too, but she had time the next day. I knew I could be at my office without worrying or calling her about little Nidjo, for Virginia was here.

"I didn't push the envelope. I think I'm going to learn more and more about Professor Dingle soon enough. Besides, I need the credits," Giselle whispered, and then kissed me after I turned out the light and we slept peacefully all night, except Nidjo got some titty in the early morning.

The smell of fresh-baked bread was overpowering. We followed our noses to the kitchen breakfast nook. Virginia had Nidjo laughing at her attempts of pretending to be a buzzing bee with a tiny baby spoon with his first attempts at real food. We watched as Nidjo laughed at her, then she skillfully slipped in a quick spoonful. Nidjo liked the Gerber's cereal, kicked, and reached out for more. We had very big smiles on our faces as we sat down to eat. I wanted oatmeal. Giselle liked poached egg. Virginia had a makeshift calendar taped to the fridge, so we could get in tune with her cooking and eating times that she was planning and preparing to make for us.

I ate, showered, and dressed for work. Giselle stayed in her house robe and sat on the sofa reading her new class work assignments. A kiss from Giselle, a goo-goo from Nidjo and I was off to CMEN.

I needed to spend my complete time there uninterrupted to oversee the purchasing of supplies and get a new contract on the paper rolls that always arrived daily.

Our distribution had grown in leaps and bounds, because I hired an outside person on contract to search for more advertisers who lived outside our immediate area, but could benefit from our popular 70, 000 circulation…up from 62,000 only three months prior. CMEN was growing.

I had the ball rolling. Claire Upshaw was living in Southern California on her father's horse ranch, enjoying her freedom. She never called.

Meanwhile, Nigel began to search the background of Professor Dingle. He discovered he was a well-educated man from Griswold University in Saskatchewan, a school noted for producing superior psychology teachers. He did a three-year stint in the Queen's Navy and possessed a present membership in the Bird Watchers of the Americas' Club. It was all there on his list. There were also subscriptions to several off-color nudie magazines.

Nigel also discovered, through the traffic department, several parking tickets issued in the red-light district of the Calgary slum area. He found a misdemeanor charge of 'soliciting a prostitute' quashed in the court system only recently. That caught Nigel's attention quickly and he drove out to the dens of iniquity, those nightclubs, whorehouses and gay bars where the professor's after-hour rendezvous seemed apparently recent and frequent.

Nigel showed his badge as required upon entering, but had to bend the rules and not arrest any of them when he found five women offering him their bodies for sale. Their clients had not arrived yet and Nigel told them he could sit there with his badge out all night and every night until they helped him. If they voluntarily cooperated, Nigel told them, he was just walking out. They were suspicious of this Inspector-Gadget-looking man, but spoke out when his needed info was only that of one regular client, Professor Dingle. They moved in and they all crowded around him.

"Oh, he means the gentle old professor…yeah, we all know him. Is he a real professor?" one scantily dressed lady of the evening asked Nigel.

"Yes, ladies, I'm afraid he is," Nigel advised them.

"The old bird is a duck and quite strange, but always tips us well…never hurts us. He's a friggin' foot freak," she continued. "He sometimes comes up to the younger ones, never the pros. You know what I mean?" she asked, while suddenly lifting her leg up onto a chair to expose herself with no panties, and showing her very bushy pussy to intrigue Nigel in and attempt to lure him.

"The old guy has this peculiar fetish thing he does," she then quickly continued when Nigel frowned and had that angry look in his eyes, as if he were about to arrest her. "Be cool now…he likes to wash our feet, pop peppermint candy drops in his mouth and very excitedly lick our toes. He sucks on them and everything, then has his great big moanin' orgasms…geeeze it's creepy…but as I said, he never hurts us and he pays us good…besides that's not the worst guys try to do to us…and I can wash my feet easier than douchin'," she smiled.

"What's your pleasure, detective?" one questioned with designs on Nigel. Nigel arrogantly pitched her twenty bucks and told the girls to buy soap, they stunk a bit, he told them. They were pissed, so Nigel exited with his pride still in tact from being unable to arrest them all.

Nigel knew the only clue left was secret to most of the murder victim's autopsies. There was a substance of sucrose and mint found on over half the victims' vaginal areas, possibly other parts of their anatomies. He was going back to review the old autopsy reports with the doctors at the different providence coroners' offices.

Nigel felt regenerated and thought Dingle could be his man. If Nigel could somehow combine the clues, a teakwood desk, that monkey sculpture in Dingle's residence like Professor Grebe's, and ultimately the murder weapon, they may tie him to the other deceased criminals, Dorr and Wheeler.

Doing that, and connecting Dingle with Grebe, might solve all the crimes at once; thus, ridding the area of a twenty-year plague. Then finally, Nigel could really rest and close the case.

It still irked Nigel; no Professor Grebe evidence had yet surfaced. The detective had begun to doubt his better judgment that just maybe Grebe was a wildcat pervert on his own. Nigel began to reconsider. In addition, peppermint sticks were still legal, unlike of course, the mutilating murders of the victims.

Nigel had a plan. His 'Special Officer' would have to help him. There were no choices left to stop this long-time, sometimes intermittent killing spree that he knew was only halted for lack of a victim and willing assistants.

Most women had gotten campus police protection everywhere on the university property, limiting this predator from selecting his victim off the sidewalks. He had to take them inside to his den and not being physically able to attack a healthy young woman alone, he would have to have his assassins' help.

Nevertheless, away from the campus, one clandestine, toe-sucking, fetish killer might find his next young female victim. Nigel had to expedite.

Several weeks passed, while Nigel met with coroners across the providence to research their autopsy reports on each suspected serial killer murder victim. It became conclusive, that at least seven females, over a twenty-year-span, had sucrose present in their autopsy reports. Several had larger amounts than others did about their vaginas, and yes, their toes. Dingle was in fact the prime suspect. What a creepy thought! However, who actually murdered his prey? This was a big 'who'.

Now the detective-sergeant had to devise a plan to get his man without too much difficulty, because he was the only detective left assigned to this case, and heat was on Nigel to close it without further expenses.

Returning to the house of ill repute, so named, Candy's Corner, where Nigel had last visited, he met with the prominent Madame Candy, one of the five women who he had insulted. Candy was her fictitious street and business name. She was reluctant to speak to Nigel, who then realized he had burned his bridges behind him. Therefore, he had to be wiser.

"Look, Candy…one of your girls might be a victim. I need your help, but it is what you don't do, that will help solve this thing. I need you all to refuse Professor Dingle's business, all his loving, any toe sucking…refuse everything. I do not know how you are going to do it gracefully, but believe me that is going to bring him out looking for a victim, and I'll be there waiting for him. You have to help me," Nigel pleaded.

"I don't have to do nothin' for you, detective," she sassed. "But I'll do it for my girls," she concurred. "What can I do for my girls?" she asked.

"Thanks…now here's what I need you to tell your girls…"

Nigel laid out a simple request.

"Deny Dingle of his sexual pleasures, by refusing him. When he leaves, call this number. I am on the other end and close by. This is all I need, except, I and all of Canada will find respect for you," Nigel promised.

"Hey, you mean like Aretha Franklin's R-E-S-P-E-C-T, kind of respect, or some cash crossing my palm for these twenty minutes I wasted talking to you, while my girls sit idol waiting for you to leave?"

"If there is some kind of reward, I'll see to it you get yours. How's that?"

"I'm doin' it for my girls and R-E-S-P-E-C-T," she told her girls strutting back to them. "Get movin', while there are still some stars in the sky and nighttime left, girls, it's costing us a small fortune," she said, swaggering back and forth to them, waving her feathery wrap in the air. Then she turned back to Nigel in her sexiest pose.

"Ain't changed your mind about contributing to our IRAs, have ya, detective?" she teased, while the girls all giggled.

Nigel took a deep breath, then turned and walked away, making certain he did not burn any more bridges. He needed those whores' help.

Meanwhile, back on the college scene, Giselle started getting more advances from Professor Dingle. She was slowly gaining his confidence that she would need his assistance.

Giselle deliberately failed his first test and went to him franticly wanting to know if there was someone who tutored his classes. She found him very willing. He explained his calendar was full on the weekdays, but on a Saturday, she could possibly find him at home reading a book with nothing to do, he told her. He encouraged her meeting him for dinner the next Saturday. She consented and used her sexuality and feminine ways to entice his imagination. Her low cut blouses made his blood boil. With the girls down in the red light district sending him away as being too old, he asked Giselle if she thought he was too old.

"In what way, professor? I personally like a more intelligent, more mature man, sophisticated, and who knows how to treat a woman...I think you are rather handsome," she told him, squirming around, which almost made him cream his pants. I know I would have. Anyway, the trap was set for Saturday night, at seven.

At CMEN, I took a walk through the whole plant to see the operation at work. The "Hi, boss!" outnumbered the, "Who's that?" so I was satisfied, until I walked into the Eleanor Bigglebottom love ad office. Eleanor, bending over the keyboard at the secretary's desk, typed madly, pounding out her next column. However, there was no secretary present.

So, I watched from the hallway as she typed, used the computer, opened mail, and sipped coffee in that order, done at high speed. When I walked in, Eleanor did not even turn around, or skip a typed key. She thought I was the mail clerk. Without looking back, Eleanor told me, "Just leave the mail on the other desk."

She was definitely working much too hard, but I liked her resolve.

I sat there watching her perform, not wanting to disturb her concentration. However, when she asked herself aloud, while sucking a pencil in her mouth, and said, "Darn, how do I spell, intriguing, with or without the E?"

I spelled it as she was thumbing her Webster's.

"Intriguing…I-N-T-R-I-G-U-I-N-G…intriguing, no E," I told her.

Eleanor spun around so hard that she spun around twice, stopped, and caught herself, then looked surprisingly at me.

"Hey, boss, what brings you over here? Did something go sour?" she asked.

"Where is your secretary, Eleanor?" I questioned.

"Well, the temp agency sent me six young girls. I rejected them all. None could do anything right or as swiftly as what I wanted, so I ran out of temps!" she smiled.

"And you have been turning out those marvelous columns by yourself then?"

"Yep...me, myself, and I, boss."

I sat down in her desk and we discussed her overworking. After she said she just did not want any help at all, I told her I would give her an additional raise equivalent to a secretary's salary.

"You've earned it, Eleanor. I am telling the bursar this afternoon to raise your salary from $50,000 to $80,000."

"Gee, boss, that's awfully good of you. I love my job and if I don't fulfill your requirements, please tell me before you decide to let me go."

"That'll be the day."

"You mean you won't give me notice?"

"No, I mean that will be the day I ever think of letting you go," I told her. "Thank you for making my job easier, Eleanor. I thank the day you came in here. Someday, you'll get my job," I continued.

I left Eleanor busy finishing her work. She was a rare employee and I wished I had just a few more like her. Nevertheless, not one of my supervisory personnel was a slouch.

While driving to meet Giselle and thinking about calling home, wanting to hear Nidjo's happy goo goo, Giselle called me to tell me the gate opened. She was dining with the professor at seven on Saturday night. I told her we would talk after dinner, and she must call her dad. I immediately had reservations about my wife doing this. I picked her up at our usual meeting place and we headed home.

CHAPTER 22

On Wednesday, I had taken the opportunity to let Virginia do her personal shopping at my expense. I gave her my credit card and told her to make certain to buy herself everything she needed and an appropriate toy for Nidjo. Giselle called Kim to fill in for Virginia who had been with us all too much without a break. Virginia came home having spent only a little on herself, but had several educational toys for Nidjo.

That evening, we took Nidjo to see his grandparents who begged to see him. We drove to Nigel's for dinner and discussed his plan afterwards.

"Everything seems to be set," Nigel told us after we correlated every detail. Queenie held Nidjo and he was simply the best baby in her arms. I hid my fears of Giselle's involvement, but knew she would have it no other way.

"Look, Giss, carry your weapon on the inside of your thigh. Have Jerry duct tape it there."

"How will I walk straight?" she asked.

"Since you were a baby you've had that sway. Nobody but a fool would suspect you are carrying. If they get there, use it with deadly force," Nigel ordered.

I became a nervous wreck. My wife was giving her all to this and I had to make certain I could be there.

"Where will I be?" I asked Nigel.

"We'll wire Giss and you'll have to be in our surveillance van coordinating us by radio. We will park it as close as we can after Giss goes inside. All you have to do is listen to her conversation, and keep me in the game.

"Giss, you just say, 'Bitty Batter bought some butter; Bitty Batter said the butter was bitter; so Bitty Batter bought some better butter and mixed the bitter butter with the better butter and made the bitter butter, better butter'…Got that? We'll come charging in."

"What the heck did you say, Daddy?" Giselle asked, seriously concerned she could never say all that.

"Just kidding, Giss…you both looked up tight and I thought a little humor might ease the tensions. Giss, just say, 'Bite me!' and we're coming through the door with heat. The guys should be in place, also, to come in.

"I don't expect the professor to give you much trouble. I know you can physically take him by yourself. Nevertheless, know we are there with you and if you think he is a threat or you find out incriminating evidence you can nail him with, just announce he is under arrest and pull your crotch weapon, because he might have something we don't know about. Remember, Giss, just say, 'bite me'.

"Jerry, make certain the recording is on. It's simple and I'll get it going before I leave. I'll try to find a place for you close by on the street, but we must go into position as soon as Giss gets in there. The professor will undoubtedly have all his attentions on Giss.

"I will make my way to be around back and get inside, if I can. There's no pets allowed where Dingle resides, so I will not have to worry about big dogs. A few of the officers volunteered on this thing, but I do not know where they will be, yet. We will have to improvise. Remember, we have to get in there ASAP, on Giss' call, 'bite me', anyway we can. The boys are bringing the heat and a door jam. Saturday night, guys and girls, and I'm certain we'll have our man," Nigel boasted.

Nigel was serious, very thorough, and sure, but I got sick to my stomach worrying about Giselle, who seemed to think it all was a piece of cake. I guess it was from her police training. I had none and I was afraid I would screw things up. That would be disastrous.

It seemed like the world took one giant step forward and it was Saturday already, late afternoon. I was with my love in our bedroom, working hard under Giselle's sexy-looking dress, but this time it was not pleasure. I had duct tape, securing a small Lady Smith to her inner thigh. It had to be secure, but she had to be able to get to it, if she needed it. I was ready to call it off, but I could not get the nerve, because she and Nigel were so set on this.

Nigel showed up in an old 60s Hippy-looking, painted van, and asked if we were ready. We all went outside as Nigel gave me a once-over on using the radio. Behind the van, there was another car parked with four officers inside. When I kept looking at them, Nigel said they were the volunteer help. I began to feel more at ease with the extra men and one woman. Their faces were stern and looked like they were serious. They were all packing heat.

The radio was simple enough and all I had to do was key the mike to talk. I breathed easier, until Nigel upset the cart.

"Look, Jerry, we're going in on this one without a whole heck of a lot of planning…sometimes things happen you don't plan on, no matter how well conceived the plan. Ours is a quickly put together plan, no run-through. I think it is good. Nevertheless, what I am saying is this…if things go down bad, we have to remain calm and keep our heads. The idea is to come out alive with our suspect also alive. However first, we have to see that Giss is safe and that no harm comes to her of any kind. Now, let's meet the other guys," Nigel said as we walked back to greet them.

"Thanks, guys…this is my son-in-law, Jerry, he'll be on the radio, and you all know Giss. Jerry, this is Nick, Regina, Ortiz, and Moen. We are all a team tonight, so let us rid our community of some filth. Giss, you have anything to add?" Nigel asked.

"Let's went, Poncho!" she cheerfully chimed. It was Giselle's favorite assertion to vacate quickly.

The Canadian sun was at sunset as we eased up on Churchill Place, the street where Professor Dingle resided. His home was on a cul-de-sac, facing straight on from where I could see. At 6:55 p.m., as Giselle passed us by in our white Tahoe, she said over her body mike, "Wish me luck, honey," and then parked in Dingle's drive.

As Giselle got out of our high step Tahoe, I noticed her shortened hemline and revealing neckline, both accented everything she physically had. I was reminded what a prize she was. She had her books and things in a backpack and held it in her hands. She did seem to walk funny with the pistol between her legs, but carrying the backpack seemed to equalize her swaying, wide-legged approach. It was still extremely sexy. She could tempt any man on the face of the Earth and it might stem on entrapment using such gorgeous bait as she was.

As soon as we heard Dingle's voice welcome Giselle inside, rather gentile-voiced-like, I was certain I could hear and record their every word clearly. The small mike, taped between her large breasts, caused me concern, because I imagined that those bosoms might smother the sounds. I was relieved somewhat, but still jumpy. I could actually hear the beating of Giselle's heart pounding, and then it seemed to settle down. It was a warming sound, which I had heard many times making love to her. I felt it then pounding against my chest, and I could almost feel her emotion in her every heartbeat.

As he stepped from the van, Nigel was outside on foot immediately, but headed in the wrong direction. I looked in the rather dirty rearview mirror, seeing the other police exit their unit as they also dispersed. I continued to listen as the professor began speaking to Giselle. She thanked him for seeing her and once again for helping her with her chair as she sat down at the dining table.

Giselle kept conversation going between them. She was describing her position in the house by telling me in a roundabout way what she saw. Giselle remarked on his furnishings and that his home was beautiful, very elegant, with such high ceilings, a beautiful dining table with huge candelabras. She raved to him about them all and I got the picture in my mind of the inside.

The conversation went to many things, mostly his travels, but nothing led to any evidence that might expose the professor. This went on for an hour or more as they dined, and then they both went to his study. Giselle continued to elaborate freely ad libbing as she walked with him. It was a masterpiece of ingenuity on my Giselle's part, describing every movement.

Suddenly Nigel's voice came over the radio talking to one of the other officers. He advised him not to fall out of that tree. I took a double take when I could barely see a man using binoculars, and holding a sniper's rifle, wedged up in the fork of an adjacent big tree next to the home.

Then Nigel spoke to me to tell me to give him more play-by-play. Therefore, I began doing so, relaying each conversation. It began to seem all very disruptive, for as I repeated, Giselle spoke, and I was losing some content.

Several hours passed, when a car drove up in the driveway. A tall young man got out and went to the door of the professor's, did not knock, but walked right in. I heard Giselle sound startled by his sudden appearance and she remarked, "I thought we were alone."

"Giselle, this is Darnell. He is a rookie police officer friend of mine from Edmonton. He also is a graduate student who helps me grade papers."

I heard Giselle's heart beat begin to quicken. I did not know if she thought he was handsome, or if she knew him and he might reveal her cover. Nevertheless, her heart certainly remained beating faster and louder.

The professor and the young man left the room, Giselle whispered. "Nothing's happening. He still hasn't done anything nor asked me to have him help…"

Giselle stopped talking, then said, "What a beautiful desk I saw in your study, professor, is it teakwood?"

"Yes, my dear. I had it shipped in from South America…Brazil in fact," he noted. "May I offer you something cordial to drink? Wine, bourbon, just club soda?" he offered.

"Maybe a diet soda, please…any kind you have will do," Giselle told him.

Then Giselle whispered, "That new guy is freaky…he keeps acting strangely, looking at me funny and keeps coming down and then going back upstairs like he's waiting for something to happen…when he comes down, he…Oh, thank you, professor…what about my study help?" Giselle had stopped short, and then spoke out to the professor again.

I actually could hear her breathing and swallowing as she sipped the drink. Nigel broke the radio silence and asked Moen if he could see what the young guy was doing upstairs.

"I don't like this, sarge…he's got duct tape and rope. He's tying ropes to the rungs of the bed like there's going to be some kinky shit about to take place…hold on, he's got a big black Uzi in his waistband, also. I just put my riflescope on him, but he's moving around too much."

Overcome by Moen's explained events, I almost upchucked out of the window. I realized my Giselle was now in too deep. I listened while her heartbeat seemed to slow down considerably.

"Here, my dear…would you like another one of my specially imported, Swedish peppermints?" spoke the creepy professor's voice, almost sounding clandestine, just like 'Snidely Whiplash' did in cartoons. "They're really, oh so refreshing, dearest, after a fine cuisine… and you'll find them oh so refreshing, right before sex, too," the now Professor Snidely-Dingle told Giselle. She did not answer him and that was alarming. Giselle's heartbeat was still very slow now. I listened intently for anything.

"I'm sure you don't mind this, pretty Giselle, as you sleep now, but soon you'll know why I like them, my dearest. You have such beautiful feet, my dearest…you are an extremely beautiful girl…"

"Nigel, something's going on in there…Nigel! Answer me!" I shouted. I clicked the mike and saw it had disconnected from the radio. The cord had somehow snapped. There now was no communication to him, but I could hear Giselle's soft words…"What was in that drinkkkka…?"

Then I heard her sigh and a breaking glass hitting the floor. Everything was going wrong and I knew he had doped or poisoned my Giselle.

"Darnell…come down here!" the professor yelled out.

I heard sudden footsteps and Darnell saying the upstairs was ready.

"Are you just going to suck on her toes, professor, or fuck her? Get up, so I can carry her upstairs. This is going to cost you plenty," Darnell warned. "I don't think I can carry this big bitch up the stairs by myself," he continued.

"What's this…she's got a pistol in her crotch!" Darnell sang out as he apparently dropped Giselle. I heard her deep breathing again.

Where was Nigel? I could not communicate with him or anyone, so I hollered out the van's window just as loud as I could, "Bite me!" which was Giselle's signal to come in quickly, if she could have. I could not see Nigel or the others anywhere, so I did what I thought only the best I could do to get to her quickly to save my helpless wife.

I sped the van at break-neck speed, right across the front yard, knocking out shrubs and then plowed right between two of the big outside pillars, crashing through the huge front door, and then flew into the foyer. I should have thought of wearing the seat belts first. That sudden stop was unkind.

I came out staggering, bruised, dazed, dizzy, and disoriented. I squeezed through the jammed driver's side door as best I could, away from the smoking van. It was totaled. The radiator spewed hot vapors into the room from the crunched up radiator, bent up hood and front end. There was a huge cloud of dust blinding my vision and chocking me. The van had halted, up against an inside wall shaking the whole house, including disturbing the big chandelier still swaying dangerously overhead. It was a tremendous crash; I hoped I had not killed anyone.

"Giselle! Giselle!" I hollered out through the debris and dust, beginning to search for her.

As I yelled out for Giselle, I heard chairs being turned over and feet shuffling when suddenly Nigel hollered loudly, "God damn it, look out, the young bastard ran upstairs, and there goes the professor… he's got Giss' pistol headed down that hallway…they're both armed now with two revolvers and an Uzi! Get Giss outside quick, Regina… through the window if you have to…call for back up and EMTs," he ordered her from another room and very out of breath. I guess he, too, had breathed in some of that floating plaster dust.

Through the dust, I saw Regina trying to help a very groggy Giselle stand up. I ran to Giselle and swooped my wife up into my arms. Regina then led our way out, her service pistol in hand, exiting through a kitchen doorway and into the big garage. Regina hit the inside remote buttons to lift the big door, when I heard sporadic shots being exchanged inside behind us.

I heard Regina calling out on her radio asking for assistance and emergency help on Churchill Place. Giselle became limp and out of it. I feared she was poisoned, rape-drugged…but at least she was alive and unmolested, except for her toes. They were sticky without her shoes, which remained inside. I heard more shouting and continuous shooting. Apparently, neither the good nor bad could hit home.

Regina told me quickly that Nigel had slipped inside somewhere, watching Giselle, and had called her right before he tried to stop the aggressive advance of the professor. When she and Ortiz came in, a gun was being held at the head of Giselle by the professor and an Uzi on Nigel by the guy from upstairs. Moen, our sniper, was out of position. Therefore, she and Ortiz surrendered and were disarmed, too.

Suddenly Nick rushed inside, unaware of his immediate danger, and was shot dead by the Uzi.

"Everything looked really, really bad," Regina quickly told me. "If you hadn't come crashing through that door, and knocked everyone down, I think we all might have been blown away. The tall guy from upstairs has a 9mm Uzi. We were no match for him and never expected this at all," she shouted, as the EMTs arrived.

"Is she OD'd or shot?" one EMT called coming with his medical case in hand and on the run. "That's Giselle Gray for God's sake!"

"I think it was a date-rape drug in her drink," Regina told them. "She wasn't shot."

They got to us and immediately carried Giselle into their unit and began their work. A tube was inserted into her nostril and down into her throat to prepare to begin pumping her stomach.

I continued to hear more shots, then a burst of fire erupted that must have been fifty shots all at once. It was loud and long.

"That was the Uzi," Regina yelled out.

We feared the big guy had opened up on the other policemen and they might already be dead.

I just had to find a way to help them. I wanted a piece of the man who tried to molest my wife, and was probably Rita's kidnaper-rapist.

No sooner had the big doors closed on the emergency vehicle, and Giselle rushed away safety to a hospital under red lights with siren wailing, a squad car slid in near us with two officers. One was none other than Rita Tory. She was shocked to see me there.

"Boss, you injured bad? You look as if you have been involved in an accident, you're bleeding," she immediately spoke.

I pointed to the van wedged into the doorway.

"No, I'm all right, Rita, but the guy Nigel thinks kidnapped you, Professor Dingle, is inside there with another big guy named Darnell with an Uzi shooting at Nigel, Nick, and Ortiz if they're still alive…

be careful. Moen was up in that tree with a sniper rifle, but I can't see him now. There's been so much gunfire I don't know if Nigel or any of them are dead or alive. Remember, that big tall guy in there has an Uzi," I told Rita, just as that Uzi fired out with a loud burst again. Rita quickly ducked, and then moved back to her squad.

I immediately saw the look of rage in Rita's face. My words besieged her when she realized at least one of them inside, maybe both were the persons who kidnapped-raped her. Her face was now ashen white. It was a grimacing expression, frightening, horribly angry, and something that I had never seen in it before.

Rita and her partner, Rick, quickly opened their squad car's trunk and each retrieved a riot shotgun. They both ran back to my side of the house and peered inside through a shattered window. As more shots rang out, Rita motioned to someone. She evidently saw Moen in the tree and motioned that they were going in. I don't know what she told him, but sure enough they entered through the hole in the doorway I had made with the van. Regina immediately moved up and took a position to cover them.

It was quiet for several minutes. Then suddenly shotgun blasts erupted against the rapid sound from the automatic Uzi's burst. One shotgun hit the floor, rattling as if it was used up and empty. Then I heard Rita's voice hollering over her radio, "Officer down, officer down!" Rick had been hit.

The eerie nighttime setting of the cul-de-sac made it difficult to see. It was surreal with the outside yard lights turning off one by one. I saw lights in the neighbor's upstairs rooms and people's heads bobbing up and down, peeking over their windowsills at the deadly occurrence.

Suddenly, I noticed a silhouette run past Dingle's upstairs window. A loud shot rang out and I saw that silhouette come crashing through the upstairs window, as if the person had jumped through it. He had. It was the tall guy with the Uzi and he hit hard and lay sprawled out upon the asphalt drive, squirming, bleeding profusely.

Rita's partner Rick came limping outside and grabbed the Uzi, just as the creep struggled to get to it. Rick cuffed the guy behind his back and left him lay there. Then he himself sat down, incapacitated by his heavy loss of blood, running down one sleeve.

Squad cars burst onto the scene from everywhere as I stood there frozen, because they all had shotguns and pointed them everywhere and several times sweeping at me until I wasn't a threat. One officer attended to Rick's needs. Another uniformed officer came to me and quickly asked if Nigel was in the house.

"Nigel, Ortiz, Nick and Rita Tory and an armed Professor Dingle, is in there, too. I don't know their situation. Rita just went in and that's Regina by the window. There's a guy who used an Uzi lying over there on the drive, but there's at least one more armed man inside, that's Dingle," I yelled out repeating, while watching the activities around the house as all the other officers left me to surround it.

Nobody told me to stay out of the way. So I ran up to the house next to Regina and Moen who had just come down from the tree. He had shot the tall person, he admitted.

As we peered inside into the large library, I spotted a wild-looking Professor Dingle crouched and hiding behind that large teakwood desk of his. He had Giselle's pistol in his hand, pointing it at the doorway, just as if he were waiting to shoot anyone who entered. He had blood on his clothes.

Several officers came out; one had another on his shoulders in a fireman's carry. I thought it was Nick. Then another officer assisted a wounded Nigel outside. Nigel looked to be in bad pain, bleeding several places from the blast of the Uzi. Regina went to help move Nigel to an emergency unit. He was alive then, but barely walking with the help from the officers. That really pissed me off seeing him that way.

When I noticed a human shadow on the hallway's wall, just outside the library and the professor's kneeling position behind his desk, I saw Moen struggling to get a shell loaded into the breech of his German Mauser sniper rifle to shoot him.

I saw Rita pass quickly in front of the doorway on a sweep technique as the professor ducked down.

It happened much too quickly. I never thought I could do it. Nevertheless, as Rita cautiously walked into the room, searching slowly, suspecting anything from anyone in there, the professor had his pistol cocked, aiming, and about to shoot the unsuspecting Rita.

I do not remember doing it, but I grabbed Moen's revolver from his holster, as he desperately tried to remove a shell from the breach of his rifle, which apparently jammed because his extractor bar had broken.

I just pointed and fired quickly, and blindly, through the broken window at the professor, before he could pull the trigger on Rita. The blast from that .357 magnum tore a hole in him the size that my fist could enter. He could not do much else, as the shock-power from the powerful slug lifted him up and over onto the top of his desk. Nevertheless, he still was alive and trying to shoot her. How Rita resisted from finishing him off, I do not know, but she kept him in her sights, hammer cocked.

Rita looked over hard at me quickly to see who fired, and after seeing me, she continued to move towards Dingle, pointing her weapon at him.

"Go ahead, you slimy bastard, make my day, please, please!" Rita pleaded and screamed at Dingle, her face still cringed in madness, as she approached him, step by step. "Remember me, asshole? Look at my face! Payback's a bitch, you perverted, son-of-a-bitch, isn't it?" she continued, as Dingle stayed upright there gasping, wildly clawing, and scraping everything in front of him off onto the floor. He was still trying to get up straight to fire that pistol at Rita, which he held cocked in his badly shaking hand. He coughed, spit up dark red blood bubbles, choked hard on them for a moment, and then the professor got a horrible look upon his face, as he became limp, slowly collapsed, and slid off onto the floor...Dingle was definitely dead.

Rita grabbed up the pistol, and then looked at me as she stood over his body. She uncocked her own pistol carefully; holstered it, and then bent down slowly fixated on something. She then retrieved something I knew offended us both. Next, Rita held it up for me to see. It was a statue, identical to the monkey-skull statue in Grebe's home. I knew then that very same desk had been used to photograph those naked young women before their vicious murders.

"It's over," I sighed to Moen. "Is that big guy you shot dead over there, too?" I asked.

"Yeah," he spoke, looking disturbed at all the blood on my face.

Moen was fretful, because immediately after I fired Moen's loud pistol, impulsively he spun around and his Mauser's steel butt stock inadvertently crashed into the side of my noggin. It took a few seconds for me to realize I wasn't shot, nevertheless, I was rendered dazed and bleeding profusely about my head. The warm trickling blood began blinding my vision as it streamed down on my shirt. It was my red badge of courage for that life and death gun battle.

Rita came outside, as more police wearing swat team attire entered quickly, armed with riot shotguns to sweep the upstairs. When Rita saw my bleeding, she helped me over to an arriving emergency vehicle.

"You saved my life again, boss," Rita said holding me tightly.

"Yes, but the last time I was late, you told me, remember?"

CHAPTER 23

It was quite a sight at the hospital. There we were, Nigel, my darling Giselle and I, our closest kin gathered around us, just one happy family, in the recovery infirmary. We were lying side by side, recuperating, as the news cameras rolled. We all wore those terrible hospital gowns with our butts hanging out. Only Giselle looked fabulous, as she got up, closed the curtains, and sat near Nigel to hold his hand. She had fully recovered from the date-drugging attempt, but she was being held for observation.

I had a slight concussion and a subdural hematoma, a gift from Moen. I was x-rayed for the concussion, and received six hairline stitches.

Nigel suffered multiple gunshot wounds; however, all of them were non-life-threatening, struck down by the Uzi six times on that first long sweeping, loud burst of fire we heard. Nigel had returned fire, which chased both the professor down a hallway and Darnell up the stairs, before Nigel finally collapsed. Nick was hit in that same burst also, but he died instantly.

We learned from Nigel how everything went down, except I did not understand how Professor Grebe was found shot to death inside.

"We never even knew he was there," Nigel began. "The S.W.A.T. team's sweep found him later. Apparently, Grebe was already there before we had arrived. Birds of a feather, see what I told you people?

Nevertheless, he planned to participate, we believe. Our guess is he must have recognized Giselle as an officer, we think. He hid, lurking in a closet, masturbating, while apparently watching Giselle. I suppose he was waiting for her to go lights out so he could attack her body. I knew he was in this somehow."

"Ha! I thought about that lot of times," I jested to a very worried looking Nigel.

"Ah hem, anyway!" Nigel continued looking at me seriously. "Grebe got caught…you're kiddin' me, son, aren't ya?" he asked me in disgust. "Is that all you ever think about is my daughter?" he asked, shaking his head and looking at Giss.

"Oh, Daddy!" Giselle sounded off.

"Continuing…Grebe had his pants down for the last time, I guess. That same wild burst of the Uzi that hit me, accidentally caught Grebe behind the door, right between the eyes.

"Our guys found him shot dead in a closet in a pool of blood," Nigel said, acting pleased to tell me. "And the university is advertising for two new professors," he ecstatically quipped, as he sipped some orange juice, and then continued.

"I took the liberty of retiring my previous 'Special Officer' secretary," Nigel said squeezing Giselle's hand. "I petitioned Rita Tory to take her place."

Giselle saw it coming and thought it was a great idea, since she would be off on leave repeatedly, she concurred. She then told Nigel of her new pregnancy. He shook his bandaged head at her and then me and asked us quickly while laughing, if we had not learned anything from Giselle's sister Diana, who drove Queenie and him half-crazy constantly with her rebellious attitude. Diana was there and stomped out of the room.

"You do not get what you hope you're getting sometimes," Nigel warned us, now uncomfortable watching Diana's distain.

"Yes, but three out of four is good, and soon Diana will outgrow that stage and make you proud as Giselle has," I told him.

Giselle and I both left the hospital the next day, but Nigel remained for several more days and came home that next Thursday. We picked him up.

Lots of news developed for the CMEN. The Police Superintendent praised Detective-sergeant Nigel Gray on the TV for his efforts to halt the killings and remove the true perpetrators from our society. He never gave up.

Nigel received a promotion offer, but declined. He wanted to remain in his present position, because he did not want to get behind a desk and push pencils. He was given extended time off as his reward.

"He was a 'Detective Extraordinaire'," so advised the Prime Minister in Edmonton and commended by his immediate superiors with a plaque for his office wall. They also reluctantly overlooked my destroying their only covert vehicle, when I drove it through the professor's front door.

I was a big star, too, at CMEN, and at home with Nidjo and Giselle. Two weeks later, after I had called Mom and Dad several times promising to bring Nidjo down to their farm, my dad passed. I was saddened, especially sorry, since Joe had not seen Nidjo, although Giselle had sent many pictures. My dad meant so much to me; I had a hard time realizing he would not be there, standing as always beside Mom to greet us.

We all crowded into the big Tahoe and I drove us down to South Dakota on what would become thereafter our yearly adventure. Nigel, Queenie, Diana, Michele, Nidjo, Giselle and I, together; however, Virginia stayed behind and watched our house. She just did not like traveling and was so happy in our home; she did not want to leave, ever.

I had to rent a small covered U-haul trailer to have sufficient room for everything. That Tahoe was loaded and again, everyone and everything was searched at the USA/Canadian crossing. Before he searched Nigel, the attending border patrol officer recognized him and asked to shake his hand. However, he still frisked Nigel thoroughly and Nigel was perturbed.

A cold wind blew across the South Dakotan plains upon our arrival to spend the night at our hotel in Rapid City. However, spring was in the air and in the morning, a warm sun shone on us as we made our way out to the farm.

Mom did not stand outside to greet us, but my sister Tracey and her two children were quickly out to meet us, anxious to see Giselle and Nidjo. Other relatives had also come, but time had narrowed their numbers down to only three of Dad's relatives and two of Mom's.

Queenie and Nigel offered their condolences to Mom and she thanked them and welcomed both to her home. We laid Dad to rest on the home place that next day, under the big oak, in the family plot. Preacher Earl from Rapid City gave a nice eulogy for my dad, having known him since a young man for forty-nine years. He said my dad was most of all honest, hard working, a wonderful husband and a good father, I agreed. Dad was sixty-six.

I took Mother's hand as we placed a Sweet William bouquet on his casket. "Bye, Dad…we loved you very much," I whispered to his spirit.

We stayed over at the farm when Mom begged me to share Nidjo. As all the girls talked, Nigel and I took the shotguns from the cabinets and drove Dad's old pickup out near the stubble fields to shoot rabbits.

Rabbits had replaced the pheasant season and was about to come to an end. Nigel was thrilled when I took him to our favorite briar patch and let him shoot six cottontails. All he had to do, since he was still healing from his wounds, was sit on the old truck's tailgate, as I played beagle and chased up the hares past him. Nigel did not miss one rabbit and soon we limited out.

I always brought along my sharp Case pocketknife and several extra plastic bread wrappers. After Nigel shot one rabbit, I would quickly skin it, while the body was still warm. That helped remove their fur effortlessly. I gutted each, and then placed them individually in a bag; sometimes two in one bag, if hunting was good.

Dad just loved shooting rabbits there and I found some of his old red, spent casings lying on the ground. They were holy to me, so I picked them up, put them in my hunting coat's pocket, and left them in there to remind me of all the times we shared while hunting.

Giselle made hasenpfeffer out of all those rabbits, a German meal Virginia taught her and everyone enjoyed. We stayed another night and sat around the big wood burning stove, singing and talking. Then Mom told me privately that Dad had put me down as their sole heir to his farm to make me consider moving there. I asked about Mom's own interests in the farm. Mom said she would hire help to do the farming, or probably cash-rent it out to neighbors. We had good ground and that would be no problem, but she would refuse the Chinese representatives, as Dad had, to farm for them. They shipped everything back to China.

Well, as time passed, Giselle and I made our family grow with four boys, Nidjo, Mark, Brandon, and Gregory. For several years, the David family all attended every Stamps game and watched their mother cheering as an Outrider cheerleader for the Stampeders, until after one season, Giselle decided that was enough. It wasn't because they now mandated a maximum age limit of twenty-six; Giselle was happy being there in our home together, watching our boys grow into young men. I retired from CMEN five years later, and yes, Eleanor Bigglebottom runs CMEN yet today.

It was during this time that Rick and Rita became permanent partners. I was proud to be selected as an usher at their June wedding. The only mishap was when the bride and groom came back down the aisle together as one; Rita stepped on my toe and looked at me as if she finally had gotten even with me. I was thrilled for them both. However, we did not stay for the reception because I was limping.

Virginia was like the boy's grandmother, after both Queenie and Mom passed, and she remained healthy and strong at seventy-five.

When we all hopped into my newest white Tahoe one early morning, (we had three, mine, one was Nidjo's and one Giselle's), we drove down to the farm in South Dakota during our boys' school Christmas break.

Nigel was aging, had finally retired, and was somewhat despondent, so we took him along. I took him out rabbit hunting, as in many previous times and he really enjoyed our yearly trek to that briar patch, especially with all my boys. We had a ton of birds, rabbits, too, on the back of Dad's old pickup. I knew who would have a lot of plucking to do, before Giselle and Tracey roasted them all for our big feast.

My sister, Tracey, had divorced Gary, her first husband, and eventually remarried. She and her new farmer-husband, Don Greibel, lived in my parents' home, at my insistence. Tracey's twins, Kate and Karen, invited their boyfriends, also.

Don Greibel was an old friend of mine, for we had both attended high school together way back when. Don had always cash-rented from us, and had met Tracey on the farm, while Mom was still alive. I liked him. I decided it was better if Tracey and I shared our parents' desire just for me to have it alone. After all, they liked Don, just did not know he would someday be their kin. Tracey became the mother Mom hoped she might.

They both stood outside awaiting our arrival, being able to see the dust kicked up, as I drove down our long five-mile lane. Each held the other, waving to us, just as Mom and Dad had done; I smiled. We spent a week there hunting and reviewing the crop receipts, then returned to Canada.

Life has been good to us, and I thank the Good Lord every day for giving Giselle to me. She has maintained that sexy figure of hers by daily workouts and jogging. Her long black hair has turned a bit grey, but she still makes my heart throb remembering her as that gorgeous Outriders cheerleader I first saw on the sidelines of our victorious Stampeders.

We had invited Nigel to come live with us, after he sold his home. Just as he had every year upon his home place land, Nigel began a big garden one early spring on ours. It was his pride and joy and Virginia made fast work of its bounty. We often saw him leaning on his hoe, looking off, daydreaming of his lost love, Queenie. We always knew when he was melancholy, he shed tears, and as they ran down his dusty cheeks, they always left tracks.

One early morning, Virginia found Nigel lying face down in his garden, apparently dead from a brain hemorrhage. He was black faced when she discovered him. He was seventy-eight.

We arranged for his body to be carried to South Dakota and placed him beside Mom's, Dad's, and Queenie's graves, where Giselle had planned and thought she, too, would someday like to lay there by my side. Giselle loved it there on Dad and Mom's place.

One day, shortly after our Nigel had passed, and while going through his personal storage trunks full of his old police memorabilia, Giselle and I stopped to read his case notes from several of his hardest worked and solved crimes. One, of course, Giselle and I shared with him.

We placed Nigel's handwritten notes together by their dates, read them individually, and then decided how he had debunked them to lead him to his suspects.

I had to dry my eyes reading one of his notes. There scribbled on the border read, "Jerry and Giselle are working with me. I hope something good develops with them. I really like Jerry." It touched my heart.

We determined how Nigel eventually narrowed evidence to a single perpetrator, and then eliminated unfounded evidence and circumstantial hearsay, while he finally deduced his conclusions, all scribbled down there in his notes. A fact became very clear how the genius detective solved many of his investigations.

"Your dad was a true mathematician," I told Giss. "Nigel meticulously gathered and added up all the evidence found on a crime scene, subtracted, and divided their worth, multiplied the suspect's opportunity to commit a crime, then arrived at a summation from it all. What a piece of mathematical genius, he was!"

We uncovered Nigel's retirement plaque. There so emblazoned was an official recognition of Nigel's detective prowess, dedicated, by and large, to Nigel's solving of 'The Peppermint Files' a long twenty-three year killing spree; much praised and greatly applauded from the multitude who gathered to honor him, which made him blush the evening of his retirement celebration. It was Nigel's night.

These words are inscribed there:

"Our citizens everywhere are safer today: upon every sidewalk; in the shopping malls; parking lots and streets; disabled drivers on a lonely road; especially those young co-eds on campuses throughout Alberta, Canada, because of the efforts of Detective-sergeant Nigel Gray (ret.) an always dedicated officer, with unrelenting fortitude, who for thirty-eight years using his cunningness, sought to rid our world of **the square root of evil**."

THE END

WHO IS RE`AL "BULL" ONEY?

Find out about Philip W. Kunz, pen named Re'al "Bull" Oney, a new Midwest author whose books are at your favorite book outlet, or visit:
> Amazon.com (books)
> Barnes & Nobel.com
> iUniverse.com (browse bookstore)

Find high adventure, love & romance, murder, new science fiction and everything in between. This amazing Midwest author's books hit the publisher's lists in February 2006 and are still coming!
> "Read about your dreams," with exciting stories such as:

The Square Root of Evil

The Devil Inside Darin Drake*

Picking up the Pieces!

Relative Humidity!

Tall Tales, Half-Truths, & Big Fat Lies

Rising Up from the Dirt

Secret Places in Her Heart!

My Moody Indigo

A Trace of Death

The Miami Card Sharks

The Fifth Musketeer

Small Town Murders

The Hellions

Fat Man's Island

Visions of Grandeur!

Big Oak Mega Buck/The Knock at Our Door!/Ella's Compassion - a
> trilogy

Stink Finger